wild egg

A story of one woman's search
for her childfree life

Jennifer Flint

ISBN:

(Paperback) 9

(ebook) 978-1-913590-57-4

Cover design by Lynda Mangoro

The Unbound Press

www.theunboundpress.com

Hey unbound one!

Welcome to this magical book brought to you by The Unbound Press.

At The Unbound Press we believe that when women write freely from the fullest expression of who they are, it can't help but activate a feeling of deep connection and transformation in others. When we come together, we become more and we're changing the world, one book at a time!

This book has been carefully crafted by both the author and publisher with the intention of inspiring you to move ever more deeply into who you truly are.

We hope that this book helps you to connect with your Unbound Self and that you feel called to pass it on to others who want to live a more fully expressed life.

With much love,

Nicola Humber

Founder of The Unbound Press

www.theunboundpress.com

This book is dedicated to three special women.

For my mam
You are my craggy rock.
I love you and am so lucky to have you.

For Jessica Watson
You lit the fire beneath my feet.
I am honoured to know you.

For Aunty Kate
You enriched my life in so many ways.
Thank you for the razzle-dazzle.

Wild Egg Endorsements

"A powerful story and page-turning must read novel for women feeling the pronatalistic push/pull of motherhood as an expected choice. (And, equally important to those who love them unconditionally.) Along the way, Wild Egg will have you wondering if you're happy or joyful and if you're the egg or the eggcup. Brava!"

Marcia Drut-Davis, author of "Confessions of a Childfree Woman" and "What? You Don't Want Children?" and childfree pioneer.

"This book is beautiful, brilliant, serious and funny. Flint gives us the gift of Hollie, a lovable, courageous role model for the childfree choice. Flint also uses original language and metaphors to depict the frustration, determination and creativity of parenthood/childfree decision-making. Readers will feel seen, heard and less alone in their own decision-making. I highly recommend Wild Egg to my coaching clients, readers and social media followers"

Merle Bombardieri, MSW, LICSW, author of 'The Baby Decision: How to Make the Most Important Choice of your Life', psychotherapist, and international decision coach.

"A brilliant and touching exploration into one woman's greatest decision. Men should read this too."

Michael Heppell, Sunday Times No1 Best Selling Author

Acknowledgements

They say it takes a village to raise a child, and this has certainly been true of *Wild Egg*.

Firstly, I would like to thank **John Buttery**. I am deeply grateful for our marriage and the call to adventure on the kitchen-floor that night which irrevocably changed my life. With deep and abiding love, always.

I would also like to thank *Wild Egg*'s four godparents ... **Michael Heppell**, since we first met in 2005, you and your work have inspired me to fulfil my wildest dreams. My wonderful coach, **Jacqui Sjenitzer**, for being a magical midwife and holding the mirror to my golden shadow. **Paul Fiddaman** (CEO of Karbon Homes), for letting me sit by your still reservoir and enabling me to take a leap of faith. **Veronika Sophia Robinson**, thank you for your wonderful heart-led celebrant training which unlocked the door to my creative self.

Next, special thanks to a host of people who have been an important part of the journey ... **Julian Bird**, for unleashing my creative kraken. **Jane (Wifey) Rowe**, for riding those horses and helping me keep my faith in the magic; your friendship sustains my soul. **Hannah Penn**, **Nessy Brassey**, **Kev Gray** and **Kathleen Chingles**, for your creative inspiration and cheerleading. **Oly Blackburn**, for the beautiful egg you gave me that came to feel like destiny. **Helen Young**, for listening to me when I was in existential hell. **Zara Cordella**, for helping me get me out of my head and back into my body. **Stella Kodjer** for some of the most important conversations of my life; your friendship continues to be a holy blessing. **Tracey Watson**, **Lorna Jeromsen**, **Rachel Finn**, and **Margaret Barlow** – you helped me find strength and courage when I felt lost, and the space you hold continues to enrich my days. **Charley Morley**, your 'Embracing the Shadow' retreat was the most profound and catalytic experience of my life. **Cecily Maher**, for conversations about the S-word and helping me finally come out of the closet! **Carmel Parry**, for our weekend in Manchester when I took the red pill. **Penny George**, for our trip to Samye Ling and conversation in the

Tibetan tearoom. **Keith Tadd** for the greatest reframe of my life, and so many beautiful gifts. **Ildiko Spinfisher** for your phenomenal life retuning session that unblocked my creative pipes! **Gordon Sinclair**, for all the easter eggs and inspiration, especially the lighthouse story you told me that night. **Angela Mitchell**, my *Wild Egg* birthing partner, thank you for commenting on the early draft and courageously sharing your experience. **Erin Hurley**, for sharing your perspective and bringing your awesome vibe to the *Wild Egg* party. My Oasis buddies – especially **Jo Ray** and **John Sammons**, for helping me emerge from my creative shell and dream big. All my Write That Book Masterclass buddies for your energy, encouragement and big hearts, in particular **Alan Rafferty, Fiona Setch, Sarah McGeough, Melanie Wellard, Gayle Hubble, Christine Beech, Steve Dobby, Karrie-Ann Fox, Maria White, Charlotte Grand, Kate Rodwell**. And **Rachel Kenny**, thank you for your invaluable advice… you were right!

The Unbound Press team, who have been a joy to work with – **Nicola Humber, Jesse Lynn Smart, Jo Gifford, Sarah Lloyd**, and **Lynda Mangoro**. **Marcia Drut-Davis**, thank you for your pioneering work as a leader in the childfree movement and allowing me to stand upon your shoulders. And finally … **Elizabeth Gilbert** – everything changed after I read your book *Big Magic, Creative Living Beyond Fear* and took my own holy vows to creativity in 2015.

Contents

'Tell me, what is it you plan to do with your one
wild, precious life?'

~ Mary Oliver

Part One

Ending the Story
of the Mind

Mother's Birthday

'We did it!' Hollie said aloud, looking in the mirror as she applied her expensive new primer. It glided across her skin like silken fudge and smelled like a dentist's surgery.

At last! came a reply in her head.

Her midlife upgrade was complete.

She had reached the summit of herself and planted a flag of self-confidence in it. No longer drifting, lost, and unfocused. No longer chasing her elusive potential. She had finally claimed it.

Age forty-one, she had reached a place of sanctuary, a resting place where the relentless daily tides of self-doubt could no longer buffet her.

Her marriage was on solid ground after a few rocky years. The house was how they wanted it. And now she had a job commensurate with her ability, and a feeling of direction and purpose.

Everything was on track.

And she deserved it all.

She had (quite literally) walked over hot coals. Rewired her mental programming. Invested her own time and money to become the best version of herself. She had left no stone unturned in a bid to maximise her potential and was … finally … enough. From here on in, it would simply be a case of maintenance. Of keeping all the plates spinning.

Hollie watched as the creases round her eyes magically blurred and disappeared. It reminded her of the Etch-A-Sketch she had as a kid, smoothing out and re-coating the screen to make it pristine again, erasing all the lines and mistakes.

'Hollie Hardwick, Director of People,' she said, still feeling a thrill at hearing her new job title. She moved closer to the mirror and peered into her own eyes, wanting to capture this moment like a Polaroid.

She looked healthy, vibrant, alive.

For the first time in her adult life, she felt confident about her appearance. Maybe now, she hoped, she would be released from the grip of crippling self-consciousness and the constant need for vigilance. With sufficient income to maintain it to this standard, she could relax a little and learn to smell the roses.

This evening was about celebrating her mother's sixty-fifth birthday, but it was her night too. The first opportunity to celebrate her promotion and let it really sink in. Hollie smiled, reflecting on the symmetry of her mother retiring at the very moment she was stepping up in her career, simultaneously crossing a threshold. Yes, she would have to dig deep in this new job, but she was good at that. She knew how to work hard. But feeling comfortable in her own skin, this was entirely novel.

Perhaps, thought Hollie, this was what people meant when they talked about the boon of midlife? She finally had all her shit together and had become a proper grown-up. She suddenly felt excited and hopeful for her all that her fabulous forties were going to bring.

Hollie opened a section of her custom-built fitted wardrobe and surveyed the rails of clothes, organised like a Farrow and Ball colour chart. She was so glad she had invested in having her colours done a few months ago. She was convinced it had been a factor in securing her promotion. 'Dress for the job you want, not the job you have,' Lizzy, the style consultant, had said. 'When you discover your colours and personal style and wear them with confidence, they will enhance your essence. People will be able to see and meet the real you.'

Since her consultation, Hollie was well on the way to completing her wardrobe and looking forward to buying some new pieces to address a few outstanding gaps. Lizzy was right about confidence, Hollie thought as she pulled out an emerald-green tailored dress, orange belt, and pair of red patent leather heels. Previously, she would never have worn such vibrant colour combinations, not wanting to stand out or be too seen. But now, she felt emboldened. She worked hard enough at the gym, why not stand tall and be proud of her body, instead of always criticising and hiding it?

Once dressed, Hollie looked again in the mirror. She looked good. But did she look as though she was trying too hard? She had never been to the Angel Inn before and was unsure of the dress code. She turned this way and that, trying to make up her mind. 'Time to go, babe,' Hugh called up to her. 'Okay,' she shouted back.

'Fuck it,' she said to her reflection. 'Be the woman you want to see in the world!'

~

Later that evening, Hollie and Hugh were propped up on their elbows, facing each other on the kitchen floor. Glasses of fizz in hand and surrounded by party detritus, they basked in the afterglow of a successful evening. Everyone had come back to their house and carried on until a little before midnight.

'I'm so glad we stuck with those tiles,' Hollie said, looking at the Italian patterned floor tiles they had used on the walls in their new kitchen.

'Yeah. Remember when you had a meltdown and said we were going to have to re-do the whole lot?'

'I know. So glad you talked me out of it. They really set off the walnut worktops. Everyone commented on them this evening.'

'Yeah. And the bathroom. Everyone loved the wallpaper.'

'Courtesy of my mood board!' said Hollie.

'Yes, babe.'

'I have to say, though, I'm so glad it's all finished and the house is back to normal. Don't think I could have coped with the stress for much longer.'

'I still think the finishing touch was those skylights,' said Hugh, gazing up at the ceiling. 'Amazing how much they elevate the roof and make the whole room feel bigger.'

'Yes, okay, I acknowledge your design genius!'

'About time!' said Hugh.

'Listen to us, I think we're having a smug-married-moment!' said Hollie, taking another sip of her champagne.

She smiled at Hugh, sinking into this satisfying moment of domestic bliss. It felt comforting, like the faint whirr of a washing machine cycle on a lazy Sunday morning.

'Babe …'

'Yes?'

Hugh paused and looked down into his glass for a moment.

'I …'

He took a gulp.

'What is it?' said Hollie.

'I …'

'Are you going to say something mushy?'

Hugh put his glass down on the floor and looked tenderly into her eyes.

'I … I *really* want a baby.'

Hollie stared back.

She could feel her mouth hanging open.

22

She felt instantly sober, as though someone had just slapped her face. Really hard.

Somehow, she knew it was not the alcohol talking.

'I've been thinking about it a lot recently, and I just think it would be amazing.'

'But ...'

'I know, babe. I know we talked about this before, but we've never really talked about it, have we?'

'What do you mean?'

'I know you said you thought you didn't want to have kids, but you have never said you definitely don't.'

'I suppose not ...' said Hollie, trying to absorb the full weight of what he was saying.

'What if you've kept your options open for a reason?'

'I ...'

'What if, deep down, part of you is hoping you might change your mind?'

Hollie was reeling.

'Sorry, probably not the best time to bring this up,' Hugh said, looking sheepish.

'It's okay, I can see this is important to you,' Hollie replied, hearing the longing in his voice.

'I know I said I was happy with whatever you decided. And I am. I still am.'

'So, what's changed?'

'This evening ... I don't know ... maybe being at the Angel put a spell on me or something.'

'Very funny. I thought you didn't believe in that sort of thing?'

'It's just … we had such a lovely time. And everything is going so well for us. And the house is complete, like a lovely nest. And I just kept looking at you tonight, so beautiful, thinking how much I love you and how happy I am to be your husband, and how proud of you I am. And I just pictured us having a baby. I felt like it would be … a seal on our love.'

'But I'm forty-one, and you're fifty-one. Aren't we a bit old?'

'Maybe. But we're fit and healthy, there's no reason not to.'

Hollie opened her mouth to say something, but Hugh continued.

'Plenty of people have children when they're older these days.'

'But I just got promoted. How would I do this job and be a mother?' Hollie noticed her voice had gone up an octave and took a deep breath.

'I could be a stay-at-home-dad.'

'What?'

'I've been thinking about it. The business isn't going so well anyway, and I'm getting tired of pandering to clients who expect you to bust a gut, but never appreciate it. Maybe it's time for me to do something else? I'm not sure running an advertising agency was ever my life's dream, to be honest, anyway. And with your new salary, we would be okay without it. And I expect, knowing what you're like, you'll be promoted again before we know it.'

Oh my God, Hugh really had been thinking about this! Hollie thought.

'I …'

'More than anything, I love you, and I want us to be together. So, if you don't want to, I understand. And we can have a good life. I just thought … maybe it's time to make a decision. You know, once and for all.'

Hollie took another sip of champagne.

'I just *really* love you.'

'I love you too,' Hollie said and leaned over to kiss him.

'Are you okay?' said Hugh.

'It's just a lot to take in, that's all.'

'I know. Sorry, babe.'

'But you're right. I suppose I haven't really thought about this. Not *really* really.'

'Perhaps not the best time to start right now, eh? Probably need to get off to bed. I know my timing might not be the best, but I just couldn't help it,' said Hugh.

'It's okay. Let's talk about it some more when we've had some sleep.'

When Hollie woke up later that morning, she felt that her world had tilted one hundred and eighty degrees on its axis. Like there had been a glitch in the matrix.

Hugh had left a note on the pillow.

Gone to football with Dad.
See you later x

She pulled the duvet up round her neck and replayed the scene from the kitchen floor.

They had talked about having children when they got together five years ago. Hugh had been married before. He and his ex-wife had had a son and, much to his later regret, Hugh had an affair when his son was three years old. Enraged, his wife had thrown all his belongings onto the pavement, changed the locks, and refused access. Heartbreakingly, this had continued for years, and Hugh had never had any meaningful contact with Stephen, who was now grown up and living in Australia. Hollie had been engaged before and had eventually ended the relationship after realising she was unsure about having children but was sure she did not want them with Colin. So, when Hugh had told her he was not keen to become a father again, and she had said, *Okay*, Hollie had assumed this was it.

Job done.

Conversation over.

Decision made.

But in the wake of Hugh's heartfelt plea, Hollie now realised she had never stopped to deeply consider what this meant for either of them. Deep-down, she had always suspected her answer would ultimately be no. Yet now Hugh had confronted her so directly, she found herself unexpectedly jolted. For the first time, she was stopping to ask herself, genuinely and deeply, *Hollie, DO you want to be a mother?* and was shocked to discover there was not a clear *no*.

Somewhere, there was a seed of doubt.

Was there, as Hugh had suggested, part of her that had been waiting to be persuaded?

Hollie thought about her mother, younger sister, and almost all her friends who had children. She was practically the only woman she knew who did not have kids. Over the years, she had become accustomed to being the odd one out. On the outside looking in. Every time she met someone new and they asked, 'Do you have children?' Every time she found herself marooned inside a conversation about how to get kids to eat their greens. And every time she stopped to think about how everyone around her was consumed with raising their families.

Being the 'other' had become like static in the background of her inner life.

From time to time, she had talked to other women about having children, usually those awkward moments when conversations turned invasively towards what great parents she and Hugh would make. She had learned to deflect their questions by asking, 'How did you know you wanted to become a mother?' And on numerous occasions, she had watched women searching for their answer, as if the question was not something they had ever entertained.

Then, they would describe this visceral, embodied sensation – a kind of primal communion from within the marrow of their being – that had spoken to them with clarity, certainty, and confidence.

A kind of *ug*.

Hollie had never had the *ug*.

All she had ever heard was echoing silence.

But lying here now, Hollie suddenly realised she had never deeply engaged with the question of whether she wanted children. It had simply been a big ball of ambivalence she had kicked into the long grass. She had assumed she would not have children but had not wholeheartedly *decided*.

'Shit,' she said aloud.

She replayed the moment Hugh had looked at her last night. Those clear blue eyes, brimming with such love. The tenderness in his voice.

Babe. I *really* want us to have a baby.

There had been such earnestness, such longing in the word really. Something about the way he had spoken had penetrated deeply. The force of this insight hit her hard again. Like a buckle moment, when someone kicks you in the back of the knee and you crumple to the floor. For the first time, Hollie envied her mother, sister, and her friends their knowingness.

One thing, however, was now crystal clear.

She had to make a choice.

A definitive choice.

To abdicate what seemed like *the* most important choice of a woman's life suddenly struck her as a failure of duty to herself, and to her marriage. If she did not wish to become a mother, she needed to say a definitive, unequivocal, empowered, 'No, thank you,' to the Universe.

As a professional, educated woman, this should be a choice made *by* her, not *for* her.

Apart from simply being jolly good manners, saying a polite, 'I really appreciate your invitation, but after due consideration I've decided to ...' would be good for her mental health. A clear decision would ensure no loose ends were left dangling in her psyche. It would be the psychological equivalent of sewing her tubes together with nice, neat stitches, making a sturdy seam between a future childfree life and the fictional one in which she became a mother. That way, she would not be tempted to pick at the frayed edge of regret in later years.

At the very least, she owed it to Hugh to fully engage with this question. To reach closure. Also, Hollie mused, it was not beyond *all* possibility that a genuine enquiry might locate this seed of doubt, perhaps uncovering a surprising yes to motherhood. Was it possible that she had simply not been ready until now? And if there was a yes, she would need to hurry up and try to get pregnant because in all likelihood, the shutter of her biological egg shop was already closing ... or perhaps, had already closed? She had no idea. She had been on the pill since she was seventeen.

Sitting here in the cold light of day, she knew one thing for sure. Age forty-one, she needed to make the most profound decision of her life.

And fast.

Hollie started feeling anxious.

Without this clarion call from her *ug*, how would she decide?

How would she discern what was her authentic choice, versus what was social and cultural conditioning?

How would she know the difference between what she thought she should do to fit in and please Hugh, versus what she actually wanted?

How, in other words, could she trust herself?

'Come on Hollie,' she said aloud. 'You're a director, for goodness' sake. You can figure this out!' She was good at getting things done. All she had to do was galvanise herself.

'Right!' she said.

Hollie climbed out of bed and went downstairs, feeling full of resolve. She would take this task seriously. She would make sure she was a competent and diligent wife. After breakfast, she would get to work and figure this out. She would simply sit down and write a pros and cons list.

Yes, she thought, perhaps this was simply the passing out parade for her midlife upgrade.

Ambivalence Deadlock

Three months later, Hollie opened the porch door and looked at the doormat. There it was, a red envelope addressed to her, in her own neat handwriting.

Her last ditch attempt.

She laid the envelope on the dining room table and walked into the kitchen to make some coffee, glancing down at the floor to the place they had lay down that night. She still felt no closer to making a decision, and if this red-envelope trick did not work, she would be well and truly out of options.

She stood at the white Belfast sink and gazed out of the window as she filled the kettle. She loved that their kitchen was so high up and enjoyed looking out over the vale. The steep road was a nightmare in winter when it was icy, but at this time of year and from this vantage point, looking out at a canopy of treetops, red tiled roofs and chimney stacks, it was a delightful place to live, especially so close to the city.

Hollie opened a packet of freshly ground coffee and inhaled the smoky smell before pouring a generous amount into the glass cafetière.

She needed a strong cup this morning.

She felt flat and tired.

As well as covering her old vacant post and, in effect, doing two jobs, she had exhausted herself in the process of unsuccessfully trying to break the deadlock of her ambivalence. She had begun list-making with great gusto and hope, naively assuming the whole matter would be quickly resolved and life would move on – swiftly and neatly concluded, thanks to the application of logical reasoning. Initially, it had been a surprising and interesting exercise, seeing her pros and cons committed to paper, although few of the things she had written had come as a surprise. It had felt more like meeting a familiar friend and getting acquainted on a deeper level. And yet, she had not realised how much certain things meant to her until she had really begun to examine them. The exercise had seemed to confirm that Hugh had been right: whatever the outcome, it felt important to be coming off the fence and really engaging with this question.

The only problem was, having completed her lists, Hollie was stuck.

Well and truly stuck.

Overall, the pros and cons were equally balanced.

It was stalemate.

Sometimes, on days when her lists had not balanced, she had wondered whether it was a sign that divine providence was revealing her true decision. On occasions when her pros list was longer, she had begun to question whether her deep, unacknowledged longing was to say yes.

But on days when the cons won, she had found herself concluding that no was surely her honest answer. She had also berated herself for being ridiculous. 'Just because one side has more points than the other, Hollie, this doesn't actually mean anything, for fuck's sake!' she would say out loud. But in the very next moment, found herself beginning to wonder … *I know, but what if?*

On other occasions, she had employed a kind of *final answer approach*, scrutinising each list, and challenging herself as to whether she had *really* got everything out. If she outed *every single tiny thing*, no matter how trivial or embarrassing, she thought, perhaps the gap between the pros and cons might be more definitive and tip the scales one way or the other.

'Are you sure, Hollie?' she had said. 'Are you sure you're being really honest with yourself here? Come on, it is just you and me here, you can tell the truth!' When this failed to work, she had tried a kind of weighing-scales method, carefully prioritising each item to sort the wheat from the chaff, thereby giving her better visibility to what really mattered and enabling meaningful like-for-like comparison.

She had also attempted to inject some competitive spirit, with the aim of determining an overall 'winner' (game, set, and match) by comparing a pro and con and asking, 'So, Hollie, is this more important than that?' Each time one was more important, it gained more points, and points (as everyone knew) made prizes. The problem, though, was that trying to compare something like 'seeing the world anew' against 'the traumatising effects of soft play' was hard to weigh up fairly.

She had even tried to get Hugh involved, to see if he could bring a fresh perspective. They had sat in bed reviewing the lists together, but all they ended up with was a no-score draw, going round and round the same conversation. 'At the end of the day, I just want what you want, babe,' Hugh would say.

'So what you're saying is you'd *really* like us to have a baby, but you're also fine if we don't?'

'I think it would be amazing to be a little family, but I just want you to be happy.'

Hollie would feel herself becoming tense.

'That's lovely, but I need you to say what you really want. It's important.'

'I already told you …' Hugh would respond, his voice rising and becoming edgy. 'I want what you want. It's your decision, I don't know what else you want me to say.'

Hollie invariably wanted to shout, *I want you to take fucking responsibility for what you want and stop making me responsible for everything*!

But she said nothing.

'You're doing your deep breathing thing. You're angry, aren't you?' Hugh

33

would say. Hollie would lie, telling him she was 'fine' and 'just thinking'.

'Okay, help me understand a bit more ...' she would say.

'Here we go.'

'What?'

'That tone. Why do you have to make everything so complicated and difficult?'

Hollie's hands would ball into fists and Hugh would look like a sulky child.

'Let's say we have a child. Tell me more about how we'd set things up, practically?' she would ask.

'I thought with your career taking off it would make sense for me to stay at home and be a full-time dad.'

Hollie would feel herself becoming more tense.

'So you get to hang out with yummy mummies, while I slog my guts out doing long hours, and then our kid hates me and loves you? Sounds great.'

'I just thought you wouldn't want to stay at home, it would drive you mad.'

'Yes, but ...'

'But we can figure another way if you'd prefer. I just want us to be happy.'

That phrase again.

Hollie felt like punching him.

He was the one who had sprung this on her when her biological clock had almost stopped ticking. How had he expected her to react?

'I know,' she would say, trying to manage her face.

'We can just forget the whole thing if you want. Things can be great without a kid as well.'

Hollie envied Hugh's lightness. His seemingly casual, *I fancy a baby*, then, *It's okay, I'm not that bothered*. It was like he had thrown an existential grenade over her fence, walked off, but then had been surprised when there was an explosion. She never felt quite sure whether he was pretending to be more equivocal than he actually was, or genuinely did not mind. She suspected the former but felt nervous about probing too deeply for fear of opening the wound of his estrangement from Stephen. Yet, at the same time as feeling angry with him, it also felt unfair to chastise Hugh. Here he was, saying, 'I love you and I want to make a family with you,' and she was giving him a hard time. It was all so complicated.

Over and over, the same questions kept going round in her mind.

Why is something instinctive to others so elusive to me?

Why am I so closed off to my own knowing?

Why can't I just be easier and nicer?

Is there something missing in me?

Am I selfish?

What if I regret not having children?

Frustrated and feeling out of options, Hollie had remembered this letter-posting technique from a coaching workshop a few years ago. Everyone was invited to write a card to themselves saying what they were committing to in terms of applying their learning, then had put it into a sealed self-addressed envelope. At some random date, the facilitators had posted their cards, on the premise that the message would arrive at a future serendipitous moment. Expectantly, Hollie had bought a card at Kings Cross station on her way to a work conference, popped her lists inside, stuck a second-class stamp on it, and asked a slightly bemused colleague to post the envelope when she felt called to do so.

She poured a mug of thick coffee and stirred in a teaspoon of organic honey, then opened the envelope. She smiled at the appropriateness of the card – a yolky yellow colour with a fried egg on the front with writing underneath … *Husband, you always crack me up*, it said. She unfolded the yellow lined notepaper inside. Like opening a time capsule, she hoped seeing her lists afresh, with the benefit of some time and distance, might give her new perspective.

Becoming a Mother: Cons

1. No try-before-you-buy option

As she read this again, a phrase came to mind … *post-purchase dissonance.*

It was a marketing term she remembered from a conference years ago, used to describe buyer's remorse when a product you bought turns out to be a disappointment. Surely, she thought, as children were completely non-refundable and there was no try-before-you-buy option, the chances of post-purchase dissonance were high? Whilst she and Hugh could borrow kids and have them over for weekends to 'try on' parenting, it was never going to be anywhere near close to the actual reality of becoming a mother. With a husband, you could divorce them if it did not work out, but once you had a child you were bonded for life, regardless of who you got, or how they turned out.

And what if your child was disabled?

What if they had terrible behavioural problems?

What if they had a dreadful personality?

Or what if they ended up in prison or addicted to heroin?

All of these things seemed, to some extent, a complete lottery.

Whilst rationally she understood that however their child turned out, she would love them, it did not mean it would be a remotely enjoyable experience. In some ways she felt mean-spirited for thinking this, but equally it seemed like a hard truth, and the thought of not being able to change her mind was terrifying. She had always been an options-open kind of person and she feared feeling trapped.

2. Loss of freedom

Loss of freedom still felt like a potent con. She loved being able to do what she wanted, when she wanted, like lying in bed this morning and sauntering down to make coffee. She could also be terribly impatient and was the type of person who strode around purposefully wherever she went. From what she had observed, everything became slowed down with children. Even something as simple as *going for a walk* was no longer actually going for a walk but more like going out to, well, *stand around*, for a while, holding coats then return home, inch by excruciating inch, frequently accompanied by wailing. Whilst she could frame this as an exciting developmental opportunity to learn how to be more zen, Hollie feared she would be in a permanent state of simmering resentment, with an ever-growing to-do list of things not getting done.

3. Environmental impact

She smiled as she read this again.

When it came to being 'green', she always thought of her father. Growing up, they used to buy chewy, brown wholemeal loaves, which came in thin white paper bags that her father used to recycle by smoothing them out and cutting them into squares to use as toilet roll. It was like wiping your bum with greaseproof paper, mostly unabsorbent, so pee would run onto your hand if you were not careful, and highly embarrassing when friends came round. Hollie knew she was woefully inadequate when it came to being a conscious consumer but could not help thinking that bringing another child into the world when there was already a growing population crisis was actually the selfish thing to do. There were already plenty of children who needed a good home – why add another one to the list?

As her father had always said, 'We are living on a finite planet experiencing exponential growth – something has got to give.' He had given her a book called *The Limits to Growth* to read in her late twenties. It had chilled her to the bone to read the analysis of experts modelling future scenarios that combined birth rates, dwindling natural resources, and mortality rates. If she had a child, what kind of future would they have? The facts were alarming. With over seven billion people already on the planet and worsening climate change, wasn't it perhaps ultimately selfish to bring more children into the world? And after all, there were already plenty of abandoned kids in need of a loving home. Was helping them more of a moral duty than contributing to overpopulation? Every time she thought about it, she had apocalyptic visions, which Hollie suspected might be connected to having read a book called *Z For Zachariah* at school set in the aftermath of a nuclear holocaust.

4. Pregnancy and giving birth.

On the subject of things post-apocalyptic, she was still repelled by the idea of being out of control of her own body.

And, honestly, she was afraid of childbirth.

She was not proud of this, recognising in herself an element of vanity, maybe even cowardice. After all, giving birth was totally natural. But she had decided it was important to be brutally honest with herself and keep it on the list. Once again, she recalled a graphic film of childbirth they had watched at middle school in Religious Education, and wondered whether her fellow classmates had been similarly traumatised. Every time she thought about pushing a baby out of her vagina, she replayed the gory images from that film and felt herself recoil in horror. And it was not just the giving birth part, either. It was what happened afterwards. The high school story of Jenny's mum had also burned itself into her brain. She could still see her friend's face that day when she described how her mother's stitches had dissolved in the bath after her caesarean, and her innards had fallen out. Every time she thought about it, Hollie pictured Jenny's mother desperately trying to push a string of giant sausages back into her belly, like a scene from *Alien*.

5. *Impact on work*

She reflected on the week she had just had at work. Even if Hugh was a stay-at-home dad, she could not imagine how she would maintain the level of productivity needed to be successful if she also had a child. The fact was, women always seemed to end up doing more of the emotional and domestic labour, and she could not shake images of herself looking stressed and haggard, working harder to keep up, whilst her confidence gradually ebbed away. Thinking about it again now, Hollie could feel the anxiety in her body as she projected herself burning out. She was so not good on a lack of sleep and feared descending into a pit of post-natal depression. She imagined being off sick and people talking about her. 'Did you hear about Hollie Hardwick? Had a complete nervous breakdown, apparently. Couldn't cope with having a baby. Not up to it.' Not being able to cope seemed like the worst kind of incompetence. She had read about these high-flying women who had several children and held down big jobs but, in her bones, she just did not feel she would be one of them. She was already struggling to keep her head above water as it was. It felt like having a child would tip the balance, and she would sink.

Fast.

6. *Impact on marriage*

Impact on their marriage was a difficult one. Now that Hugh had declared his hand, it seemed to Hollie there was a negative impact either way. If she decided she did not want children, how would Hugh reconcile himself with never having the chance to fully enjoy being a father? But if she decided she did want to become a mother and was unable to cope, how might that change the way he saw her? As a mother, would she be a disappointment to him? Would she become lesser in his eyes? And if Hugh stayed at home, how would that change things between them? Having less quality time together seemed to be an inevitable consequence of children. It also struck Hollie as an irony that when you became a parent you ended up spending less time with the person you actively chose to spent time with in the first place, in order to spend time with someone you were tied to but who you might not actually like. And what would happen if they split up?

7. Being old parents

She still could not shake the thought that when their child was ten, she would be in her early fifties, and Hugh his early sixties. Whilst she liked to think she was not hung up on age, this did seem a bit long in the tooth. What if they were simply be too tired to be good parents? Content to plug their child in to electronic devices rather than spending quality time colouring in and working Play-Doh together like you were supposed to do for their development. And then there was the whole question of navigating the burgeoning, murky, and complex world of social media. She imagined Hugh and herself getting to a point where they were too old to even understand what was going on.

8. Long-term impact on my body

Hollie thought of Aunty Audrey, who had once confided in her that she had ongoing health conditions 'down below' after giving birth, which meant she always had a stock of Tena-Lady in her cupboard. The thought of her vagina not going returning to its original honeymoon-fresh condition was bad enough, but contemplating it being permanently misshapen and leaky seemed quite another. She was still unsure whether she was willing to take the risk.

9. Financial responsibility

Hollie had once heard an eye-watering figure about the cost of raising a child. Yes, she and Hugh were lucky to be in a good financial position now, but things could change. It was an unstable world. She also hated the idea of having to stay in a job she might have otherwise left because she could not afford to leave. She often heard parents say this at work, and seeing people chained to a job they clearly loathed, just trying to 'hang on until the kids had finished university', was soul-destroying. Also, these days, kids no longer seemed to simply go to university and then make their own way in the world like she had. With house prices continuing to rise, the likelihood that they would have a boomerang-kid living with them as an adult seemed high. What if they never got their house back?

10. Enforced family fun

Unlike Hugh, who seemed able to let things wash over him, Hollie had little tolerance for doing things she did not want to do. When she asked colleagues about their weekends at work, they would often describe excruciatingly dull activities, rounding off with the comment, '…yeah, but the kids had a great time and that's what matters,' as if their personal enjoyment was no longer a relevance or consideration. The thought of having to acquiesce to the noise, smell, lighting, and garish colours of soft play centres and sit in urine-filled swimming pools filled her with dread.

And children's birthday parties. WTF was going on with these? It seemed to have become obligatory to invite your kid's whole school class and give everyone a goody bag full of shit, plastic presents and fluorescent sweets. Recently, she accepted an invitation to the party of her friend's daughter, thinking it might help in her deliberations as well as show support and interest. 'Please come, Hollie,' her friend Anna had said. 'Katie would love you to be there, and I hardly see you these days.' Katie was five and in truth, Hollie had thought, would not give a rat's ass whether she turned up. And the reason she never saw Anna anymore was because every activity she wanted to do together revolved around her daughters or spending time talking incessantly about them. Hollie had gone to the party, but had resented eating the cheap, crappy, beige food from plastic trays to assuage the tedium of half-snatched, fragmented conversations with Anna who was too distracted to talk to her anyway. And, after presenting a gift to Katie, she had (as predicted) not seen her for the remainder of the party.

Hollie remembered how she had come home feeling tormented. On the one hand she had been angry with herself for not being, well … nicer … for not finding a way to relax into it and enjoy the experience. On the other, she had felt disappointed that so many interesting, thoughtful friends who used to be good company had given in to investing their time in banal activities, doing what was expected of them because everyone else did it, and – worst of all – trying to convince her this was 'fun'. She wondered whether when it was her own child these kinds of activities might be tolerable, maybe even enjoyable? 'When it's your own, it's different,' was what people always said. She supposed it was possible, but sitting here right now, she remained sceptical.

11. More housework

Hollie looked around the pristine room and imagined how it would look different with a child. She pictured dirty handprints on the walls, her expensive moisturisers squirted hilariously over carpets, mess and stickiness everywhere, and a general increase in volume of domestic chores. Hugh was good around the house, but he nonetheless did man-cleaning: cursory wipes around things rather than deep sparkle-cleans. It seemed inevitable that her workload of domestic chores would significantly increase if they had a child. Perhaps a small price, but nonetheless a due that would have to be paid.

12. School uniform shopping

Hollie laughed looking at this con again. She had forgotten it was on the list. For some reason, the ritual of shopping for school uniforms always seemed fraught. It was a subject that periodically became a hot topic in the HR office at work as all the mums shared the trauma of this thankless task. School uniform shopping, as far as Hollie could tell, was one of those parental activities that was necessary, costly, and painful, for which you rarely got any thanks in return and, due to growth spurts, had to be relentlessly repeated. Kids did not want a school uniform but had to have one, and invariably, as Hollie recalled from her own school days, they wanted something infinitely more racy or trendy than was permissible or affordable. It was a lose/lose situation. Like some of the others on the list, she reflected, school uniform shopping was emblematic. It symbolised the unsatisfying sacrifices parents so often made, and the ingratitude they had to swallow in return. Whilst this could be a good experience in teaching her to give with no expectation of return, it seemed to her this was all well and good in theory, as opposed to the actual practice.

13. The teenage years

She feared a kind of karmic revenge for her teenage years. It seemed to Hollie that unless you were supremely lucky, there was an inevitability about having to let go and watch your little boy or girl morph into a smelly, sullen, inconsiderate git to some degree or another, whilst resisting the urge to say, 'I told you so,' when they did not listen to your sage advice. After all the years of sacrifice and investment, it still seemed to her you could do everything right, but your kid could still turn out wrong. As external forces played an increasing role in moulding the person your child would become, you had to hope to God that the lottery of life turned out in your favour. And even if nothing particularly bad happened, you might still end up with an adult you did not get along with or have much in common with. It seemed like a risky return on investment. She only had to look at poor Hugh to see this. As far as she knew, he had made one mistake and been punished for the rest of his life. It felt terribly unjust, yet he was not the only person she knew who was estranged from their children. She suspected it was more common than people liked to admit.

14. Grandchildren duties

Hollie had noticed a pattern amongst many of the older women, that they were often automatically expected to be willing to give up their freedom later in life to perform free childcare. What if she did not want to do this? She knew this was something that might not even happen, but in the end had decided to retain it on her cons list because it reminded her that having a baby meant a commitment for life. The expectation that care-giving was a lifelong obligation seemed to her something worth considering, especially as she knew women at work who had fallen out with their own children over this issue.

At the end of the list of cons, there was nothing she wanted to add or remove. She felt satisfied, if not entirely proud, of her candour.

Hollie boiled the kettle again and looked out the window. Reading the cons again, she thought she sounded like a woman who did not want children.

Was this her truth?

What if this whole exercise was simply a ruse?

What if she liked the idea that she was the kind of woman who *would want* children? That wanting children was somehow ... *nobler*? A better, more meaningful, more expansive choice? It was hard to know whether she actually believed this or had been conditioned to feel it. It seemed difficult to separate the two. Or perhaps she just feared missing out. Or she was in denial because of fear? Fear of losing control. Fear of being overwhelmed. Fear of being found wanting. Of not being enough.

The kettle boiled and Hollie added some hot water to the cafetière.

She sat back down and turned to the next page.

Becoming a Mother: Pros

1. Personal growth and seeing the world anew

She still imagined re-connecting with the wonder you felt as a child to be one of the most beautiful aspects of being a parent. Like the moments when, as a little girl, she had opened the door to the front room and gasped as her eyes had surveyed the neat piles of Christmas presents left by Santa and his helpers. Hollie remembered this feeling of enchantment: as if the very moment she had entered the room, the last glittering particle of fairy dust had just disappeared into the air, yet the lingering magical sparkle of its invisible presence remained hanging palpably in the atmosphere. She imagined vicariously re-living those moments, watching her own child's reactions and experiencing the delicious momentary pleasure of remembering what wonder felt like before the careworn, old coat of weary, seen-it-all-before adulthood had numbed this innocent joy.

She sat back in her chair, remembering the recent workshop in

44

London. They had done an exercise on personal values, and growth had been top of her list. What if having a child and watching them grow was the most powerful and profound personal development experience you could have as a human being? Was she really prepared to forgo this? Was it true that becoming a mother was the highest expression and fulfilment of womanhood? If she decided not to become a mother, did this mean she was not as committed to personal growth as she liked to believe? Or again, was all of this just what she had been conditioned to think? It suddenly struck Hollie that whatever choice she made, it was important that she moved *towards*, not *away from* something.

Towards freedom. Towards an alternative way of life.

Not away from fear.

Yes, she thought, she did not want fear to be the reason for choosing not to do something

2. Passing on learning

She had not yet totted up all the money she had spent investing in her own personal development over the years, but she knew it was considerable. She believed in the adage that you only *really* learned something when you were able to teach it to someone else, and loved the idea of sharing her insights and wisdom to nurture an emotionally intelligent, well-rounded human being, who might live a luminous life, and even do some good in the world. But then who was she kidding? Perhaps this was the fairy tale all parents were sold, only to be disappointed by the reality of their kids discounting and dismissing anything they had to say.

3. Deepening my bond with Hugh

This still felt tricky. On the one hand, she was not sentimental enough to buy into the commonly-held view that children 'made a marriage'. In fact, from what she had observed, they often seemed to have the reverse effect. Yet despite this, there was something undeniably seductive about producing a biological child together. She imagined seeing a mirror image of herself and Hugh fused together, embodied in another person, and felt a pull at her heartstrings. Whatever happened in life, having a child would mean them always being bonded together in the deepest and most irreversible way. She welled up as she replayed what Hugh had said about 'sealing their love' and saw his beseeching eyes looking at her. She was certain he would be an amazing father and imagined it would be a fulfilling experience to observe him growing into this role, in tandem with her learning to be a mother. She also reflected that this might help Hugh heal from the sadness of Stephen.

4. Experiencing love

She had gone back and forth on this one several times when writing her lists, but in the end decided to leave it on. Right now, however, she noticed her rational self remained less persuaded.

Get real, Hollie, the love a child has for their parent is totally conditional, for goodness' sake, it said. *If you don't feed and clothe and give them your full attention, there is a good chance they will end up hating you. And even if you do, they might still loathe you anyway. There's a reason 'They fuck you up, your mum and dad' is such a well-known poem, you know!*

Yet, powerful cinematic images of herself cradling a baby were simultaneously playing in her mind. Eyes brimming over with love as she gazed down adoringly at her tiny bundle. She had seen this look of adoration on her sister's face when her nephew was born, and it was burned into her retinas. She had also seen this expression in films sufficient times to vividly imagine the expansive, breathtaking rush of unconditional love flooding through her body. She imagined it as waves of ecstasy, like when you come up on a pill at a rave, only pure and grown-up and grounded. But surely such moments were fleeting? The director's cut of the film – the bit that always ended up on the floor of the editing suite – would probably show the baby squealing the place down seconds later, having filled its nappy! She knew all this, yet some deep part of her, something beyond the rational self, could not shake the idea that growing and giving birth to another human was an ultimate expression of love.

Having a baby would mean literally and metaphorically being cracked wide open, and there was something undeniably compelling about this idea.

5. Smelling my baby's skin

Whimsical as it sounded reading it again, this idea had become a kind of metaphor for her, capturing something of what she imagined the visceral experience of motherhood to be. Whilst she was not the cooing, maternal type, she could not deny the allure of soft, freshly talcum-powdered baby's skin. There was something about little children coming out of the bath, being patted dry with a fluffy towel and put to bed that evoked something deep inside her. A kind of wide-eyed, hazy nostalgia. She had smelled her nephew and the babies of friends (when they were trying to convince her of the joys of motherhood) enough times to have this fragrance clearly recorded and stored away. It was one of those evocative smells – like suntan cream on sun-kissed skin or paint pots being washed in the corner sink of a classroom. An olfactory experience that bypassed your brain and lured you into a promised land of afternoon naps and long summer evenings playing out, that seemed to cast an irresistible spell, evoking a kind of Arthurian-legend version of childhood. She recognised part of her wanted to have this experience, to claim it as her own, and add it to her book-of-life memory store. She felt sad thinking about missing out on this deeply intimate experience of communion.

6. Buying tiny clothes

Like smelling baby's skin, she had written this 'pro' as a shorthand for a certain texture of experience she imagined came from having children. It seemed there was something in the act of providing for your children – feeding, clothing, and supporting them – that was somehow … *ennobling*. A role that bestowed you with a satisfying largesse and confirmation of your own grown-up-ness. Hollie imagined this is what people referred to when they talked about parenthood making you 'selfless', that you prioritised your resources to care for your children and gained a sense of satisfaction from this sacrifice in return. At least when they were little anyway, she imagined buying tiny shoes and dinky dungarees and adorable jackets and diddy school uniforms would be utterly charming. Hollie sipped her coffee and wondered whether her own mother had felt like this when she was a baby. Undoubtedly, her mother had not enjoyed the experience when Hollie was older, when she used to spend money on good quality school shoes only to be met with derision and resentment, and – on one occasion – a screaming tantrum in the middle of the shop!

7. Bedtime stories

Hollie had been an avid reader from a young age, reading books by the light of a pocket-sized torch under her duvet. She imagined there were few things better than snuggling up in bed next to your own child, saying those immortal words – *once upon a time* – and clicking a key into the lock of their imaginations, then watching them fall asleep into otherworldly enchantment. She would be good at bedtime stories, enacting all the voices – from the deep, reverberating *fee-fi-fo-fums* to the fluttery fairies and the cackling witches – and introducing her child to the magical kingdom of books. It was a role she relished the thought of playing.

8. Providing comfort and soothing

It seemed to be a universal impulse that whenever people were in danger or really unwell, they always called out for their mother.

I want my mum!

Something about the idea of someone calling out this phrase to her evoked a deep feeling of tenderness. It made her think about all the times her mother had comforted her with homemade chicken soup. She remembered a time when the toddler of one of her friends had hurt themselves in the park, having come down the slide too fast. Her friend had gone to top up the parking meter at the moment it happened, and consequently her little boy had run towards her as the only familiar person in sight and thrown himself in her arms.

It was the one and only time a child had ever done this to her, and she had been taken aback by the feeling of encircling him in her arms. It was a moment of exquisite tenderness that had stayed with her, and Hollie had reflected there was something deeply powerful about being the person someone else runs towards when they are tear-streaked and vulnerable. She was surprised to find this impulse within her, yet it was undeniably there now she was looking more closely. As surely as if that little boy had left an imprint upon her that day.

9. Being in the motherhood club

Being able to bond with her mother, sister, and friends remained a powerful pro. Then at least, she would feel like she fitted in with all the mothers complaining endlessly about how hard it was raising children. She would no longer be the 'other'.

The outsider.

Someone who did not belong and did not understand.

She would be a spoke in the wheel of life like everyone else, able to exchange baby wisdom and child-rearing advice, and part of a community of mothers who were all in it together. There would be no more awkward silences when she was asked, 'So, do you have children?'

It would be easy to join in, show pictures of her kids, and always have something in common. She imagined the sweet relief of not feeling the need to justify herself anymore or wonder whether there was something wrong with her, and whether she was missing out.

10. Scrapbook firsts

She loved the idea of building a mental scrapbook of those initiation moments that parents always waxed lyrical about. First steps. First day at school. Learning to ride a bike. Graduation. Even falling in love. If they had a child, she and Hugh would have their own scrapbook, just like everyone else, filled with those special Kodak moments that recorded all those milestones along the path of life.

11. Being part of the family tree

Her mother loved genealogy, and since retiring, she had started researching and mapping the family tree. Every time she had gone round lately, her mother relished telling her about another long-lost relative she had added, and every time she looked at the family tree, Hollie was acutely aware of the absence of a line coming down from her name on the structure chart and the lack of photographs of her children proudly displayed on the mantelpiece. Since having her son, her sister had rekindled relationships with cousins they had barely seen for years, now with children in common to unite them. They had met up a few times for playdates, and Hollie felt a stab of envy at not being part of this unfolding tapestry. If she and Hugh had a child of their own, Hollie would be woven into the unfolding future generations, her place secured and substantiated in the extended family. Without children, she would remain as a full stop on the family tree, where everyone else was part of a continual, expanding flow.

12. Being more outwards

'You think too much,' her mother had always said to her growing up. It was a phrase colleagues at work had also used when referring to her tendency to analyse problems from three-hundred-and-sixty-degree angles, and something Hugh frequently commented upon. In part, it was what made her good at her job, but it was also a characteristic that condemned her to live inside her head, where she would often ruminate and sometimes disappear down shadowy rabbit holes. As one colleague had once said, 'For God's sake, Hollie. Stop walking around in sackcloth and ashes and just chill out!' Hollie expected that becoming a mother would naturally pull her towards being more outward-facing and imagined herself becoming grounded and rooted in the external world, like her mother and sister, helping her to be better balanced and connected.

But … as an introvert, would she actually enjoy this?

13. Old age

Revisiting this, she wondered about the rhetoric versus reality. 'But who will look after you when you are old?' was a question she had been asked many times when people discovered she did not have children, along with, 'How does your husband feel about that?' and, 'Why not?' It always surprised her how her not having children seemed to empower people to ask the most probing personal questions. She would never dream of asking, 'Do you ever worry your kids won't look after you when you are old, after everything you've done for them?' Yet this kind of rudeness was so acceptable the other way round that people would actually become offended when you did not respond, as if it was their right to know the answer. Having children, it seemed to her, was no guarantee of being looked after when you were old. If you were lucky, your children might visit you in your care home, if (of course) you were not estranged from them altogether. But by choosing not to have children she would be almost guaranteeing there would be no one who felt duty-bound to help her when she was old. She had to admit this felt vulnerable, especially as, on balance of probability, she was likely to die after Hugh.

But was this a good reason to have children?

14. Leaving a legacy

Just yesterday, she had seen a friend's post on Facebook: 'List of things to do so you have no regrets when you are old,' and noticed most of the items related to spending time with your children. Leaving a piece of yourself after you died felt important, and having a child, it seemed to her, was undoubtedly a way to take care of this. Like everyone else, she wanted to matter, for her life to have meant something. She loved the idea of passing things on, she and Hugh creating their own unique traditions and rituals with a child of their own that would ripple forward in time to become part of an unfolding future history after they had gone.

Hollie sat back in her chair.

There was nothing else she wanted to add to her pros list either.

Reading the pros again, there were definitely aspects of motherhood that tugged at something deep inside her, yet she could not shake the feeling there was a strong thread of whimsy woven through the pros lists, whereas the cons seemed somehow more grounded and real.

Was she holding up a romanticised, fantasy-version of motherhood? The kind of vision that was sold to you in adverts of adorable, gurgling babies? A beautifully packaged and carefully sterilised version of motherhood that lured you into believing motherhood was a biological imperative and caused you to forget that having a baby was only a momentary flash in the journey of a lifetime's commitment?

Maybe this was why having an *ug* was so important. Because if you really sat down and thought about having children, it was a terribly difficult choice to make rationally.

Maybe NOT having an *ug* was her answer?

That the absence of an *ug* was itself proof she did not want children?

But somehow, she still could not accept this.

There was still a seed of doubt.

What if she regretted closing the door forever?

What if there was something missing in her that she needed to find?

What if her *ug* was just different, lying somewhere dormant, waiting to be unfurled?

What if this was her chance to become a better, less selfish person?

What if motherhood really was the pathway to becoming a woman of substance?

Hollie heard the key turn in the door.

'Hi, babe.'

'You back from swimming?'

'Yeah. Gruelling training session this morning. What have you been up to?' Hugh said as he dumped his sports back in the hall and came through the door, smelling of chlorine.

'Reviewing my motherhood pros and cons lists. Again.'

'You still on with that?'

'Yeah. I posted the lists to myself to see if reading them with a fresh pair of eyes might give me a breakthrough'

'Impressive.'

'Thanks.'

'Mind you, I suppose I shouldn't be surprised. You're nothing if not thorough!' he said, kissing her on head. 'So, did it work?'

'Not sure. I just finished reading the reasons to become a mother and can't decide whether I really believe them, or they're a romanticised version of what I've been programmed to believe. And when I look at the cons, I think I'm just being a cynical doom-and-gloom merchant projecting all these things that might not happen.'

'What's this?' Hugh said, picking up the card. '*Husband, you always crack me up*. Are you saying I drive you insane?'

'You definitely do that!'

'Or I have cracked you open? Like an egg,' said Hugh, laughing.

'I don't know about that,' she said, 'but I definitely feel like a sticky, yolky mess. I just keep thinking … what if I regret it?'

'I don't know what to say. Maybe if you don't know, that's a decision in itself?'

'That would just feel like giving up.'

'So what are you going to do?'

'Honestly, I don't know.'

Maybe-Baby FM

Hollie put her key in the ignition of her VW Golf. The 2-litre diesel engine growled into life. She decided to drive the scenic route to work. It was the last day of the school holidays, and the roads would still be quiet. She switched on Radio 4. The cost of family holidays was being debated. Interviewees were arguing about whether the school calendar needed to be re-imagined due to the exorbitant price hikes and she realised she had not included the additional cost of holidaying with children onto her cons list.

Was this the universe giving her a sign?

Maybe the envelope technique had worked after all? This morning was she finally connecting to her truth?

Maybe she already knew her decision deep-down?

She did not want to have children.

She smiled to herself.

Yes, this was her decision.

She felt relieved as she reached forward and switched off the radio. This morning, she would just savour the peace and quiet for a change and enjoy the drive The sun was breaking through the clouds. She put her foot on the accelerator and the car responded instantly as she passed a sign indicating the national speed limit. She could feel the power beneath her feet. Whilst technically you could drive sixty miles an hour here, most people stayed around forty because of the bends. This morning she revved up to sixty. The car stuck to the road like glue.

She felt free.

Twenty minutes later, she was almost at work when the traffic suddenly slowed down. She wondered what the delay was. After crawling along for a while, she saw the road was down to one lane as preparations for a new housing estate were underway. The foundations of a show home were taking shape, flanked by two large billboards featuring two attractive couples and smiling children.

Coming soon, beautiful three and four-bedroom family homes.

Hollie thought about the estate agent who had showed her and Hugh round their house when they bought it. 'And this is the nursery,' he had said, opening the door to the box bedroom. The wallpaper was a muted yellow with a pattern of tiny white, brown, and orange owls. 'The owners only just finished doing it out, so it's all ready for a new arrival. Boy or girl.' She remembered he had looked at Hugh and winked. She had not really paid attention at the time, but retrospectively felt annoyed by his easy and insensitive presumption that they, like everyone else, would have kids.

No, she did not want children.

She was grateful for having made her decision.

Hollie pulled into the carpark and glided into a spot near the reception. The door made a satisfying clunk when she got out and locked the car. She made a beeline for the HR office to check in with her team and walked into the midst of an animated conversation about the trials and tribulations of entertaining kids during the school holidays.

'Chloe and Jack want to go to Flamingoland, but …'

Everyone in the room was a parent except her and momentarily she felt acutely aware of it as the conversation fell silent. 'Don't let me stop you, please carry on,' she said.

'… but have you seen how much the tickets cost? By the time we factor in getting there and back, paying for lunch and rides, it's going to be a small fortune,' said Jackie, one of the HR officers. 'They take your eyes out at these places. Know they've got a captive audience,' said Julie, the payroll clerk.

'Yeah, desperate parents!' Jackie retorted.

'No. Desperate mums!!! My Dave would never be seen dead at Flamingoland. I always end up taking the kids to these places,' said Jess, the recruitment administrator, to a chorus of knowing laughter.

Yes, thought Hollie, this was further confirmatory evidence, she was grateful not to be in the motherhood club.

'Hollie, I bet you're listening to all of this, thinking, "Thank goodness I don't have all this stuff to worry about,"' said Sandra, one of the HR managers. 'Yeah,' she said, imagining none of them would think for a second that she had been seriously contemplating it. Hollie lingered. She was always mindful of waiting long enough to show an acceptable level of interest in these conversations that she was never part of, before feeling able to divert the discussion onto work issues. As she had arrived a little earlier than usual, she tried to relax and listen a little longer before moving the conversation on.

Jess reminded everyone about the staff discount scheme and pointed out there were some great money-off vouchers for school holiday activities currently being advertised, which led to further discussion about all the great things you could do on a budget, and the atmosphere quickly changed.

'But when you see their little faces, you still end up thinking it's all worth it don't you?' chirped Julie.

Everyone agreed. Even Jess, with comical begrudging. 'Have I shown you this photo of our Daisy?' said Julie. 'At her birthday party last week. Dressed as a princess. Melts my heart every time I look at it.' Julie scrolled through her mobile phone and passed it around. Within a few moments, everyone in the room was sharing photos of their children and trading funny stories, turning moments of frustration and calamity into great anecdotes that Hollie imagined would be shared at future dinner table conversations as an easy way of building rapport and connection. Oddly, she noticed herself beginning to feel envious as she listened to their descriptions of family life in all its ordinariness and chaos.

Wouldn't it be lovely to be part of these conversations? Maybe I am missing out on this, the real stuff of life?

Reeling at hearing this voice inside her head, Hollie made her excuses and retreated to her office.

Later that morning, she struck up a conversation in the kitchen with a colleague from another department.

'How are you, Angela, I haven't seen you for a while?'

'Don't ask, Hollie.'

'What's up?'

'Teenagers, that's all I'm going to say.'

'Oh dear.'

Hollie wondered whether this level of daily conversation about children was normal, and she had simply become more tuned into it; or whether, like some kind of cosmic joke, the universe had begun broadcasting Maybe-Baby FM 24/7 inside the echo chamber of her mind.

'My daughter's fifteen and she's a nightmare. Asked if she could have some friends over the other day. I stupidly said yes. They camped in the garden and stayed up all night, traipsing in and out of the house, opening and closing the fridge. In the end, Hubby got up in the middle of the night and shouted at them, and now all hell has broken loose. I haven't slept a wink.'

'That sounds so hard, Angela. Teenagers, eh? I remember what I was like at that age.'

'Count your blessings you don't have to worry about this stuff. Seriously, Hollie, never have kids.'

Hollie walked back to her office. *Well, that settles it*, she thought. *I don't need this kind of stress. It sounds bloody exhausting. No, I don't want children.*

Later that day, Louise from Procurement turned up with her new baby, drawing a large, cooing crowd of women into the open plan area which Hollie could hear through her door. Despite the fact people usually couldn't bear Louise, she was now a new mother, so her status was instantly elevated.

As the senior 'people person', Hollie felt it was important to show her face at these pass-the-baby-parcel rituals, but today she stopped what she was doing and approached the gathering with renewed interest. When the inevitable opportunity came to hold the baby, unusually, she said yes. Cradling the fuzzy, sleepy, swaddled two-week old, she allowed herself to soften into the milky sweetness of the moment, trying to ignore the nods and winks from colleagues as they suggested she was 'getting broody'. On Maybe-Baby-FM, she heard a Suzanne Vega song start to play …

It won't do
To dream of caramel,
To think of cinnamon
And long for you.

Omigod … Hollie thought as she leaned closer to the infant … *maybe I do want a baby!'*

~

That evening, she and Hugh went to her mother's house for dinner. Her sister and brother-in-law were visiting from Harrogate.

'Hi, Sis, you look fancy in your work stuff. Is this your director upgrade?' said her sister as she walked into the kitchen.

'But you look tired, and a bit too skinny if you ask me,' her mother chimed.

'Nice to see you too,' said Hollie, trying not to sound too defensive.

'And what have you done to your hair, Sis? Very glossy. Is this you power dressing? Seriously, how did you get your hair like that?'

'Er, I just had a special conditioner put on,' said Hollie.

She was keen to avoid this discussion, not wanting to say how much she had *actually* paid for this new treatment. She knew it was likely to lead to entrapment in another awkward conversation about how selfish she was, always spending money on herself.

'Look at the state of my hair, gone to pot a bit since this one came along.'

Hollie felt like her sister said this with a certain pride. A kind of … *look at me, I'm a better person now I've let go of the shallow things I used to be concerned with before I became a mother and a woman of substance.*

It was hard to know whether this was a deliberate dig at her, an accidental jibe, or whether she was just being oversensitive.

Hugh handed her a gin and tonic.

'Wow, that's strong.'

'You look like you need it,' Hugh replied.

'Here. Before you drink that, say hello, Aunty Hollie,' her sister said, holding her fourteen-month-old at arm's length. Before Hollie had time to take a sip of her drink, she found herself awkwardly holding her nephew. His cherubic face was smeared with snot and what looked like the aftermath of pesto and pasta. It felt like watching her interacting had become a kind of family sport. Right on cue, her brother-in-law walked in.

'Ooh, look at you, all dressed up and only here to go! Is that the sound of your ovaries clacking I can hear, perchance? Only joking, take no notice of me. I mean, frankly, who'd want one of them? Look at the state of him. Congratulations on the promotion, by the way.'

'Thanks,' said Hollie.

'Sorry, Sis, I can see you've had enough already. I better take him back before he messes your lovely suit.'

Hollie handed her nephew back. She felt relieved, but also ashamed that she was not better at cooing.

'Did I tell you Aunty Ruby is here?' said her sister.

'No.'

Hollie was often the last one to find things out. Her mother and sister spoke several times a day since Jack had arrived. Even though she didn't want to speak to her mother every day, she felt an unreasonable stab of jealousy at their closeness.

'One of the people she married last year has just had a baby and she's come over to see them.'

Aunty Ruby lived in America and had her own business as a wedding celebrant.

Hugh took Hollie's glass. 'Want some more ice in that?'

She nodded, grateful to feel she was being taken care of.

'Shall I make a salad, Mum?' Hollie asked.

'Probably better had, I know the ones I make are never good enough for your high standards.'

'Yeah,' her sister reinforced with a conspiratorial laugh.

Hollie began chopping red peppers, taking a big gulp of her Spanish-measures gin.

'Steady on, Hollie, you know what you're like when you're tired and mix alcohol.'

'Yes, Mum.'

She noticed her mother never seemed to comment on what her sister drank. She could not help thinking it was because she did not have kids and therefore seemed less responsible.

Hugh gave her a little squeeze. 'You okay?'

'Yeah, I'll be fine after more booze and something to eat.' She smiled weakly.

The doorbell rang and Hollie heard Aunty Ruby's distinctive American-with-a-Northern-English accent down the hall.

'Hi darling, oh don't you look glamourous,' she said, hugging her in a haze of Chanel N°5 as she entered the kitchen. 'I don't know how you do it, but you seem to look younger and more beautiful every time I see you, Hollie. You must tell me your secret.'

'More money and no kids,' her sister shouted over.

Everyone laughed.

'Yeah, that's it,' Hollie joined in, wondering why she felt embarrassed at being complimented.

'So, tell me, darling, I hear you got a big promo—'

Aunty Ruby stopped and screeched as her brother-in-law walked in holding Jack, cleaned up and freshly nappy-d.

'Oh my God, look at him! Give him here. Isn't he just gor-gee-ous, to die for, the most handsome boy I ever laid eyes on in my life! I swear, I just want to eat him up.'

Hollie escaped upstairs. She walked into her old bedroom and looked at herself in the full-length mirror on the wall, staring at her reflection.

Mum is right, I do look tired.

She forced a smile.

Come on, Hollie, loosen up.

Stop being so prickly.

You're being over-sensitive.

Back in the kitchen, she continued preparing the salad.

She looked over at her aunty, mother and sister, watching their easy conviviality with envy.

'Did you hear about your cousin's stepdaughter Laura? She had a baby girl. Isn't that just the most wonderful thing? I'm going down to visit in a few days and I just can't wait.'

'Yeah, Aunty Ruby,' Hollie's sister said, holding her pregnant belly. 'We're hoping this one will be a girl.'

'How exciting!' Aunty Ruby trilled.

'I figured we may as well go for it. I mean I'm not getting any younger, am I?'

'So, will it be you next, Hollie, with this gorgeous husband of yours?' Aunty Ruby said, kissing Hugh on the cheek.

'Maybe,' he said sheepishly.

Hollie shot Hugh a look.

'Maybe! What do you mean? You're actually thinking about it, Sis?'

'Well, I guess at some point we all have to think about it, don't we?' Hollie said, trying hard not to sound defensive.

'No, most of us didn't think about it, we just did it,' her mother said, rolling her eyes.

'Well, if you are going to, you better hurry up, Sis. You know your fertility already dropped off a cliff a few years ago, don't you?'

Hugh brought Hollie's drink over and offered to finish the salad. She sat at the table, willing herself to lean into the conversation.

'So how did you know you wanted children, Aunty Ruby?'

Her Aunt looked at her blankly. She recognised the look. It was the same expression her mother and sister had given her in answer to the question.

'Well, honey, I guess I just always knew.'

As she said this, Aunty Ruby touched her body in the place where the top of a pregnancy bump typically ends. There it was again, Hollie thought, the elusive *ug*.

'You think too much, Hollie, that's your problem,' her mother said. 'You either do or don't want a baby. If you don't know, it seems to me it's probably best you don't have one.'

'Yeah,' her sister added. 'You'd hate it anyway, the whole pregnancy thing.'

Hollie felt like she was being pulled inside her own stomach by a kind of inner suction causing her to fold in on herself, like being swallowed in a vacuum.

She felt awkward inside her own skin.

Out of synch.

Misplaced.

Hollow.

What is wrong with me? she thought. *Why can't I just be like normal people?*

Maybe her mother was right.

She should not drink gin.

Or have a baby.

~

The next morning Hugh woke her up with a cup of tea in bed.

'What time is it?'

'Nearly nine. I thought I'd let you have a lie in.'

'God, I feel like death.'

'You did drink rather a lot last night.'

'And my mouth tastes like an ashtray.'

Hollie had noticed her alcohol consumption slowly creeping up over recent months, and she had started smoking again, which often happened when she got stressed. She suspected it was a way of trying to turn back the clock to her student days when everything seemed lighter and more fun.

'I didn't do anything awful, did I?'

'You got a bit heated, but only towards the end. I think it might have been something about an interview on *Woman's Hour*. Are you okay?'

'Not really. I had a weird dream. I was staying at my cousin's house. Sleeping on a bed outside in the garden. I cut my finger, but couldn't find anything to wipe it on, so I ripped a strip off the bedsheet, hoping my cousin wouldn't notice. And I was trying to balance an egg on the headboard for some reason. The next thing I remember, the egg had been splattered down a bright red wall.'

'Sounds very Margaret Atwood. Budge over.'

Hugh climbed back into bed and snuggled up.

'You feeling horny?'

'Definitely not.'

Sex was the last thing on her mind at the moment.

'Are you okay? You just seem really tense and distracted. I'm worried about you.'

'I'm wondering if my mum is right? Maybe motherhood is not for me. I just don't seem to have the *ug* like everyone else.'

Hugh spat out his tea.

'What's an *ug*?'

'That thing my mum, sister, Aunty Ruby and all my friends seem to have. That inner knowing, like something that speaks to you from your womb. The voice that says, *Yes, I want a baby*. Maybe you're supposed to have this and if you don't, it's a sign that, deep down, you're not meant to become a mother? What if there's just something wrong with me? What if I'm just a selfish cow?'

'That's harsh, babe.'

'It's what a lot of people think.'

'Well, maybe, but they don't know you. And I love you, so you can't be all that bad.'

'Maybe you just have terrible taste?'

'Very funny.'

Hollie took a sip of tea.

'I'm sure there are more women like you than you think. Maybe you just don't happen to know any?'

Hugh had a point. Maybe she needed to find one of these maybe-baby women?

'Or maybe you're just thinking too much about this whole thing? I hate seeing you so stressed.'

'But surely if ever I was going to really think about a decision, it's got to be this one? I mean, a child is the one thing you can never give back. No try-before-you-buy. Ultimately, even a husband is return-able, but a baby isn't.'

'Thanks,' Hugh said with a half-cocked smile. 'You really know how to make a man feel wanted.'

'You know what I mean. Once you've given birth, you're always a mother. End of. For life. So if ever there was a decision to get stressed-out about, surely it's this?'

'Maybe we should just forget the whole thing,' Hugh said, kissing her on the cheek.

'No, I'm not saying that. I just mean it's a big deal.'

'But I have to say, if I'm honest, babe, it doesn't sound like you want one.'

Oh God, Hollie thought. He had those Bambi eyes again.

'I don't know. Maybe I do. What if I'm just in denial? I'm not made of stone, you know. There are moments when I think how wonderful it would be. I imagine myself pregnant, and picture scenes of us with a child. I can see that too, you know.'

'Me too.'

'I just feel so stuck with it all. Paralysed. Everything is getting on top of me. Learning my new role, still covering my old job, wrestling with all this. Making a decision about anything right now feels almost impossible. Even on things that should be quite straightforward at work. It's really affecting my confidence. I went to our senior team meeting the other day to sort out an issue about the new employment contracts and I ended up lying because I was so ashamed to admit I didn't know the answer to a straightforward question. I've never done that before, Hugh.'

'Who hasn't done that? You really need to learn to give yourself a break. Maybe you need to stop thinking about this for now. Leave it for six months until you've passed your probationary period, then we can talk about it another time.'

'I don't think that's a good idea.'

'Why?'

'Much as I hate to admit it, my sister is right, I probably don't have long left, biologically speaking. I feel like the clock is ticking and it's about to strike twelve.'

'Okay, in that case then, we better get on with it,' Hugh said, kissing her, 'and hurry before your womb turns into a pumpkin!'

~

In the following weeks, Maybe-Baby FM continued to blare a nonstop playlist. It was like being trapped inside a private torture chamber, pulled this way and that … *yes-no-yes-no-yes-no* … day after day, with no way to switch it off.

Hollie wanted to hang the blasted DJ.

She spoke less to Hugh about her torment, and never mentioned it again to her family. It felt too humiliating. Having failed to make a breakthrough with her lists, she found her mind increasingly searching through the personal archives of her upbringing, hunting for clues in the motherhood back-catalogue. She had been blessed with a wonderful childhood. Financially poor by today's standards, but culturally rich. Hollie thought about their Sunday afternoon ritual, before her sister was born, when she had gathered round the hi-fi with her parents and spent a couple of hours recording onto tapes. Her father would plug in a microphone with a long cable that looked like something Val Doonican might use whilst propped casually against a high stool, and they would read poetry or sing along to a folk song.

She had also loved designing elaborate games with her friend Lucy. They would pretend to be detectives, hunting for clues to solve the mystery of the ghostly presence of a cleaner who was said to haunt their school. According to legend, the cleaner had been working in the girl's toilets one evening and met a grisly end, condemned for eternity to lurk in the toilet bowls as a disembodied pair of marigold gloves waiting to pull unsuspecting bottoms down to a watery death … like a kind of Hammer House of Horror meets Moaning Myrtle. She had also loved roller skating, *Twinkle* comics, and playing house. Like most girls, she had owned a few dolls and enjoyed tucking them in at night in the wooden cot her grandfather had made.

Unlike her, Hollie's mother had known she wanted children from an early age and applied herself fully to the role. She had taught Hollie and her sister their times tables before they started school, cooked meals from scratch, visited all the elderly relatives every weekend, kept the house spic and span, and completed home improvements – like the time she hand-sewed hessian carpet tiles together to make a hard-wearing fitted carpet for the hallway. Her mother was the parent who, when the school lollipop lady became gravely ill, stepped up and volunteered to caretake the job like it was her civic duty to maintain safe crossing for all children.

When it came to enjoyment and personal self-care, however, her mother was far less dedicated. Date nights had consisted of sharing a bar of chocolate, drinking a few cans of McEwans Export, and playing a game of Scrabble. Or, if her parents were really splashing out, a bottle of German wine. Investing in your own wellbeing was, in her mother's eyes, tantamount to self-indulgence: something flaky, middle-class people did. Her mother always put others first, and Hollie wondered whether she could give of herself in this way?

Did she possess the capacity to be so selfless?

Could she balance a demanding and often stressful job, with being deeply engaged and present at home?

The thought of doing either incompetently was anathema to her. And, unlike her extrovert mother, she needed lots of me-time. Hollie began to wonder whether her mother's example had influenced her more deeply than she had realised. If this was her motherhood blueprint, it was a lot to live up to. Inspiring and intimidating in equal measure.

She thought about the other women in her lineage and their relationship to motherhood. Her mother's mother, Margaret, had been a hard-working mother and was also utterly selfless. Until the day she died, she refused to let anyone do anything for her without paying them, even something as trivial as going to the corner shop for a paper when she was crippled with arthritis. Conversely, her father's mother, Lilian, had been an opera singer who cavorted with theatre folk and was a distant and neglectful mother. She had emigrated to America when Hollie was young, so she did not remember much about her except that she wore fur coats, smoked through a cigarette holder and was always 'bloody freezing'. Then there was her favourite, Aunt Edna, whose flat had always smelled of lemonade and freshly baked empire biscuits. She had married relatively late and, tragically, her husband had died in a shipping accident. Heartbroken, Aunt Edna had sold her sweet shop, never remarried and never had children. She was viewed in the family as childless, yet childlike. Playful, but slightly pitiful.

Hollie began to wonder whether the feeling of connection she felt with Aunt Edna, her only childless female relative, might be more meaningful than she had realised?

The only other significant motherhood-memory she could find was from sixth form college. Seventeen years old, she and three friends had been sitting together just outside the smoking lounge (a stinking bit of corridor where you were allowed to smoke 'tabs' as they called them in those days). For some unknown reason they were each separately squashed into a wooden locker, imagining what they might do when they 'grew up'. The consensus was that Freya would be a hippy and have children (she became a yoga teacher and had two daughters). Sarah would be a teacher and have children (she became an educational psychologist and had two daughters) and Izzy would be an actress and have children (she married a film producer and had two daughters). Hollie however, despite being a moody, painfully self-conscious and overweight goth, was apparently going to be a 'business-woman', even though none of them really understood what this meant, which she could only surmise was inspired by her modest success as an Avon Lady. She was also the only one predicted not to have children.

Looking back, she wondered whether her friends had somehow discerned, even then, a future she could not fully grasp.

~

Having failed to make a breakthrough on her own, Hollie decided to see if she could find a 'maybe-baby woman' to talk to, and reached out to her friend Jodie, the most networked person she knew. Jodie hung out with women who wore printed scarves, invested in high-quality footwear made of natural materials, and listened to *Woman's Hour*, so she seemed the most obvious choice. Hollie sent Jodie a text.

Help! Desperately seeking like-minded, ambivalent-about-having-children forty-something professional woman for intimate conversation. Willing to travel to meet right person and pay for dinner.

Within a few days, Jodie messaged back to say she had found the perfect date: a friend called Rosie who was the same age and had recently had a baby after, according to Jodie, 'really wrestling with her decision'.

As an extra bonus, Rosie also had the same Myers Briggs personality type as Hollie, INTJ, a type characterised by a high need for competence, and an abhorrence of confusion, mess and inefficiency.

A few weeks later, Hollie found herself parked around the corner from Rosie's house, in a leafy street of neat Victorian terraced houses about eight miles from where she lived, feeling flustered and anxious.

What are you doing, Hollie? You hardly know this woman. And here you are about to interview her!? I mean, who does that?

She wondered what Jodie had said, suddenly feeling annoyed for not double-checking and being better prepared. She had considered going in with a set of questions but decided against it. Whilst it might effectively be an interview, it seemed important to avoid making it *feel* too much like one, so she had decided to aim more for a Lorraine Kelly chat show vibe, rather than a Jeremy Paxman cross-examination. Sitting here right now, however, she felt far from chilled and chatty!

So, Rosie, I know you were ambivalent about having kids and then latterly decided to have a baby. As someone with the same personality type as me, can I just ask ... do you regret your decision?

This was the question she wanted to ask, but who asked this, let alone answered it? She could not help imagining that somewhere, buried in the dark web, there was a secret society of mothers who found each other and eventually met in a basement in a circle of chairs, bonding through the shared shame of the ultimate taboo as they introduced themselves in hushed tones: 'Hi, my name is Mary, and I regret having children.' Surely it stood to reason that, as you could not meaningfully try out having children, and once committed could never go back (like taking the red pill), some women must know that given the choice again, they would choose to forgo the whole experience? But even if this was true, it was clearly *not* the done thing to saunter into a stranger's house and ask them.

Hollie wondered what the point of their coffee date was. What was she really hoping to learn? It had seemed a good idea at the time, but now she was not at all sure what she was doing here, yet it would be rude not to show up. 'Come on, Hollie, think,' she said aloud, attempting to gear herself up. 'You're going to have to get out in a minute and knock on that door. What do you want to know?' Maybe, if she could uncover the thought process that had led to Rosie making her decision, it might illuminate something she had overlooked, a killer point that would tip the balance one way or the other? Perhaps if she listened to Rosie's story and understood how she had unpicked the deadlock of her ambivalence, she might be able to apply this process to her own situation?

Or, Hollie mused, was she secretly hoping for some sage advice, for Rosie to tell her what to do? Was part of her hoping she might lean over and whisper, 'Look, between me, you, and the gatepost, I'd say don't do it, sister.' Or conversely, 'Hollie, I implore you not to miss out on this most enriching human experience.'

It seemed unlikely either would happen.

Hollie took a deep breath. At least Rosie being the same personality type was likely to mean there was some common ground. She was desperate and out of options, so what was the worst that could happen? Hollie got out of the car and rang the bell. Her heart was pounding.

'Hi, Hollie, I've been expecting you. Come in,' Rosie said and ushered her down a tiled hallway and into a large dining kitchen at the back.

'Would you like a drink. Tea or coffee?'

'Yes, that would be lovely. A chamomile tea if you have one.'

Rosie looked like the sort of person who would have the loose flowers variety.

'Thanks so much for agreeing to let me come round and speak with you, Rosie. I really appreciate it. Especially as I imagine you have your hands full with your new son and juggling work.'

'Yeah, it's pretty intense, but you know, you get used to it. You can see for yourself the house is a bit of a mess.'

Hollie had noticed but tried to avoid automatically using this as evidence to reinforce the downside of kids. After all, she did not know Rosie and had no comparator for what it looked like BC, *before child*.

'Here you go,' Rosie said, sitting at the table and placing down a beautiful pot of tea and metal strainer.

'So,' Jodie said, 'you're debating whether or not to have a baby?'

'Yes.'

Hollie could have kissed her for just coming straight out with it, putting the issue right out on the table so matter-of-factly.

Very INTJ.

'How can I help?'

'Good question,' said Hollie, trying to buy some time to gather her thoughts. 'I guess I wanted to meet you because I've always been ambivalent about having children and have suddenly found myself needing to make a definitive decision. I feel completely stuck and hoped it might help to talk to someone who has recently been through this kind of journey, to get some insight that might help.'

'I understand. I was the same,' said Rosie, pouring her own tea.

Hollie felt herself relax a little.

'To be honest, Hollie, if you'd asked me, I probably would've said I would not have kids either. Not really the maternal type, you know. I was that person when people brought their babies in to the office, I'd avoid it or feign interest. I just thought … so what? … anyone can have a baby. Women in Africa have them every day living in extreme poverty and just get on with it, without the big fuss we make over here. I find all that cooing sentimentality nauseating. I know that probably sounds harsh.'

'I'd say it sounds honest,' said Hollie, feeling relieved to hear someone else admit this.

'My partner, Simon, wanted kids, and eventually we got to the point where we just needed to make a decision about what we were doing with our lives. Simon had left his job and I was coming to the end of a contract, so it felt like a natural pause for us to consider the next stage. Age-wise I was entering into the realm of biological now or never, so we talked through the options.'

'My husband wants a baby too, which triggered this process for me. Can I ask, were you stuck over the decision, Rosie?'

'Not sure I'd describe it as being stuck, but I certainly spent a lot of time thinking about it and weighing up pros and cons. I went through a phase of writing lots of lists.'

'Oh God, me too!' said Hollie.

'I'm passionate about the environment and having kids massively

74

increases your carbon footprint, so I was really conscious of this. I was determined not to use disposable nappies but, as you can probably see from that pile on the table over there, I totally failed. Having a baby is so exhausting, there are just some things you have to give in to.'

'I can appreciate that.'

'And the tiredness sucks, to be honest. I've aged a lot recently.'

Hollie took a sip of tea and stayed quiet.

'I'm just fucked all the time. It's like having a permanent hangover, but without the booze. The thing is though, I know it'll pass, and it is getting better. Silus is eighteen months now and more interactive. I mean babies are pretty boring, right? I'm looking forward to when he's a bit older and we can take him out camping and teach him stuff. That's when it will get more interesting.'

Hollie smiled, inviting Rosie to continue.

'Simon's been amazing. He does a lot of the childcare. He knows how important my work is to me. Being subsumed by domesticity was never going to be my thing. Or being defined by being a mother. I'm a person first and foremost and he gets that. I wouldn't have wanted to have a kid if we weren't parenting with equal responsibility. You do have to watch yourself slipping into calling each other Mum and Dad, though. Bloody ridiculous and annoying, but surprising easy to do! … Sorry, is this helpful, Hollie?'

'Yes. Definitely. Were there any other things you weighed up?'

'Oh yes, lots of things but I think I've deleted it all now. Have to conserve my brain power.'

Hollie felt a stab of disappointment. She would have loved to know more about Rosie's lists.

'How are you finding work?'

'I went part-time after having Silus. I was thinking about it anyway and probably would have done it at some point. I was always travelling to London and just didn't want to be doing that anymore. Financially, it's been challenging with Simon also working less, but you just find a way to manage. And we don't go out these days now anyway!'

Hollie wondered whether this was Rosie's subtle way of saying she regretted it. Was she trying to give her a hint, albeit unconsciously?

'Coming back to your question, I remember worrying about whether I'd be an incompetent mother. I'm not the most emotional or effusive person and I wondered whether I'd be the kind of person who could give to someone else when I felt empty? You know, have that kind of selflessness.'

'I know what you mean,' said Hollie, noticing the words landing in her body.

'But now I realise being a mother can show up in lots of different ways, and I think I'm not bad at it. I'm learning, and I'm okay with that. I think too many mothers get so self-absorbed and focused on the family that they don't pay attention to the outside world, and I never wanted to be like that.'

Rosie put her hand in the air to stop the conversation and turned her head.

'Sorry, baby monitor. I can hear Silus. Hopefully, he's just moving around. Should be okay for another ten minutes or so.'

Hollie was starting to feel conscious of taking up Rosie's time.

'Sounds like he's settling,' she said, bringing her attention back to Hollie. 'I'm not sure I've been helpful.'

'You have. Honestly. Apart from anything, it's just really refreshing to have an honest conversation.'

'Is there anything else you want to ask?'

Yes! thought Hollie. *Do you regret your decision?*

'I'm curious about what tipped the scales towards having a baby. You talked about weighing up pros and cons before. Was there something that, in the end, trumped all your concerns?'

'Good question. I think it was just a combination of things. Simon was keen, so that was definitely a factor. Often blokes have to be persuaded, so I was lucky, you could say. I think I just got to the point of just thinking, "Why not?" Like, slowly, the idea of being guided by something other than my own wishes grew and I began thinking having a baby might be a pleasure. Something different. I thought, maybe having a kid would be a bit of a wild ride for us. I mean ultimately, we try to be all rational and mature but when you boil it down, life is messy and complex, and we make all our decisions from a mixture of courage and fear. I wouldn't be without Silus, but it is hard work, Hollie, I'll not lie. There are good days and bad days. I don't think it's better or worse to have kids, or not have them. At the end of the day, it's just a personal choice.'

Hollie excused herself to go to the bathroom. She sat on the toilet and surveyed the room. Rubber toys in the bath. Piles of nappies on the windowsill. Packets of baby wipes and tubes of cream strewn on the floor. It was a far cry from the peace of her neatly arranged pots and potions. Did Rosie regret it? It was hard to tell. Would she want to give Silus back if she could? Who knew? She certainly wasn't selling motherhood in the way many women Hollie had spoken to seemed to, as if they were not telling the whole truth. But nor was she saying, *It's terrible, don't do it.* Asking the 'regret' question was an impossible thing to impose on anyone. And even if Rosie were to say she regretted it, how would that help? She might say yes in this given moment, but undoubtedly other days her answer would be a definitive *no*.

Back in the kitchen, they talked a little longer about Jodie and a few mutual friends, while Hollie finished her pot of tea.

'I probably should be heading off now. I've taken up enough of your time.'

'Before you go, I dug a book out for you. I did lots of research and found it really useful when I was having a similar debate with myself. You're welcome to borrow it.'

Rosie retrieved a book from beneath a pile of baby detritus on the kitchen bench. 'Here,' she said, handing it to Hollie.

'*Maybe Baby*. Good title. Thanks, Rosie.'

As Hollie drove home, she reflected on the conversation. She was not sure it had moved her any closer towards finding her *ug*, but she felt a little less alone and freakish. And she had to admit, there had been something grounded and beautiful about the way Rosie had talked about her small family unit, a feeling difficult to put into words but tangible, nonetheless. *Was Rosie giving me this book a sign?* she wondered. Had she nudged slightly towards the 'maybe-baby' zone?

That evening, she was sat up in bed, reading.

'What's that you're reading?' Hugh asked as he climbed in.

She showed him the front cover.

'*Maybe Baby*,' he read aloud. '*Twenty-eight writers tell the truth about scepticism, infertility, baby lust, childlessness, ambivalence, and how they made the biggest decision of their lives.* Sounds like a light read, babe.'

Hugh laughed.

'What's funny?'

'You. You're just so … *you*. In everything. I've never known anyone as diligent. Speaking of which, where's your pencil and highlighter?'

Hollie was one of those people who always underlined passages and annotated in the margins, so books often wound up tattered like an old pair of trainers. A small, satisfying rebellion against her usual perfectionism. It was also the reason why Jodie would never lend Hollie anything from her own extensive personal library.

'Not my book.'

'Whose is it?'

'A woman called Rosie. A friend of Jodie. I went to see her today.'

'What about?'

'I …'

Hollie paused and smiled, pursing her lips.

'I guess I interviewed her about how she decided to have her baby. Like you said, I found someone who was ambivalent like me.'

'Seriously?'

'Yeah.'

'That's next level, even for you! Did it help?'

'Yes and no. It didn't wave a magic wand. But talking to someone I could relate to definitely made me feel less of a freak.'

'That's good.'

'It also made me realise there's a whole genre of books on the subject I never even thought to read, for some reason.'

'Just what we need, more books. How many have you ordered?'

'Three so far,' Hollie said.

'And how will you know when you've read enough?'

'Good question. I assume I'll just know. I'll feel satisfied I've thought about it from all angles.'

'Sounds like hard work. I still have an even better idea, you know, whenever you feel like it.'

'What's that?'

'Just come off the pill and see what happens.'

'You mean, basically, have sex?'

'Well, yes, that would be part of the equation.'

'That's not a decision. It's abdication.'

'Huh?'

'It's saying I can't made up my mind, so I'm going to throw caution to the wind.'

'I don't get it.'

'On the balance of probability, coming off the pill and having sex means it's highly likely a baby will be the result. To my mind, this is tantamount to deciding *yes, I want a baby*. Or at least deciding I'm open to having a baby.'

'Not sure I agree,' said Hugh. 'You aren't even sure you *can* get pregnant. I think coming off the pill is like saying, *I am surrendering to letting nature take its course and am open to whatever the outcome is.*'

'Still feels like giving in. If I come off the pill, I want it to be a choice, that I am saying yes to becoming a mother and then seeing what happens. Rather than saying, *I can't make a choice, Mother Nature, please decide for me.*'

'Rather you than me,' Hugh said.

~

Hollie raced through the book Rosie had lent her, and quickly devoured the ones that arrived in the post. The more she read, the more she felt validated that choosing whether or not to be a mother was a deeply personal subject that was nuanced and complex and far less binary than simply wanting or not wanting children. There were women who had not wanted children from a young age and never wavered from their strong inner knowing. Women who had been ambivalent like her – wrestling, as one author put it, with choosing between forever and never – who had come off the fence in many different directions. Women who had struggled with infertility, through illness or by marriage. Women whose life circumstances had never aligned. Women who had suffered the heartbreak of miscarriage.

On and on.

Yet despite their different circumstances, there was a shared experience of feeling out of synch and questioning what kind of women they were. Hollie felt relieved to know there were other women out there like her. And the more she read, the more the daily Maybe-Baby FM broadcasts became tolerable, as if someone had turned down the volume down so she could at least hear herself think. It was a blessed relief.

And yet, to her surprise, the pages of the books she bought remained unusually pristine. Reading them felt like grazing on tapas, sampling small dishes of women's personal experiences, and common themes harvested from many individual stories. But Hollie wanted a full five-course meal. She wanted a deep, intimate, raw story.

She began to wonder whether all this reading was becoming a way of stalling. A kind of sleight-of-mind, fooling her into believing she was making progress when in reality she was just going deeper into stalemate. Was her truth that she did not want to become a mother, and this was a way of putting off the frightening finality of this decision and all it would mean? It certainly felt possible. But then again, she had felt something when she was with Rosie. A stirring that was hard to put into words. What if there was something there, locked deep down in the vaults of her psyche? What if she just needed to find a key to open her safety deposit box?

Even if it was empty, she needed to know.

Maybe buying more books was not the answer.

Maybe she needed something more immediate, insight that was more real and gritty.

~

The following Saturday, while Hugh was at the football, Hollie walked into her study and sat at her computer poised to explore the world of online blogs. She felt like a kind of Peeping Tom, intent upon lurking in rooms where she could listen to conversations she was never party to in real life. She wanted to hear it all. Like Alice stepping through the looking glass, she wanted to enter this alternate unfamiliar world beyond the mirror to see what emotions might be stirred.

As her computer booted up, Hollie looked out of the window over the garden at the front of the house. Once again, the image of the estate agent who had shown them round when they bought it came to mind, and that queasy, conspiratorial wink he had given Hugh. They had never bothered changing the décor, given it was to their taste. Hollie liked the idea of it being the 'wise owl room', which seemed a good motif for her study space. Looking at it again now, she appreciated the irony of this moment.

'What kind of woman are you anyway, Hollie Hardwick?' she said aloud. 'The kind of woman who values working and studying over raising a family?'

Perhaps, she thought.

She wondered whether Hugh ever opened the door to this room and looked longingly at the wallpaper, remembering what the estate agent had said? She took a sip of her coffee and typed into the search engine:

Blogs about motherhood.

She had that guilty feeling of walking through customs with nothing to declare, which struck her as odd. After all, it was not like she was asking The Google to recommend porn sites. Within a few clicks, Hollie had disappeared like Alice down the rabbit hole and landed in a weird and alien Stepford-Mom world, one where women defined themselves by the term *mom, mommy,* or *mummy* and seemed obsessed with creating the perfect experience for their 'bundles of joy'. In this realm, a pervasive undercurrent of anxiety seemed to flow through all the conversations about whether they were getting motherhood right enough. They seemed so wrapped up in pursuit of a pot of gold at the end of a perfect family rainbow that Hollie imagined them having major midlife-breakdowns or drugged up on Prozac further down the line. She couldn't help feeling a bit sorry for them. Reading their posts reminded her of the feeling she used to get when she ate a whole selection box in one go on Christmas day … sickly and having consumed something of zero nutritional value.

Curious to explore other avenues, Hollie opened a different virtual doorway and followed a trail of breadcrumbs that led her into another realm: the *Motherhood Fanatic Zone*. Motherhood Fanatics were groups of women united by an unshakeable belief that any woman failing to use her uterus for the procreation of God's children was not only less than fully actualised but was, effectively, inviting the devil to fill the void of her barren womb with corrupting, evil spirits. 'Fuck you fascist bitches!' she shouted at the screen. 'So much for the sisterhood, eh?'

It was one thing to contend with being labelled as selfish and permanently othered, but she had never considered that not having children might be seen as morally bankrupt. Hollie sat back in her chair, reeling from the thought that she could be judged this way were she to become a childfree woman, and enraged for all the other women who might want to have children but were not be able to for whatever reason. It seemed even more unjust for them to be castigated.

How dare these motherhood fundamentalists cast stones?

She glanced out of the window and saw her neighbour, Kathy, puffing on a cigarette at the bottom of her garden, which was directly opposite theirs.

She needed a smoke.

'Hi, Kathy.'

'Hello, Hollie.'

'Can I pinch a cigarette from you?'

'I don't smoke,' said Kathy, winking as she offered her packet whilst looking furtively back towards her house. 'Promised George I'd given up. Terribly naughty of me.'

Hollie liked Kathy. She was in her sixties, but still had a glint in her eye. She was a glass artist and played the banjo in a folk band.

Hollie lit the cigarette and inhaled deeply.

'You working? I saw you up at the window,' said Kathy.

'Yeah, kind of.'

Hollie paused, wondering whether to say anything about what she was doing.

'Can I ask you a personal question, Kathy?'

'Of course.'

'Did you always know you wanted children?'

'D'ya know, I don't think I ever really thought about it. In my day, that's just what you did. Why, are you and Hugh thinking about starting a family?'

'We're talking about it,' Hollie said, feeling this was not exactly accurate. It was more like she was talking to herself.

'I think there's a lot more choice these days. Although having said, that my Sally got pregnant when she was eighteen, so it didn't really come up for her. I imagine the longer you wait, the harder it is. You have more to lose when you are older and already have a career like you, Hollie.'

'Yeah ...'

Hollie took another puff of her cigarette.

'Not sure what I would have done in your shoes, if I'm honest.'

'Have you ever thought you might not have had them, given a choice?'

'Now there's the million-dollar question,' Kathy said, stubbing her cigarette out. 'I don't know. I loved having kids, and I love being a grandma. But it's not for everyone. And it's not an easy path to take. Sorry, Hollie, that's probably not very helpful, is it?'

'Like you say, it's a big question.'

'I think you just need to follow your heart in the end. Good luck,' Kathy said and walked back up the garden.

Hollie sat back in front of the computer. Kathy was probably right, she thought, but that was exactly her problem, how to listen to her heart and not her head. She clicked on another link and began reading a blog written by a new mother talking about the birth of her fourth child which had garnered hundreds of me-too comments, then followed links to other sites they had recommended. This led her into a kind of *Motherhood Blitz Spirit* community, made up of women who reminded Hollie of her sister: women who had taken motherhood in their stride and were navigating the trenches of baby-rearing together with a matter-of-fact acceptance and communal generosity. Conversations were confessional and educational: they talked about leaky boobs, first bowel movements after birth, the wreckage of their ve-jee-jees, how they noticed their sphincter tightening when they heard their babies cry, and how giving birth felt like being hit by a truck. Hollie loved their honesty, but at the same time their conversations unnerved her. They brought back memories of that film in Religious Education and the story of Jenny's mother and her sausage innards in vivid technicolour. The more she read about the realities of childbirth and the postpartum period, the greater Hollie felt her respect for these women grow, but the more she found herself questioning her own ability to cope.

Finally, for completeness, she spent another hour lurking in communities where women who were avowedly childfree pitied and pilloried so-called *breeders*. These women celebrated freedom from the tyranny of visiting theme parks on bank holiday weekends, congratulated themselves on their under-appreciated contribution to a less crowded planet, shared their intolerance for the mess and noise of children in public spaces and argued passionately that the definition of unconditional love ought to be diversified to include 'fur babies'. There was also a great deal of discussion around the endlessly awkward pregnant-pause moment after answering the insensitive question, 'So, do you have kids?' and plentiful advice on what to say in response. Their views resonated, but their righteous anger and judgement of women like her sister made her feel uncomfortable. One particular woman vented her spleen over feeling abandoned and betrayed by friends who had become born-again moms, saying things like, 'I just worry about who will look after you when you're old,' and, 'It would just be so lovely for you to have a baby, you'd make an amazing mother.' Hollie empathised with her feelings of alienation and the fury of being patronised, but hoped she was more understanding.

By the time she heard Hugh's key in the door, she had been sitting in the same position for several hours. He shouted up for her, and she quickly closed the screen. She felt satisfied with her own due diligence in considering motherhood from many different angles, but there was still no word from the *ug*. If anything, she seemed more likely to be childfree, but still sensed something lurking beneath the surface.

Something important, as yet unearthed.

A small tug.

Maybe, as Kathy had said, if she wanted to be really sure it was time to hear the quiet whisper of her heart.

Wading into the Swamp

A few weeks later Hollie was sitting in the foyer of a local community cinema with a gin and tonic, waiting to meet her friend Diane.

Diane was a coach and her only friend who did not have children.

Over the two years they had known each other, they had become their own childfree support group, a safe place to share their resentments and psychological scars without fearing judgement. She was exactly the kind of person Hollie might have hired to help her work through her maybe-baby crisis

Hollie took a sip of her drink and glanced up as she heard someone approaching. From the corner of her eye, she noticed a poster advertising the film they were going to see, *Now You See Me*. The title felt like a metaphor for her elusive *ug*.

'Sorry I'm late, Hollie,' said Diane as she arrived at the table.

Hollie stood up and hugged her.

'It's *so* good to see you.'

Diane sat down just as her phone rang.

'So sorry, Hollie, I just need to take this call, I'll be with you in a minute.'

'No problem, let me get you a drink.'

'Large g and t.'

Hollie watched Diane on the phone from the bar. She was clearly agitated. Hollie knew she was in the middle of a big break-up and wondered if it was connected to this.

Diane ended the call as she returned to the table and put down the drinks. She immediately picked up her glass and took a large gulp.

'What's going on?'

'Just Darren and his bullshit. He's now done a U-turn and is refusing to move out of the house.'

'Shit.'

'Yeah.'

'Do you want to talk about it?'

'I will, but not just now, to be honest. I'm sick of hearing myself.'

'I know that feeling.'

'To make matters worse, I've fallen out with one of my oldest friends.'

'I'm so sorry, Diane, that's really tough. What happened with your friend?'

'Fucking kids.'

Diane was classy and sensitive. The sort of person who rarely swore. Hollie knew it must be bad.

'What happened?' she asked, leaning in a little closer.

'I've mentioned my friend Sam to you before I think? We've been friends a long time. Since school.'

'I remember you mentioning her.'

'She's got a daughter, Maddy, just turned thirteen. When Maddy was younger, I used to go round quite a bit, and make an effort to do things. I showed her how to bake as Sam is useless in the kitchen, and Maddy and I would do crafty things together. I tried really hard. I knew if I didn't, I would never get to actually see Sam, but this last year I've been so busy with work and everything going on at home that I haven't really been round.'

'Totally understandable,' Hollie said, nodding thoughtfully.

'And if I'm honest, Hollie, it sounds awful, but it's been a relief to have an excuse. It feels like I always make the effort to see Sam and deep down I think I've been getting a bit resentful that it's all one-way.'

'I totally get that,' Hollie said. 'It's like you're automatically expected to develop a relationship with your friend's kids and are made to feel like a bad person if you don't want to hang out with them.'

'Exactly,' Diane said, taking another gulp of her drink. 'Anyway, Sam rang me a few weeks ago asking me to come to Maddy's birthday party. They had splashed out on a venue, you know, the full works. I told Sam I wouldn't be able to come as I already had plans for dinner, but she went on and on about it, saying how upset Maddy would be if I didn't go. Seriously? She's thirteen years old, the party will be full of her friends, boys, entertainment … the lot, and she will be devastated I'm not there? As sure as God made little apples, I don't think so. So, I said no.'

'Well done, that can't have been easy.'

'Damn right. I mean, you know me, I hate letting people down, but there just comes a point. But get this … Sam told me I'd let her down and now she's refusing to speak to me or answer my messages!'

'That seems extreme.'

'You're not kidding. I can't believe how she has behaved.'

'Good for you for holding your boundaries, though.'

'Yeah, but it fucking hurts, Hollie. All the effort I've made to keep the friendship going. It's like if you don't have kids, whatever you do doesn't seem to count as much.'

'I know, hon.'

'Sorry, not a great start to our catch-up.'

'It's fine. I seem to remember you listening to me having a good old rant last time!'

'Thanks, I feel better already for getting it out.'

'Better out than in, eh? As you always say.'

'So, what about you? Let's talk about you, and then I'll calm down so I can enjoy the film later. How are things? And how's the new job since you got your promotion?'

Tormented, deranged, exhausted sprang to mind.

'It's funny you've brought up the subject of kids, because I'm now officially at war with myself over this very issue. Everywhere I go, I'm tormented by it.'

Hollie downloaded for half an hour, telling Diane everything that had happened since the kitchen floor moment and the search for her *ug* began: the conversations with Hugh, the incessant Maybe-Baby FM broadcasts, the books and blogs she had read, and the interview with Rosie.

Diane listened intently

'It's like I'm being tossed about on a sea of ambivalence day after day … *yes-no-yes-no-yes-no*. It's like in the space of a few months I've moved from one epoch to another – from BC … *Before Children* became all I think about, to AD … *Ambivalence Deadlock!*'

As awful as it was to hear herself, Hollie felt better just by saying it all out loud. Seeing Diane's reaction, her clear blue eyes full of kindness and empathy as she listened, was like a soothing balm.

'Omigod, Hollie,' Diane said in her lilting Edinburgh accent when she had finished, 'you're freakin' hilarious. That's such an intense logic process, no wonder you feel bloody exhausted! You're definitely playing true to your personality type there, full-on Doctor Spock mode, trying to outrun your mind!'

Hollie nearly spat out her gin.

'And I can't believe you actually went and *interviewed* someone. That's awesome commitment!'

'I suppose it is kind of funny,' Hollie said, grateful to see the lighter side for a change.

'But can I be honest with you?'

'Please do.'

'I have to say, I'm surprised that you are really considering having kids. I guess from all the conversations we've had in the past I assumed you didn't want them.'

'Me too.'

'So what's changed? I mean, I understand you genuinely wanting to respond to what Hugh said, and I appreciate what this means to him, given what you've told me before about being estranged from his son, but still ...'

'I've asked myself this same question. Over and over again. I guess deep down I hadn't expected to find any doubt when I confronted myself with whether I wanted to be a mother, and it really freaked me out. It's made me wonder whether there might be unexamined longings that I've just buried.'

'I can relate to that,' Diane said, looking thoughtful.

'I'm terrified by the idea that I might regret it later, and it keeps gnawing away at me. I just want to make absolutely sure my answer is a definitive no, before it's too late. And, weirdly, the more I have thought about it, the less certain I feel.'

'Too late for what?'

'Too late to have children, because nature will have decided for me.'

'Remind me, Hollie, how old are you now?'

'Forty-two next week.'

'Oh yes, I have something for you,' she said, rummaging in her bag and handing her a card and gift.

'Thanks, Diane.'

'I hope you like it.'

Hollie opened the envelope. It was a moody black and white image of a lighthouse.

'I know how you love lighthouses.'

Hollie turned the card to read the back. *Storm Brewing*, it said, with commentary beneath from the artist.

'It's perfect. I love it.'

Hollie began peeling open the neatly wrapped gift.

'A scarf, I think?' she said.

'Predictable, I know, but I just saw it and thought of you.'

Hollie pulled out a bright yellow scarf with small white flowers and polka dots.

'It's beautiful, thanks. And yolky yellow, very apt!'

'Glad you like it and yes … getting back to what we were talking about a minute ago, you're not past it yet.'

'Maybe not, but apparently, I'm verging on being an old hag in terms of egg quality!'

'Women do have children well into their forties you know. Look at Cherie Blair, she had her fourth when she was forty-five.'

'True, but I can't help feeling that time is ticking on. Everyone assumes they will be able to get pregnant, but what if that's not the case? And Hugh is almost fifty-two.'

'Woah, back up a moment. Seems you are putting a huge amount of pressure on yourself here. You're off into the future, when right now, it seems to me, step one is making your decision.'

'Can I ask you a question, Diane?'

'Fire away.'

'Do you have any regrets? About not having had children, I mean?'

'No. But unlike you, I always knew I didn't want them, and never had a stable enough relationship where having children was really on the cards anyway, so I never wrestled with ambivalence. To be honest, when I look at some of my friends, like Sam, I see a lot of striving and struggle and hard work. And I think if you're a woman, you often end up having to do motherhood alone, muddling your way through with no one to teach you how to be a good parent and feeling trapped, having to do things you don't really want to do for the love of your kids. I miss my friends and how they were before, and still feel left out at times, but in the end, as much as I respect their choice, I wouldn't trade my life for theirs.'

'Thank you,' Hollie said. 'Being friends with you saves me a fortune in therapy!'

'I'll send you my bill later! Actually, it's helping me to have something else to think about, and reframing the situation with Sam. My empathy is coming a bit back online,' Diane said, chuckling. 'And speaking of bills, it's my round. Same again? We've probably got time for a quick one.'

God bless you Diane, Hollie thought as she watched her friend go to the bar. She felt a little guilty for not asking more about what was happening with Darren and made a mental note to ask later.

'So back to you and your decision-making, Doctor Spock,' Diane said when she sat back down. 'I was thinking to myself at the bar, I bet Hollie *hates* the feeling of being incompetent, of being unable to make a wise, clean decision. Am I right?'

'Abso-bloody-lutely!'

'And I bet you are telling yourself you *should* be good at this because you're a people-development person who helps other people when they're stuck?'

Hollie nodded, feeling her cheeks flush.

'Yep. Me frickin' too! At the bar, I was just reflecting that I've been feeling exactly the same thing about me and Darren splitting up; the old, "Why can't I just …?" It totally sucks.'

'Totally.'

'But seriously, Hollie, I hate to break it to you, but I feel you're not going to have a breakthrough by writing endless pros and cons lists, or any other kind of logical thinking, sweetie. I think you need to get in touch with your intuition.'

Hollie thought of her conversation with Kathy in the garden, about following her heart.

'I definitely don't feel in touch with my intuition just now. I don't think we've spoken in a while!'

'And remember, Hollie, as an INTJ personality type, logic is the *passenger* of your car, but the driver of your personality is intuition. Right now, it sounds to me like the passenger has taken over the steering wheel, so no wonder you're careering all over the place. You're like a proverbial driverless car!'

'Bloody hell, I hadn't thought of it like that!' said Hollie.

'And you know what this means don't you?' said Diane leaning in and dropping her voice to a whisper.

'What?'

'I think it's time to take a deep breath and …'

Diane paused and looked straight at Hollie with a playful look on her face.

'…*feel* your feelings.'

'Jesus, you mean I haven't already?'

'Nope. I would say you are still *thinking* about them, sweetie.'

'Shit!' Hollie said, immediately feeling the truth of what Diane had said in her body.

'Exactly! I'm afraid, grasshopper, if you really want a breakthrough, it might be time to wade into the messy swamp of your emotions, my friend.'

'Bugger!'

They both fell silent for a moment.

'See that poster?' Diane said, turning round and pointing.

'Yes,' said Hollie, looking at it again.

'Look at the tagline for the film. *The closer you think you are, the less you'll actually see.* That's like a description of your motherhood journey so far with your ingenious use of logic. The more lists you make, the further away you're getting from any kind of clarity.'

'I get it,' said Hollie, feeling like a balloon that had just been pricked with a pin.

Now it was her turn to take a huge gulp of her gin.

'So, how do you suggest I connect to my intuition?'

Diane looked mischievous.

'Have you heard of bodywork therapy?

Hollie could feel herself pulling a face.

'Don't worry, it's not what you might think.'

'Naked psychotherapy?'

'Very funny. I've been having it and as you know, I'm hardly one for taking my clothes off in front of people. I mean, I'm bloody Scottish, Hollie!'

'True.'

'Think deep massage meets a type of reiki. It's about working with the body's electromagnetic field to promote a stronger mind-body connection. I thought it sounded a bit woo-woo at first, but a friend recommended it, and well, I was desperate! It's really helped to ground me and hold myself steady during the last few months with Darren. The place I've been going is near where your mum lives. Here,' she said, opening her purse and handing Hollie a business card. 'The contact details are all there.'

'Embody Healing,' Hollie said, looking at the front of the card with the image of a woman's head.

Diane paused and smiled.

'What?' said Hollie.

'I've been told it's especially good for people like you as it bypasses the rational brain and works deeper in the unconscious.'

'Like me, how?'

'Highly cognitively defended.'

'Thanks,' Hollie replied with mock-sarcasm. 'Now you're just sweet-talking-me!'

~

A week after her forty-second birthday, Hollie rang the doorbell of Embody Healing.

An elf-like woman with a deep suntan and wavy chestnut hair opened the door. She looked as though she had just woken from a nap.

'You must be Hollie?'

'Yes.'

'So lovely to meet you. I'm Phemi. Welcome. Come in. I'm just finishing off with another client. Take a seat and I'll be with you in a tick.'

Phemi had sparkly eyes and a look of mischief.

The reception room was white and sparsely furnished. Pieces of driftwood, pebbles and shells adorned the windowsill, and wicker hearts on ribbons hung round the walls. It smelled of lavender and oils.

Hollie's eye was drawn to a poem hanging in a white wooden frame. She stood up to read it. 'The Invitation' by Oriah Mountain Dreamer. She stopped on a passage that made her stomach lurch.

It doesn't interest me to know where you live

or how much money you have.

I want to know if you can get up

after the night of grief and despair,

weary and bruised to the bone

and do what needs to be done to feed the children.

Hollie thought about her sister who had just given birth to her second child, a healthy boy called Jacob. She and Hugh would be going down this weekend for a flying visit.

Phemi returned with a cup of fennel tea, smelling faintly of tobacco.

'Beautiful, isn't it?'

'Yeah.'

'She's a Canadian poet and writer. Wrote this after leaving a party early apparently, frustrated by the usual tedious small talk, and just poured out this amazing poem.'

'I can relate to that.'

Phemi disappeared to attend to the other client and Hollie sat with her cup of tea. She imagined her sister, bleary-eyed, getting up just as their mother had done to soothe her screaming baby.

Am I the kind of person who could get up weary and bruised to the bone and attend to the children? she heard a voice ask inside her head.

Five minutes later she followed Phemi into a warm, dark room lit with soft uplighters and tealights in glass jars on the floor.

It felt like a womb.

'So how did you come by Embody Healing?'

'My friend Diane recommended you.'

'Lovely Scottish Diane?'

'Yes.'

'Great. I always love it when people come through word-of-mouth.'

'Can I ask, is Phemi short for something? It's an unusual name.'

'Yeah, my actual name is Euphemia Rose Dae. My mother was a gypsy with a fancy for dramatic names. Wasn't the easiest name to have at school though, I mean I look like a Romanian refugee anyway without needing a name like that. I've always shortened it to Phemi, even though it sounds a bit like a sanitary product!'

'Wow, Euphemia Rose is epic. I'm Hollie May Hardwick.'

'Well, I'm very pleased to meet you. So, Hollie Hardwick, you've come for bodywork therapy?'

'Yes.'

'Have you experienced it before?'

'No, but I read a bit about it on your website, which is very good by the way. I loved what you said about *our bodies having stories to tell that require a deep kind of listening.*'

'Thanks, and yes, listening to your body is really important and something none of us are taught to do very well in my experience. Especially as women. We're programmed to criticize and disassociate from our bodies so it's not easy to make friends with it, never mind actually respect what it has to say!' Phemi looked Hollie up and down before continuing. 'I think we should just dive in if that's okay with you? I'm going to mix an oil and then we can get started.'

Hollie was relieved that she did not press for further information.

'I think we need lots of lemon today,' said Phemi as she began mixing tinctures in a pestle and mortar on a high table in the corner of the room.

Hollie was intrigued. What had she interpreted in her glance that had said *lemons*?

'This session will basically be like a deep, relaxing, massage. The difference is I work with your energy body.'

Phemi paused as if waiting to see her reaction.

Hollie simply nodded as if this was all entirely normal.

'To be honest, I like to just get stuck in, and say more about it afterwards if that's okay with you?'

Hollie nodded again.

'If you want to remove your clothes down to your underwear and make yourself comfortable on the massage bed under the towels, I'll be back in a few minutes.'

As she began five minutes later, Hollie felt Phemi pressing firmly onto her back as she instructed her to take deep breaths and sunk into the comfort of the firm bed and thick, burgundy towels. She felt oil being smeared over her skin with skilful hands. It smelled like a Greek summer.

Hollie soon drifted off ...

She was flying.

Heading north.

Hugging a rugged coastal landscape, like the opening sequence of a documentary.

Below, there was a small hut on a hill.

Suddenly she was inside.

A simple room, with wooden floors and sparsely furnished.

If felt important.

Somewhere she was meant to be.

A place enveloped in love.

An hour later, Hollie heard Phemi's voice calling her back.

'Wow,' she said as she slowly returned to the room, feeling felt drowsy and disorientated. It was hard to believe their session was already finished.

'Take your time,' Phemi said, placing a hand gently on her arm. 'I'll get you a glass of water.'

Re-dressed, Hollie perched on the end of the massage bed, sipping the water.

Phemi sat in a chair opposite.

'What did you experience?'

'I definitely went somewhere,' Hollie said and described her vision

'Interesting,' Phemi said, nodding sagely. 'I noticed a couple of things. There was a lot of stuck energy in your right leg. I don't know if you noticed, but I spent a lot of time working on this. I was pushing really hard at one point. And your head – woah! The energy coming off this was unbelievable. Probably the most powerful I've ever worked with.'

Hollie was unsure whether this was a good or bad thing.

'I think you might be someone who lives in your head a lot?'

'You could say that,' Hollie smiled.

'I'm not kidding. I had to hold myself really steady just to be with your energy. It felt a bit like one of those glass globes with lightning bouncing around inside. I had to stay there for ages. It must be bloody exhausting for you! I feel like it would be good to come back for some more sessions, help you ground yourself into your body and calm the energy in your head.'

'I definitely could do with being more peaceful up here,' Hollie said, touching her forehead.

Phemi looked at her for a moment. She seemed to be debating something.

'You know, some people find this a bit weird, but I'm going to say it anyway and you can decide whether to take it or leave it, Hollie.'

'O...kay?'

'I guess it's probably not going to come as a surprise to hear me say something that might sound a bit out there, but given what you've told me about your vision, I figure you might be a bit ... well ... cosmic, anyway.'

'Cosmic!' Hollie laughed. 'I haven't heard that word like that used about me for a long time. Not since I was a student.'

'Cosmic Hollie Hardwick. Has a certain ring, don't you think?' Phemi cackled, emitting a laugh that sounded like it came straight up from her boots.

It felt so good to hear someone see her differently to the serious, stressed person she felt trapped inside.

'You know, when I work with bodies, they often speak to me. They all have their stories to tell.'

Hollie had never heard of this idea, but it sounded intriguing. Whilst Phemi was undoubtedly a bit out there, she exuded a commanding presence that made her want to listen.

'When I lay my hands on people, or even when my hands are alongside someone's body working with their energy, I'm like a channel. Messages get communicated to me. Sometimes, pictures appear in my mind. Other times, I get a word or phrase that suddenly pops into my head. I don't know what they mean, so I just offer them to clients and let them decide whether they make sense or not. And, even then, what comes through may not mean anything until much later.'

'Did my body speak to you?'

'Can I ask you a question?' replied Phemi.

'Of course.'

'Do you have children?'

Hollie felt a chill run down her spine.

'No. Why do you ask?'

'Because I've laid my hands on a lot of bodies, and when I had my hands on you, I got a strong sense that came through, really clearly, that you have ...'

Phemi paused and looked at Hollie, as if somehow she intuited the magnitude of what she was about to say.

'... a mother's body.'

Tears fell down Hollie's cheeks.

'I'm sorry, I didn't mean to upset you,' Phemi said, handing her a tissue. 'Take your time. Spooky stuff like this can happen sometimes.'

Hollie wiped her face, then looked back at Phemi. Her story came tumbling out.

'No wonder your head energy is off the scale, Hollie,' Phemi said when she had finished. 'It sounds like you are going through a very unique and private kind of torture in there!'

'You could say that,' Hollie smiled.

'I salute you for it.'

'Really?'

'Damn right. I got pregnant when I was seventeen. Knew nothing. I was completely ignorant. And now, age forty-three, I'm already a bloody grandmother! Me, for fuck's sake.'

'Wow, that's hard to get your head round.'

'You're telling me. But you know what, my daughter chose to have a family relatively young and that's great, because it's what she wanted, and what she chose. Me, I never even knew I had a choice, Hollie. Becoming a mother just happened, and I got on with it. So I think all power to your elbow that you are deciding what you really want, not what anyone says you should do.'

'Thanks, Phemi, I appreciate that.'

'But I can also see this is hard,' she continued, 'to actually sit down and think about it properly. I don't know how you do that.'

'I'm beginning to come to the same conclusion, to be honest, which is why I'm here. To get out of my head and into my body, to see if I can find my inner knowing. As I said to Diane, I don't think we've spoken for a while.'

'Sounds very wise. And yes, I think to make a conscious decision you need the whole of you on board, and to cut your poor head some slack.'

'It's so good to be able to talk about this. I usually find it difficult to speak about what's going on, so thanks for listening, Phemi.'

'You're welcome.'

Hollie glanced at her watch.

'Omigod, I can't believe it. I've been here for an hour and a half! I feel awful taking up all this time.'

'It's okay, you were my last client today.'

After they arranged their next date, Phemi showed Hollie out.

As she opened the door the tinkling bell rang again. It had a lovely old-fashioned sound, the kind she imagined her Aunty Edna would have had at her sweetshop to signal when a customer had entered.

'Thanks, Phemi, I feel so much better.'

'You're welcome, Hollie Hardwick. I like you already,' Phemi said with a cheeky grin.

~

Four weeks later, Hollie was back in Phemi's treatment room, sitting on a low chair, holding a steaming mug of sweet apple tea.

Since her last visit, several Moroccan lamps had appeared, made of brass and stained glass in colourful mosaics of red, green and blue, and were casting intricate patterns on the walls. She could easily have been inside a fortune teller's den, hidden deep inside a labyrinth of alleyways in an ancient bazaar.

'So, how have you been keeping?' Phemi asked.

'I don't know. I kept thinking about what you said, about having a mother's body, over and over, wondering what it meant. Then, a few days after our session, something spooky started happening. I was driving to work with the radio on, not really paying attention, just off inside my head, thinking about all the things I had to get done. Then suddenly, I had strange sensation, like something was apparating next to me, at the edge of my peripheral vision. A kind of ... *presence*. The air felt tingly, and I remember I turned my head as if half expecting to see someone in the passenger seat …'

'Go on,' said Phemi, looking straight at her with intense focus.

'This strange expectant feeling continued, off and on for another week, until one day, I turned and saw a clear image of a young girl, about five years old, sitting there next to me, chatting away, as if she had been conjured from a genie's lamp. I had an inkling that if I stopped the car to take a closer look, she would disappear, so I continued driving, looking out of the corner of my eye and seeing her projected there, and this feeling of exquisite tenderness flooded my body.'

'Did anything else happen?' asked Phemi.

'A memory came to me. Ten years ago, I was sitting on a bench in the city centre near my office, eating a sandwich. It was a beautiful, blue-sky sunny day, and I was enjoying watching the world go by, when a gnarly old gypsy woman sat down next to me. She looked homeless, you know, had that smell like she was sleeping rough. I waited for her to ask for money or food, but she didn't. She just sat there for a few moments, enjoying the sunshine on her leathery skin. After a short while, she stood up to leave and had begun to walk away when she suddenly stopped, turned back around, and looked straight at me. "One day, you will have a daughter," she said, then walked off without a backward glance.'

'What did you make of that?'

'I thought it was completely bizarre. I imagined she entertained herself by pretending to be a seer, wandering the streets, planting random ideas into people's heads. Or that she just had mental health issues. But after what you said about me having a mother's body, I started to wonder, what if she was psychic? Even though rationally I keep thinking it's ridiculous, the idea is like a mind-worm I can't stop thinking about!'

'I said you were fucking cosmic, Hollie!' Phemi said, throwing her head back and cackling with laughter.

'Seriously though, is this normal when people get bodywork therapy?'

'It varies a lot to be honest. Everybody's energy is different.'

'What do you mean?'

'When you get down to the quantum level, we're all pulsing with electromagnetic energy. And our bioenergy field, which has a conscious intelligence, extends a few feet out from our physical bodies. Did you know it's actually shaped like an egg, funnily enough?'

'No, I've never heard of it before.'

'I know this stuff sounds woo-woo, Hollie, but science is catching up with it all now, all the stuff the gypsies and hippies have been saying for years.'

'Okay.'

'Information is being communicated through our energy fields all the time, moving back and forth. I don't profess to know the ins and outs. All I can tell you is that I work with energy, and I feel it channelling through me and know there's a deep intelligence in it that, personally, I believe is far wiser than our rational mind.'

'But how does it communicate?'

'Through dreams, visions, intuitions, prophetic feelings of deep knowing. It happens a lot. Beyond that I don't really know how to describe it, Hollie, and I'm not too bothered about having language for it. People either get it, or they don't, and that's their business.'

'Fair enough.'

'It seems to me, you are highly visual and intuitive, and I suspect that as you quieten your ridiculously busy mind, it will open space for this deeper embodied intelligence to communicate with you.'

'I definitely feel my mind has already quietened down compared to what it was,' Hollie said.

'We can work on that some more today,' Phemi said, getting up and moving to the corner of the room where she started mixing an oil. 'I'm going to use frankincense. Good for grounding.'

'Tell you what else I've noticed,' Hollie said. 'Before I came to you, it felt like everything was speaking to me. Everywhere I looked and everything I listened to seemed to be constantly broadcasting … *yes-baby, no-baby, yes-baby, no-baby*. Every time I turned on the radio or went into the office at work, I would seem to walk straight into a conversation about the pros or cons of having kids. Like a constant barrage. I started calling it Maybe-Baby FM.'

'You know what that is, don't you?'

'What?'

'The part of your brain that filters out what is and isn't important. Like when we decide to buy a red soft-top sports car and suddenly see them everywhere. I can never remember what the letters stand for, though.'

'It's called the Reticular Activating System. RAS for short.'

'Yes, that. But I reckon it's also more cosmic, something to do with what Einstein called *spooky action at a distance* … the way we magnetise and repel people and things that resonate with certain frequencies in our energy field.'

'Go on …'

'Well, in your case, your energy field has changed because the question of motherhood is now important to you, so your brain's primed to filter in data that relates to this, which previously would have gone unnoticed. And, as the Buddha said, with our thoughts, we create the world, so energetically speaking, you are now creating a new reality. Your thoughts are magnetising things towards you that resonate on the same frequency.'

'You really are quite the philosopher, Phemi.'

'I know. I really should get paid for this shit!'

'But I'm not sure I understand the idea of things resonating at the same frequency? Like, how does a conversation in the office about taking kids to Flamingoland vibrate at the same frequency as the thoughts inside my brain?'

'I don't know, I'm not that clever. I just know from my lived experience, and all the people I've worked with over the years, that this shit is real and I'm happy with that. I'm not like you Hollie, I don't need to know all the theory. Too much like hard work. I just trust energy and the intelligence of energy. That's it. Plain and simple.'

'Sounds great. I wish I could stop thinking so much. Sometimes I think I even wish I hadn't overthought the whole question of having children and just done it, as crazy as that sounds.'

'That's exactly why you've come to me!'

'Indeed.'

'I think we really should get started in a minute. I just have one more question, if that's okay?'

'Fire away.'

'Have these visitations shifted anything for you?'

'They haven't convinced me motherhood is my path if that's what you mean. But I do feel like something is ... *opening* within me.'

'As though you are opening emotionally to the possibility of motherhood?'

'I guess so. I think this must be what Diane meant when she said I needed to actually start feeling my feelings!'

The Egg Room

By late November, after a total of five sessions with Phemi, Hollie had not found her *ug* or made a definitive decision, but she felt noticeably less stressed and scattered.

In the last session she had fallen asleep for almost the whole hour, and Phemi suggested they had gone as far as they could.

'I think it might be time to work on some deeper issues,' she had said, 'and I have just the man for the job. A psychotherapist. He lives locally, and he's very good. Been around the block, if you know what I mean. Semi-retired now. I've been seeing him for a while, to sort out some ongoing shit with my mother.'

Phemi had rummaged in her bag and handed Hollie a tattered red business card with white writing.

Julian Finch

Counselling and Psychotherapy

MBACP Senior Accredited

UKRC Registered Practitioner

It seemed the time had come to travel down into the vault of her deepest self and open the safety deposit box.

~

Two weeks before Christmas, Hollie arrived for her first session, in a pleasant but non-descript housing estate.

It had just started to snow as she turned off the engine and parked in front of a bungalow.

She sat for a moment to gather her thoughts, preparing for the inevitable, 'So what's brought you here?' question.

She gazed out of the window and noticed a sticker on the back window of the car in front.

Baby on board.

She hated these signs. As if you were going to change how you were driving because you were okay with the idea of maiming or killing a human being, providing it was not a child. Right now, however, the sign seemed like a metaphor. Was she, or was she not, going to emerge from psychotherapy with the decision to take a baby on board?

She stepped out of the car, put her hood up, and rang the doorbell.

The "Greensleeves" tune played inside the house. She thought this seemed oddly sentimental for a psychotherapist, without really knowing where this judgement came from.

After a few moments, a balding man opened the door.

'You must be Hollie,' he said, reaching out to shake her hand.

He was dressed in a cheap work shirt and trousers and had a bushy, seventies-style moustache. Hollie thought he looked like a cross between a chemistry teacher and radio DJ Steve Wright. Perhaps, she thought, this was a sign that she had come to the right place to change the playlist on Maybe-Baby FM!

Hollie entered a hallway through a small porch. A deep crimson carpet with tiny gold crests dominated the otherwise beige and white space and a high shelf was littered with china figurines and cups. It felt simultaneously chintzy and clinical.

She followed Julian Finch into the living room which had the same décor and crimson carpet, a modest bay window, and a gas fire with fake flames.

He motioned for her to sit on a sofa whilst he settled into one of the matching adjacent armchairs. There was a glass of water on the highly polished wooden coffee table in front of her, resting on a gold coaster.

'So, Hollie, tell me a little bit of who you are and what's brought you here today?' he said with a reassuring air of authority. Hollie thought she could detect a faint Midlands accent.

'Phemi at Embody Healing recommended you. I've been having some bodywork therapy with her as I'm struggling with the decision of whether or not I want to have children.'

Hollie could feel Julian Finch's small, attentive eyes watching her closely. Not smiling, not nodding, just observing and inviting her to continue.

'I'm forty-two and hadn't thought much about children before. I had kicked the whole issue into the long grass, and just assumed I wouldn't have them. But now I've really engaged with the question, I feel completely stuck, and I need to make a decision quickly because I don't even know if it's possible for me to get pregnant, or how long I have left. I'm trying to peel off the layers of what I think I *should want*, to understand what I actually *do want*, but I just can't seem to access my own answer. That's why I'm here ... I need to find a way through, to find my *ug*.'

'And what may I ask, is an *ug*?' Julian Finch said with no hint of a reaction.

'It's a thing I've noticed women with a strong maternal instinct seem to have. A primal knowing. A kind of pull which seems to bypass any *do I or don't I want a baby* questioning.'

'So you want to access your inner knowing with regards to whether or not you want to become a mother?'

'Yes.'

'And what prompted you to engage in the search for this elusive *ug*?'

'My husband said he really wanted us to have a baby. Completely out of the blue.'

'I see. And you love your husband?'

'Yes.'

'And what prompted him to say this?'

'He said it would *seal our love*. We have come through some rocky years, and he thought this would be the icing on the cake. He is estranged from his son from a previous marriage, so I suspect it's also about helping to heal this wound.'

'And this had a powerful effect on you?'

'It jolted me awake. Part of me was angry that he waited until my biological clock had almost stopped ticking, just as I'd been promoted and felt like everything was settled. Yet another part of me feels grateful, because I think if he hadn't said anything, I was in danger of this decision being made for me, not by me and I suspect I might have always been left wondering, *what if…?'*

'And what are you expecting from me?'

Hollie paused and took a sip of water.

'I need a way to break through this stuckness. I need to …*feel my feelings* … but I don't know how to.'

'I see. And may I ask what it is you do for a living, Hollie?'

'I'm a people director for a large mental health trust.'

'A very demanding job, I imagine. And you've been recently promoted?'

'A week before Hugh said he wanted us to have a baby. I remember because it was my mother's sixty-fifth birthday.'

'Potent timing. So, you are on a big learning curve whilst wrestling with this profound choice. A lot to contend with.'

'Yes,' Hollie said, feeling grateful for the positive stroke. It felt good for someone to appreciate how hard this all was for her.

'And when you are stuck in other situations, how do you *feel your feelings* then?'

'I …' Hollie looked down to her lap and smiled, 'I think my way into them, I guess.'

'Can you say more about this, please?'

'When someone asks me how I feel, I struggle to find the data. It's like I have to go inside my head and say, *Hollie, how DO you feel?*'

'So you're a very self-aware person, with good insight into your own mental processes. And you place primacy on being rational and thoughtful and using logic to understand your feelings.'

'Yes.'

'And what are your feelings about this issue of becoming a mother?'

'Is that a trick question?'

'Make of it what you will, Hollie.'

Julian Finch was not smiling. She was unsure whether he was irritated, teasing her, or if this was a test.

'Bodywork therapy has been interesting. I went specifically to bypass my logic brain. After a few sessions, I started to get this well … *presence* … next to me. A little girl. I know it sounds odd, but it felt like it might be the manifestation of a future daughter. As if something inside me was slowly cracking open. A feeling I've not experienced before.'

'What specifically was this feeling?'

'An exquisitely tender longing,' she said slowly.

'Hmm. And is there anything else about how you feel?'

'Embarrassed,' Hollie said

'In what way?'

'I keep thinking, how can I not know what I want? As an educated, intelligent, well-developed woman, how can I not know my own mind? Why am I so paralysed by self-doubt? How can I not tune into my own wisdom and find my answer?'

'Do you like to know everything?'

Julian Finch said this with a wry smile, cocking his head to the side. He looked like a bird sitting on a branch. Curious and observant.

Hollie laughed and felt herself relax a little. She could see why Phemi liked him.

'I don't need to know *everything*, but I do like to know my own mind.'

'Sounds like you know your mind very well, Hollie. Perhaps what you know less well is your own heart. And I wonder whether your heart is what is slowly starting to open?'

~

'What is most alive for you today?' Julian Finch asked after she sat down and removed her coat at the beginning of their second session.

'Well, it's a new year, and I'm thinking I have to get on with this. It's been almost eight months since this process began, and I need to make a definitive decision.'

'So, you are arriving full of resolve. Anything else?'

'I keep thinking, it's like I'm standing at a crossroads, looking at two diverging paths, motherhood and un-motherhood, and I don't know which one to take.'

Julian Finch picked up an A4 pad and drew something.

He placed it down on the coffee table and turned it towards Hollie, pulling his armchair closer.

A straight line leading to a circle, with two lines going off in different directions.

'So, if this is the crossroads and these are the two paths, where are you in relation to them?'

Hollie stared at the drawing.

'Standing at the crossroads, walking round and round saying, *I don't which way to go, I don't which way to go … which way should I go?*'

Julian Finch picked up the pad again and drew a clock face right next to the crossroads and placed it back down.

Hollie heard a loud, involuntary gulp.

'What just happened?'

'I felt that in my body. Tick-tock. As soon as you drew that clock. In my head … *Come on, come on, come on … tap, tap, tap … you've got to make a decision, Hollie. What if you only have a month's worth of eggs left? And here you are pissing about. What if in two months you say yeah, I want to try for a baby, and the shop's already shut?* It horrifies me.'

'Horrifies? That's a strong word. Say more.'

'Because I should have thought about it sooner.'

'I'm noticing that *should* in there, Hollie.'

'I need closure. There's this part shouting at me to make my mind up, but I can't see ahead. And that vision of the little girl next to me in the car, I can't get it out of my mind. I keep wondering, was that real, or did I just make it up?'

'Why would you make it up?'

'To experience a tenderness I don't really feel? To pretend to myself I am more gentle and loving than I really am? But then another part of me is like, *How am I even having this conversation with myself?* And so it goes … I just keep on and on and on, layering and layering the conversation, creating echoes in a hall of distorted mind-mirrors. And I'm so pissed off because I know *I'm doing all this to myself.*'

'So you're giving yourself a hard time, and not allowing the process to unfold because the clock is ticking so loudly? A bit like trying to make a decision at one minute to midnight, before the glass slipper turns back into a turnip?'

'Yes,' Hollie smiled, grateful for a little humour.

'How about we separate the part of you that's shouting *hurry up*, and the part that is wanting to lean into whatever is unfolding?

'That would be nice!'

Julian Finch ripped a piece of paper from the pad, re-drew a larger clock face in the centre and wrote *NOW* in large letters above it, with an arrow pointing to twelve o'clock.

He stood up, moved the coffee table and armchair against the wall, placed the piece of paper on the crimson carpet and opened a set of glass doors revealing a tidy dining room.

'Please stand over there,' he said, pointing to boundary between the two rooms.

'Let's say that where you are standing now is the beginning of your thought process, and this piece of paper here is your last egg,' he said, pointing to the piece of A4.

'Last egg! Calling Hollie Hardwick's last egg!' he said, cupping his hands around his mouth, announcing these words like an efficient train station master.

Hollie stared at him.

'What do you need to do between where you are now, and where this piece of paper is, to help you make a decision?'

She was glued to the spot, her eyes fixed on the piece of paper.

'Hollie?'

'The only thing happening right now is ... there's a voice inside my head shouting, *OMIGOD, MY LAST EGG!* I never even thought about having eggs and now *the last one is going!*'

'Okay … Turn around and imagine you are looking back at yourself with a few hundred eggs to go. What advice are you going to give that Hollie?'

She paused, becoming tearful as she gazed into the blackness of the windows that overlooked a back garden.

'Not sure. I'm just getting upset.'

'What's the upset about?'

Hollie turned to face back into the living room. She felt a flutter of anxiety in her chest.

'I always assumed I would just … *know.* I think I'm angry with myself, that as somebody who wants to live intentionally, I haven't engaged with this question and now it's almost too late.'

~

That night, Hollie had a dream.

She was standing inside the centre of a large stone room, shaped like an egg.

It felt deep underground.

The air was still, yet there was an intense aliveness in the room.

From floor to ceiling, a series of evenly spaced stone shelves adorned the outer circumference.

On every shelf there were hundreds of gleaming brass eggcups, lined up with great precision, like a neat army of golden soldiers.

Most egg cups were standing empty. But some, dotted here and there, contained tiny eggs.

Hollie could see small doors behind each eggcup, like the kind you find on a cuckoo clock. In the dream, she knew those trapdoors opened at random every month and more eggs would disappear.

She approached one of the shelves and picked up an eggcup, holding it in the palm of her hand, feeling its cool texture and reassuring weight. Silent tears fell down her cheeks as she saw there were delicate inscriptions etched into the metal.

Boy. Brown eyes. Brown hair. Olive skin.

She picked up another eggcup.

Girl. Green eyes. Red hair. Pale skin.

Hollie stood back in the centre of the room, surveying the depleted stocks.

A primal scream burst from deep inside her.

STOP!!!!!!!!!!!!!!!!!!!!!!!!!!!!!!!!!!!!!!

~

'What did you discover through the life scripts exercise I gave you last time?' Julian Finch asked at the beginning of their third session.

'To be loved, I must be clever, competent, and in control; and I live in a world in which I will be continually judged by my appearance so I must be vigilant at all times.'

'And how might this relate to your decision to be, or not to be, a mother?'

'Becoming a mother is the most out-of-control thing I can imagine. Your body is no longer under your control during pregnancy, and you can do everything right as a mother but not necessarily end up with a great kid, or a good relationship with them. There are too many variables. Looking at my scripts, feeling out of control undermines my self-worth.'

118

'Anything else?'

'I don't know how I would balance being successful at my job with being a good mother. I imagine myself trying harder and harder to do everything right – running myself into the ground without, of course, *appearing* to be trying too hard. Then at some point, I imagine everything falling apart.'

'And tell me about appearance.'

'This is connected to my father. He had an accident when I was three years old. Cut his face open and ended up with terrible scarring. He became painfully aware of being judged on his appearance. *Beautification* … he used to say … *is the highest form of capitalism.* He said beauty, nature's signalling system, has been weaponised to keep the ugly truth at bay.'

'What truth?'

'That we are destroying the beauty of the earth by plundering the natural resources and, in effect, making the planet ugly. So we manufacture a fake beauty to gloss over the ugliness. My dad called it *The Titanic Effect.* We focus on furnishing beautiful homes, buying beautiful clothes, cooking beautiful food, driving beautiful cars, emulating beautiful celebrities … making it look lovely in our little bubble so our minds refuse to believe the ship is capable of sinking.'

'A kind of consensual hypnosis?'

'Exactly.'

'Your father sounds like a man with a unique mind. What did he do for a living?'

'History professor. Probably would have been one of those academics who ended up on TV if the accident hadn't happened.'

'And he's still alive?'

'Yes. In a care home, he has dementia now,' said Hollie, feeling a stab of guilt that she hadn't visited him for a while.

'I have a sense that you are wrestling under the weight of your father's powerful intellectual narrative, Hollie. I wonder, what does this mean to you and motherhood?'

'It's a conundrum. Having a baby puts pressure on your resources. You have less available to invest in your appearance, at the very same time your appearance is most ravaged – by a lack of sleep, worry, more demands. You're stepping into the natural beauty of bearing a child and the transformation of becoming a mother but having to work harder to maintain your outer appearance to avoid being judged … *Ooh, doesn't she look tired? Ooh look at her struggling to get rid of her baby weight. She's aged ten years since having kids.* All this stuff eats away at your confidence, but then you are made to feel vain for even thinking about something deemed to be trivial, so then you have all the shame of this layered on top.'

'And what does this mean to you, personally? What is *your* relationship with *your* appearance in this context?'

Hollie felt her jaw tightening as a flush of shame washed over her.

'I know this is not easy, Hollie. I'm only pushing you because this feels important.'

Hollie lent forward towards the coffee table and took a tissue from the box that was housed inside a decorative case. She blew her nose, then fiddled with the tissue in her lap.

Thick silence stretched out. She felt her heart beating in her throat.

'I saw a memory.'

'Go on.'

'I'm about seven years old, looking in a full-length mirror, crying.'

'Why?'

'Because I hate my reflection'

'And how might this relate to motherhood?'

'I don't know,' Hollie said, looking down at her lap and fiddling with a tissue.

'What if you *did* know?'

'Know what?' Hollie said, feeling irritated.

'How this might all relate to motherhood, needing to be in control of your appearance?'

'I don't know'

She was beginning to feel tired. She wanted to leave.

'Maybe it's because I am shallow, and I spend my resources making myself and my life look good to such an extent that I can't contemplate being a mother.'

'Why not?'

'Because it would upset the carefully constructed façade I have worked hard to create in order to feel enough.'

Hollie felt like she wanted to shout fuck you at Julian Finch.

'May I offer a hypothesis?'

'Go ahead,' she said, feeling almost brazen.

'It sounds as though part of you believes that if you have a child, your carefully controlled and curated sense of self might not survive intact – especially not the outward projection of yourself that you work hard to maintain in order to function, belong, and feel enough. To become a mother is therefore to risk becoming out of control, posing a threat to your ability to succeed in a world that will judge you by your outward appearance, ultimately perhaps impacting on your mental health. Another part of you, however, is unwilling to accept what you perceive as shameful vanity. This part believes a story that becoming a mother is to somehow become authentically beautiful. Staying deadlocked in a double-bind of ambivalence is a completely rational response to this dilemma, and understandable in the context of your father's experience.'

Hollie was jolted.

Like that night on the floor with Hugh, it felt as if Julian Finch had just slapped her awake.

~

Just before the Easter holidays, Hollie had her final session with Julian Finch.

'So, how are you as we begin today, Hollie?'

'Not too good, to be honest.'

'Why is that?'

'Rough day at work. I had a run-in with a colleague. He's a particularly aggressive and toxic person and I feel as though he has it in for me. It's been brewing for several months. I finally plucked up the courage to challenge him and he went for me in a meeting, in front of everyone. It was so embarrassing.'

'In what way?'

'Because I nearly cried.'

'I can imagine that was tough. What made you so upset?'

'Because I knew I was right to challenge his behaviour, but I didn't keep my cool, so I felt I was the one who ended up looking foolish.'

'How did your colleagues react?'

'There was a dreadful silence, but eventually one of them stepped forward and said he was out of order.'

'So you were vulnerable and provoked your colleagues to step up. Isn't that what you have been working towards?'

'Yes, but …'

'But what?'

'But I should have done it better. At this level, as a director, I should be better at this stuff.'

'There you go again, should-ing all over yourself!' Julian Finch said, smiling like a wise old owl.

'I know.'

'Interesting this happened today, the day of our final session, don't you think?'

'What do you mean?'

'Well, you could say that it's a validation of all the work we have been doing together.'

'I don't understand.'

'You came here to feel your feelings, to learn how to tap into them and express yourself. And here is an example today, of you leaning into difficult emotions rather than shying away from them, in the midst of a highly charged situation.'

'I hadn't thought about it like that,' said Hollie.

'What if,' he continued, 'this is a great sign of progress?'

'I don't know,' she said. 'I just feel really tired. I thought after seeing Phemi and now you, I would have made a decision. I would know what to do. But I don't. When I got promoted I felt on top of the world, and now here I am, almost a year later, and I just feel like a failure. It's like, finally when I felt self-confident, just for one brief a moment, it all got taken away in an instant and I had to start all over again.'

Julian Finch had cocked his head to the side again, like he did the first time they met.

'Anything else?'

'Yes. And it's Easter and there are fucking eggs everywhere. Wherever I look, I see eggs in all shapes and sizes, and I keep thinking about my last eggs, gradually dwindling while I'm sitting here paralysed by self-doubt. Like those nightmares where a monster is coming towards you, but you are frozen, unable to run.'

'And is there anything else about *fucking eggs*?'

'I keep thinking about death and rebirth. That I need to choose now. Am I allowing my eggs to die forever? Or am I going to use my eggs to create new life? It's like I'm still at the crossroads, but now it feels like I am strung up, crucifying myself. And then I think, *For God's sake Hollie, stop being so bloody dramatic!*'

'This is good progress,' Julian Finch said, smiling at her kindly.

'Really??'

'Yes, because it sounds as though you are allowing yourself to experience your own feelings more deeply. I can feel it as you are speaking. There is a different energy.'

'Rage!' Hollie said, half joking through gritted teeth.

'And what might be underneath this?'

'I still keep thinking, *What's wrong with me?* Why don't I have an *ug*?'

'*Ug* being your word for the maternal instinct, that gut knowingness, that you want a child?'

'Yes. It's a visceral inner knowing of your own truth, I guess,' said Hollie.

'How does the *ug* work for women who know categorically they do not wish to become a mother?' said Julian Finch.

'I assume they also have a clear inner knowing. A way their truth speaks to them.'

'So is this *ug* really maternal instinct, or about being in dialogue with your deeper self and experiencing your own truth?'

Hollie stared down at the crimson carpet a few feet in front of her. It was as if her brain had just commanded her whole body into perfect stillness, like a statue. Her awareness narrowed to swallowing, blinking, and breathing.

What if ug is not maternal instinct?

What if the ug is my truth?

What is my truth?

Hello, Ug

'What's this?' Hollie asked as she walked into the dining room and saw a huge bouquet of white roses in a vase, with a white envelope propped up against it.

'Open it, babe,' said Hugh.

She put down her briefcase and handbag next to the table, sat down, and opened the envelope.

To my darling wife.
Our love is already sealed.
Hugh xxx

'That's so lovely, thank you, but …'

Hugh walked over from the kitchen with a glass of fizz in each hand.

'Before you say anything, I know it's a school night, but one glass won't hurt,' he said, kissing her on the lips.

'Okay,' Hollie replied, taking a sip. 'So, what's all this in aid of?'

Hugh pulled out a chair and angled it to face her.

'Well, I know it's your mum's birthday today, and I know you've been a bit upset recently with things being tense between you two.'

'I spoke to her again today. I rang from work at lunchtime to try and arrange something for her birthday and she said she didn't want to think about it because she was staying at my sister's longer to help her with the baby. Fair enough, but it was her tone that got to me. She was just so dismissive.'

'She's probably just a bit preoccupied.'

'Yeah, I suppose.'

'Anyway … I was thinking it's the anniversary of your promotion and I know how hard you've worked, and I just want you to know I'm proud of you.'

'Thanks.'

'And … I was talking to Dave yesterday. I told you him and Marie are splitting up, didn't I?'

'As in business-partner Dave?'

'Yes. And she doesn't want custody of the kids.'

'Yes, you said.'

'Dave was saying he didn't think she ever really wanted kids, but she just had them because it was what you did. And there was a lot of pressure for grandchildren, apparently.'

'Happens a lot. I always thought she seemed quite bitter,' said Hollie.

'And now her girls hate her.'

'There's always an expectation that children stay with their mother, so this must be hard to take.'

'Yeah, and talking to Dave, it made me realise how lucky I am already, and that I don't need us to have a baby to seal our love. I just want you to know that I really mean it. I would love us to have a child together, but if you don't want to, it's okay. And you don't have to feel you need to make up for what happened with Stephen.'

Hollie leaned over and hugged him tightly, feeling herself welling up.

'Funnily enough, I've been thinking …'

'You're always thinking!' Hugh said smiling at her.

'Well, I might surprise you then,' she said.

'Don't tell, me. You have decided you do want a baby?'

'Not exactly.'

'What then?'

'I'm going to stop taking the pill.'

'Really?' Hugh said, his face suddenly lit up. 'Is this because of the psychotherapy?'

'It's hard to pinpoint to anything specific. And I can't really explain it rationally. It's just … a feeling that's been brewing. Maybe I have exhausted my mind and my intuition is finally speaking to me.'

'But I thought you said something about coming off the pill being like abdication?'

'I did, but now I'm not sure I believe this. Who knows if I will be able to get pregnant at my age anyway? From what I've been reading, it's not as easy as you think. For all we know maybe I only have one egg left in the egg room!'

'One wild egg,' Hugh said.

'I just have this really strong feeling that I need to let go of something.'

'Let go of what?'

'I don't know. It might be the pill. It might be the idea of motherhood. It might be my ambivalence. Who knows! All I know is that I feel like I can't wait anymore to make a decision, so this seems like the most obvious option. Also, something Diane said a while ago keeps going round in my mind.'

'I always liked Diane,' Hugh beamed, raising his glass in the air as if toasting her.

'She reminded me that logic is the passenger of my car, but the driver is intuition. I think I need to put intuition back in charge of the steering wheel and she is whispering to me to come off the pill.'

'Well, whatever that means, I like it,' said Hugh.

'What does your intuition say about us taking the rest of this bottle and going upstairs?'

Hollie smiled.

'She says yes.'

~

Three months later, Hugh was propped up on his pillow, gazing at her as Hollie opened her eyes.

'Morning, babe'

'Hi.'

'I didn't want to disturb you. You looked so peaceful.'

Hugh leaned over and kissed her.

'Better get going, I'm picking my sister up soon, she's coming for lunch today.'

'Oh yes, I forgot,' said Hollie.

'Actually, you look really beautiful this morning.'

'What, as opposed to unlike other mornings?'

'Very funny. You still need to work on accepting compliments after all this therapy then!'

'Work in progress.'

'I don't know, you look … *glowy*'

'Good word.'

'You couldn't be pregnant, could you?'

'I doubt it. That would be quick, given I only came off the pill a couple of months ago.'

'Stranger things have happened. Maybe you're right, perhaps I just have the eyes of love on today. Anyway, best get up and at 'em.'

'Ok, see you later,' she said, wrapping the duvet back around her.

Hollie's mind was turning over.

Glowy … Could it be possible?

She took a sharp intake of breath as she recalled a scene at work a few days earlier. She had been feeling queasy one morning, moments before walking into the kitchen where Sandra had collared her by the kettle.

'Are you feeling okay today, Hollie?' she had asked.

'Why?'

'I've been up on the toilet all night, being sick. I wondered whether it was food poisoning from what we ate yesterday, when we went for lunch. Didn't we eat the same thing?'

'Yes. I must admit I am feeling a bit off-colour this morning,' she had replied,

But now Hollie's mind was racing. If she had not seen Sandra, she would undoubtedly have wondered whether it was morning sickness but had dismissed the idea. She needed to get a test.

Hollie slowly got out of bed and got dressed, feeling as though she were in slow motion. She drove to the nearest supermarket and headed for the aisle where she imagined they kept the pregnancy tests. It was part of the store she had never visited before. She stood staring vacantly at the shelves. She was finally here. Standing on the threshold they said was the one you crossed to become a fully actualised woman. She suddenly felt hyper-real, as if all her senses had been dialled up, profoundly aware of the potential spark of life inside her.

Inside her brain, she could almost hear instructions being communicated, telling her body what to do …

Reach arm out at forty-five-degree angle towards shelf.

Curl fingers together to grasp product.

Rotate wrist to read packaging instructions.

It seemed as if part of her wanted to slow down and savour this moment, to record every sensory aspect of this unexpected rite of passage, as she moved within touching distance of the mysterious temple of motherhood. She suddenly felt a sense of communion with her mother, sister, Aunty Ruby and all her friends who had stood here before her, inside this moment, and all the other women who would do so again.

She lingered, standing in the aisle staring into space with a Clear Blue & Easy twin pack in her hand, like an actress awaiting her cue from the director.

So Hollie, what do I want the result to be? she heard a voice whisper.

If ever there was a moment when her truth would rise, surely it would be now? She observed herself intently for a sign, but there was still nothing. She glided towards the checkouts and the next thing she knew, she was back in her ensuite bathroom, peeing on the white stick. Hollie laid it down on the floor in front of her and stared at the white tiles round the bath, dotted here and there with cute frogs, wondering whether, against the odds, one of Hugh's tadpoles had fertilised a last egg. Adrenalin surged through her body as a blue mark began to form in the results window.

A blue cross appeared.

'No. It can't be true. I must be reading it wrong,' Hollie said aloud. She opened out the tightly folded instructions, like a delicate tracing-paper map, to double check the detailed instructions. She surveyed the three images denoting a positive result, each showing a version of the blue cross, then looked back at her stick. It was the same as picture B.

If you are still unsure of your result see Q7 for full details, the instructions said.

Hollie went to Q7 and read the wording using her forefinger to follow the tiny copy, guiding her eyes carefully along from left to right, like she had done at school when learning to read for the first time.

For your result to be positive there must be a blue line in the control window and a '+' symbol in the result window within 10 minutes of performing the test.

She looked again at her stick.

Blue cross.

'No, it can't be. Maybe it's faulty. I better check.' Extra carefully, Hollie opened the second packet in the box. She removed it from the foil wrapper like a technician in a laboratory, ensuring there was no accidental touching with her hand or the toilet bowl that could possibly contaminate the result.

Blue cross.

Hollie looked at the leaflet again. The words had not changed. She was sure she was reading them correctly. 'Okay,' she said aloud, doing her Pilates breathing. 'I need words. Not just a line in a window. I need words. Unambiguous words. Not symbols.' Half an hour later she returned from a second trip to the supermarket with a Clearblue Digital Pregnancy Test.

Feeling sick that morning …

Glowy …

Blue cross …

The film montage played over and over in a loop, but she couldn't take it in. She sat on the toilet seat again, watching the Smart Countdown on the small screen, which indicated that the test was working. It looked like a mobile phone battery charger symbol.

Pregnant.

There it was, in black lettering.

Unmistakeable.

'Omigod! … I'm pregnant! Me. Hollie. Pregnant. A baby…. Omigod.'

She just sat there. Gawping.

A couple of hours later Hugh arrived back with his sister, Sharon. Hollie had prepared lunch in a daze and greeted them both before excusing herself to go to the toilet. Hugh followed her upstairs into the bathroom.

'What's up?'

'What do you mean?'

'I mean you look like you are working *really* hard trying to act normal. Is everything okay?'

'I'm … pregnant.'

Hugh's face broke into a radiant smile. He looked at her with those eyes again, like that night on the kitchen floor. 'Egberta,' Hollie said, touching her abdomen in that way she had seen so many other women do before. She liked the literalness of this name as she thought about the tiny embryo inside.

'Hello, Egberta,' Hugh said, hugging her tightly.

From the moment Hugh's sister left a few hours later, Hollie threw herself into full project management mode, galvanised into action by the shock of seeing those words in the window. Emotionally, she felt oddly neutral, as if the enormity of Egberta was too much for her to hold. And for now, it seemed irrelevant.

Hugh was thrilled.

She was pregnant.

There was a job to be done.

And she was nothing if not competent.

She opened her laptop and began reading voraciously, digesting everything from pregnancy vitamin supplements, to what happens during each trimester, to the latest baby names.

It all felt very grown-up.

~

Ten weeks into the pregnancy, Hollie still felt oddly neutral.

Everything was progressing as it should and, as seemed to be customary, she and Hugh had agreed not to tell anyone until they had passed the first scan. She had taken to avoiding her mother as much as possible in an effort to keep the news under wraps and minimise the temptation to blurt it out, just to see the look of shock on her face.

Hollie assumed it was normal to feel a strange sense of neutrality whilst your pregnancy was still, in effect, a secret. It was like she was standing behind a pane of glass watching herself. Removed and oddly surreal.

Then, one Saturday morning, she suddenly woke up alone with severe cramps.

Hugh had already left to go swimming. She went to the toilet and saw she was bleeding a little. Tiny spots. Hollie went into the study and opened her laptop to check the medical advice. It seemed that it may, or may not, be something to worry about. She noticed she still felt detached. By the time Hugh arrived home, the bleeding seemed to have become heavier. Unlike Hollie, he seemed alarmed and suggested they call the doctor. Within a few hours, she and Hugh were sitting holding hands, waiting to be called in for a scan in an alcove off an empty corridor of the local hospital.

'To be on the safe side,' her GP had said, 'given your age.'

'Are you okay, babe?' Hugh asked with his arm around her protectively. 'Is the pain getting any better?'

'No change,' said Hollie, wincing with the cramping which had significantly increased. 'It's like extreme-sport period pain!'

In a funny way, she was grateful for the pain.

Even now, when it seemed there was really something to worry about, she still felt strangely neutral about being pregnant. As if it was happening to a version of herself and she was elsewhere, at a distance, observing. She wondered whether this was a bad sign. Perhaps, she thought, she deserved the pain? A nurse in light blue scrubs came out of a door opposite and approached them.

'Mrs Hardwick?' she said, standing in front of Hollie.

'Yes.'

'And you must be Mr Hardwick?' she said to Hugh.

Hollie noticed her name badge.

Marie Fenwick.

She thought of Dave's wife, Marie, and pictured her vinegary face. Hollie wondered how she had felt about her pregnancies when she went for her scans.

The room was dark, a little chilly and virtually empty apart from this bed on wheels, a washbasin, and some medical equipment. Hollie lay on the trolley as instructed and unzipped her jeans. Hugh was sitting next to her in a chair.

'So, I am going to put some gel on your tummy. It will be a little cold. Then we can have a look and see what's going on in there. How far along are you?'

'Ten weeks.'

'And you have been having some bleeding and cramps?' she said whilst rubbing the gel on Hollie's stomach. It reminded her of cheap hair gel she had used in the eighties.

'Yes.'

'Okay, let's have a look,' the nurse said with one hand guiding the scanner and another looking at the TV screen to her left. Hollie again had the feeling of being inside a movie of her own life, as though she were watching this iconic cinematic moment of pregnancy as a scene, but not fully participating in it.

'There we go,' said the nurse. 'There's your baby. Can you see it? About the size of a grape.'

Hollie peered towards the monitor. You could just make it out. Hugh squeezed her hand, gazing between the screen and her adoringly. She could see his eyes were becoming watery. 'Wow. She's real,' Hollie said, somehow feeling as if she was trying to psych herself up into being fully present in the moment, willing herself to act her part.

'And yes, we have a good heartbeat. Can you hear it?'

She wondered if this was normal. Were other women unable to absorb the magnitude of what it meant to be growing another human being inside themselves? Or was there something wrong with her reaction? Hollie continued staring at the monitor and concentrated her ears.

Boo-bum-boo-bum-boo-bum.

A distinct and clear underwater beat. It reminded Hollie of the muffled sounds and otherworldly atmosphere of scuba diving.

'Okay, that's it, Hollie. Everything looks as it should. I will give the results to the doctor, so if you would like to wait outside, he will call you in shortly.'

'Wasn't that amazing, babe? Seeing our baby?' said Hugh when they sat down.

'Yeah,' Hollie said.

'You okay?'

'Just the pain,' Hollie lied.

About fifteen minutes later, Hollie was invited into another room off the empty corridor and spoke briefly to the doctor.

'Looking at the scan results, everything looks normal, Mrs Hardwick,' he said after asking about her symptoms, which had begun to ease off. 'But given your age and stage of pregnancy, I must warn you that the chances of miscarriage are high. That said, many women in your situation go on to have healthy babies, so for now there is nothing to worry about. I suggest you go home, rest, and keep an eye on things.'

'It's going to be okay, you know,' said Hugh as they drove home. 'I mean, I know we might lose Egberta. And obviously I hope we don't. But at least we know you can get pregnant now, so that's good isn't it?'

'Yeah,' said Hollie, trying to sound convincing as she gazed out of the car window.

'Are you upset?'

Hollie nodded, not wishing to open a conversation. In a way, she thought, she was upset – upset that she did not feel upset in the way she thought she should. She kept conjuring the image of the tiny grape in her belly, and the underwater sound of her baby's breathing as if repeated viewing would help to trigger a reaction. First contact. This was supposed to be a joyous moment, wasn't it? So why had she not felt anything? Why did none of it feel real?

Was she preparing herself for the worst?

Or was it something else?

Something she was missing?

When they arrived home, Hollie put her pyjamas on and went to bed for the rest of the day, hoping to get some respite from her thoughts even more than the stomach cramps. But by the early hours of the morning, she was awake again, bleeding heavily and in pain. She crept out of bed and sat on the toilet. She pulled down her bloodied pyjama bottoms and removed them to wash in the sink before having a pee and wiping herself.

And there she was.

Egberta.

Lying on the white toilet paper in a splat of gooey blood, like one of those dead baby birds she and her friends used to find on the road when they were kids. Spuggies they had called them. Splatted and broken after they had fallen out of their nests. She called into the bedroom for Hugh and held out the toilet paper like a tiny shroud.

'It's Egberta. She's gone,' she said flatly.

Hugh knelt on the floor by her feet.

'I'm so sorry, babe,' he said, peering at the bloody mess.

Hollie didn't answer.

'I really hoped it was going to pass.'

Hollie nodded, still staring at the tissue paper, as if forcing herself to keep looking would somehow jolt her back into her body so she could feel something.

She wanted to cry. Felt she should even.

But there was nothing.

'Like the doctor said, it's really common for this to happen.'

'I know.'

Hollie was unsure what to do. Simply flushing Egberta away seemed too matter of fact. Perhaps they ought to do something ceremonial? Something to honour what had happened. But what? She had no idea. And contriving something might seem melodramatic, and equally as inappropriate. She stared again vacantly at the toilet paper shroud.

'Say goodbye to Egberta,' she said, cupping it gently in her hands as she looked at Hugh.

'Bye, Egberta.'

'Goodbye, Egberta,' she said.

Hollie stood up, dropped the tissue into the toilet bowl and with a final glance, flushed the spuggy body away. Life had been inside her, and now it was gone. They went back into the bedroom and lay on the bed.

'We can try again,' Hugh said, hugging her tightly.

'I know,' Hollie replied.

She felt numb.

Hollie went to work the next day and carried on as normal. She did not say anything to anyone about Egberta. She felt like she was underwater. Holding her breath. Every time she thought of the word *miscarriage*, and how this was an experience which had happened to her, it sounded oddly hollow and distant. As if the substance of its meaning had been surgically extracted and stored neatly in a jar on a shelf behind a wall of opaque glass.

'At least we know we can get pregnant,' Hugh kept saying, trying to be helpful. 'We can try again.'

And every time Hollie had nodded vacantly.

'Yes,' she said, 'we will try again,' even though she could feel an emptiness behind her words.

Mercifully at least, Maybe-Baby FM seemed to have gone off-air. What she did not tell Hugh, could not tell anyone, was that part of her felt oddly … *legitimised*. She was no longer simply an alien, 'other' woman who did not want children. She had entered, albeit briefly, the sacred temple of motherhood. She had opened herself up.

~

In a bid to cheer her up, Hugh organised a surprise holiday to

Santorini, just after the schools went back.

'A change of scene will do you the world of good,' he said.

It was a beautiful place, and they had a stunning hotel with an infinity pool and spectacular clifftop views. Yet Hollie continued to feel oddly detached. Like she was watching herself on a travel programme.

Shortly after they returned, Hollie was in the ensuite bathroom one Saturday afternoon. She flushed the toilet, washed her hands, and turned to leave, when suddenly her right hand reached out and grabbed the small silver knob on the door of the bathroom cabinet. Without any prior intention or forethought, she wrenched it open so hard she almost pulled the door off its hinges, then watched as her fingers reached to the back shelf and scrabbled to find a packet of contraceptive pills. Deftly, her fingers popped open a foil window, and removed one of the tiny lilac-coloured pills.

She swallowed it dramatically, with a loud gulp.

Hollie stood immobilised on the spot.

Her mouth was hanging open in shock.

She held her hands up in front of her face and turned them over slowly, looking at them as if she were an alien who had suddenly just landed inside this human body. Her mouth still hung open as she tried to re-embody herself and process what had just happened, waiting for her brain to come back online.

The air around her was tingling.

She had made a decision. No argument. No weighing of pros and cons. Just the full-body sensation of a crystal-clear insight landing in her body.

A deep knowing had suddenly risen from the depths of her seabed, like a mighty kraken, and punched its way through her thick glass wall.

Motherhood is not my path.

She heard her voice say this inside her head. It spoke with absolute certainty.

It did not feel so much like a choice. It felt more like … a *commandment*.

Motherhood is not my path.

Hollie felt the power of this knowing simultaneously in every single atom of her being. As if that tiny pill had set off a chain reaction lightning up every cell – *ding, ding, ding* – in a stunning sequence of pinball wizardry.

'Now *that* … was a decision!' she said out loud as she stood staring into the bathroom cabinet, still rooted to the spot.

Finally, her *ug* had spoken.

And she had heard it … loud and clear and unmistakeable.

Motherhood is not my path.

This was her deep truth. She knew it without a shadow of doubt. She knew it with a whole-body certainty that transcended way beyond her rational mind. She knew this was the stunning moment of clarity she had been searching for ever since the kitchen-floor-moment. She knew that through the act of ingesting her tiny lilac pill, she had just swallowed the most powerful full stop of her life.

The doorway to motherhood had been firmly slammed shut.

Suddenly, a new question arose in her mind.

Now what?

Part Two

Transitioning in the Birth Canal

Departure Board

'I'm so glad we're finally catching up,' Diane said after they had ordered food. 'You've been on my mind a lot.'

'Sorry it took so long to get a date, been crazy at work. Don't know where the time is going. I feel as though life is racing past in a blur. Maybe because I now spend my life in bloody meetings!' said Hollie, inwardly cringing as she heard how cliched and worn she sounded.

'Living the executive dream, eh? Rather you than me, sweetie.'

'Yeah. The art of trying to convey what you mean, without actually saying what you think!'

'I'm so glad to be out of all the corporate politics, it was never my strong suit.'

'I'm already wondering whether it's mine, to be honest, Diane. My workload has gone through the roof. I never realised how many people would want a piece of you when you get to this level. Feel as though I've aged ten years overnight.'

'Are you still managing to keep up your gym routine? I'm always so envious of how self-disciplined you are.'

'It's slipped recently. I know I should make myself go, but I feel so shattered at the end of the day. And I'm working in the evenings a lot as well.'

'You need to watch that, Hollie.'

'I know. Must do better.'

'No. Must be *kinder*.'

'Yeah, fair point.'

The waiter came over. He was handsome. Early twenties, Hollie guessed. Probably looking at her thinking she looked middle-aged, she thought, like his mother.

'So, what's been happening since we spoke on the phone?' Diane said after they had ordered. 'I'm so sorry about Ebgerta. Had you decided on a proper name for her, if it's okay to ask?'

'Amber Rose.'

'Beautiful. I think there's something important about naming your baby in a miscarriage.'

Diane paused and looked directly at Hollie. She seemed to be scanning her, taking her all in, like a kindly nurse asking a patient to open their mouth and say *ahhhhh* then peering into their eyes and ears to check for signs of a healthy reaction.

'And it sounds like you found the ug and made your authentic decision. How are you feeling about it all now, after your Incredible Hulk routine with the bathroom cabinet?'

'Like I'm in suspended animation.'

'Go on …'

'The door to motherhood definitely feels closed. For good. And I feel okay with that. It feels right. The problem now is I realise I'd *literally* seen two paths stretching out beyond the fork in the road. Route A was motherhood, clearly marked with milestones along the way, but route B is just a blank.'

'Route B being the path of un-motherhood?'

'Yeah. I think I had in my mind that something would happen once I had made a definitive choice, you know. Probably sounds a bit stupid.'

'Stupid how?'

'I had this sense that a new journey would begin. You know, that making this decision would be catalytic and spark something else. But all I feel now is a kind of … *nothingness* in front of me. Like I'm in an empty departure lounge, waiting to catch a flight to my future.'

'You've moved from being at a crossroads, to sitting in a kind of existential airport?'

'Exactly! It's like I'm waiting for a flight to be called, but the departure board is blank. There have been no announcements, and zero passenger information, and it all feels a bit eerie.'

'Sounds like an episode of *Twin Peaks*!'

'It definitely has a David Lynch vibe,' Hollie chuckled, grateful to see the funny side. 'Frankly, I want to bang on the desk and complain to the airline, but there's no one available to speak to and no bloody way out!'

Diane laughed just as the waiter arrived with their sushi starters and bottle of sauvignon blanc in an ice bucket.

'What's funny?'

'You,' Diane said, pouring the wine. 'It's been, what, a matter of weeks since you made a momentous decision that in effect slammed the door to motherhood shut after a deep, yearlong enquiry that resulted in … oh by the way, a wee miscarriage … and you've already morphed into a frustrated passenger tapping your feet in an airport expecting to have boarded a plane to Plan-B and pina coladas!'

'Oh God, I hadn't thought of it like that!'

'Cheers, my dear, and belated happy birthday! This is my treat today,' Diane said, raising a toast.

'Cheers.'

'Here's to brilliantly sitting in your patience,' said Diane.

'Very funny. I suppose when you put it like that …'

'Seriously though sweetie, put your glass down a minute.'

Diane grabbed hold of Hollie's hands across the table and lowered her voice.

'You've had a … *miscarriage*.' She mouthed the word slowly, enunciating each syllable, then paused as if wanting to make sure the weight of it had sunk in. 'So there's probably some grief you're going to need to process.'

'I had a few tears the night we flushed Egberta down the toilet.'

'Yes, Doctor Spock, I hear you. But I'm talking here about something deeper than a quick cathartic cry. This is a frickin' big life ending. I know you said you're at peace with your decision, but don't underestimate the emotional impact of this, Hollie. Maybe this feeling of emptiness is an expression of your very real physical and emotional loss?'

Hollie suddenly felt embarrassed. She bought herself a minute by picking up a salmon roll and popping it in her mouth. Was she really shallow after all? Just a selfish childfree woman? She had had a new life growing inside her and now her baby was gone, and she was trying to move on to the next thing. What was wrong with her?

'What's that look?'

'What look?'

'That one where you look away and go in on yourself. Let me guess, now you're giving yourself a hard time at not being competent enough at grieving?'

Hollie felt her cheeks flush.

'Am I right?'

'How are you in my head, Obi Wan Kenobi?'

'We Scottish folk, we have special powers! You should know that by now, Hollie.'

'It's like dinner in the psychiatrists chair.'

'I know, and you love it, admit it.'

'Maybe a bit,' Hollie smiled.

'Listen. I know you're incredibly resilient, Hollie, but friends I know who have been through miscarriage found it really tough. Whether you are conscious of it or not, at some level you will have been creating hopes and dreams of an imagined new future for you, Hugh and Amber Rose, and you can't just turn those emotions off like a tap. Not even you!'

'In other words, you're saying I need to lean into this feeling of nothingness?'

'I'd say that embracing this eerie betwixt-and-between place would be a good starting point. So instead of trying to project-plan your way out, maybe try settling into the departure lounge, buy some snacks, find a comfy chair, and tuck into reading a good book.'

Hollie smiled, took another sip of wine, and gazed out of the large picture window looking out over the river.

'I don't know, Diane. I feel okay about the miscarriage. Honestly. I know in every cell of my being now that motherhood is not my path. But this empty feeling, I think there's something more to it.'

'More than what?'

'More than processing my miscarriage.'

'Say more …'

'I keep hearing the same thing, round and round in my mind … *This can't be it*!? Surely, there must be more to life than just, *carry on as you were*. Do you know what I mean?'

'The gap?'

'What's that?'

'That feeling of not being enough. If I am not a mother, then what am I for?'

'You have this too?'

'I went through a period of feeling like this last year when I hit the menopause. Even though I never wanted kids, there was something sad about the finality of the whole thing that I just couldn't seem to shake. A palpable feeing of emptiness. It was probably tied up with me and Darren splitting up as well. I just kept thinking, what had my life amounted to? What will be left behind when I'm gone?'

Diane pulled a handkerchief from her bag and wiped her eyes.

'I'm sorry, Diane, I didn't know all this was going on for you. And here's me banging on about my stuff.'

Hollie wondered whether she had been a terrible friend. Had she been so self-absorbed that she had missed cues about what was going on for Diane?

'It's okay, honestly, Hollie. I wanted to say something but couldn't bring myself to. How ironic is that? I'm great at giving you advice, but I felt so ridiculous about the whole thing I just couldn't talk about it. And I guess my hormones were all over the place. To use your analogy, the shutter on my egg shop had well and truly closed, but somehow I couldn't face finally handing in the keys!'

'So, Obi Wan, you are still wading into the swamp of your emotions?'

'Oh yeah. Pot and frickin' kettle!'

'What a bloody relief!'

'When I started seeing Phemi, this was the beginning of my real grief work.'

'And how do you feel now?'

'I ebb and flow. I can get triggered by all the normal stuff ... the *so-do-*

you-have-kids? questions, and the *but-you-would-have-made-such-a-great-mother* comments. Not because I wish I had children, I'm totally at peace with that. In fact, I'm actually really glad I don't have them. It's more because of the constant expectations to justify yourself when you don't have kids, and the fact that everyone seems to want to point out there's a gap … it's hard not to start wondering whether there is actually one! So, I've now decided, as a fifty-something single woman, my new mission is to work on cherishing my freedom and really make the most of it. I'm taking the view that each decade is going to be my best yet, and believing I'm exactly where I'm supposed to be.'

'Such an empowering belief. I can feel the energy of it as you're talking.'

'Let's face it Hollie, we make shit up about our lives all the time, we usually just choose to make it up really bad and convince ourselves the crap version is more "realistic" … that it's the "real world". Well, I say *bollocks* to that! We create our own reality, so from here on in I'm going to be the author of my own life and become the most holy-shit version of myself I can!'

'Holy-shit version of yourself,' Hollie said, raising her glass. 'I'll drink to that!'

'*Slan-ge-var*, as we say in Scotland!' Diane said, clinking her glass.

'*Slan-ge-var!*'

Diane took a gulp, put her glass down and leaned forward in her chair, lowering her voice again.

'To be honest, Hollie, I've begun to wonder whether feeling empty isn't just the nature of being human anyway?'

'Why are you whispering?'

'I don't know,' Diane said, chuckling, looking around the restaurant like a spy, checking there was no one listening before she revealed a state secret. 'Maybe, because we don't have the distraction of children, we notice and experience the emptiness more keenly? I reckon it's probably the same thing that happens to most women later in life, when their kids fly the nest, and they suddenly think, *Who am I? … What's my purpose? … What's life all about?*'

'I never thought about it like that before,' said Hollie, nodding thoughtfully.

They fell into silence for a few moments. The waiter came back over.

'Everything okay? Is there anything else I can get you two ladies?'

'Other than plane tickets to somewhere exotic, no thanks,' Hollie quipped.

'It looks like you have already been somewhere nice,' he said, looking at her.

'Santorini.'

'Lucky you. Always wanted to go there. Anyway, enjoy, ladies,' he said and walked over to another table.

'How was your holiday, I forgot to ask?'

'Santorini was stunning. Like a big white wedding cake of a place, perched on a cliff face.'

'As beautiful as it looks in all the photos?'

'Yes. But to be honest, it felt oddly vacuous.'

'It was only a few weeks after your miscarriage.'

'Yeah, maybe that was it, I had this feeling that I was there, but not really *there*. As if I was watching myself on television. We had a beautiful hotel looking out over the sea, but our room smelled of drains and they couldn't move us to another one. It felt like a metaphor: picture perfect on the surface, but like something was off below the surface. Maybe I just need to learn to be more grateful for what I have?'

'How has Hugh taken your decision, you haven't really said?'

'We haven't talked much. He was sad about the miscarriage but says he's okay with us not having children if that's my decision. Not sure I really believe him, though. I suspect he wanted to be a father again far more than he's admitting, to heal old wounds, you know.'

'As in, being estranged from his son?'

'Yes.'

'I seem to remember you saying his son is in Australia now? Heartbreaking, isn't it. This is the part they never tell you about becoming a parent, about all the things that can get messed up.'

'Hugh definitely messed up, but, let's face it, nobody is whiter than white. It just seems so unjust that this is the consequence of one mistake. I know he tried hard to re-establish contact when Stephen was young – sending gifts, showing up at the school – but nothing he did worked and now I think he feels it's too late. He was hoping by the time his son became an adult he would reach out, but for whatever reason it hasn't happened.'

'That's so sad for Hugh, but you know it's not your job the rescue him, right? He has to find his own way through this. You can't feel guilty for making your own decision, even if it's not what he wants.'

'I know, but it's hard. Anyway, enough of me moaning, I feel like I'm being terrible company.'

'Don't go adding managing me to your list of woes! Anyway, you still have plenty of credit in the emotional bank account after you helped me last year when I had my meltdown.'

'When you threw the toilet seat at Darren? I still can't believe you did that!'

'I know … another relationship down the swanee. Literally! He turned out to be another avoidant attachment type. At least I think, age fifty-three, I'm getting better at spotting them!'

'What's happening with you and Darren now?'

'We can talk about that in a minute, Hollie,' Diane said, sounding momentarily like a headmistress. 'But before you try to completely change the subject, just one more thing I want to say about your miscarriage and what you said before, about feeling empty.'

'Okay,' Hollie said, wondering what she was about to say.

'Have you seen an email from Phemi she sent out recently?'

'No. Not looked at my personal emails for a while. Why?'

'She's starting up a mindfulness group. I just thought it might be worth you going. Maybe help you process all of this stuff while you're sitting in the departure lounge.'

~

A week later, Hollie rang the bell of Embody Healing again. She had worked late and come straight from the office. Phemi invited her in, and Hollie followed her into a small, dimly lit room at the back of the building. There were five other women of varying ages assembled in a wonky circle of chairs, cushions and a battered sofa. Three mismatching chintzy lamps were perched on side tables and an incense stick was burning. On a grubby white wall, a large, framed picture of a female Buddha was hanging at an angle next to a crumpled piece of flipchart paper with one word written on it in large scrawl.

Vulnerability.

It felt unnervingly intimate. Suited and booted, Hollie felt like Bridget Jones arriving at the vicars-and-tarts party in fancy dress, realising everyone else had got a different memo. She sat to the right of Phemi on a threadbare yet surprisingly comfy armchair, aware of the stark contrast with her expensive woollen coat and trouser suit.

'Welcome. I'm so excited to have you here, for you to meet each other,' Phemi began, sitting cross-legged on a large cushion. Dozens of thin, coloured bangles jangled as she gestured.

'I don't know exactly how this is going to work, but I feel in my bones this is going to be a really special group.'

Not sure about that, Hollie thought glancing round the room, hating herself for being so judgemental. None of the other women looked like her ... *professional.* Hollie imagined Diane looking at her sweetly, telling her to be more self-compassionate. She removed her heels, placed her feet flat on the floor and tried to relax. Her feet were sore.

'I think for this evening we should just do some introductions and explore what you want to get out of this group, then take it from there. Before we start though, I want to talk about this word,' she said, pointing to the flipchart paper. '*Vulnerability.* The courage to be vulnerable is essential for our development, and to be fully present in our lives, which is essentially what mindfulness is all about. So, I want us to make this a space where we can be vulnerable with each other, knowing what is said here stays in the room. Think of our sessions as being like visiting a well – a place we can drop down beneath the surface of our chattering minds and fill our buckets with the still, fresh water of our deeper knowing.'

By the end of the introduction, it seemed to Hollie that Phemi had only the vaguest notion of how the 'programme' of five sessions would work, informed by some previous experience of running youth groups, a brief stint as a mental health worker, and having read some articles about mindfulness. From what she could gather, Phemi was proposing to introduce a theme or a quote that had 'emerged for her' in the weeks, days, or even minutes before a session, using this as a catalyst for conversations. And, well, basically, seeing what happened! Hollie reflected that were she to even consider running a group that people paid money to attend, she would need a postgraduate diploma in mindfulness, fifty hours of practice, and several days of rehearsal. Yet here was Phemi, blithely holding court, completely at ease, seemingly comfortable to run a programme balanced precariously upon a single metaphor – with no notes, no session plan, and no clear objectives.

Hollie couldn't decide whether her casual approach was astonishing arrogance, or enviable chutzpah.

'Any questions before we begin?' Phemi said with a beaming smile as she stood up and removed the incense stick from its decorative wooden box, wafting it in the air around the head of each woman as if trying to smoke out questions from inside everyone's heads.

Cheesy, thought Hollie, feeling a slight inner clench as Phemi waved a trail of smoke around her in figure of eight, like she was wielding a wand. Phemi sat back down on her colourful cushion and looked at each woman in turn with her hands in the prayer position, doing a little bow.

'Okay, let's begin.'

Hollie had been wondering whether to ask if they were actually going to do any mindfulness practice but feared her tone of voice would come across as too critical and didn't want to embarrass Phemi or ruin the vibe, so she stayed quiet. Phemi went first, sharing an eye-watering account of her life. A raw collection of hell-and-back tales that would have been at home in a gritty Ken Loach film. The connective thread seemed to be an unshakeable self-belief that whatever shit happened, it was always for a reason and her highest good.

'If you follow your inner compass,' she said, 'everything will work out okay in the end.'

Hollie thought she didn't so much have an internal compass, as an unreliable weathervane, spinning round in the wind. She admired Phemi for her raw candour but could not help but wonder whether this was a safe psychological space for such heavy stuff to be shared.

'I'll go next,' an older lady said who was sitting to one side of the battered sofa. She looked like someone who set her hair in rollers and went to bed in a hairnet. She reminded Hollie of Petunia Dursley from *Harry Potter* and she felt an instant dislike towards the woman as she watched her edge forward and clear her throat as though preparing to give a speech.

'I'm Mary,' she said. 'I'm here because …'

She started to cry.

Phemi handed her a box of tissues. 'Take your time Mary. It's okay.'

'I have twin girls and neither of my daughters speaks to me anymore. It's been going on for years and I don't want to talk about the reasons here, but I'm …'

Mary blew her nose noisily.

'… heartbroken. I feel like I've lost everything … even my faith in God. I feel cast adrift, suffering, with no one to guide me. I've been coming to see Phemi for a year now to try and make peace with it all. I don't know what I want to get out of this group, but I'm happy to be here.'

Mary made the sign of the cross and sat back, still sobbing.

'But it's really nice to meet you all. Sorry. That's all I have to say,' she added.

'Thanks for sharing, Mary,' said Phemi, gently leaning forward and touching Mary's leg. 'I think suffering is a very powerful word.'

Or just melodramatic, thought Hollie.

'In Buddhism they have this idea of the four noble truths. They believe suffering is the nature of our existence, providing a gateway to our spiritual growth.'

She liked Phemi, admired her even, but this already seemed less like a mindfulness programme and more like a spiritual AA meeting for people who seemed, frankly, a bit tweaked in the head. She imagined her senior colleagues walking in the room, rolling their eyes, and asking what the hell she was doing here with these misfits, hippies, and bible bashers, and cringed as she imagined herself trying to explain. Perhaps she had been too trusting? Too desperate?

'I'll go next,' said a young, burly woman with a broad Geordie accent.

She was sitting in a sturdy armchair at the opposite end of the room to Hollie. She looked like she would punch you if you glanced at her the wrong way.

'I'm Lesley from Bensham,' she paused. 'Rough.'

She said this with a slightly upturned lip that made her look a little bit like Elvis. Phemi snorted with glee. Everyone else, including Hollie, emitted slightly nervous noises, not feeling quite confident enough to laugh.

'I'm thirty-two. Don't believe in God. But if there is one, he's a warped motherfucker in my opinion. No offence, like,' she said, looking at Mary.

'Quit my job a few months ago. Was working at the local college. Couldn't handle it anymore. So I said, "Fuck this shit," and walked out. Right there and then. Always thought I was thick. Done crappy jobs. Didn't do well at school. Not clever enough to study. My dad was an alcoholic. Beat my mam about. I used to go round the town at night, looking for fights to watch. But then I accidentally ended up in one and got the shit kicked out of me. Just as well, really. Woke me up. Realised something needed to change. Anyway, recently I've been having a few anger issues again. My wife persuaded me to come and see Phemi and try to get in touch with my feminine side!'

Lesley from Bensham looked round the room as if testing everyone's reactions.

'Yeah, I'm married. I bet you're looking at me thinking who would fancy her? Fat ugly bitch. I guess I got lucky! That's me.'

'Tell them what you are doing now, Lesley,' Phemi said, giving her a little wink.

'Doing an access course so I can go to university and get myself a degree. English literature. Realised I'm not as thick as I thought I was after all.'

'And … go on, say it out loud, Lesley.'

'I'm following my dream.'

Momentarily, Lesley from Bensham looked coy, like a little girl pulling adorably at her sleeves.

'Used to write stories as a kid. Before it all went tits up at home. I'm interviewing women about their triumph-and-tragedy stories. Women who have overcome hard things in their lives. I'm writing a book. Just fucking doing it.'

'And tell them who has already agreed to be interviewed.'

'Phemi, man, stop embarrassing uz.'

'Shall I say?'

'Alright man. Let's just say I am in discussion with a female Paralympian and leave it at that for now. Don't wanna jinx it, like.'

The room erupted with spontaneous applause and Lesley from Bensham turned a bright shade of red.

'Take a bow Lesley, you legend!' said Phemi, emitting an impressive ear piercing, fingers-in-mouth whistle.

Hollie felt electrified. *Note to self,* she thought, *must remember to stop being so judgemental.*

'And what are you hoping to get from the group, Lesley?'

'I dunno. I'm just here because you persuaded me, Phemi, with your wily ways! But I suppose if I have to say something, it would be your word on the wall here. How to be better at vulnerability. Which – for the record – I fucking hate!'

'Fair enough,' said Phemi. 'I think we can all relate to that, as you can see by the nodding heads around the room right now. Who's next?'

'Don't imagine anyone else wants to follow Lesley, so may as well get mine over with, save everyone the bother,' said the woman sitting to Hollie's right, in a chair that reminded her of her nana's commode.

'Hello, everyone. My name's Pat. I'm fifty-one years old. Married. Got three sons. Born and bred up here. Lived in the same house for most of my life. I feel like a fraud compared to all yous.'

'There's no comparison here, Pat. We are all equals. No one is any better or worse than anyone else,' Phemi interjected.

'Aye, I know, Phemi. It's just, everyone is so amazing.'

'So are you.'

'Don't know that there's much else to say. Used to work in a fish and chip shop, then got diagnosed with cancer. Am in remission now, thankfully. Been coming to see Phemi after my sister told me about her. To be honest, I thought I was just coming for a nice massage.'

'Me fucking too, Pat!' said Lesley from Bensham.

Everyone laughed.

'Trying to take better care of myself. Never been very good at it. That's about it, to be honest.'

'And what would you like to get out of this group, Pat?'

'I'd like to learn how to be more assertive. I'm like a skivvy for me family. Always cleaning up after them, then losing my temper because they don't lift a bloody finger round the house. So, being more assertive, and calm as well, that would be good.'

'Yes. I think as women we give, give, give. Somehow are conditioned to think self-care is selfish. I know because I'm crap at it too, but I'm learning to get better,' said Phemi.

'Who would like to go next?'

'I'll go, Phemi,' another woman sitting on the battered sofa mumbled.

160

Very slight with short, mid-brown hair and pale skin, she was sitting squashed into the far-right corner, hunched-up, as if trying to take up the smallest possible amount of space. Her eyes were lowered to the floor.

'I'm Chris. I'm forty-five. Live alone. Haven't been out of the house for over a year. I have chronic fatigue. Find it hard to talk. Hard to be here at all.'

Chris stopped and an uncomfortable silence descended.

Hollie wondered whether this was all she had to say. Had she simply run out of words, having become out of practice, or was she re-charging after the effort of a few sentences?

'I want to congratulate you, Chris,' Phemi said. 'I know how much it has taken for you to be here this evening. I know this is huge progress. And I just want you to really appreciate yourself for this. There's no pressure. You can say as little or as much as you want.'

'Thank you,' Chris said, still looking at the floor, which seemed to indicate she had finished.

Phemi appeared to be completely relaxed and not in the slightest bit phased by Chris's semi- catatonic state.

'I'll go next,' said a tall, slender woman with long, brown hair curled in perfect waves sitting on what looked like a dining-room chair next to Lesley from Bensham.

'I'm Yvonne and I'm a self-employed hairdresser. I'm forty-seven, single, and in the menopause. Been really struggling with it, which is why I came to see Phemi after a friend told me about her. I don't have kids ...'

Yvonne hesitated and looked down in her lap for a few moments.

'Take your time, Yvonne,' said Phemi.

'Always thought I would have children, but never met the right guy. I would get into a relationship, everything would be great for a while, and then I would find out he had an alcohol problem, or gambling debts, or something. I just seem to attract nutters. I've been internet dating for about a year, and I tell you, it's like a zombie apocalypse out there! You wouldn't believe the sorts of profile pictures blokes use. I've seen guys standing in urinals, blokes holding fish, and guys sending me photos of themselves in leather underpants as if to say, *Look at my packet, ladies*. It's grim. To be honest, I don't know why I keep putting myself through it.'

'Because you're a sadomasochist?' Lesley from Bensham said jokingly.

'That's sounds about right, Lesley!' Yvonne replied with a half-smile, and a resigned look in her eyes. 'I'm starting to think I would be better off on my own, but I just get overwhelmed by feeling lonely sometimes.'

Yvonne heaved a deep sigh.

'And what would you like to get from our group?' said Phemi.

'To find the confidence to make some decisions. Stop wallowing in regret for what I don't have.'

'Okay, Hollie, that just leaves you. I'm so glad you've joined our group. Adding a touch of class to our motley crew,' Phemi said.

Hollie smiled, hoping she looked sincere. She was still unsure she wanted to be here. Slipping away unnoticed, however, was clearly not an option.

'But, ladies, don't let this polished professional exterior fool you. Hollie is positively cosmic!'

Cosmic.

Hollie had forgotten this word. Right now, she felt anything but. Judgemental, uptight, awkward, self-conscious ... but *cosmic*, definitely not. She wasn't sure what was worse: feeling embarrassed by the idea that these women were looking at her wondering how the hell this corporate suit could be cosmic, or accepting that beneath this polished exterior was a vast, starry wilderness trying to escape.

'Erm ... where do I start?'

Hollie tried to get her thoughts in order, quickly sorting what she was, and was not, prepared to share.

'Anywhere, Hollie, just go for it,' Phemi said.

'Okay,' she said, feeling slightly irked. 'I'm Hollie and I'm forty-two. I'm feeling vulnerable this evening, having arrived somewhat over-dressed. I came straight from work. I'm a people director for a mental health trust. Very busy, demanding job. I'm married, no children.'

Hollie paused and glanced at the flipchart paper.

'Children and vulnerability brought me here. A few months ago, I decided I'm not going to be a mother, after a soul-searching journey. I was always ambivalent and had kicked the question of motherhood into the long grass until, out of the blue, my husband said he wanted us to have a baby. As a rational, analytical person, I tried to think my way through the decision until I completely exhausted myself, and finally came to see Phemi to bypass my brain so I could make a wholehearted choice. I'm at peace with my decision, but the problem since I closed the proverbial egg shop is—'

Lesley from Bensham guffawed.

'Proverbial egg shop, love it. I'm totally nicking that! ... Sorry, Hollie.'

'That's okay, Lesley,' Hollie said, feeling slightly irritated to have been interrupted. 'The problem is, like Chris, I keep thinking ... *This can't be it!* There must be something more to life than the rinse and repeat, nine-to-five. It feels like I'm waiting for life to begin, stuck in a big empty departure lounge, waiting to catch a plane from the Plan-B runway to some unknown destination.'

'God's waiting room,' said Mary.

'I don't believe in God,' Hollie replied a little too curtly. 'My parents are atheists. In fact, my dad once said he would disown me if I ever turned to God.'

'That's intense. What made him say that?' Phemi asked.

'No idea.'

'Maybe he saw you were totally cosmic?'

'Fathers, eh, Hollie?' said Lesley from Bensham. 'A lot to answer for.'

'Yeah. And, like you, Lesley, I always wanted to be a writer. Years ago I started writing a book, inspired by my dad's life.'

'What was it called?' asked Lesley from Bensham.

'*The Lighthouse Keeper's Ransom.*'

'Did you live in a lighthouse, like?'

'No, but my dad was a lighthouse keeper before I was born. He went there as a kind of retreat, thinking he was going to write a book that would *shine a light on human thought*, as he put it.'

'Right on. Out-fucking-rageous. Did he ever get published?'

'He had academic papers published as a history professor, but he never finished his book. I guess I had this crazy idea that I would somehow carry the torch for him.'

'And did you?' Lesley from Bensham asked, leaning forward in her armchair.

'Sadly not. I kept trying, and failing, and falling off the wagon, then eventually gave up. Now I don't have time to write. Probably wasn't a good idea anyway … sorry, how did we get talking about this?' Hollie said, aware this was not what she had intended to share.

'And what would you like to get out of our time together? Apart from a first-class seat on the next available airplane?' said Phemi.

'I liked what you said earlier, about having an inner compass. If I could find my compass and get a sense of direction, that would be a good start. In the meantime, to get better at sitting in an empty departure lounge and staring at four walls without going insane would be useful.'

'Sounds like an advert off the back of *Mindfulness for Dummies!*' Lesley from Bensham said, smiling at Hollie. 'I think Phemi was right about you, Hollie,' she continued. 'You look right la-dee-da and that in your posh suit. But underneath, I reckon you're definitely a bit fuckin' cosmic!'

Surrender

A few weeks later, Hollie let herself into her mother's house.

'It's me, Mum.'

'I'm in the back room.'

Hollie walked in.

'Is that another new coat, Hollie?'

'Er, yes. I got it a few weeks ago. Do you like it?'

'It's very striking. Cerise, I think you call that colour?'

'Yes, it's one of my colours.'

'Bet that set you back a bit?'

'I got it reduced,' Hollie lied.

'It's very nice but I don't see why you needed another coat. You've already got plenty.'

'Well, I work hard, and I can afford it, Mum,' Hollie said, trying hard to manage her tone of voice. 'Anyway, how are you feeling today?'

'I'm okay. Still in pain but I'm feeling a bit better again.'

'I guess it's only week two and they say it can take a while to recover from a hysterectomy. I can see about taking more time off it you need me to be here for another week?'

'I'm sure I'll be fine. I know you're busy.'

Hollie felt a stab of guilt, like one of those parents who showered their kids with gifts to make up for not spending quality time together.

'Honestly, if you need me, Mum, I'll just take the time. Work will have to wait for once.'

'It's okay, your sister said she could come back up if I still need help.'

Maybe she deserved not to be the person her mum relied on, Hollie thought.

'What were you watching on telly?'

'*One Born Every Minute*. Me and your sister love it. It's filmed in the maternity hospital where your sister gave birth to Jack. So fascinating. It's just started if you want to watch it.'

Hollie had heard of the show. The team often talked about it in the office at work, but she'd never seen it. She wondered what other things her mum and sister shared that she didn't know about. Her mother un-paused the TV and Hollie sat down to watch a woman having contractions. She still hadn't told her mother about the miscarriage, or anyone in her family. Was this a sign telling her to say something she wondered?

Within ten minutes, she was fidgeting. There was something about daytime TV – the formulaic intonation of the presenter's voices, the bad puns – it was almost as if she could feel her brain slowly calcifying.

Breathe, Hollie. Just chill out, for fuck's sake. What's wrong with you? Surely you can sit and just watch one TV programme!

'You got ants in your pants? Keeping you away from work?' her mother said.

'No, I think I just need a cup of tea, I'll make a pot.'

'Don't suppose you want me to pause it?'

'No, thanks, you carry on.'

Hollie paced the kitchen while the kettle boiled. Like being childfree, an inability to tolerate daytime TV felt like another micro-indicator of how socially awkward and unwoven into the fabric of normal everyday life she was. She imagined telling her mother about the miscarriage.

I've got something to tell you, Mum. I came off the pill a few months ago and got pregnant ...

Part of her wanted to see the look on her mother's face, but the other part didn't want to go through the whole *You? But I thought you didn't want kids* conversation.

And there was something else.

A deeper discomfort.

Every time she pictured the scene, her faced looked wrong somehow.

Not ... sad enough.

She feared part of her would *enjoy* telling her mother and that her face would betray this. She would no longer be an awkward, childless woman. She would be a woman who had had a miscarriage. She would, theoretically at least, belong in the club of women who knew the pain of a failed pregnancy. She would be ... *legitimised*.

Hollie felt a flush of shame wash over her.

No. She mustn't say anything. She couldn't trust herself.

'I've made a pot, Mum. Nice and strong, how you like it.'

Hollie poured the tea and tried to relax.

'Did I tell you I'm going to be starting a big project to review our performance management framework? I know you did something similar before you left work and wondered whether I could pick your brains?' Hollie said when the programme had mercifully finished.

'Oh God, I don't want to talk about work, that's all done and dusted now. Rather stick pins in my eyes!'

'Fair enough,' Hollie said, feeling embarrassed by her failed bid for connection. They sat in silence for a few moments, then her mother picked up the remote and began scrolling through the TV menu. She tried to find something else they could talk about.

'I started a mindfulness course the other day.'

'Oh. What, like meditation?'

'I think the idea is to become present to your own thoughts and feelings and to practice self-compassion and self-awareness. To get to know and accept your deeper self without judgement.'

'Sounds like a lot of mumbo jumbo. How can you not know yourself? I've always known who I was. Knew what I did and didn't want to do. Always knew I wanted children. Had them. Knew I didn't want to be a teacher, even though everyone said I should, and I didn't. Never let anyone tell me what to do.'

'That sounds nice. Maybe you're just lucky?'

'I just got on with things.'

'Yeah,' Hollie said, feeling this was not a good avenue to keep exploring. 'The mindfulness group is definitely an … interesting group of people.'

Hollie emphasised the word *interesting* and paused, waiting for her mother to respond, hoping she might be curious to know more. But she just looked at her blankly.

'There's a young woman writing a book. Got me thinking about picking up my idea again. Remember *The Lighthouse Keeper's Ransom*?'

'Not that again. Remember what happened last time. You started off full of enthusiasm and ended up tearing your hair out. Just like your father. And you don't want to end up like him.'

Her mother continued scrolling through the TV menu looking for something else to watch.

'I guess, it's just …'

'What?'

'I feel like I need something to …'

'Haven't you already got enough to do, Hollie? You have a busy job, a husband, a lovely home. What more do you want? You're always working anyway, so I'm not sure how you expect to write a book as well. You'll just drive yourself mad! I thought the whole point of not having children was to have your freedom. Why don't you just try and enjoy it? Practice acceptance of what you already have, isn't that what mindfulness is about?'

Hollie noticed she was clenching her teeth and tried to slacken her jaw.

'I just keep thinking that—'

'That's your problem, Hollie. You think too much.'

'I …'

Her mother's phone was ringing.

'It's your sister. She's Facetiming.'

Hollie heard her sister's voice.

'Someone wants to send you a big kiss and say get better soon, Grandma. Show the card you made, Jack.'

Hollie watched her mother's face break into a beaming smile, her tone of voice instantly changed.

'Thank you, darling,' she said and blew kisses at the screen.

'Is Nurse Hollie looking after you well, Mum?'

Hollie could hear the sarcasm in her sister's voice.

'We know how she loves to change nappies and deal with anything messy!'

'Well, she hates *One Born Every Minute* as well. Don't you, Hollie? Say hi to your sister.'

'Hi, Sis,' Hollie waved as her mother briefly turned the screen round.

'What? *One Born Every Minute* is brilliant! Not highbrow enough for our Hollie, you reckon?' her sister said.

Hollie resented it when they talked about her as if she wasn't there. But she knew saying anything know would come across as horribly passive-aggressive. She excused herself on the pretence of needing the toilet.

Upstairs she stared at herself in the mirror.

She had that feeling again.

A feeling of having no substance.

Of being empty inside, folding in on herself like a collapsing black hole.

Hollie, what's wrong with you?
Your mum's recovering from an operation, give her a break.
You're being oversensitive again.
GET A GRIP.

'Thanks for ringing, that's really cheered me up. Speak later,' she heard her mother say as she ended the call.

Hollie resolved to jolly herself up. To try and be an uplifting presence.

'Can I get you anything else, Mum?' she said brightly, making a concerted effort.

'Actually, I'd really like to have a shower. What do you think? Do you think I should?'

Relieved to have the opportunity to do something useful, Hollie spent the next ten minutes discussing the doctor's advice, asking her mother how steady she felt on her feet, exploring the tiny practical details of getting upstairs and into the shower.

'Okay, sounds like a good idea,' her mother said after they agreed their plan.

Hollie stood up to help but as she stepped forwards, her mother held up her hand up in a STOP signal, like a traffic warden.

'No. Wait. I think I'll ring your sister. See what she says. She'll know what to do.'

Hollie felt as though she had been punched in the stomach. She tried to suppress tears she could feel welling up as she watched her mother call her sister back.

Her sister who was currently nearly one hundred miles away and *not in the room*.

Her sister who hadn't been present in the room now for three days.

Here she was, the daughter with first-hand insight into how her mother's recovery was going at this point, but it felt like her opinion was not good enough. Her mother was ringing her *younger* sister for a consultation, for a solid and reliable opinion. It felt like further evidence that her opinion held less weight. As though by having children, her sister was a more responsible and trustworthy adult. Having made a definitive decision at the crossroads of motherhood, she had hoped – maybe even expected – that this feeling of otherness would disappear.

But here she was again, painfully aware of the emptiness of her own womb.

Of being an un-mother.

~

Surrender.

Hollie saw the word on the flipchart in large blue letters as soon as she opened the door to the back room. She had come straight from work again. Everyone was sitting in the same place.

'Wow, look at you!' Phemi said, coming in for a hug as Hollie removed her coat. 'You look stunning. Even your lipstick matches your jacket!'

'Thanks,' Hollie said, now wishing she had gone home to change and just turned up a bit late. She felt like a high-definition Dulux commercial in a world of grey.

'Dunno how you can be arsed to look like that every day. This is posh for me,' Lesley from Bensham said, tugging at her branded hoodie. 'Clean.'

Everyone laughed except Chris, who was squashed into the corner of the sofa. She looked like a waxwork dummy, resembling how Hollie felt inside.

'I've been interviewing for new board members,' Hollie said, feeling the need to justify her appearance.

'I've been with clients all day,' said Phemi, grinning. 'Just stuck my hair up and put this sparkly top on.'

Hollie looked at Phemi enviously. Her heavy hair was piled on her head in a way that looked effortlessly cool, like she had just had wild sex, smoked a few French cigarettes, stuck on some kohl eyeliner, and left a lover sprawled and satisfied in bed.

'Make yourself a cuppa, Hollie, we're just chilling for five minutes before we get started.'

'Thanks,' Hollie said as she put her navy leather handbag down by her chair.

'Fucking Mulberry. Jeez. How much did that cost?' said Lesley from Bensham. 'Probably more than my car!'

Hollie felt her cheeks flush.

'It was my present to myself when I got promoted,' she said, hoping Lesley from Bensham would not pursue this line of questioning.

'Take no notice, Hollie,' said Phemi, chuckling. 'Lesley has no filter.'

'Aye, sorry, take no notice of uz, Hollie'

Hollie forced a smile and walked to the kitchen. She fished out a packet from a selection of herbal teas. A *moment of calm* it said. Just what she needed.

'So, this evening I thought we would explore the idea of surrendering,' Phemi said, pointing to the flipchart. 'I thought you'd be impressed with me, Hollie, I bought some of that special adhesive stuff that you can re-use, like a mobile whiteboard!'

'Very impressive,' Hollie said, noticing it was not stuck on straight.

'And you'll see I surrendered to the need to get the piece of flipchart straight!'

Hollie wondered whether her judgement was written on her face as she took off her boots and stretched out her legs.

'Before we begin, let's take a moment to get present in the room with a little breathwork,' said Phemi. 'Sit in an upright position so your spine is nice and straight. Imagine sitting in the saddle of a horse in a dignified pose.'

Hollie inhaled and exhaled, trying to tune in to her body, and noticed her left leg was aching. She started thinking about the forty-odd page pension strategy report she had to read for a meeting in the morning …

Before she knew it, Phemi was calling them to open their eyes.

God, I'm shit at this, Hollie said to herself.

'Does anyone want to share?' asked Phemi, looking round the room.

'Just found that really hard,' said Pat. 'Kept thinking of all the things I've got to do this week round the house and that. Not very good at things like this. Just sitting still, doing nothing.'

'Me too,' said Hollie.

'This is very common,' said Phemi. 'We are trained to be human doings, not human beings. I would suggest the first step is to just be kind to yourself and try not to judge your thoughts.'

Phemi rummaged in a large, worn carpet-bag. It reminded Hollie of Mary Poppins and she half expected her to pull out a cockatoo in a bird cage for a live demonstration. Instead, Phemi pulled out some dog-eared paper and an assortment of pens with the names of various hotels on them, which she dumped in a pile on the floor and invited everyone to write or draw something in relation to the word *surrender*.

'Who would like to share?' she said ten minutes later after the timer on her phone went off.

Lesley from Bensham held up an image that could have been a piece of graffiti on a wall. A big, hairy hand pointing a gun and a pair of arms held up in the air.

'Wow, Banksy from Bensham, you have a talent for drawing!' said Hollie.

'Wouldn't go that far, like. It's allreet, I suppose,' she replied.

Phemi looked at her like a kindly teacher. 'Lesley, remember what we talked about? Learning to accept compliments. Hollie just gave you a gift and you shoved it back in her face. Think of it like at Christmas when your aunty gives you a hideous pair of earrings. Thank her, even though you know you are going to take them to the charity shop as soon as it opens.'

'Aye ... Thanks, Hollie.'

'So, can you tell us about your drawing Lesley?' Phemi asked.

'Surrendering is a tactic for not getting shot. When you know it's hopeless trying to resist.'

'A kind of self-defence?' Phemi said, nodding thoughtfully.

'Yeah. My mam used to do this. I remember one time when my dad had her by the throat. I was screaming at him to get off her. And then there was this moment when she suddenly stopped trying to fight or resist. She went all limp, and then he stopped. Proper freaked him out.'

'I'm so sorry to hear you had to witness such a dreadful thing, Lesley,' said Mary. 'You poor thing. I just want to give you a hug.'

Hollie felt herself cringe, like Mary had just slimed all over her.

'Divvn't feel sorry for uz, Mary. Just is what it is. Shit happens, you know. That's just life. Me dad had a shit upbringing. Wasn't his fault.'

Hollie interjected in the hope of preventing Mary emoting any further. 'I wrote, surrender is giving up, admitting defeat, losing the battle, feeling powerless, being out of control, alien, and *lazy* with a question mark.'

'Mine was similar. But less good words,' said Pat.

'Yvonne, how about you?'

Yvonne was holding her piece of paper about a foot away from her, staring at it. She looked pinched and tense, the way Hollie imagined she looked when she felt herself collapsing into her inner black hole.

'Sorry, I need a cigarette,' Yvonne said and walked out of the room with her handbag.

'Should I go after her?' asked Mary.

'She'll be fine. We need to trust Yvonne is giving herself what she needs right now,' replied Phemi, who turned towards Hollie. 'Why have you written *lazy*, question mark?'

'I was thinking that if I just surrendered, nothing would get done. My immediate reaction was that it seems like an appealing word to sex up doing nothing and make the easy option sound cool. But, listening to Lesley's story, I imagine what her mother did took immense courage.'

'I agree,' said Pat. 'If I surrendered, nowt would get done round the house and we'd end up living in a bloody pigsty. And what would people think if they came round, and the place was a fleapit?'

176

'That may be true Pat,' said Phemi, 'and yet I wonder, are there some things you could stop doing?'

Pat looked thoughtful.

'What if you surrendered the need for your family to be grateful for everything you do? What if you accepted you are doing what you do because it matters to you, but surrender the need to make it matter to them?'

'I see your point. But letting go is hard,' said Pat.

'Yes, but sometimes holding on is even harder. We're very conditioned to be in control, but if we mindfully choose to stop resisting something that's hurting us, like Lesley's mam, it can be a kind of tactical withdrawal. Instead of being in push, push, push energy – strive, work harder, faster, better – we can see surrendering as being a pull energy. Being in flow and seeing what wants to emerge and just noticing what comes towards us.'

'Pull, not push,' Mary said, looking straight at Phemi as though a whole stadium of floodlights had just switched on inside her.

'Do you think this applies to relationships as well?' she asked.

Phemi nodded, encouraging her to say more.

'I've been working so hard to try and repair the relationship with my daughters, trying to get them to speak to me again, hoping beyond hope for things to go back to how they used to be, but what you're saying is to surrender, and let all that go? Accept I can't turn back the clock? Open my heart to loving them anyway, even though they are hurting me?'

'Exactly, Mary. I'm sure this will help you to find some peace.'

Hollie instantly thought about her mother.

'I relate to what Mary said. Since my mother retired and my sister had children, I feel our relationship has changed. They are closer, but I can't seem to connect with her anymore. My mum and I used to talk about work stuff, but now I feel nothing I do is very interesting to her and that my opinion doesn't count as much because I don't have kids. Like I'm not enough.'

'Do *you* feel you are enough, Hollie? As a childfree woman?' asked Phemi.

'Not when I'm with my mother.'

'And when you are not with your mother, you do feel enough then?'

'Intellectually, I want to say *yes*, but I feel in my body the answer is *no*. I have this feeling of being hollow and insubstantial, like I'm an empty shell.'

'Jesus, if you are not enough, Hollie, what hope is there for the rest of us?' said Lesley from Bensham. 'I mean look at you, for fuck's sake!'

'What if you surrendered to the emptiness?' said Phemi, turning back to Hollie.

'It's not that simple.'

'Isn't it? What if you surrendered needing to have a relationship with your mother like the one your sister has? What if you could accept her for the way she is and love her anyway, even when she doesn't see you the way you want her to?'

'I'm very moved by what you've shared, Hollie,' said Mary. 'I never said this out loud before, but I never felt enough as a mother. I didn't want children, but I wasn't taught about the pill. When I got pregnant, I hated the idea of having a baby and wanted to have it aborted, but it was too late. I remember thinking, this is what we are supposed to do, have children, but I don't want this. One day, I poured my heart out to my mother and she told me it was terrible I should feel like that. "Children are God's gift," she said, "and you should be grateful."'

'Thanks, Mary, I really appreciate you saying this,' said Hollie, feeling surprised to hear this confession from Mary. Lesley from Bensham clapped. 'Yeah, too right. Shit just got real!'

'And on that note, I feel like this is a good moment for us to pause and take a tea break,' said Phemi, grabbing a packet of tobacco and some papers from her bag.

The group reconvened ten minutes later, including Yvonne who had come back inside with Phemi, reeking of smoke and body spray. Hollie noticed her eyes were puffy and red.

'I'd like to show my picture now if that's okay?'

There was a hearty chorus of support from the group as Yvonne unfolded her paper and held it up. There were six eggcups in the middle of the paper, each holding an egg with a thick red cross drawn over the top of them.

'As I said last time, I'm single, and have never been married. In fact, my longest relationship so far has lasted about eighteen months. I wanted children, but somehow the circumstances were never right. Three years ago, I decided to take control of my situation and had some of my eggs frozen.'

Lesley from Bensham looked as though she was bursting to speak but managed to hold herself together and stay respectfully silent.

Hollie glanced at Mary, whose mouth was hanging slightly open, willing her to keep quiet.

'About six months ago, my GP confirmed I'm in the early stages of menopause, so it's now biologically impossible for me to have children of my own, and pointless to keep on paying money to store my eggs. But there's part of me struggling to let go. I know it probably sounds stupid but … it's the finality of the whole thing, the idea that the possibility of creating a new life is gone. Forever. Even though I know the chances of this happening were ridiculously slim in the first place.'

Phemi passed Yvonne a tissue.

'It's like something precious has slipped through my fingers, and I feel so humiliated that I wasted the best part of ten grand on fool's gold, waiting for the perfect relationship that never arrived.'

'You made an empowered choice that felt right at the time. You took control of your own fertility and gave yourself more options. I think that's bloody brilliant,' said Phemi.

'Yeah,' said Lesley from Bensham, unable to contain herself any longer. 'It's a lot of money and that, but you might have spent this on a new bathroom or a few holidays anyway, so good for you!'

'True,' Yvonne said dolefully, wiping tears from her cheeks, 'but at least I'd have something to show for it if I had a nice new bathroom.'

'What happens to your eggs now?' Lesley from Bensham asked.

'I have to sign some papers. They have asked me whether I want to destroy the eggs, donate them, or give them up for research and training.'

'Eeh, dunno how I'd make that kind of decision,' said Pat. 'What are you going to do?'

'I was thinking about donating, you know, the sisterhood and all that, but I keep feeling weird about it, worrying I won't have closure. I just haven't been able to make a decision and am really struggling with it all, which is why I came to see Phemi. What I realised earlier, when I drew this picture, is that I need to surrender ... it was a bit of a lightbulb moment.'

Phemi was leaning forward on her cushion.

'What light has switched on, Yvonne?'

'It's time for me to let go of motherhood.'

Hollie felt something move inside her. A kind of inner click as she heard those words ... *let go of motherhood.*

Mary clapped her hands together loudly in an oddly exaggerated manner. 'Not sure why I just did that,' she said and then immediately looked up and to her right.

'What is it?' asked Phemi.

'I think it's God's seal of approval,' replied Mary staring with a bewildered look on her face.

'So what you're saying is that when you clap like that, like a performing seal, it's a sign of God's approval?' said Lesley from Bensham. 'Fucking mental.'

Hysterical laughter erupted in the room, breaking the tension for a few moments. Even Chris seemed to be enjoying herself and started to move a little, rocking back and forth on the sofa, looking up and smiling at everyone.

'God, it's good to laugh for a change,' Yvonne said.

'Yeah,' said Hollie, trying to compose herself, 'I know what you mean.'

The room became quiet again after a few moments, but there was now a feeling of freshness in the air.

'So, do you know how you might let go of motherhood, Yvonne?' said Phemi.

'I think I'm going to have my eggs destroyed. To use Hollie's analogy, I'm going to close the shutter on the egg shop, lock it up, and hand in the keys. For good.'

'And how do you feel hearing yourself say this?' asked Phemi.

'Relieved. Lighter,' Yvonne said. 'Like I could even take on a zombie apocalypse!'

'I'll happily lend you some ammo!' quipped Lesley from Bensham.

'I'm so proud of you. Come here,' Phemi said, gesturing to Yvonne to stand up.

Yvonne obliged, and the two women stood for a moment in the centre of their wonky circle, embracing in a joyful hug while the rest of the group clapped and whooped.

'This group is amazing!' said Pat. 'Can you lend me some ammo too, Lesley, I might just surprise my lazy lot the next time they expect me to run around after them!'

'I'll get right onto my dealer,' Lesley from Bensham said, making a phonecall hand gesture.

'Okay,' Phemi said in a commanding tone after she sat back on her cushion. 'Before we start plotting more acts of violence, I feel it would be good for us to take a minute now, to pause and go inward after all that's been shared. So, let's take a moment to ground ourselves. If it's good for you, you can close your eyes. And take a deep breath in, then allow that breath to gently exhale out …'

Hollie took a few breaths and saw herself projected onto a screen in her mind. She was sitting in white space on a green velvet sofa, legs crossed. She smiled, recalling what Diane had said at the restaurant. Maybe this was a sign she was starting to make herself comfy in the liminal departure lounge?

Either way, she knew one thing. She was grateful for being here and part of this oddball bunch.

Laying Down the Armour

When Hollie walked in for their third session, there were two small, fake white Christmas trees on the side tables, and a question on the flipchart with green tinsel taped round the edge.

Is your armour preventing you from growing into your gifts?

'Just to let you know, Chris can't make it this evening. She sends her apologies,' Phemi said.

'Is she okay?' said Mary.

'I'm sure she will be,' replied Phemi.

Mary moved forward as though she was going to say something else but thought better of it and sat back again.

'I feel it's time to dive a bit deeper into vulnerability, so I dug out this quote as a little provocation,' said Phemi as they all settled in their usual seats.

'Yeah, great Phem,' said Lesley from Bensham, 'just what I fuckin' need today. I don't need to take my armour off, I need to put more on! Like … proper chainmail.'

Hollie pictured Lesley from Bensham wearing full knight's armour, galloping along at a jousting tournament, helmet open, wearing an expression of pure rage.

'Do you want to talk about it, Lesley?' Phemi asked.

'Na.'

'Okay. Is there anything you need before we begin?'

'I'll be fine Phem, divvn't worry about uz.'

Phemi nodded.

'Vulnerability, as Lesley has demonstrated already, is a feeling that scares all of us,' Phemi paused and glanced at Lesley from Bensham in a way that simultaneously seemed to convey she was on her side, and checking she was not about to kick off. 'We want to avoid being uncertain in life, we want to fit in, and we want to feel safe and secure, so we armour up to try and protect ourselves. Through her work, vulnerability researcher Brené Brown suggests there are three types people use, and I thought it might be interesting to think about which one is our go-to place in the armoury.'

Phemi rummaged in her Mary Poppins bag, removed three folded pieces of paper, and opened one out, laying it down in front of her.

Perfectionism

'This one is described as the twenty-ton shield. If I do everything perfectly – look perfect, act perfect, be the perfect mother, the perfect wife etc. – then I won't be judged.'

'That's definitely not me!' said Lesley from Bensham, glancing in Hollie's direction.

Phemi unfolded the second piece of A4.

Numbing

'This is about using things to avoid how we are really feeling, as a kind of distraction. Over-eating, boozing, taking drugs, being a workaholic, things like that ...'

'Enough said!' Lesley from Bensham said, grabbing a roll of fat around her stomach.

Phemi unfolded the third piece of paper.

Foreboding joy

'This one is about predicting everything that can go wrong before anything has actually happened, as a way of preparing for the worst. It means you end up living inside the energy of dread, never allowing yourself to really enjoy life and expecting everything to fall apart at any moment.'

'Aw God, that's me, like,' said Pat. 'I do that all the time. Especially this time of year, when you're run off yer feet trying to get everything done for Christmas.'

'I think since I lost my faith, I've been foreboding joy, asking what I did to deserve all the bad things that have happened. I think I closed my heart to the joy I used to feel when I felt guided. I forgot how to trust,' said Mary.

'I find it hard to trust people, I've been let down so many times I just expect it to happen now,' said Yvonne. 'I never really thought about this as armour before, though.'

'And Hollie, what resonates most for you?' asked Phemi.

'Perfectionism. I'm a work hard, get all As type of person. I have a very strong inner critic voice. Like today, I didn't feel I handled a meeting at work very well and went into an internal dialogue about how I should have done better ... *Why didn't you do x instead of y, Hollie. You don't deserve this job. They are paying you all this money and THAT'S IT? That's all you've got?* Then I made up conversations other people were having about me, talking about how I screwed up and how they felt embarrassed for me. And I do this shit to myself all the time! I call this voice my inner witch.'

'I'm shocked, Hollie,' said Mary, her eyes out on stalks. 'To be honest I ...' Mary looked down at her lap and fiddled nervously with an embroidered cotton handkerchief. 'I find you intimidating. You come across as so clever and glossy and together, with your big job and your successful career. If I'm honest, I've wondered what you are doing here. I felt as though you looked down on us a bit ... Sorry.'

Hollie sensed the others shifting nervously in their seats.

Phemi extended a protective hand across her and looked as though she were about to intervene.

'It's okay, Phemi,' said Hollie. 'Please continue, Mary, I respect your honesty,' she said. 'Even if I'm having a buttock clench moment over here!'

'Ha ha, nice one, Hollie!' said Lesley from Bensham.

'Sorry, I probably shouldn't have said that,' said Mary, turning red. 'But I feel like this is important because I never say things like this.'

'Go on, Mary,' said Hollie.

'Every time we've met, I've sat here and looked at you and thought, *Why can't I be more like Hollie?* Even this evening, you have walked in dressed casually, but you still look so stylish with everything beautifully co-ordinated. I thought you must be so confident and really think a lot of yourself, and how nice that must be. Suppose I felt a bit jealous. But now, you're saying all of this, that it doesn't match how you feel inside?'

'Correct,' said Hollie.

'But you are a ... *director*? I thought people like you were full of confidence.'

Hollie winced a little, thinking Mary could really use some training on how to give feedback.

'This is something called "imposter syndrome", Mary, and it's very common,' said Phemi.

'Well, this is a revelation, right here,' said Mary.

'Praise the fucking Lord!' said Lesley from Bensham, throwing her head back.

Hollie was unsure whether Lesley from Bensham was taking the piss out of Mary, or simply grateful to hear truth spoken.

'I'm sorry if I came across a bit harsh, Hollie.'

'It's okay. It's NOTHING compared to what already goes on in here,' Hollie said, pointing to her head. 'In fact, I'll share this with you.

I never told anyone before because, well, I thought it was a bit too intense and weird ...'

Lesley from Bensham leaned forward with her arms stretched out and fingers interlocked. Hollie could feel the intensity of her stare.

'A few years ago, I decided I needed to get rid of my inner witch character once and for all. I was doing a personal development course at the time, and I did an exercise where we used an object to represent the thing you wanted to get rid of. I chose an orange as it was the most acidic thing I could find. I kept it at home on a mantelpiece as a reminder until one day, I decided to go a step further and bury my witch, finish her off for good. So I drove to the coast near the lighthouse, held a funeral ceremony, and buried the mouldy orange.'

'What do you mean, you held a funeral ceremony?' Lesley from Bensham said.

'I lit a candle, thanked my inner witch for her efforts in trying to help me become a better person, and explained she could now rest in peace because I didn't need her anymore. Then I buried the orange, read a poem, played a piece of music, and wrote *RIP* on the sand over the top of the makeshift grave with pebbles, and blew out the candle.'

'That's fuckin' tweaky!' Lesley from Bensham said. 'Who would think, looking at you, you'd do something like that, eh?'

'Brilliant,' Phemi said, grinning from ear to ear.

'What a story Hollie, you definitely have to write a book, like!' said Lesley from Bensham slapping the arms of her chair. 'You could call it *From Corporate to Cosmic!*'

Corporate to Cosmic. Everyone laughed as they repeated the phrase and nodded approvingly.

'That's actually not a bad title, Lesley,' said Hollie, chuckling. 'I was deadly serious at the time but looking back now it does seem quite funny, I have to admit.'

'Bloody genius if you ask me,' said Lesley from Bensham. 'I think we should all do a funeral for our inner fuckin' witches, like a passing out parade for our mad group!'

~

The next time Hollie walked into the back room, the piece of crumpled flipchart was blank. Chris was there, sitting in her usual small space, although Hollie felt that she looked as if she had expanded slightly.

'Happy new year everyone and welcome back,' said Phemi after their chatter had died down. 'And especially welcome Chris, it's lovely to have you here again.'

'Sorry I missed the last one. I was having a bad spell. But I feel better now, and it's nice to be back.'

Chris looked around and smiled, releasing the usual grip of her arm.

Hollie felt oddly tender towards her, as though she wanted to give her a hug.

'You may have noticed there's no quote today,' said Phemi. 'In the last few days I noticed a sense of being very present in the moment without any expectation of what comes next, and it's been very freeing. It seemed to create space for more to emerge and I got to thinking … how often in life do we just allow ourselves to *be*? To be human *beings*, instead of human *doings*? So when it came to putting something on the flipchart this evening, I tuned in to what wanted to emerge, and the answer I got was … *white space* … so I decided, I'll just put this in the room and see what happens.'

Phemi took a deep breath and settled back onto her cushion. She folded her hands in her lap and, with a Buddha-like expression of peace on her face, slowly looked round the circle in a clockwise direction.

Hollie noticed she was clenching her teeth and tried to relax. She wondered whether Phemi had simply failed to prepare for the session and come up with this excuse at the last minute to make it sound intentional, but then immediately felt guilty for being so cynical. Then, in the same instant this thought went through her mind, she wondered whether this was all projection because in fact, she was uncomfortable with nothingness.

'I *hate* fuckin' silence, me,' said Lesley from Bensham, rubbing her hands together.

Phemi looked at her, encouraging her to continue.

'It's like the calm before the storm. The pause before something bad kicks off. Makes me itchy.'

'I know what you mean,' said Pat. 'I have to fill silence. I'm definitely a human-doing!'

'It makes me think of the well you talked about, Phemi, the first time we got together,' said Chris. 'It's like looking down an echoing, deep black hole. I'm always scared that I'm going to fall in and never come back out.'

Hollie had forgotten about the well and was impressed Chris had remembered. She wondered whether behind her waxwork-dummy exterior, Chris was absorbing and recording everything in the room.

'What Chris said just reminded me of something,' said Hollie. 'When I was trying to decide whether I wanted children, I kept having this sensation of a black hole opening up inside me, as if there was a vacuum at my core and I was going to collapse in on myself. I had this terrible fear that I was empty, without any real feeling or substance. Since I closed the door to motherhood, this has changed. I still have a feeling of emptiness, but it's not a black hole inside me anymore. It's more like the emptiness is all around me, a white space like a blank canvas.'

'Your airport departure lounge?' said Phemi.

'Yes, exactly. I'd never noticed until now, but the feeling of emptiness has moved, and that's important. Thanks, Chris,' Hollie said, looking across at her.

A shy smile lit up Chris's face, like a slow dawning sunrise.

'So …' Yvonne said, 'I finally confirmed with the clinic that I want my eggs destroyed yesterday. New year, new broom, and all that.'

Everyone let out a spontaneous round of applause.

'Well done, Yvonne,' said Phemi. 'That feels big.'

'Yeah. But now that I've finally let go of motherhood it feels like I'm facing this sense of emptiness, like looking into a deep, dark well. I'm frightened of falling down the hole and never coming back out, like Chris said,' said Yvonne.

Mary sniffed and blew her nose into a cotton handkerchief with her initials embroidered on the corner. Hollie imagined her sitting in a sewing circle in a church hall.

'I think maybe I need to let go of motherhood too. At least the way I thought motherhood was supposed to be when your children are grown up. I imagined caring for grandchildren and going for afternoon teas with my daughters, and I feel so bitter all of this has been taken away. I kept blaming God for everything that happened … I was just so … so …'

Mary's face crumpled, the way a small child's does when they fall over and hurt themselves.

Hollie could feel her heart pounding as she watched Mary gasp for air in stuttering, shallow breaths, quivering as she tried hopelessly to stem the swell of whatever was rising inside her.

Suddenly, a strange howl crashed into the room as Mary dissolved into an ocean of sobbing tears and everyone sat, unable to move. Hollie felt the atmosphere was like one of those eerie dreams when you want to run but somehow remain rooted to the spot, motionless and riveted.

Mary tried to quell her tears and speak but she was unable to get any words out and simply waved her handkerchief as if it were a surrender flag.

No one moved a muscle.

'I ... I ...' Mary took a deep breath and looked at Phemi.

'It's okay, Mary, let it go,' said Phemi.

'I'm trying ...' said Mary in a small, high-pitched voice, as a new flood of tears flowed and she fiddled with the corner of the handkerchief. 'I embroidered this for my husband,' she said. 'MJ ... Martin James. I always had him on a pedestal, did everything to try and please him. Kept the house spic and span, cooked his dinner every evening, ironed his shirts, tried to be the perfect wife. But I never felt like I was good enough. And then one day I found out he had been having an affair with my best friend ... for the whole time we were married. And even though he cheated, he manipulated our girls so they believed that I had driven him away, that it was my fault our marriage had collapsed because their dad was so perfect and wonderful in their eyes, he could do no wrong. And I said some things I shouldn't have, and ... well ... that's when I lost my faith ...'

Mary blew her nose and leaned back against the sofa.

'Thank you,' she said.

'This is the power of bearing witness to one another,' said Phemi, 'and allowing things to emerge by creating empty space.

~

For their final session, Phemi had baked a tray of surprisingly delicious, chewy wholefood flapjacks made of honey and oats and seeds which she cut ceremonially and dished out one by one.

Mary shuffled forward on the sofa and Hollie noticed she looked different. As if she was lit from within.

'Can I say something, please? I'm bursting ...'

'Please do,' said Phemi.

'Since we last met, all sorts of wonderful things have happened. I went on a pilgrimage to a holy place called Iona in Scotland, and it was heavenly to be back there. In the abbey, I heard a beautiful piece of music being played and it reminded me of how I used to love playing the piano. So I bought the sheet music and have started learning it. Every time I put my hands on the keys it fills my heart with joy, and I feel God speaking through me. Since I returned, I've randomly bumped into old friends and feel as though I'm slowly coming back to life and I just wanted to say thank you, to all of you, for being part of my journey'.

'I think this deserves a special Mary round of applause!' said Phemi and began clapping like a seal, which everyone else copied.

Hollie smiled to herself as she imagined one of her particularly sour-faced colleagues opening the door at this very moment, looking at their strange group in horror. She realised she no longer cared so much what they might think about her motley crew. They were her group of weirdos, and she had come to feel at home among them.

Mary waited for the clapping to subside then picked up a white paper gift bag on the floor at the side of the sofa.

'I bought you all a small gift to say thank you and good luck. Each of them has received a holy blessing.'

'Thank you,' Hollie said as she held up what looked like a comedy beard and moustache made of grubby cotton wool. 'What is it, Mary?'

'Took the words right out of me mouth, Hollie!' said Lesley from Bensham.

'A Sithean Angel,' she replied, beaming, 'handmade from one hundred per cent pure wool. It means *hill of angels*. It's believed that this is the place where St Columba knelt in prayer and was joined by angels as the sun set. Each year, special sheep are raised there now, and these angels are made from their wool to look over and protect people.'

192

Hollie thought about celebrating her mother's birthday at the Angel Inn, and how that night had led her to be sitting here in this room.

'Well, seeing as we're doing prezzies, I suppose I'll go next,' said Lesley from Bensham, grabbing a supermarket carrier bag from beside her armchair.

Hollie felt a stab of guilt. She earned significantly more than everyone else in the room, but it hadn't occurred to her to bring gifts. She'd enjoyed these sessions far more than she had expected, but it also felt time to move on. Perhaps, she reflected, she was not good at doing endings? Too hasty to wash her hands and get on to the next thing.

'I just wanted to say thanks as well. I've really enjoyed being part of our little gang and I feel like I've learned a lot. My wife even says I'm a bit calmer, so that's a big plus,' Lesley from Bensham said as she stood up and handed out cards.

She paused when she reached Hollie. 'Don't know why, but I just felt I was supposed to give you this,' she said with an intense look on her face.

Hollie opened a white envelope. Inside was a card, about the size of a playing card. On one side was an intricate, colourful depiction of an oriental Buddhist-looking figure, sitting cross legged. On the other side was a quote.

What wise person is eaten up
With doubts about happiness
In this life and the next?
Intelligent people make
Meditation the essential thing.

Hollie thanked Lesley from Bensham. She had no idea what to make of it but remembered Phemi's words about staying open and curious.

'I didn't buy nothing,' said Pat, 'but I just want to say thank you. I've told my lot that they need to do their bit round the house more and they've started helping, I actually had some time to myself the other day, just watching a bit of telly on my own and it was great. I was so happy.'

'Yeah,' said Yvonne, 'likewise, I feel I've got so much out of this group. I've decided I'm saying thanks-but-no-thanks to the zombies and taking myself out on a date! I feel so much better than when we started these sessions, so thanks, ladies.'

Everyone burst into spontaneous applause.

'I know I haven't said much,' said Chris, 'but just being here has been big for me. It's the most interaction I've had with people in years and really helped my confidence, so thanks.'

'I want to also say thanks to all of you,' said Hollie. 'To be honest, I wasn't sure what I'd let myself in for when we first met, but I've really enjoyed being part of this group. I've learned a huge amount and feel as though an important shift has happened for me … like I've gradually relaxed and settled into my seat in the departure lounge.'

When Hollie got home that evening, she stuck the little card next to her mirror with the quote facing up. As she pressed her thumb against the top to make it stick, she noticed a peculiar feeling … of an inner compass pointing north.

Make meditation the essential thing.

She felt attracted to meditation, yet never practiced it, and began to wonder whether there was a resistance to stillness and going deeper?

She pulled the card back off the wall and turned it over to look at the figure on the other side. Beneath the figure was a name, written in tiny calligraphy.

Atisha 982-1054

She typed this into the search engine on her phone.

Atisha (982-1054), the great Buddhist Master and scholar who founded the Kadampa tradition and who re-established Buddhism in Tibet. He composed and taught Lamp for the Path to Enlightenment, the first text written on the stages of the path, Lamrim.

Lamp for the path to enlightenment … Hollie felt an inner click again.

She typed again.

Meditation and Scotland.

A place popped up. A tiny island with an ancient spiritual heritage off the west coast.

Ker-chunk.

She felt something land in her body.

A knowing.

Finally, after months of sitting in the departure lounge, the departure board had whirled into life and assembled a series of letters to spell her destination.

Footprint Island.

This was where she was supposed to go.

Footprint Island

The journey to Footprint Island felt like a pilgrimage in and of itself. Three trains, two ferries.

It struck Hollie that people who came here did not arrive by accident.

They were greeted by an enthusiastic welcoming party waiting on the small wooden jetty. A man and a woman who looked about Hollie's age, and a striking shaven-headed nun dressed in maroon and gold robes. 'Footprint Island welcomes you,' the nun said with a slight bow. The man and woman began lifting luggage out of the ferry as the nun gazed serenely across the water. It looked as if she was hovering slightly off the ground, expecting to apparate somewhere at any moment. The ferry driver offered Hollie his hand for support as she stepped out of the boat. 'Enjoy the island,' he said with a little wink and tone of voice that made it feel like an instruction rather than a passing pleasantry.

The instant her feet touched the jetty, Hollie experienced a deep feeling of being held. As if the island itself – a live, pulsing being in its own right – was welcoming her.

I've got you. This is home.

She stayed quiet as the party made its way up an incline towards the centre – a large farmhouse-style building with whitewashed walls and wooden window frames painted red and orange. She felt as though her senses were suddenly more finely attuned, noticing the chattering choir of voices, the sound of suitcase wheels turning as they swished over grass, the rise and fall of her feet and the fluid transfer of her weight.

The earth beneath her feet felt like a memory foam mattress.

Did the grass really feel softer here, or was it her imagination?

On their left, they passed a row of alternating white stupas and prayer flagpoles in front of a curved stone wall, lined up like a series of sentries. The flags flapped and whipped in the wind as though they were clapping, saluting their arrival. The ferry party filed in through a gate beneath an archway of roses. They walked along a path called *Avenue of Joy*, bedecked with a vibrant array of flowers and bushes and alive with chirping birdsong. Other than hydrangea, Hollie didn't know the names for anything, and it suddenly struck her that she could tell you the brand names of people's luggage and clothes just from the logos – North Face, Barbour, Gore-Tex – and their relative value, but had little clue when it came to the natural environment around her.

To the right, they passed an opening signposted *Magical Mandala Garden*. Hollie would not have been at all surprised if it had said, 'Enchanted wood, enter if you dare.' She felt like she wanted to hold her breath in case she disturbed a flock of fairies about to fly round the corner.

A sharp left turn took them into a courtyard with a large building on the right and accommodation set out in a horseshoe formation to the left. They were ushered into a large dining room with yellow walls and lots of windows.

After queuing politely for hot drinks, they were invited to sit down for a group briefing. A man in jeans and a woolly brown jumper stood up and dinged a singing bowl to get everyone's attention. 'Welcome to Footprint Island. I'm Grayden, the centre manager,' he said and proceeded to brief the group on housekeeping matters, stressing several times the importance of signing up for the daily washing-up rota. Hollie had the impression that Grayden was distinctly un-woo-woo. If anything, surprisingly dour. He reminded her of one of the IT managers at work.

'So, a little bit about the island for those of you who haven't been here before. Footprint Island has a long spiritual history stretching back to the sixth century. Nowadays, it's under the ownership of the Tibetan Buddhist community who established it as a place of sanctuary for people wanting to come on retreat, and a space for interfaith dialogue – although you don't have to have a faith or religion to take part in the community. At the south end, there's a lighthouse surrounded by a compound of buildings. This is the Inner Light retreat, where a community of nuns are undertaking a three-year closed retreat, and it's not open to visitors.' Hollie was disappointed to hear this. She had seen the lighthouse from the ferry and had hoped to get up close.

After the briefing, volunteers showed people to their rooms which were configured into three two-storey blocks. Hollie smiled as she saw the yellow nameplate on the door of hers: *Wisdom*. She thought of the meditation card Lesley from Bensham had given her. It felt like a good sign. Her room on the ground floor was simply furnished. A single pine wardrobe, a desk, chair, reading lamp and a sink. The single pine bed reminded Hollie of the one she had slept in as a child. It felt cosy and familiar. She hung her clothes, packed a small rucksack, and headed out to get some fresh air while there was still daylight.

Half an hour later, Hollie reached the Inner Light retreat and lingered by a white, walled garden, craning her neck to see inside. The notion of a closed retreat seemed mysterious and bewitching, real-life Rapunzels who had willingly cut off their hair and chosen to be locked up together. She imagined what it would be like to speak with one of them. Maybe they might break their silence, feeling compelled to say something profound, life-changing and holy? She wondered what it was like living with only women. Did they argue? Did they ever pine for their hair, or pretty clothes? Sex, even? What were the individual journeys that had led them to this place? And what did they *do* all day?

Disappointingly, there was nobody around. The place seemed deserted.

Hollie continued and followed a path which hugged the end of the island, ascending upwards. A lush carpet of purple heather and ferns covered the slope, and she could see a few hobbity-looking homes built into the side of the hill with spectacular views. She passed a man photographing a robin, and two women deep in conversation, but none of them acknowledged her. She hunkered down as a strong wind picked up but within about ten minutes it had gathered such force that she was struggling to move forward and feeling nervous about the prospect of being blown off, so she turned back. She passed the lighthouse retreat again, when an intense tirade burst into her head, stopping her in her tracks.

Look at you, with your fashion boots, wearing make-up.

You are vain and shallow.

You are an empty, ridiculous woman.

People here will feel your bad energy.

No one will want to speak to you.

You have nothing to contribute.

Why are you here?

Stop trying to 'find yourself', creating drama as a poor substitute for not having children.

Sitting quietly, being forced to listen to your pathetic drivel, over and over.

This is going to make you more depressed, Hollie.

'Holy shit!' she said aloud, stunned by the tone of the inner monologue. 'What the fuck just happened?'

An image came to mind of the Rapunzel nuns sitting in a circle, holding hands, humming – like some kind of sonic voodoo ritual. Was humming even a thing in Tibetan Buddhism? She had no idea. Another image appeared. She was back in the room at Embody Healing, replaying the scene where Phemi told her about the mindfulness technique ... *the trick is not to become attached to the thoughts; name what you notice and be a detached observer.*

Hollie began walking again, narrating in her head.

Okay, so I'm noticing judgement about my appearance.

Oh ... and there's another thought about how empty I am as a childfree woman.

Like magic, the voices began to quell.

A few minutes later, Hollie saw a woman bounding towards her. 'Hi. I'm Krystina, we met earlier,' she said, rosy-cheeked and with a beaming, megawatt smile, 'at the ferry landing.'

'I remember. I'm Hollie.'

'Pleased to meet you, Hollie. You here for the retreat?'

'Yes.'

'I'm staying as a guest, doing a bit of volunteering in the garden. Just come out to spread my legs ... Oh God,' she said shaking her long wavy hair and flapping her arms, 'I meant ... stretch my wings.'

She looked at Hollie as if she couldn't believe what had just come out of her mouth.

'I mean ... STRETCH MY LEGS!'

The two of them looked at each other in a momentary pause, before dissolving into hysterical laughter. For several moments they tried to compose themselves, laughing with tears running down their cheeks whilst holding their stomachs and slapping their thighs.

'Krystina ... that was the best introduction anyone has ever given me in my entire life!' said Hollie as she finally came to a juddering halt.

'Yeah,' said Krystina, grinning from ear to ear, 'I think after that introduction we'll have to be lifelong friends!'

'Definitely!' replied Hollie.

'How far did you manage to get round the island?'

'I started climbing up, but the wind was too strong.'

'It can be like that sometimes. I think I'll just go as far as the Inner Light Retreat. I love peering over the gate. Fascinates me, that place.'

'Me too.'

'Reckon you could do it, Hollie? A three-year retreat?'

'No idea. I'm only at the mindfulness-for-dummies stage so that seems way out of my league!'

'Definitely next level isn't it! Ani Zopa just came out a few weeks ago.'

'The nun in the robes?'

'Yeah. And you know Grayden, the centre manager? His wife is in there. Think it's a bit of a sore point.'

Hollie nodded, thinking it might explain why he seemed a bit grumpy.

'Listen to me, terrible gossip, probably not very Buddhist, eh? If you are free sometime, maybe we could take a walk around the island together?'

'I'd love that. Thanks.'

'Okay great, catch you later,' she said.

'Enjoy spreading your legs, Krystina!'

'Cheerio!' she waved back bounding off again, chuckling to herself.

~

After soup that evening, Grayden stood up again. 'I have an important announcement. Your course leader Edith was taken ill yesterday. We're confident she will be okay but is sadly not well enough to be here. I imagine this is disappointing news, as I know many of you have travelled a long way to be here. However,' Grayden held his finger in the air like an orchestra conductor, 'as ever, Footprint Island finds a way. By stroke of luck, or perhaps the hand of fate, we have Ani Zopa with us who has just completed a three-year retreat here on the island and kindly agreed to step in. It won't be the programme as advertised, but it will focus on mindfulness and meditation. The programme will now begin after lunch tomorrow, so you will need to decide by breakfast if you wish to leave. We have a weather warning for high winds from early afternoon so unless you leave before then, you are likely to have no choice but to stay. What I would invite you to consider is this … the island may not be giving you the programme you wanted, but perhaps is offering what you need.' Hollie excused herself from the table and went to use the payphone in the hall. 'Didn't you get my text messages? I sent them a couple of hours ago,' Hugh said when he answered.

'No. I don't have a signal. Is everything okay?'

'I was in the kitchen and the photograph of us fell off the wall. I was worried it was a sign.'

'That's not like you,' said Hollie.

Hugh usually took things at face value. A picture falling off the wall was a faulty fitting or some imperceptible movement of the walls, nothing more, nothing less.

'How's the pitch coming along?'

'Okay, I suppose. Not feeling too hopeful given my run of luck lately. Seem to be losing more clients than we're winning. I think the prospect of Brexit isn't helping.'

'Do you want me to come back? The course leader is unwell so the programme I signed up to isn't going ahead. A Buddhist nun is going to improvise something instead.'

'My preference is always for you to come home, but it's your choice, and you have already gone all that way. What's the worst that can happen?'

'Getting stranded. Stormy weather is on the way which means the little ferry can't get across.'

'As long as you don't shave your hair and decide to become a nun, babe!'

~

Hollie had a strange dream that night.
She was in a white room with curved walls.
Shelves were built into the walls, housing thousands of books.
She was slowly pacing the room, running her hands along their spines.

A space opened, revealing a white spiral staircase.

White light shone down onto the stairs, and she climbed into a large lantern room.

She spread her arms out and levitated up, out of the tower, until she was hovering in the sky.

Pieces of paper were fluttering past, as if the pages of a book had been cast into the wind.

~

The following day, four people left on the morning ferry. Everyone else, including Hollie, remained and made their way to the large hall after lunch. The entrance was up a flight of white steps and there was a blue plaque on the wall, *Serenity Hall*. To the left, a large brass gong hung in a frame in front of a long wooden bench where you sat to remove your shoes and left them tucked underneath.

Inside, Hollie walked across the parquet oak floor in her socks. It was sparse but felt warm and inviting with handsome wooden panels halfway up the walls, and cheerful turquoise paint above. A deep skylight was set into the middle of the roof with the Footprint Island symbol, golden crested waves against a turquoise sea, painted next to it. She sat cross-legged on one of the bright red cushions, expectant and curious. There was a centrepiece in the middle of the circle, a clear glass vase filled with flowers. She recognised branches of honesty plant. Her mother had always kept a vase of them, and Hollie had always been fascinated by their papery, otherworldly quality.

'Good afternoon,' said Ani Zopa. She was sitting on a cushion positioned at twelve o'clock in the circle, her arms inside the sleeves of her robes, with an expression of benign neutrality. Hollie had often been told she had a resting-bitch-face and thought how lovely it would be to know that your face was just sitting there, kindly and inviting all by itself when you weren't paying attention.

There was an uncomfortably long pause as Ani Zopa stared off into the distance. Hollie could feel herself twitching as the silence stretched.

Was this part of the lesson, or had Ani Zopa just run out of words after so long in the enclosed retreat? A faint smile passed Ani Zopa's lips, and she seemed to give an almost imperceptible nod, as if having received an instruction from above. She turned to face the man sitting next to her in the circle and looked at him for a few moments, holding his gaze before moving on to the next person.

In complete silence.

Hollie was sitting at ten-to-twelve on the clock-face of the circle and began to feel oddly nervous as Ani Zopa's creeping-death-stare came towards her. She watched how others reacted. Some people seemed to bask in the luminous glow of Ani Zopa's greeting. Others twitched uncomfortably and looked as though they wanted to run away. One or two even became a little tearful, as if they had received a holy blessing. Hollie thought back to her inner tirade. What if it was true that these nuns could see *through you*, into the essence of your nature? What if their senses had become so finely attuned through years of isolation that they had developed spiritual x-ray vision and they could see into your soul just by looking at you?

Ani Zopa stopped and looked at her.

Hollie saw her eyes were shining, as if they were backlit by a beautiful, radiant light. Penetrating, yet warm and curiously soft. She looked in a way no one had ever looked at her before, with a gaze that seemed to take in *all* of her, an expansive version of her that stretched beyond the physical boundaries of her body and down into the depths of her being.

For a fleeting moment Hollie felt ennobled.

Ani Zopa smiled and moved on.

'You are most welcome here,' she said, after silently greeting the last person. 'All of each of you is welcome.'

Momentarily, Ani Zopa drifted off again before seeming to remember where she was. 'Thank you for your patience as we have adjusted the programme. I have spoken to Edith on the … tele-phone.' Hollie thought there was something about the way Ani Zopa said *telephone* that made it sound like a piece of new-fangled technology. 'She told me what she had in mind, so we will aim to follow a similar flow. We will begin in the morning with a short teaching, then a silent meditation. In the afternoon we will have a guided meditation, and a mindfulness activity. It's up to you what you choose to participate in. No obligation to attend anything. Simply an invitation.'

Ani Zopa paused again.

'Today, we will prepare for starting in earnest tomorrow. Does anyone have any burning questions at this stage?' No one spoke and Ani Zopa looked satisfied. 'Then let us begin,' she said, picking up the singing bowl perched on an embroidered cushion. She struck the bowl then rolled a small wooden mallet round the outside rim, making a vibrating wave of sound that echoed across the hall. 'The ultimate purpose of our practice here is to become more awake, more aware, more kind,' she began. A few people in the circle picked up notepads and pens and began writing. Hollie glanced at her journal lying in front of her. Ordinarily, she was the first to begin making notes, studiously trying to capture everything that was said, highlighting key words and phrases. But suddenly it felt almost … *inappropriate*. No, she decided, she was going to trust herself to remember whatever was important. She would try to really pay attention and listen to Ani Zopa.

More awake. More aware. More kind.

Hollie repeated the words in her mind.

'To become awakened to our Buddha nature, the seed of enlightenment that is at the core of every sentient being. To become aware of the mind poisons that obscure our Buddha nature and make us cling to the construct of the self we create. And to learn to be more kind to ourselves so that we, in turn, may extend compassion to all living beings.'

Ani Zopa leaned forward and pointed to the vase of flowers in the centre.

'Some of you will recognise the plant in the vase here. I picked it from the garden this morning. It's called *lunaria*, more commonly known as *honesty*,' she said. 'Observe the delicate, papery pods … look closely.' Hollie craned her neck. 'See how each pod contains a dark seed? This seed is like our Buddha nature. The more we remove the veils that obscure our true nature, the more we see. The more we surrender our ideas of perfection and our attachments to external things – our cars, houses, achievements – the more we perceive through the eyes of truth. The more we release ourselves from fear and anger, from desire and jealousy, the more translucent everything becomes. We come to see what is so simple and so close, we almost miss it.' Ani Zopa paused and looked off into the distance again, as if she were savouring what she was about to say before releasing it from her lips. 'The ultimate emptiness of enlightenment.'

Emptiness?

Hollie had imagined becoming enlightened would be a holy thunderbolt-and-lightning kind of affair. And surely, feeling empty, was not a good thing?

'That in the essence of our being, we are already luminous, perfect and whole. Just like this seed.' Ani Zopa rocked back on her cushion and returned her arms inside her robes. A man put his hand up to ask a question. Hollie had noticed him immediately when she had walked in earlier. Swarthy skin, wavy dark hair and dark brown eyes. Handsome, in a Shirley-Valentine-meets-hot-Greek-fisherman kind of way. 'Can you explain what you mean by Buddha nature? Is this the same as the soul?' Ani Zopa looked directly at him, hands still inside her sleeves. 'No,' she said with a beatific smile on her face. The man was visibly rattled. He had the look of someone who had never experienced anyone saying no to him in his entire life. 'I'm sorry, Ani Zopa,' he said. '*No, as in, no, it's not the same? No, you can't explain? Or both?*'

She looked at him again.

'Just no,' she said, with kindly eyes, and no change whatsoever in the even tone of her voice.

Hollie could feel her buttocks clenching. She had never seen anyone say a no like this in her life and was sure the man's cheeks had become a little flushed. 'I see,' he said with slight tension in his voice. Ani Zopa did not reply and made no effort to relieve him, or to address the discomfort in the room. It simply hung there for a few twitchy moments. Hollie wondered if Ani Zopa saying *no* like this was part of today's lesson?

'That is our teaching concluded for today. We will now have a fifteen-minute break and afterwards you are invited to join me for silent sitting meditation.' Ani Zopa struck the singing bowl again. Hollie's thoughts raced as the sound reverberated. Was her saying *just no* a teaching technique to show how much we cling to certainty? Was wanting to intellectually understand something a mind poison? Ani Zopa stood up, bowed to the circle, and walked briskly out of the room, almost as if she deliberately wanted to avoid any further questions or interaction.

Hollie had never seen anything like it.

Perhaps she was still coming back online after emerging from the alternate realm of the lighthouse? Or was it possible that Ani Zopa was simply an enlightened arsehole?

~

Hollie returned later for the silent meditation.

Just No Guy, along with three others, did not.

'Who among you already has a meditation practice?' asked Ani Zopa. About three quarters of the room put their hands up. 'For those of you less familiar, or with no experience, there are a few important points to be aware of before we begin.' Hollie had never sat for an hour in silence. Frankly, it sounded like torture, but she was determined to try. 'Meditation gives us a way to access the silent centre of our awareness. A way to unhook from our ego's constant need to be always doing, doing, doing. All the programming we have about being busy, being productive, and working those lists!' Hollie wondered whether nuns ever made to-do lists? It might be all well and good not having them in a lighthouse retreat, but she would not be able to survive without them in the real world. Had Ani Zopa ever worked hard and been properly busy? It was hard to imagine.

'When we meditate, we tap into our ability to just BE. To be with silence and emptiness.' The hairs on the back of Hollie's neck stood up. 'We believe emptiness is something to fear. We are afraid of the unbearable weight of emptiness.' Hollie could have sworn Ani Zopa glanced at her as she said this. 'Yet emptiness is not something to be feared, or even healed. Emptiness is a portal, a gateway into expansive awareness, to the inner stillness that is the very *ground of* our being.' Hollie was not entirely sure what she meant by the ground of being, but for some reason she could feel tears starting to well up.

'It's our *fear* of emptiness which is really the problem.' Ani Zopa took a deep breath in and out. It looked like she was breathing the whole room through her body, absorbing the truth of those words through her skin. 'Through meditation, we train ourselves to tolerate emptiness. We allow the mind to finally be at rest. This takes practice, so it's normal for your mind to squeal like a pig when you begin!' A ripple of knowing laughter surfed around the circle. 'Thoughts will continually arise. The important thing is not to judge them as good or bad. Simply accept what is there with loving kindness. And when the mind wanders off, just come back to the breath.' Ani Zopa looked around the circle and smiled like a kindly shepherd looking at her flock. 'I think that is sufficient for now,' she said. 'Make yourselves comfortable and we will begin'

Hollie sat cross-legged and closed her eyes. She listened to the echoes of the singing bowl, imagining the sound stretching to the outer corners of the room like undulating waves.

Emptiness is a portal, she heard in her mind.

All this time, she had been searching for a way to become a woman of substance, yet this nun was saying substance was already there, like a tiny seed waiting to be discovered inside the emptiness. A rich emptiness that was there waiting, lurking in the depths of everyone – childfree women and mothers alike.

~

Later that afternoon, Hollie and Krystina met for a walk. The air was fresh and still as they set off. The predicted stormy weather had yet to arrive.

'Beautiful isn't it?' said Krystina.

'Yes. Feels vividly alive, like stepping into a painting,' said Hollie.

'I know what you mean. I've been working in the garden for a few hours today. I just love being in nature, listening to the birds, getting my hands in the soil. Makes me feel connected to the living pulse of the island.'

'How long have you been a volunteer?'

'I'm not a proper one yet, just come for a few weeks. You can stay as a guest and volunteer for a few hours a day, which gives you the best of both worlds. Anyway, how was your session with Ani Zopa?'

'It was ...'

Hollie searched for a way to sum up what had happened.

'Intense, eh?' Krystina interjected.

'Yeah.'

'Sorry, I interrupted. Terrible habit of mine. I'm like an overexcited puppy sometimes.'

'It was weird and wonderful and confusing all at the same time. Part of me thinks she might be a brilliant teacher. But on the other hand, she seems rude and dismissive. I can't work her out.'

'I know what you mean,' said Krystina. 'Seen it before with a few of the other monks and nuns. We have this idea that people who are enlightened are going to be all love and light, but from my experience, they can be quite fierce, especially with their personal boundaries.'

'What's that about?'

'Maybe having a heightened sense of your own sacred space makes you fiercely protective of it?'

'I suppose that makes sense,' said Hollie.

'Did Ani Zopa share her story?'

'No. She didn't really introduce herself at all.'

'Apparently, before she became a Buddhist, she was a real high-flyer. PhD in applied maths, brain the size of a planet. Worked in the city. Big glass office, mega salary, the works.'

'No way!' said Hollie, trying to picture Ani Zopa in heels and a designer suit.

'But something happened. No one knows what exactly. From what I gather, she had some sort of road-to-Damascus experience. Walked out of her life to follow a spiritual path, and eventually became Ani Zopa.'

'Woah!'

'Yeah. Talk about your life turning upside-down, eh?'

'That certainly puts a different perspective on things,' Hollie said, feeling chastened. Once again, she had been reminded of how quick she was to judge.

They walked in silence for a few moments and Hollie imagined Ani Zopa standing in a glass tower, looking out across the city of London. She wondered what her eyes had looked like then, in that parallel universe, in her other life.

'Can I ask you something, Krystina?'

'Go ahead.'

'What made you invite me to come on a walk with you? I'm glad you did, I'm just curious.'

'No idea, really. Just came out of my mouth, right after I told you I was off to spread my legs!'

'Yeah, you definitely made a big impression with that one!' Hollie said, laughing.

'Actually … no, wait. Let me tune in.'

Krystina paused a moment and closed her eyes.

'There was something else. I felt … a pull.'

'What do you mean?'

'Like this,' Krystina said, pinching the material of her jacket between her chest and pulling it forward with her thumb and forefinger, in the same way a small child might tug at your trouser leg. 'I call it the *holy heart tug*.'

Hollie's eyes widened.

'Holy heart tug?'

'Have you heard of chakras?' said Krystina.

'Yes.'

'Right here is your heart chakra,' she said, cupping her hands over the centre of her chest. 'And whenever I feel a pull here, I pay attention. It's like my body telling me to move towards the person or thing, like I'm being guided by a force – call it higher self, the universe, or whatever floats your boat.'

'I think a holy heart tug brought me here,' said Hollie.

'Me too,' replied Krystina. 'This is my second time on the island. First time was seven years ago after my mother died suddenly, just before her sixtieth birthday.'

'I'm so sorry.'

'Thanks. We were very close, and I was devastated. Completely fell apart. I was living in a crummy flat in London at the time, doing youth work and I just couldn't get myself together. I tried to go back to work, but I couldn't do it. Everything just unravelled. All I could think of was that I needed to find somewhere I could grieve with grace, if that makes sense?'

'Absolutely.'

'Somewhere I could be with people if I wanted, but also be alone. A place of solace. And, through a series of synchronicities, I stumbled on this place. Never heard of Footprint Island, and knew very little about Buddhism, but there was just something about it. I felt myself pulled towards it as soon as I went on the website, like I was meant to come here. As soon as I stepped off the ferry, it felt like home. And even though this place is miles away from London and my mother never visited, it was like I could feel her presence more strongly here.'

'That's a beautiful story,' Hollie said.

'I stayed for a couple of months and began volunteering in the garden, working with Billy. Have you met him yet?'

'No.'

'I'll introduce you. Billy's in charge of the Mandala Garden here. He's an amazing gardener, cultivated the whole thing from scratch. Planted it so there would always be something flowering, all year round. He is also completely bonkers, and one of the wisest people I know. Took me under his wing, like a surrogate father.'

'I'd like to meet him.'

'It's a must, Hollie. Billy's an island legend! He saved my life in so many ways. Helped me realise I'd become disconnected from myself. My grandmother, my mother's mother, was a Lithuanian peasant. Came to this country to escape Nazi persecution. As you can imagine, she had a very different perspective on life to most people. I spent a lot of time with her when I was a little girl. We would go to the woods together and forage for wild plants and mushrooms and make all these healing potions and poultices and rose petal jam.'

'I love the sound of her.'

'I used to think she was like a kindly Baba Yaga character, a bit ancient and supernatural. She taught me about the importance of being in communion with nature, and about trusting the earth, but I forgot all this after she died, and I went on a bit of a bender.'

'What was her name?'

'Lena … After I returned from the island, I decided to become a herbalist. Sold my flat, left my job and went to university. To become qualified, you have to complete a science degree first, so it took me six years. Given my witchy ancestry, it wasn't really my thing, but I was determined. I finished a few months ago – exhausted, penniless, and a bit broken – so I returned here, to get my hands back in the soil, re-witch, and decide what to do next.'

'Re-witch, I love that! I imagine your mother and grandmother would have been very proud.'

'Yeah … So how about you, Hollie? What brought you here?'

'The holy heart tug and serendipity, much like you.'

'It seems to be a common thing with people who end up here,' said Krystina.

'About two years ago, my husband said he wanted us to have a baby. I had always been ambivalent and suddenly knew I needed to make a definitive choice before nature decided for me. I probably expected my answer to be no, but when I honestly asked myself the question there was just this terrible, echoing silence.'

'That's tough. I don't have children, but was always clear I didn't want them, even though everyone banged on about what a great mum I'd be. How did you make a decision?'

'I started with pros and cons lists!'

Krystina laughed.

'I know. Totally anal. And completely useless.'

'Bless you.'

'When that failed, I had bodywork therapy and then psychotherapy, which ultimately led to me coming off the pill. To my surprise, I got pregnant, but had a miscarriage at about ten weeks.'

'Sorry, Hollie. So you decided you wanted children after all?'

'Not exactly. I just got to a point where I was exhausted by trying to outrun my mind, the clock was ticking, and I had this intuition that I needed to come off the pill. I guess you could say I surrendered and decided to see what wanted to emerge.'

'And did you try again?'

'No. A strange thing happened. A few months after the miscarriage, I was in the bathroom at home. I was about to walk out when, completely out of the blue, I practically ripped the door from the cabinet and swallowed my contraceptive pill without a single premeditated thought.'

'Your body made a decision.'

'Yes. It was like every cell in my body shouted, HELL NO! As I swallowed the pill, I heard a voice speak clearly inside my head. *Motherhood is not my path*, it said.'

'Sounds like your higher self spoke to you.'

'I think so, yes. But after the door to motherhood slammed shut, I was left with an acute sense of emptiness, like I was waiting for an alternate life without children to begin. I kept thinking … *Now what? What am I for if I am not a mother? What's my purpose?*

'And this feeling brought you to Footprint Island?'

'Yes.'

'Maybe this is our connection?' Krystina said as she stopped and turned to face Hollie, extending out her arms. 'Give me your hands, my darling.'

Hollie did as she asked and looked into Krystina's clear blue eyes. They were filling with tears.

'I came here to grieve for my mother. And it sounds like you have been called to grieve for motherhood.'

Motherhood Energy

The following morning, Hollie was sitting alone with a second cup of coffee staring out of the window, watching gathering grey clouds being whipped together by a lashing wind.

'Okay if I join you?'

It was Krystina holding a breakfast tray.

Hollie nodded.

'Looks like the stormy weather has arrived,' Krystina said. 'One of the volunteers says she loves it when the wind picks up on the island. Brings change, she said. Clears what needs to be swept away.'

'I hate wind. I end up looking a bit *Absolutely Fabulous* after a night of binge drinking. But I like the idea of it bringing an inner spring clean. It's a good reframe.'

'I enjoyed our walk yesterday,' said Krystina, sitting next to her.

'Me too,' said Hollie.

'You got me thinking about not having children. I remembered a book someone recommended, when I decided not to have kids, and it really helped. I knew becoming a mother wasn't my path either, but I remember feeling this force of nurturing energy inside me that I didn't know what to do with. Then I read *Cave in The Snow* by Tenzin Palmo, one of the first Western women to be ordained as a Buddhist nun. At a young age she rejected the conventional path of marriage and motherhood to follow a spiritual calling and ended up living in a cave 13,000 feet up in the Himalayas. On her own, for twelve years! Can you imagine that?'

'Bloody hell, that's hardcore.'

'She set herself a goal to achieve enlightenment in this lifetime to encourage other women on the spiritual path. Her book really inspired me because she had this nurturing, motherhood-energy too. It opened my eyes to many ways this can be expressed.'

'Motherhood energy ... I love that idea,' said Hollie.

'Yeah, it completely flipped how I thought about the whole idea of mothering. Now, I see how I mother all sorts of things into existence, through working with plants and helping to heal people, and it really nourishes me to think about how I'm expressing my mother's heart.'

'That's so beautiful, Krystina.'

'Last night, I had this strong feeling that it was important to tell you this. I think you have motherhood energy too. I can tell because you have kindness in your listening.'

Hollie stared at Krystina.

'Can I give you a hug?'

'Of course. I'm a great hugger!' Krystina said, pulling Hollie towards her bosom.

Hollie sank into her generous embrace, allowing herself to feel enveloped in the warmth of her friend while the wind rattled the windows.

'Thank you,' she said, wiping tears from her cheeks as she pulled away. *Kindness in my listening* ... is one of the loveliest compliments I've ever had. No one has ever said I'm kind.'

'Well, I have, so now it's official! After I finish this, I'll take you to the library before your session this morning and we'll find *Cave in The Snow*. I'm sure they have it.'

Hollie took another sip of coffee. Maybe the winds of change were already blowing something through her?

Half an hour later, carrying a dog-eared copy of the book, Hollie made her way to Serenity Hall, head down against the wind. She sat on one of the wooden benches and quickly removed her shoes before going inside. Ani Zopa was sitting on her cushion, in the same place as yesterday, eyes closed, so still she could have been made of wax.

Hollie hesitated by the door for a moment. She was a little early and wondering whether to apologise for interrupting. Ani Zopa opened her eyes and beckoned her, smiling. Hollie grabbed a cushion and tiptoed over as Ani Zopa closed her eyes again. She gently laid the book on the floor in front of her and stared at Ani Zopa.

How old was she? Her face had a youthful glow, but her neck suggested she was older. Late fifties, early sixties possibly? It was hard to say. She was certainly supple for her age. Maybe nuns practiced yoga? Or, Hollie mused, perhaps being enlightened made your limbs move more fluidly?

Ani Zopa opened her eyes and glanced at the book on the floor in front of Hollie.

'I met Tenzin Palmo once. Many years ago when I was in great pain and fighting many demons. And you know what she said?'

Hollie could tell this was a rhetorical question and stayed quiet.

'She told me I needed … weapons.'

Weapons!

Hollie resisted the urge to shout … *WEAPONS* … *no way!*

'She taught me the Green Tara mantra … *om tare tuttare ture soha*. "Use this to call on the power of Tara," she said. "Green Tara is compassion in action, the mother of all Buddhas. The female Buddha always ready to come to our assistance and sit with us inside our darkness as we face our fears."'

Ani Zopa looked at her. It was a look brimming with love, the way a mother might look at her child.

'What is your name?'

'Hollie.'

'You should look it up, Hollie …. *om tare tuttare ture soha*. Now, would you like to ring the gong and call the others? It's time to begin.'

Hollie went outside, picked up the mallet, and struck the large brass gong. She stood there for a few moments listening to the reverberating, ancient sound, feeling like an extra in a sequel of *The Last Samurai*. Just No Guy walked out of the dining room towards her. He smiled as he approached the steps as she bashed the gong enthusiastically for a second time.

'I see you've been ordained as chief gong ringer today, suits you!' he said, smiling with his lovely dimples.

'Thanks,' said Hollie, feeling her cheeks flush slightly as he walked past and removed his shoes.

'Good morning,' said Ani Zopa when everyone was gathered inside. 'Yesterday, I spoke about the purpose of our practice – to become more awake, more aware, and more kind – and the innate potential we have to realise our Buddha nature. Just as the sun is always shining, our Buddha nature is ever-present, but sometimes obscured by clouds in our minds. The more we let go of our attachments – the need to have all the answers, to intellectually understand everything, to predict how others will react, to control and perfect – the more we can rest in a state of radiant awareness.'

Hollie thought again that this must have been the reason Ani Zopa had not answered Just No Guy's question yesterday, to help him let go of the need for answers.

'Today, I will talk about awareness. If we want to be happy, we need to become more aware of our mind poisons. In Buddhism there are three mind poisons which cause negative states. The first is ignorance, or delusion. We see things as fixed and permanent, but this is not the nature of reality. Neuroscience tells us this now, catching up to knowledge that was known two thousand years ago.'

Hollie thought there was something supremely surreal about sitting in this hall summoned by a gong, listening to a nun talking about neuroscience.

'The nature of reality is impermanence. Things are always changing. Life, is energy in motion.'

Ani Zopa lifted her right hand and rotated it at the wrist, gazing at it as if for the first time.

'Each of us is made up of energy and space. Our hand, our arm, the cushions we are sitting on, even this hall … are all space and energy at a quantum level.'

Hollie had that feeling again, like the moment when she had stood in the supermarket aisle in front of the pregnancy tests. The same surreal feeling of being inside a movie of her own life.

'And space is all pervading. You cannot say this is my air, you may not breathe it in. We are all interconnected with everything, which is always in a cycle of death and rebirth … in a constant state of becoming. By clinging to our deluded perceptions that everything is solid and permanent, we create suffering.'

Hollie thought about her own suffering in the departure lounge of un-motherhood. Was this what she had been doing, waiting for a flight to escape from emptiness? Searching for a place where she could make herself solid and real, a place she was now being told did not exist?

'The second mind poison is greed, our attachment to things. We buy cars, houses, fancy clothes to elevate our status, to satisfy the ego. But do we possess things, or do they possess us? Grasping is like drinking salty water: the more we drink, the thirstier we become.'

Images floated into Hollie's mind. Her shiny car, her burgeoning colour coordinated wardrobe, the new furniture she had bought for the house recently.

'And the third mind poison is fear. We envy what others have and we strive to get more. Or we become fearful that what we have will be taken away.'

Had she been buying things to fill the emptiness? To become a woman of substance? She had never stopped to think about it before.

'We can enjoy things, of course. The point is to lose our fascination with comfort so we may have gratitude and appreciation for what we have, but without clinging to it. When good things happen, we can feel happy. And when bad things happen, we can also feel happy. We can learn to welcome *everything* with loving-kindness and acceptance.'

Ani Zopa paused and looked slowly round the circle, smiling. Her hands were folded lightly across her chest as if offering everyone a blessing as the skylights overhead rattled with the wind. As she made eye contact with her, Hollie wondered how she would feel if she was stripped of her possessions and career. Who would she be then?

'What questions do you have?' said Ani Zopa.

A middle-aged woman raised her hand.

'I'm struggling with the idea of accepting all experiences equally. I lost my mother to cancer last year and am still coming to terms with this. But I think what you're saying is that I shouldn't be sad, that her having died is no different to if she had recovered? I'm sorry, but that sounds cruel to me.'

'I am very sorry for your loss … and I understand heartbreak is a very real and very painful kind of suffering,' Ani Zopa said, looking directly into the woman's eyes with kindness.

She paused for a few moments as if trying to transmit the sincerity of these words into the woman before continuing.

'What I am saying is that grief can be a pathway to joy and peace. That loss and suffering can offer us powerful tools for our growth. That does not mean this is easy, but if we are able to face up to our own suffering, and meet it with equanimity, we can make space for these experiences and allow them to become our teachers.'

Hollie thought about grieving for motherhood. Perhaps if she figured out how to do this, she might be able to find her pathway to joy and peace.

~

The wind had just died down as Billy emerged from his cabin at the top of Avenue of Joy.

He cut a striking figure. Over six feet tall and wearing trendy black glasses, he was dressed in sleeveless red robes and a fur trapper hat with the side flaps turned up.

Hollie thought he could have been comedian Harry Hill's handsome older brother.

'You must be Hollie,' he said, extending his hand. 'So nice to meet you.'

Hollie could not fail to notice his shapely biceps and wanted to ask if he worked out, but stopped herself, wondering it if was wrong to think a monk was hot.

'Likewise, Billy. I've heard a lot about you,' she said, shaking his hand.

'So, this is your first time on Footprint Island?'

'It is.'

'How wonderful. And you are on the retreat with Ani Zopa?'

'Yes.'

'Very good. Very good indeed.'

Billy stooped slightly forward, looking at Hollie as if he was breathing her in, then became upright again.

'Have you had a good day so far?' he asked.

'I have, yes. It's been very interesting. And you, Billy, have you had a good day so far?'

'I suppose it depends on how you think about a good day … Do you like *Star Wars*, Hollie?'

'I do.'

'I think about it like this: you can have some days when the mind poisons win, you know, like when you've gone over to the dark side and Darth Vader has taken over inside you. And then there are other days when you manage to conquer your mind and stay on the Jedi path. So that's how I tell if I've had a good day or not, whether I have managed to steer clear of the Death Star. And on that basis, yes, I'm having a good day today.'

'Wow! That's a great way to look at it, I shall remember this!' Hollie said, laughing.

Billy grinned at her.

'I like this one, Krystina,' he said, smiling at her friend. 'Shall we walk?'

Without waiting for a reply, Billy began striding exuberantly towards the gate.

The three of them naturally fell into a line with Billy in the middle. Krystina began talking enthusiastically about the gardening she had been doing that morning and asking Billy advice about a poultice she was making for one of the volunteers. Hollie listened, enjoying eavesdropping on a conversation that was at once interesting and alien. *Yarrow, Black-Eyed Susan, Evening Primrose*. She tried to make a mental note of the names of plants she assumed must be in the garden.

After twenty or so minutes of walking, they stopped and climbed a set of mossy flagstones to a hermit's cave. Hollie wondered whether this was like the one where Tenzin Palmo had lived in the Himalayas.

'Did you know that when the Tibetan Buddhists first bought the island, they sent someone to produce an energetic map of the land to help them decide what kinds of work were best done on different parts of the island?' said Billy.

'I never heard this before,' said Krystina. 'Told you Billy was a mine of information, Hollie.'

'This area, for example, has powerful, wrathful energy,' Billy said, gesticulating in front of him as they stood inside the cave looking across the water.

'Seriously?' said Hollie, her eyes growing bigger.

'What is it?' asked Krystina.

'Remember when we met?'

'Of course. Don't think I'll ever forget that!' Krystina said, chuckling.

'Just before I saw you, I'd had this outburst inside my head just as I was passing here. Came out of nowhere. This loud, shouting voice telling me I didn't belong here, that I was empty and worthless.'

'Yes,' Billy said with a beaming smile, 'this happens often to people who are open to the energy of the island. Footprint Island holds up a mirror for us to truly see ourselves as we are. A bit like that scene in Star Wars when Luke Skywalker goes into the cave and chops Darth Vader's head off only to see, beneath the mask, his own face looking back at him. It happens all the time here. If you ask me, Hollie, I think the island has offered you a great blessing.'

'I can vouch for this being true,' said Krystina. 'Both times I've come to the island, lots of my shit has been brought to the surface. Only way we ever get to heal is to look it in the eye, I reckon. But it's not easy, that's for sure.'

'Before coming here, I would never have thought like this but I'm beginning to understand what you mean,' said Hollie. 'Can I ask, Billy, does this kind of thing still happen to you, after being here a long time?'

'Let me see … I've been here fourteen years now, I think. Don't know exactly to be honest, I stopped keeping track a while back.'

'And how did you come to live on the island?' said Hollie.

'I did many things before I came here. Moved around a lot, but never felt I was altogether wired for the outside world. I never expected to be successful, but I was always open to risk-taking and not too concerned with being accepted by other people.'

Hollie thought this sounded like a kind of superpower.

'One day, I heard this voice telling me to take a flight to the UK and head north. I was teaching in Africa at the time, but this voice was so clear and so insistent, I just knew I had to follow it.'

Hollie thought about the bathroom cabinet and her Incredible Hulk moment. It seemed this kind of weird experience of hearing an inner voice might be more common than she'd thought.

'Coming back to your question, Hollie, I still have my moments, but there is more stillness now. Less chatter. More space.'

They descended the steps and headed back towards the centre.

'Well, it's been lovely meeting you,' Billy said when they arrived back. 'It's so great that you're here, Hollie. An opportunity to clean away what is no longer useful and start anew. No need to analyse or go back over things. Just clean up, pick up your lightsaber, and begin afresh.'

Just as he finished, the gong sounded for the afternoon session and Billy did a little bow as he shook Hollie's hand, bid farewell to Krystina, and disappeared up the path back to his cabin.

Hollie said goodbye to her friend and made her way to Serenity Hall.

'This afternoon, we are going to use the mantra *om mani peme*. This chant is taught to children in Tibet as a form of prayer and recited by Tibetans as part of their daily practice. We use it to transform our mind poisons by opening the wisdom mind.'

Hollie wasn't sure what *the wisdom mind* was, but it sounded good. Like a Jedi mind.

~

By the time Ani Zopa dinged the singing bowl to signal the end of the chanting half an hour later, Hollie felt energy slowly circling upwards inside her, like an awakening serpent coming to life.

'Now, I would like to invite you to follow me outside for some silent, mindful walking. Ideally in your socks or, if you prefer, bare feet. Allow yourself to remain in the resonance of *om mani peme* as you slowly place your feet on the ground, noticing their rise and fall. Pay attention to the present moment, and allow thoughts to pass like clouds across the sky of your mind. We will go out of the hall to the right, round the back of the building, past the sacred sycamore tree and through the mindful garden, then back in here.'

One by one, people began leaving the hall in silent procession, naturally falling into single file. Hollie followed a French woman called Francoise, and Just No Guy fell in behind her. She thought back to arriving on the island and all she had experienced since stepping off the tiny ferry. It already seemed such a long time had passed, as though the time here was more expansive. She felt revived in spirit. Less scattered on the inside. More still, just like Billy had described. She let out a long sigh and sank into a comforting feeling of peace, grateful to be here, right now, in this moment watching the rise and fall of her feet. Perhaps, she mused, she was finally learning to be with the emptiness. Where previously there was a black hole that she was desperate to escape from on the first flight out, now she was slowly constructing her own inner Serenity Hall, to be entered into reverently.

Their slow procession continued forward, passing a colourful hand painted sign, *Sacred Sycamore Tree*. As they came into a clearing, Hollie saw a large tree with a wooden bench positioned in front of it. Just as she passed the bench, Hollie became aware of Just No Guy's presence behind her, as if he had closed the gap between them. She imagined feeling his breath on the back of her neck and suddenly, unbidden, an image of them flashed into her mind: the two of them, naked and entangled, making wild love on the grass beneath the tree. How the bejesus had she managed to move from inner peace to sex within a matter of seconds? As if somehow, in between breaths, she had slipped through the portal of emptiness and accidentally taken a wrong turn into a parallel universe of erotica!

Was this another lesson from the island? The holy tree cutting her down to size, reminding her of her base desires just as she was beginning to get a glimpse of her Buddha nature?

Clearing Space

The next day Hollie was sat in the circle again, enjoying the quiet hum of conversation. She was thinking about *Cave in The Snow* which she had been reading the night before. She'd been particularly struck by a description of what Tenzin Palmo called 'the voice' … an inner voice that had spoken to her, time and time again, at what she called 'strategic points' in her life, guiding her on a path that she hadn't necessarily understood, but always followed regardless. It sounded just like what Billy had described when he'd been teaching in Africa.

Hollie looked up and saw Just No Guy sat opposite, taking the last empty space.

He smiled at her, and she smiled back.

Yesterday evening they'd played Scrabble with a few others, then talked over a pot of tea. His name was David; he was a widower and ran a charity for veterans. He was also here serendipitously, having taken the place of a friend who had persuaded him to come, albeit reluctantly, at the last minute. He confided he'd also struggled with Ani Zopa at first, but that her saying no to him had been powerful in forcing him to confront some things. They'd joked that perhaps Ani Zopa possessed spiritual x-ray vision. Hollie had eventually excused herself to go to bed. After her erotic vision, even saying the word *bed* in a sentence to him had felt like a thrilling, illicit flirtation. She'd wondered whether he'd also experienced something passing between them at the sycamore tree.

She was sure he'd gazed at her lingeringly as they'd talked, but it was hard to tell whether she was merely seeing things that weren't there. Maybe, she reflected, the island was giving her a message to focus on her marriage. She'd been stressed and working ridiculously long hours and not very present at home for some time. Maybe, she mused, Hugh was feeling widowed in their marriage.

Ani Zopa struck the singing bowl, bringing Hollie's attention back into the room.

'Good morning,' she said, greeting each person in turn. She was sat upright and cross-legged with downturned palms resting on her knees and looked as though she meant business.

'Today, our final lesson is on kindness and compassion, beginning with the self.'

Hollie felt herself sit a little taller, as if her body was saying she really needed to hear this.

'Yesterday, I spoke about mind poisons. We are all hamstrung by our mind poisons. We are all equally struggling to find happiness, and we are all equally failing most of the time.'

Ani Zopa emphasised the word *all*. Hollie felt reassured by the thought that even all those Rapunzel nuns were still working on their own shit.

'This is why we must learn to cultivate a practice of compassion towards ourselves and, in turn, for all living beings. We must learn to look at our mind poisons and see nakedly all the things we feel, and want, and do.'

Nakedly.

The sycamore tree scene flashed briefly before her eyes again and Hollie looked at David.

He was looking straight at her.

She tried to appear as if she was staring into the distance behind him, thinking deep thoughts.

'Accept that suffering and grasping is our nature. It's not about saying, "I must not feel anger or envy." It's about honestly seeing and accepting your anger and envy, without condoning or judging them, or trying to make them any better or worse than they are.'

I see you, sycamore tryst, and I accept you and let you go, Hollie said inside her head.

'And let me be clear …'

Ani Zopa held her forefinger up in the air.

'… cultivating kindness and compassion is not about letting ourselves off the hook. Nor is it about wasting energy, chastising ourselves, saying, "Woe is me." Punishing ourselves is merely a distraction, a great smokescreen of internal drama that requires us to change nothing.'

Hollie thought back to her pros and cons lists and all the time she'd spent asking herself whether there was something wrong with her. If she'd managed to be self-compassionate, would she have reached her decision more quickly and easily?

'And compassion is not some romantic notion of being all love and light, or offering woolly sympathy, what we might call in Buddhism, *idiot compassion*. It does not mean being a doormat, or self-righteously taking pity on people. Compassion is a purifying fire that we must direct with intelligence. It demands that we practice radical self-accountability and loving-kindness towards ourselves.'

Radical self-accountability.

Hollie repeated this phrase in her mind.

She had always thought she practised self-accountability, that this was the positive intent behind her frequent self-flagellation, but now she wondered. What if lashing herself was a form of distraction?

'So, when we have a problem with someone else, instead of judging and saying, "I would never behave like that," compassion requires us to look in the mirror first. It's a practice that begins with accepting our mind poisons with loving kindness. We are then able to help others and meet their needs, just for them, because we are not striving to feel better about ourselves. We are able to say, "I love you and I want you to be happy," instead of, "I love you and I want you to *make me* happy." This is the difference between love where we attach ourselves to others to feel safe and secure, and love when we are open and fearless and give generously of ourselves – freely, without the need for anything in return.'

Hollie thought about Hugh. Did he love her and want her to be happy? Or had he wanted her to *make him* happy by having a child?

She felt as though her head was going to explode.

Under her breath she whispered, *Green Tara, please help me.*

Suddenly, a large fly began buzzing around Ani Zopa's head. Hollie looked up and noticed one of the skylights was slightly ajar.

'Observe this fly,' Ani Zopa said, moving her head around to follow it. 'If you have ever watched a fly trapped in a small room, you notice how frantically it buzzes about. The way it lands on surfaces and bashes up against objects, making a noise like a little jolt of electricity. And you see that the fly rarely stays still on any surface for more than a few seconds before moving off again. Round and round it goes. What the fly doesn't know is that the windows and doors are wide open, that the way out into freedom is right there. But the fly buzzes round and round, trapped. And you can't help thinking that if only the fly would stay still awhile, it might be able to feel a slight breeze beneath its wings and let the stream of air guide it out into the open sky.'

There was a knock on the door.

'Sorry to disturb you, Ani Zopa. There's a phone call for you at reception.'

Ani Zopa acknowledged the news with a nod of her head.

'Let us take a short break now.'

Hollie smiled, inwardly thanking Green Tara for her swift intervention (just in case it did indeed have anything to do with her).

~

Hollie skipped the afternoon session. She wanted some time alone to let everything settle before leaving the following day, and the weather was good, so she packed a small rucksack and headed out to walk the full length of the island. She opened the gate at the bottom of Avenue of Joy and smiled to herself as she looked across the still water to the neighbouring island. It was hard to believe she would be back in the office in a few days. Oddly, the outside world now seemed surreal, as if here on Footprint Island existence was more real.

She began walking across the soft, undulating grass, watching the wild goats and sheep grazing nearby. She thought about the conversation with Krystina that first day, about *grieving for motherhood*, wondering whether there was something more she needed to do before she left. Something conclusive that would clear the way to *begin anew*, as Billy had said. An intentional act of commitment that would activate her motherhood energy, whatever this might be. She was lost in thought when she noticed a figure emerge from around the edge of the stone wall as she passed the back of the boathouse. It was Billy.

'Hello, Hollie. Beautiful afternoon isn't it?' he said, walking up to her.

'It is indeed.'

'Are you leaving tomorrow?'

'Yes, that's the plan.'

'Shame you can't stay longer. Do you think you'll be back again?'

'I hope so.'

'Good. I think you must.'

Hollie smiled and nodded, unsure whether this was an invitation or an instruction.

'Did you know the boathouse shop is open? The entrance is round the front. They have some lovely gifts. Maybe you might like to take a look?'

Moments later she lifted the latch and opened the door to the boathouse, accompanied by the sound of a tinkling bell. There were four round, low coffee tables with mismatching chairs in the middle of the space that she assumed must constitute the teashop, enclosed by a series of carousel stands packed with beautiful handmade greeting cards.

On two sides of the room were carefully arranged bookshelves, piles of colourful woollen blankets folded neatly on stone recesses, and a range of singing bowls on display. To the right, a large decorative wooden sideboard was laden with notebooks, incense sticks, prayer flags, and various trinkets.

Hollie picked out two hardbacked notebooks, a greeting card, and a scented candle.

There was a pretty, young woman at the cash register. She was bare-faced and pale skinned with a dusting of freckles around her nose and cheeks, and a tumble of thick, black wavy hair piled up into a messy bun, held in place with a piece of orange cloth. Her clothing looked peasant-like and effortlessly chic.

She smiled and looked intently at Hollie as she picked up each item from the counter, scrutinising the tiny price sticker and totting up the cost on a calculator. Each movement was slow and deliberate, as if this was all new to her. She could easily have stepped out of the pages of a Brothers Grimm fairytale, Hollie thought – the beautiful young woodcutter's wife who had just gone out to pick some berries and found herself curiously transported into this boathouse and having to navigate alien technology.

'Hmm … this is …'

She sounded Eastern European. The woman picked up the calculator and showed the total to Hollie.

'Cash.'

'Keep the change,' Hollie said, handing her the money.

The woman nodded and put the items into a brown paper bag. Hollie turned to leave when the woman spoke again.

'Erm ... silent meditation ...' she said, pointing upwards towards the shrine room '... starting now ... you come, yes?'

Hollie was about to explain that she was going for a walk but thought better of it as the woman stepped down from behind the cash register, threw on a woollen shawl, and motioned for her to follow. Once again, Hollie had the feeling that the island was guiding her and decided to open herself to it's invitation. She followed the young woman round the back of the building up a grassy incline and climbed the small flight of steps. They removed their boots and entered through a small white door.

The shrine room was about seven metres long and three metres wide with a series of skylights in the roof. There was a shrine at the far end, laden with tealights, pictures of monks, and golden trinkets. Along each side of the room were a series of large square cushions and small wooden stools. Halfway up on the left was another large gong hanging in a wooden frame. Hollie followed the young woman's lead, picking up a blanket from a neatly folded pile in the corner, and walking slowly to a vacant cushion, treading lightly to avoid creaking the floor and disturbing the peace of the other four people who were already assembled, sitting cross-legged with their eyes closed.

Hollie sat in her space, wrapped the white and yellow blanket round her shoulders and closed her eyes, allowing the reverent hush of the atmosphere to infuse her. She felt much more comfortable now with sitting in silence, allowing thoughts and images to drift across the sky of her mind, like fluffy clouds.

Grieving for motherhood ...
Motherhood energy ...
Emptiness is a portal ...

Hollie drifted off and found herself sitting cross-legged in the centre of the stone egg room, the same one she had dreamt about after her first session with Julian Finch. This time, all the tiny brass egg cups were empty, yet she felt oddly at peace, comforted by the unexpected warmth of the floor, as if the presence of motherhood energy somehow lingered deep in the ground, like underfloor heating. Instinctively, she cupped her hands in her lap, palms facing upwards, and began to make a long, low humming sound inside her mind.

Ommmmm …

She began rocking gently back and forth, allowing the expanding energy to fill her.

Then, she heard a voice in her head.

Why am I here?

'To drop into your knowing,' a calm voice answered, as if the egg room itself was speaking.

What does that mean?

'Open yourself. Become the eggcup.'

Hollie heard a snore and was jolted back into the shrine room. She opened her eyes and saw the man sitting opposite had fallen asleep, wrapped in a bright green blanket, his head lolling to one side.

Become the eggcup.

The phrase circle in her mind, unfurling upwards in a slow spiral of thought as her eyes became unfocused, staring into the green folds of the man's blanket.

She had an idea.

Letting Go of Motherhood

Hollie was standing at the end of Avenue of Joy, listening to the dawn chorus. It was a calm, still morning on the day of her departure. She checked her watch. Five minutes to six. Krystina appeared at the top of the path and walked towards her. She broke into her wide, gleaming smile on seeing Hollie.

'Thank you for agreeing to come with me, Krystina. I appreciate it's early.'

'No worries, it's good to be up with the larks. Sorry I've cut it a bit fine. As soon as I woke up I felt drawn to pick some honesty plant from the garden.'

'Brilliant,' Hollie said, opening the gate.

'You know, I'm always intending to come to the Green Tara meditation in the mornings but struggle to prise myself out of bed, so it's good to have the motivation. And I'm so thrilled you asked me to come. I love a good mission, and I think I probably needed this!'

'Me too,' said Hollie, 'and I can't think of a more perfect companion, Krystina.'

'I think for today, you can call me Baba Yaga,' she said, grinning.

'It suits you,' said Hollie, bathing in the light of Krystina's dazzling smile.

They arrived at the boathouse, removed their walking boots, and entered the shrine room, quickly gathering a blanket each and finding a space to sit. There were seven people already waiting, including a fully robed monk sitting close to the shrine. The monk picked up one of the silken sheaths nestled on the small wooden stool in front of him, ceremonially undoing the ribbons. Everyone followed his lead. He struck a large singing bowl.

'We dedicate this Green Tara meditation for the benefit of all beings,' he said and began a low guttural mumbling sound that Hollie could vaguely recognise as the tiny mysterious script written on the creamy papyrus-like paper. She attempted to mimic the sounds, trying to figure out how to move her mouth to form these ancient, hypnotic words, but quickly became lost and gave herself over to the spellbinding thrum and vibration of the room.

Om benza sato hung …

About halfway through, the monk signalled to a woman sitting next to the hanging gong and she bashed it enthusiastically with padded mallets. As the crashing notes subsided, the room descended into silence. All that was left was the *click click* sound of wooden beads being counted by the monk on what looked like a large necklace, and his periodic snorting.

Eventually, the chanting re-commenced, and, at the end of the hour, Hollie walked out of the room, tingling, as if those strange hypnotic words were continuing to hum deep inside her cells.

'How do you feel?' Krystina asked as they set off towards the lighthouse retreat.

'Bigger on the inside. Like the space between my atoms has expanded,' Hollie said.

'Like a tardis?'

'Exactly,' said Hollie, chuckling, 'like I've breathed in the whole island!'

'Perfect. I think you are all set for your rendezvous with Green Tara, the mother of all Buddhas.'

'Lead on, Baba Yaga!'

Twenty minutes later they arrived at the Green Tara rock painting, about halfway between the boathouse and the lighthouse retreat.

'This is us,' said Krystina, setting down her small rucksack next to the large painted boulder. 'Beautiful, isn't she?'

'Yes,' Hollie said, laying her rucksack to the left and removing her phone to take a photograph. 'I saw her before, but never really looked closely.'

The painting was about three feet tall. A bright green female figure with a benign expression, wearing colourful Ali Baba style trousers of red, orange, and blue. She had an Oriental look and was naked from the waist up, wearing a golden headdress. Her breasts were tastefully covered with golden jewellery and a turquoise blue ribbon that coiled around her shoulders and arms like a shawl. Her left hand was held up as if she was about to say something important and her right foot was slightly forward, ready to step into action.

At the foot of the rock, Hollie saw several offerings left by other people. A few coins from different countries, small shells and stones, shrivelled flowers, and burned out tealights. Clearly, they were not the first to be performing a ritual here, which reassured Hollie – if they were weirdos, at least they were in good company.

'We're lucky that there's no wind this morning. Perfect conditions. You ready?'

'Yes,' said Hollie, 'as I'll ever be.'

Hollie reached into her rucksack again, removed the candle she had bought at the boathouse, and passed it to Krystina. Krystina reached into her pocket, took out a green lighter and passed it to Hollie.

'Very colour coordinated. I'm impressed!'

'Thanks,' said Krystina stepping closer to the rock painting, standing shoulder to shoulder with Hollie. Krystina held the candle in cupped hands, her arms outstretched towards the rock.

'Green Tara, mother of all Buddhas, we have come to you today to grieve for motherhood and to ask for your assistance in opening our mother's hearts so we may fully express the mother energy that lives inside of us. We ask you to bear witness to us as we grieve for motherhood in your presence and invite you to infuse us with your wisdom and guidance. I would now like to open our ceremony by lighting this candle in honour of motherhood, in all its manifestations.'

Krystina turned to face Hollie who lit the candle. Krystina stepped forward and gently laid the burning candle at the base of the rock next to Green Tara's forward foot. Hollie took a piece of folded paper from her back pocket, opened it, and cleared her throat, resisting the temptation to check no one was walking past.

'Green Tara, my name is Hollie Hardwick. I'm here today because I know having children is not my path in this life. I don't fully understand why, but I feel this is my truth and I'm at peace with it. Yet I feel a …'

Tears began to roll down Hollie's cheeks.

'… a longing for something I cannot name. I know I need to let go of all the things I will not have. The bedtime stories I will not read to my child. The moments I will not share with my mother, or sister, or Hugh. The community of …'

Hollie took a deep breath.

'… of mothers I will never be a part of. The first steps I will not be there for. The love I would have had for my child that I will not know …'

Hollie took out a tissue and wiped her eyes.

'Sorry, Green Tara, I need a minute here.'

She blew her nose and replaced the tissue.

'Yet I can feel this motherhood energy inside me. I don't know what this means, or how to express it and I'm here to ask for your help with this. Please show me the way. Teach me how to hold the emptiness I feel so I may become the eggcup, whatever that means … thank you.'

She folded her piece of paper away and Krystina opened hers.

'Green Tara. My name is Krystina Zukas. I first came here to grieve for my beloved mother and now I'm returning to ask for your help once more. I …'

Krystina's voice faltered and she grabbed hold of Hollie's hand. Hollie could feel her trembling.

'… I know my mother's heart is asking me to step into a new life. I know I need to let go of how I thought my life should turn out and open myself to new possibilities. I know I'm being called to honour the lineage of my grandmother by bringing healing into the world through plant medicine, but I don't know how. I'm penniless and lost. Help me to find a way. I humbly ask you to give me a sign and show me my next step along this path, Green Tara. Thank you.'

Krystina let go of Hollie's hand and they stood in silence for a moment. She turned the palm of her right hand to face them. She had written the Green Tara mantra on her hand, as if cribbing for an exam.

'Let's say it twenty-one times,' she said, 'for good luck.'

They began to chant together.

Om tare tuttare ture soha …

As they finished, a slight breeze picked up.

'Did you feel that, Hollie?'

'The wind?'

'Yes. I reckon it's Green Tara. Maybe she's trying to tell us something?'

'Like what?'

'I just had a feeling that we need to do something now, to symbolise letting go.'

Krystina turned to face Hollie.

'I have an idea,' she said. 'Let's swap our pieces of paper and rip them up. Let them fly away on the breeze, like confetti.'

They swapped their pieces of paper and turned back to face the rock painting.

'Green Tara,' Krystina said as she began tearing Hollie's piece of paper into tiny fragments, 'on behalf of my friend Hollie Hardwick, I hereby declare she is letting go of the path of motherhood and clearing a space for motherhood energy to expand inside her … like a bloody big tardis!'

Hollie laughed and watched as Krystina flung her hands upwards over the back of her head, in the style of a bride throwing her bridal bouquet. The tiny pieces of paper fluttered away in the direction of the lighthouse.

'Green Tara, on behalf of my friend Krystina Zukas, I hereby declare that she is letting go of the old story of her life, to make way for her transformation into Baba Yaga, walking in the footsteps of her ancestors.'

She ripped up Krystina's paper and flung it behind her, watching her friend's face light up with delight. Krystina reached into her rucksack and gently pulled out two sprigs of honesty plant.

'Green Tara, I give you this offering of lunaria as a symbol of my commitment to living in my truth, and with gratitude for your assistance.'

She laid a sprig down and passed the other to Hollie.

'Green Tara. I give you this offering of lunaria as a symbol of my commitment to nourishing the seed of my Buddha nature and as thanks for your assistance.'

Hollie laid her sprig next to Krystina's. Krystina rummaged in her rucksack again.

'What are you looking for?' asked Hollie.

'I was walking past the Inner Light Retreat yesterday thinking about you, and I suddenly came to a halt next to those shelves where they have the plants and tubs of seeds. It was odd because I didn't make the decision to stop. It was more like my body told me there was something I needed to do. I put a fifty pence piece in the donation box, closed my eyes and pulled out a packet of seeds from one of the tubs. Here,' she said, handing Hollie a small square packet.

'Egg tree seeds. Is this someone's idea of a joke?' Hollie said.

'Apparently not. I looked it up. Egg trees are an actual thing.'

'Who knew!' said Hollie.

'Yeah. A bit spooky, eh?'

'Absolutely!' said Hollie.

Krystina began digging the soil with her hands to make a small hole, as Hollie stared at the packet, smiling at the spooky magic of it all.

'Okay, do the honours,' said Krystina.

Hollie tore the packet open and shook the tiny seeds into the hollow. Krystina moved the soil back and patted it down. Hollie took her water bottle from her rucksack and wetted the patch of soil. Krystina stood back up, picked up the lighted candle, then turned to face Hollie, inviting her to hold it with her as they watched the flame flicker in the gentle breeze.

'Green Tara, we now blow out this candle and dedicate our ceremony to the benefit of all beings,' said Krystina.

They blew out the flame together.

Middle Earth

Hollie turned her key in the door and walked into the hall. The house felt eerily still.

'Hugh?' she called out as she put her suitcase down and removed her coat.

No answer.

That's odd, she thought, checking her watch. She was right on time. They had talked on the phone yesterday evening and Hugh knew she was coming home today. She peered through the porch door and saw his car wasn't in the drive. Maybe he'd gone out to get something special for dinner. Hollie picked up her suitcase and walked upstairs to get everything tidied away before Hugh came home. She imagined sitting at the dining room table, telling him all about Footprint Island, his eyes fixed on her in rapt attention.

She opened the bedroom door. The curtains were drawn and the air smelled stale.

Hugh was in bed.

'Hugh?'

Hollie felt a slight flutter of panic in her chest.

'Are you okay?'

He began to stir, and she sat on the edge of the bed.

'Hugh,' she whispered, gently stroking his soft blonde curls peeking out of the bedding.

She could smell alcohol.

'What ... time ... is it?' he said, his speech slightly slow.

'About five o'clock. I just got back... what's going on?'

'One fucking mistake, that's what happened. Just one … fucking … mistake …'

'Sorry, I don't understand, what are you talking about?'

'Stephen …'

'What about him?'

'Got married …' Hugh said, his voice cracking, '… and he couldn't even be arsed to fucking tell me. I'm his DAD, and it doesn't even count for anything!'

'I'm so sorry,' Hollie said, climbing into bed. 'Come here.'

Hugh folded himself into her arms like a baby, his head resting in her lap.

'How did you find out?'

'Bitchface. You should have heard her. She fucking *enjoyed* telling me, rubbing my nose in it.'

'She called to tell you?'

'She rang. Something to do with our Sky subscription still having my name on it … and she couldn't resist telling me about Stephen … just blurted it out.'

Hollie rocked Hugh in her arms and stroked his hair. Maybe this was her being in her motherhood energy, she thought, letting go of how she had imagined their evening would be and getting into action, like sure-footed Green Tara, where help was needed.

'One fucking mistake … and I have to pay for the rest of my life … I'm just so tired …'

She had no idea what to say, so she resorted to making soothing noises.

'It's not fair …'

'I know, babe.'

'You work hard … try your best … try to be a good dad … then one fucking stupid mistake and everything unravels …'

'You were young, you can't keep punishing yourself.'

'I'm not punishing myself … it's her … and Stephen!'

Hollie didn't entirely agree. She sensed Hugh was pickled up to his eyeballs in mind poisons, but decided it was best not to say anything right now.

'Where's your car?'

'And there's another thing … this morning I came downstairs and found my car stacked on bricks … some little shit nicked the wheels. Can you believe it … stole all my fucking wheels and the Mercedes badge! I didn't even know that was still a thing.'

Hollie pictured Ani Zopa listening in on their conversation, her arms inside her robes, nodding sagely. *When our car has wheels, we can be grateful. And when our car does not have wheels, we can say, okay, my car does not have wheels, what is the lesson life is offering me here?*

'You work hard to have nice things … you play the game … then some little shit comes along and takes it all … it's so unfair, I don't deserve this.'

'I know,' she said, suppressing the urge to talk to Hugh about attachment and surrendering.

'It's like everything's unravelling.'

'What do you mean?'

'The business, Brexit, our baby … I just keep thinking, what's the point? I'm not getting any younger and suddenly nothing feels secure anymore, and who knows what's going to happen if we leave the EU.'

'You really think that might happen?'

'The closer we get, the more I have a bad feeling about this referendum.'

'We are good, though,' Hollie said.

'Are we? *Really?*'

She resisted the urge to jump in and continued stroking Hugh's head.

'All this therapy, Hollie, and you going off on retreat … I've been thinking, why would you need this if you were happy? And if we don't have a kid, what is there to keep us together in the long run?'

The irony of this statement seemed to be lost on him, thought Hollie.

'Love?'

'Yeah, I thought Jill loved me and look what happened there. One mistake and it was game over.'

Hollie could feel her equanimity slowly beginning to drain away.

'All this talk about unconditional love, it's all bollocks … love is always conditional.'

'I think that depends on whether it's real love, or attachment.'

'What does that mean?'

'The nun who ran our retreat talked about this—'

'Oh great, advice on relationships from a celibate nun who doesn't live in the real world, what does she know about it?'

'I—'

'I'm sorry, but I'm not in the mood for a lecture. I just want to lie here.'

'Okay,' Hollie said, trying not to feel too disappointed.

She thought about her ceremony with Krystina.

What if Hugh needed to let go of fatherhood, or at least the idea of how he had expected fatherhood to be? Would this help him to heal? Maybe he could go to Footprint Island and find what he needed too. But now was clearly not the time to say anything. There would be time to tell Hugh all about Footprint Island tomorrow.

'Hugh.'

'Uh-huh.'

'I'm not unhappy.'

Hugh grunted.

'I think I'm just searching for something. Knowing I won't be a mother, I need to find what my alternate path looks like. To find meaning and purpose as a childfree woman.'

'But you have a good job, and our life together. That must mean there's something missing. That we are not enough.'

'It's more nuanced than that. It's like … It's like I can feel this force inside me, a seed of something that needs to grow and be expressed, a kind of … motherhood energy you might say.'

'Motherhood energy? Well, if you have this, why not try for another baby?'

'It's just not my path.'

'What does that even mean? Sounds like you're speaking in riddles.'

'It's hard to explain. It's just something I can feel in my body. A … *knowing*.'

'I don't understand.'

'Sorry, I'm probably not explaining it very well.'

'So how do you know there's this alternate path? What if *this* is it?'

Hollie looked at the gleaming brass bed frame, the art deco light fittings, the polished mahogany wardrobe and matching chest of drawers, noticing the luxuriousness of their surroundings. What if Hugh was right? What if she was missing the point and *becoming the eggcup* was about being a container for gratitude, for everything she already had? An invitation to find the deeper meaning where she already was, rather than seeking a different route. To participate in life, rather than feeling like a spectator of it, skimming the surface.

'Good question. I don't know. I just have this intuition that there's something deeper which needs to be expressed, something that needs to come from within me.'

Hugh sighed and sank further into her lap.

'So anyway, you had a nice time on Footprint Island?'

Hollie paused.

Nice.

It seemed such an inadequate word to describe her experience.

Profound. Intense. Nourishing. Enlightening. Strange. Wonderful.

Any of these words would have been much more accurate, but right now, what was the point in trying to faithfully convey what had happened?

'Yes, I had a lovely time, thanks.'

'Good. And it's good to have you home, sorry I'm being all doom and gloom.'

'It's okay.'

'I promise to cheer up by tomorrow.'

Hugh turned his head in her lap and looked up at her.

'What is it?' Hollie asked

'Just looking at you. You feel a bit different.'

'Different how?'

'Calmer. Like a Buddha.'

~

The following day Hollie walked into a large boardroom set out in a horseshoe formation. She felt as though she were levitating a few millimetres off the ground, gliding through a stage set.

'Jesus,' whispered her colleague Mike, Director of Nursing, as they sat down. 'Looks like we've landed in Middle Earth!'

Hollie tried to maintain a poker face as she suppressed the urge to laugh. On the opposite side of the table, the senior leaders of another mental health trust were assembled. Markedly older on average than their team, predominantly men with skin the colour of the old cotton handkerchiefs her dad used to keep in his pockets, dressed in drab grey suits and dull ties. They had been called to a confidential meeting following rumours of a merger and the tension in the room was palpable as each side eyed the other. White china cups and saucers and expensive looking biscuits were stationed at various points around the table, lending a genteel façade to the atmosphere.

'Welcome, everyone. For those of you who don't know me, my name is Peter Wandsworth and I'm the Chief Executive of NBW NHS Foundation Trust. Today is an important milestone in the evolution of our organisations, as we can officially announce our boards are in talks about a potential merger. At this stage, plans are highly confidential, but we wanted to take this opportunity to share some relevant context, as we will be working together over the coming months to explore how we might make this work for the benefit of patients in our region. I hardly need to tell you there are many challenges facing us: a growing mental health crisis, funding challenges, a hostile political environment, and the prospect of us leaving the EU. So it makes sense for us to explore the potential for joining forces. Before I dive into a presentation, I'd like to invite Harriett to say a few words.'

An angular, sour-faced woman stood up. She was about six feet tall with very long legs. Her mousy blonde hair was cut in a short, functional style, and she wore a formal collared shirt with the buttons fastened right to the top.

'My name is Harriett Kayne and I'm the Chief Executive for CWV NHS Foundation Trust.'

Hollie tuned out, opening a notebook she had bought from the boathouse shop. On the front was a picture of gnarly trees entwined together across opposite sides of a road, forming a verdant green archway. The road cut straight through the centre of the image and bent to the right, off into the mysterious distance. It seemed emblematic of the search for her alternate path to motherhood.

She thought about Krystina, picturing her in the island garden, dappled in sunlight. Hollie had left her contact details in the card she had given her on the jetty but had not heard anything. She wondered what Krystina's reaction had been when she discovered the gift she had left waiting for her at reception: another week on the island, fully paid for. She imagined Krystina's smile filling the small reception office with radiant light as she opened the envelope and read her card. Perhaps she would never hear from her, and this was as it should be. Maybe it was fitting that her first incarnation of motherhood energy should be to give without any expectation of a return. A simple, small act of generosity, done quietly and wholeheartedly. She hadn't even told Hugh about it. In fact, she hadn't really said anything to Hugh. She had waited for him to say *tell me everything*, but the invitation never came. Hollie tuned back into the room as she heard people starting to introduce themselves.

As the creeping death moved towards her, Hollie was reminded of the first session in Serenity Hall. She imagined Ani Zopa sitting on the opposite side of the table, dressed in a suit and killer heels with an air of confidence and authority, her penetrating eyes piercing the charade of carefully choreographed gentility, into the unseen and unspoken depths. If she had held a high-flying city job, Ani Zopa must have been in meetings like this one. What, she wondered, had happened to catapult her out of that world? Had she simply reached a point where she was no longer able to straddle the two parts of herself? Had the lure of a path leading off into the mysterious distance, become more enticing than the safety of the well-lit, well-worn corporate carpet to success?

Hollie was brought back into the room by the sound of Mike's voice cracking a joke next to her as he introduced himself with his usual charming self-deprecation, momentarily punctuating the awkwardness with nervous laughter.

'Hello, everyone, my name is Hollie Hardwick,' she said next. 'I'm the people director for NBW Foundation Trust, and I'm looking forward to working with you all.'

Her words sounded oddly hollow.

Truth and Lies

'Thanks for coming with uz, Hollie, I know it was a bit short notice,' Lesley from Bensham said as the train began to pull away from the station.

'Thanks for asking,' Hollie replied. 'Was I first choice, or last resort?'

'To be honest, you're the only person I know who'd be interested and can afford to come.'

'Fair enough.'

'Helen thinks I fancy you,' Lesley from Bensham said, chuckling to herself. 'I mean, I told her you're canny fit and that, but you're not my type.'

'Too la-dee-da?'

'Aye. Exactly.'

'Well, I'm glad that's settled,' said Hollie, watching Lesley from Bensham unpack the contents of a small grey rucksack onto their table.

'Full fat Coke and bacon and egg sandwiches, this is your breakfast?'

'Yeah. I need some stodge for this early on a Saturday. I bet you already went to the gym and had some lettuce leaves or something?'

Hollie picked up a white paper bag next to her feet and put the contents on the table.

'What's that?'

'A bagel with spinach, cream cheese, and smoked salmon. Apple compote with natural yoghurt and almonds, and an energiser smoothie.'

'Jesus, you're so middle class.'

'It's called healthy eating, Lesley. Giving your body nutrition and good energy.'

'Maybe, but I bet it tastes disgusting!'

'It's delicious. I dare you to try some,' Hollie said, unwrapping her bagel and offering it.

'Na, you're alright, I'll stick to my e-numbers, thanks,' Lesley from Bensham said as she tore the plastic from the front of the sandwich packet and took a bite.

'Can I ask you a question?'

'What about?'

'Brexit.'

'Bit fucking early for politics, Hollie,' Lesley from Bensham said, rolling her eyes. 'What about it?'

'Hugh and I were talking about it last night, after we got that leaflet through the door with all the details on how to vote. He's convinced we are going to end up leaving, and I wondered what you think about it?'

'Me? You want insight from a chav, is that what you mean?'

'Very funny. Believe it or not, I'm genuinely interested in your point of view. I'm starting to wonder whether I'm in a bubble by assuming we'll remain.'

'I reckon everyone I grew up with will vote leave. For them, the EU is for people like you; it's all bagels and feta cheese and paperwork. It doesn't mean anything. They just think it all sounds poncey and middle class. So, give them a chance to stick two fingers up at the French and Germans, they're gonna take it!'

'That's similar to what Hugh said.'

'The other thing you have to remember, Hollie, is the baddies always have better slogans.'

'Apart from *may the force be with you.*'

'Yes, apart from that ... I bet you can't even remember the one for Remain.'

'Er ... not sure.'

'Exactly. But everyone knows *Take Back Control.*'

'Good point.'

'I'm getting hot now, must be talking about politics at 6:30am!'

Lesley from Bensham removed her hoodie.

'And before you say anything, I know I'm fat and I probably should eat better, but ...'

'Actually, I was going to say I like your Superman T-shirt,' Hollie said. 'It's very you.'

'Cheers.'

'Well done for accepting a compliment, Lesley, this is progress.'

'I'm a fast learner!' Lesley from Bensham said. 'Speaking of which, did you know the Superman symbol is actually a Kryptonian symbol?'

'I thought it was just an S for Superman?'

'That's what everyone thinks. But it's actually a symbol that means hope.'

'Hope?'

'Yeah.'

'I love that,' Hollie said, gazing out of the window for a moment.

Maybe Lesley from Bensham inviting her to come on this writing course was her first step along her path, she thought. The first real sign of movement since coming back from the island. The image of the

Green Tara rock painting flashed into her mind. Maybe this was her getting into action?

Hollie turned back and looked at Lesley from Bensham.

Who would have thought this unlikely woman would be a portal to her inner journey? First to Footprint Island, and now again this weekend? The universe, Green Tara, or whatever, clearly had a playful sense of humour.

'Your T-shirt feels serendipitous.'

'What does that mean?'

'It's when a seemingly random encounter happens that feels like really good luck. Like a sign you're on the right path.'

'I felt like this when Helen bought me this workshop for my birthday. I was down in the dumps about writing, and my book, ready to chuck it all in. Kept thinking, *Who the fuck do you think you are like, Lesley, believing you could write a book*! Over and over. I didn't even tell Helen. When she gave me my birthday card, she said she wasn't sure why she had booked the workshop, but just felt strangely drawn towards it. A bit spooky.'

'Speaking of spooky, I wanted to thank you again for that card you gave me at the end of Phemi's course. It ended up leading me to a Buddhist island. I did a mindfulness and meditation retreat there a few weeks ago.'

'What's the island called?'

'Footprint island.'

'Never heard of it.'

'It was amazing. From the moment I stepped off the ferry, I felt this positive energy emanating from the earth. The whole place felt alive, as if it knew exactly what you needed.'

'Now you're definitely sounding cosmic, Hollie. You'll be wearing bangles and burning incense sticks before you know it!'

'Can you imagine!' Hollie said laughing.

'And what did the island give *you*?'

'It helped me let go and grieve for motherhood.'

'So you're not sitting in your departure lounge anymore?'

'No. Not sure where I am now, but I don't feel empty anymore. I feel infused with a kind of … motherhood energy,' said Hollie tentatively, as if she was still testing the idea.

'What's motherhood energy when it's at home?'

'It's like a longing to nurture, and express, and create. A calling towards something beyond yourself.'

'As in writing your book?'

'Maybe. I definitely have a sense there's something inside me that needs to be birthed.'

'If it happens on this writing workshop, will that make me your midwife?'

'Yeah, you can be my most unlikely birthing partner. You've certainly got the T-shirt for it!'

A few hours later they got off the tube and walked to the venue. Lesley from Bensham grabbed Hollie's arm as they stood in front of an impressive red-brick building.

'God, it looks like a Victorian workhouse.'

'Apparently it used to be a fire station. Maybe it will set our creative fires alight!' Hollie said, trying, and failing, to lighten the mood.

'Whatever you do today, don't leave me alone with them,' said Lesley from Bensham.

'With who?'

'All the middle-class people.'

'You're so chippy. I'm sure they'll be perfectly nice, and mostly human.'

'Just promise. I'm not good with strangers.'

'Okay,' Hollie said, linking arms with Lesley from Bensham as she pressed a buzzer next to a glass door that looked like the entrance.

'Hello, we're here for the writing workshop,' she said, replying to a perky woman's voice that came through the speaker. They followed signs for the workshop, ascending several flights of stairs inside a square tower. The white walls were decorated with a history of the fire station over the ages and associated stories of heroism. Hollie smiled to herself as she imagined her father climbing a huge spiral staircase within the granite circumference of his lighthouse. They entered a large, brightly lit conference room with a pea green carpet. A circle of chairs was set out in the centre. All the seats were taken apart from two.

'Shit,' whispered Lesley from Bensham behind her, 'it looks like a fucking AA meeting!'

Hollie counted fourteen other people. Twelve women and two men.

'Good morning. I'm Vivienne Tarala and it's my pleasure to be leading our workshop, *Fiction Writing: Truth and Lies,*' the facilitator said in what sounded like a New Zealand accent. Almost six feet tall with wavy, sandy-colour hair that curled round her chin in a flapper style, Vivienne had large white teeth with a cute gap in the front, and a wide smile. Hollie guessed she was in her early fifties, although there was something radiantly youthful about her.

'Everyone has a story,' she began.

She had the most beautiful voice. Soft, slow, and full bodied. A dreamy once-upon-a-time voice.

'Stories,' she said, dropping and slowing her voice even more, 'resonate … deep … in our bones.'

Vivienne Tarala paused, creating a soft silence for her words to land as she looked around the circle.

'Stories are how we make sense of our world. We *live* inside our stories, continually walking into our life from our past, seeing our world through the lens of memory – of who we have been and therefore understand ourselves to be, and projecting this identity into the future. And it begs the question … what is truth? And what lies are we telling ourselves about who we are, or are capable of becoming?'

Hollie felt as though she were being slowly bewitched just listening to her speak.

'The great news, then, is that we are all, each of us, born storytellers. And today, I am inviting you to dig deep into the raw material of your life and experience to fuse together memory and imagination, so you can become more skilful story-tailors … able to stitch together the threads of fact and fiction to weave rich, compelling narratives. To create a woven fabric from all the loose ends that seem to have no meaning or purpose.'

There was a deep hush in the room. Hollie felt as though the tendrils of the words were entwining themselves around her wrists and legs, binding her to her chair with their enchanting threads. Vivienne drew a flipchart towards her and turned onto the first page with a graceful movement, revealing a list, *The Ten Commandments of Creativity by Julia Cameron*.

'Who here has heard of *The Artist's Way* by Julia Cameron?'

Hollie raised her hand, along with half of the room, feeling a surge of recognition as she remembered a conversation with a lovely Glaswegian guy called Ronnie in the dining room on Footprint Island. They had bonded after having both witnessed a woman let out a loud fart in the middle of a meditation session and dissolved into giggles together when later recounting the incident to others in the group. Ronnie, it turned out, had been writing a book about his dad's life working on the shipyards on the Clyde and had urged her to buy Julia Cameron's book when she told him that she also wanted to write. Until now she'd forgotten all about it.

She looked at the second commandment.

There is an underlying, in-dwelling creative force infusing all of life – including ourselves.

This was the feeling she had been trying to describe earlier when Lesley from Bensham asked her about motherhood energy.

'I highly recommend Julia Cameron's book as a guidebook for liberating your creative self. I expect some of you might find her use of the word *God* off-putting and I invite you to let go of this and stay open to the idea of it being shorthand for pure creative force, rather than the Santa Claus fella at pearly-gates-dot-com.'

Laughter rippled round the circle as Vivienne sat back down and picked up a battered copy of *The Artist's Way*, littered with dozens of page markers.

'*Art*, says Julia Cameron, *is an act of the soul, not the intellect.*'

Vivienne closed the book and placed it back down on the carpet.

'I would like to invite you to think of our gathering today as a sacred circle of trust. A protective container where we can allow our most vulnerable, creative selves, to be seen and witnessed.'

Vulnerable.

That word again.

Hollie noticed Lesley from Bensham's right leg twitching next to her.

'By way of beginning, I would like to invite you to tell your five-minute story. Who you are, what has shaped you, and what has led you here.

To feel our story, and sit with the significance of it, is one of the most powerful experiences we can encounter. Only when we feel into our own story can we learn to make meaning of what has happened to us. And if we are going to learn how to tell stories as fiction writers, we need to have the courage to lean into our own story. To open our hearts in service of our work.'

Vivienne stood at the flipchart again and turned over another page.

'Who has heard of *the hero's journey*?'

A couple of people raised their hands.

Vivienne drew two vertical lines on the flipchart. In front of the first line, she wrote a single word.

Ending.

'The hero's journey is a concept by Joseph Campbell, an American author and teacher who studied all the great myths from across the world. He discovered what he called the *monomyth*, a pattern underpinning all stories that resonates deep in our psyche. A blueprint that charts the journey of the human spirit and is commonly used as the scaffolding for all good stories. Distilled down, we can think of it in three parts. First, the hero receives a call to adventure: something happens that challenges him or her to leave the ordinary world behind. This can be a literal journey, or an inner journey, which sparks an ending of some sort.'

Hollie saw the image of her and Hugh lying on the kitchen floor that night.

'Then the hero crosses a threshold and moves into another realm.'

Vivienne turned to face the flipchart again and wrote two words in between the lines.

Liminal space.

'This is where the heart of the story unfolds. Here, the hero faces challenges, meets mentors and adversaries, and goes through a process of maturation. We can think of it like being in transition, in a birth canal.'

Was this what being in the departure lounge had been? Hollie thought.

'Finally, the hero moves into a ...'

Vivienne wrote *New beginning* behind the second line on the flipchart.

'But they only enter a new beginning after they have passed through a *dark night of the soul*, a break point where they must surrender to the inner darkness of intuitive knowing if they are to move forward. At this point, there is always an ending. It can be the literal ending of a way of life, or a way the hero has known and related to him or herself. By letting go, the hero finally learns the lesson of their journey and grows into a new version of themselves.'

Hollie wondered what dark night of the soul might be lurking in store for her.

'God, that was torture,' Lesley from Bensham said as they walked out of the building to get some lunch a few hours later. 'I couldn't stop my leg from shaking. Fucking embarrassing.'

'Well done for what you shared. I was proud of you.'

'Are you patronising me?'

'No. It was powerful and raw. You could see the impact it had on people. Maybe you still have some work to do on accepting compliments though!'

Lesley from Bensham grunted and shoved her hands deep into the pockets of her jeans.

'I loved listening to everyone. Very different and unique stories but you could see the same pattern emerging in each one: a longing to dive below the surface of life, into something deeper and more vivid,' Hollie continued.

'I know what you mean.'

'Did you notice, most of the people in the room didn't have children. I wonder whether this was coincidence?' said Hollie.

'Dunno.'

'I've always thought having kids automatically bestows your life with meaning, without you having to work very hard on your own development. Like being a parent offers a kind of get-out-of-jail-free card because you can focus on your kids and avoid confronting your own emptiness.'

'You mean, the old … *My-kids-are-the-best-thing-I've-ever-done* routine … *It's hard but it's sooooo worth it.* And the … *You-don't-know-true-love-until-you've-had-children* bollocks. Really pisses me off when people say this, so fucking smug. Like women are just incubators whose whole life purpose is to produce sproggs!' exclaimed Lesley from Bensham.

'Like you're not a fully actualised human being, or able to experience real love or joy in any other way,' Hollie agreed.

'Yeah … I mean, why is it anyone's business who you sleep with, and whether or not you decide to have kids? Why do we even need to have a reason? So many people who become parents never really think about it. And surely putting another life in the world is something you should fucking think about! Surely, it's better to regret *not* having children than later regret having actually had a kid you didn't really want?'

'I completely agree.'

'Take my dad for example, Hollie. A-grade psychopath. He should never have had kids. And did he suddenly discover his compassion and empathy when he became a father? Did he shite! Try watching your mam get the crap beaten out of her because the tea isn't on the table on time and tell me that doesn't develop your ability to empathise!'

'Sorry, I didn't mean to trigger you.'

'It's allreet man. I think me blood sugars are just dropping. I get like this when I'm hungry.'

Hollie picked up the pace a little.

'When I said get-out-of-jail-free card, I was more thinking in the sense that having children gives you something outward, beyond yourself, to focus your attention and energy on. And takes care of leaving a legacy. Maybe if you don't have children, you're more likely to be confronted with the search for meaning, and thinking about what you leave behind?'

'You mean people without children are deeper?' said Lesley from Bensham, smiling.

'I think I'm wondering whether we have a propensity towards being more inward. For a start, if my experience if anything to go by, I didn't just think twice about having kids, I thought about it a *million times*!'

'Ditto. Me and Helen talked about it endlessly. She was ambivalent like you, but she eventually realised hell was going to freeze over before I'd ever have kids, and we're very contented with our fur babies now.'

'And having children pulls you to participate in the external world, whether you like it or not,' continued Hollie. 'Maybe in choosing not to have them you step away from the conventional path and become more of an observer, questioning what life's all about?'

'Well, look at monks and nuns and that, Hollie. They are celibate and childless for a reason. Anyway, enough of this philosophical talk, let's get something to eat before I lamp someone.'

~

For the final activity that afternoon, the group reconvened in the circle and were invited to share a piece of writing they had worked on.

The room fell deathly silent.

'Hollie, isn't it?' Vivienne said, looking straight at her. 'Would you like to share your piece? I think you said earlier you had been working on an idea for a novel inspired by your father's life as a lighthouse keeper, right?'

'Er, yeah,' said Hollie, feeling her palms becoming clammy.

She looked at Vivienne's open, encouraging smile. She could hardly say no now.

'O...kay,' she said, feeling her heart beating in her throat.

'This is an opening scene I wrote ...' Hollie began.

~

About half an hour later, Hollie was sitting on a bench at the side of a canal with the sun on her face when Lesley from Bensham approached.

'What the fuck, Hollie?' she said, standing directly in front of her, blocking the sun.

'I—'

'What did I say to you when we arrived?'

Hollie looked at her, momentarily thrown off balance. Lesley from Bensham's lip was curled like the first time she saw her, as though she was squaring for a fight.

'I said whatever happens, don't leave me. And what did you do? Fucking left me in there.'

'I'm sorry ...'

'Words, Hollie. Just fucking words. You're full of them, but action is what counts. You promised.'

'I'm sorry, Lesley,' Hollie said, trying to keep her voice even.

'You talked about having motherhood energy before. Well, mothers are supposed to stand by you and not leave.'

Hollie had never said she was *her* mother, but she could see Lesley from Bensham was in no mood for such nuance.

'What's the matter with you, anyway? Why'd you do a runner after you read out your writing? Yes, you got some suggestions to work on, but nobody said it was shit or anything.'

'I don't know, I … I just don't think I can do this.'

'Do what?'

'I feel like I'm trying to contrive this alternative path. Ever since I knew I wouldn't become a mother, it's like I'm searching for something … chasing this longing feeling for something I can't even explain. Trying to connect to this in-dwelling force. I guess I thought after going to the island something would happen, but now I feel more stuck than ever and so humiliated that I got my hopes up. I should just be grateful for the life I already have. Maybe like you say, motherhood energy is just bullshit. I made a choice not to be a mother and that's it. End of. I just need to move on and focus on the life I have, rather than some pretentious idea of being an author or birthing something.'

'This is what I fucking hate about all you people.'

You people.

Hollie felt the sting of her words. Perhaps she had been foolish to start believing they had formed some kind of friendship. Maybe this was another thing she was kidding herself about, and Lesley from Bensham was waking her up to the cold, hard truth, like a sobering punch in the face.

'You know your problem? Choice. Too many fucking choices. You've never had to really struggle for anything. I mean really struggle. Every opportunity is laid out in front of you and yet you sit there, agonizing … *Oooh how do I make the right choice, the best choice? What if I make the wrong choice? What if I'm not enough?* … You whine on, morning noon and night, paralysed by your own self-doubt. Well, some of us, Hollie, don't have the *fucking luxury* of self-doubt.'

Hollie looked down at the ground in front of her, feeling like a rag doll fished out of the canal.

The luxury of self-doubt.

The phrase hung in her mind, flapping like a piece of washing on a line.

'It's like you just expect to be great at everything, but you never really put yourself on the line.'

'What do you mean?'

'I bet deep down you wanted that teacher to tell you that your writing was a creative masterpiece, and you're going to change the fucking world with this book, didn't you?'

'I …'

'Well, let me tell you something about this motherhood energy, or this … what did you call it? … *in-dwelling creative force*. It's not about wearing a fuckin' pinny with matching shoes and making your house smell of lemonade, you know. Motherhood energy or whatever you want to call it is fuckin' primal, Hollie. It's howling at the fuckin' moon. It's wild and untamed. It's digging your nails in the dirt, arching your back and being covered in sweat. It's cleaning blood off a floor on your hands and knees. It's messy and tough and it breaks your heart and kicks you in the balls. And yet despite this, you do it anyway, because you can't not. There's no choice. It's like breathing, you be creative or you die. That's fuckin' living real art, not preaching about it. You can't control it or tidy it up. You have to surrender to it, like Phemi said. Be prepared to be brought to your fuckin' knees by it. Birthing something, something from deep in your marrow, tears you open and makes you shit in your bed. That's the proper hero's journey, Hollie. You have to risk it all, get past your massive ego, and be willing for the class to laugh at you and the teacher to fail you even though you have bared your fuckin' soul.'

Lesley from Bensham's body went limp, although her hands were still balled into fists by her side. Hollie looked at her, this fierce, unlikely teacher with the Superman symbol stretched across her chest. Part of her was affronted at being spoken to like this, and yet there was something undeniably invigorating about the piercing, unvarnished honesty of Lesley from Bensham.

Maybe, she thought, this was Green Tara getting into action after all, taking her forward-facing foot and kicking it right up her arse.

Maybe this was hope looking her straight in the eye and testing how serious she really was about the commitment she made on the island. Whether she really wanted some kind of transformation, or just liked the idea of it.

'So what you're saying, in summary, is that I have to get a grip, grow a pair, and stop being a control freak if I want to release my motherhood energy, creative kraken?'

'Aye.'

'Okay, I got the memo. And sorry for leaving you with a bunch of hummus-eating strangers,' Hollie said.

'It's allreet, Hollie. Think I might've over-reacted a bit.'

Rumblings

Hollie removed her sandals and felt the cool sand beneath her feet.

'Thanks for suggesting an evening walk, Diane. I hardly ever come out on a school night.'

'Glad I managed to tear you away from work.'

'You'd think with my mum living near here, I'd come to the beach more often, but I seem to forget to go outside and get into nature. I spend my life sitting in front of a computer screen.'

'I love walking barefoot, there's something so grounding about it,' said Diane

'Yeah. And I definitely need to ground myself just now,' replied Hollie. 'I've been feeling pretty dislocated and untethered recently.'

'What's going on?'

'Since I got back from Footprint Island a few weeks ago, it's like I have this sense of not being quite here.'

'The Buddhist place you went to, the one you messaged me about?'

'Yes.'

'Untethered, how?'

'As if normal life is less real. When I was on the island, I felt somehow … more *me*.'

Hollie stared into the distance towards the lighthouse where they were heading. The sky was washed with hues of pink, and the setting sun glimmered on pools of sea water left by the low tide.

'The conversations I had with people felt deeper. And somehow everything seemed infused with meaning. I felt this aliveness there, but since I've come home, I … I don't know, I'm not even sure what I'm trying to say, Diane. I guess I'm not sure what I'm doing or where I'm going anymore.'

Hollie sighed and looked at her feet, feeling the cold, compacted sand.

'You mean that feeling when you have a really great holiday and you come back and want to jack everything in, pack your bags, and go travelling? When you think there must be more to life than being on the hamster wheel?'

'I just felt I'd really made progress, you know. I did a ceremony with a lovely woman I met called Krystina, where I let go of motherhood and I had this beautiful feeling of peace about not becoming a mother. When I got back on the ferry to come home, I had such a sense of optimism, as if I was about to embark on a new beginning, to find an alternate path to motherhood. But in the last few weeks I've lost faith again.'

'Why?'

'I had this mad idea that I was infused with motherhood energy'

'Motherhood energy? That's an odd phrase. I'm not sure I would like the idea of being defined by what I'm not.'

'It's something Krystina said on the island, and it just really resonated. The idea that there is a deep-seated need to create that's hard-wired into us, as women. A creative, in-dwelling force. I thought of it as giving birth to something from inside myself, creating something that continues to grow out there in the world after you've gone.'

'You mean leaving a legacy?'

'I suppose so. Leaving something behind feels like it's becoming more important.'

'You know, I've been thinking about this a lot lately, the whole idea of what we leave behind and what the most holy-shit version of me looks like.'

'Oh God, I love that phrase. I remember you talking about this at the restaurant.'

'Me too. I've concluded the legacy I'll leave behind is through all the lives I've touched, all the small kindnesses I've bestowed, all the acts of generosity I've made, and all the people I've inspired and encouraged, and the ripples that will continue to flow outwards from each of these long after I've turned to dust.'

Hollie stopped walking and turned to Diane.

'That's one of the most beautiful things I've ever heard, Diane. As you said that, I had an image of each tiny act being like a point of light, illuminating the whole planet like a great Christmas tree,' Hollie said. 'I'm totally stealing this idea.'

'You're welcome,' Diane said, beaming with satisfaction. 'But getting back to what you were saying a minute ago, what happened to make you lose faith?'

'I went on a writing course a couple of weeks ago, thinking I could rekindle my forgotten dream of writing a book, but the workshop leader told me what I'd written was pretentious crap.'

'She actually said that to you?'

'Not in so many words, but she implied it. She challenged me in front of the whole group, and said I needed to dig deeper, that I was trying too hard and needed to go into the emotional core of the story and unearth what it means to me personally.'

'So, she didn't actually say it was crap?'

'I suppose not. But it felt so humiliating. I'm starting to think the idea of writing a book is just a ruse to distract myself from feeling a failure at work, and I should just work harder, be grateful for what I've got, have fun, and stop searching for more. I think that's what Hugh wants me to do.'

'It sounds like you're going through a classic midlife crisis, the old *what's-it-all-about*. If you were a bloke, you'd probably be flicking through a Harley Davidson catalogue by now!' Diane said with a playful grin.

'Very funny,' said Hollie, wondering whether she might have a point.

'So, is work still stressful?'

'Yeah, and it's really ramping up. We're preparing for a merger, so the workload has tripled overnight. Even more meetings, and everything has become hyper political with people jostling for position. If it goes ahead, I'll be leading on the biggest project of my career – developing a new brand, building a new organisation structure, and creating a new set of terms and conditions, all in negotiation with four trade unions.'

'Nightmare. No wonder you feel like heading for the hills!'

'It's the equivalent of disassembling two huge airplanes and simultaneously using the parts to build a new one whilst they are all in flight, without any blueprints. And, at the same time, trying to keep all the passengers happy.'

'Jesus. Hope you have plenty packets of peanuts!'

'Good point,' said Hollie with a half-smile.

'Seriously though, I know it was a big promotion and a hell of an achievement to get this job, Hollie, but it doesn't seem as though you've ever really enjoyed it.'

'I know, but I keep thinking maybe if I could just find a way to hold on to this elusive thing called confidence, it would be okay, and I could learn to enjoy it and stop feeling like I'm these two selves, at war with each other,' Hollie said, gazing into the distance.

'So, you are leading a merger at the same time as feeling split apart?'

'I know, and would you believe the merger is called *Stronger Together*! Like the universe is trying to tell me something, eh?'

'Speaking of which, there's something I need to tell you.'

Hollie stopped and turned to look at her friend.

'I've decided to move back to Scotland.'

'You're leaving?'

'I've been thinking about it for a while and with Brexit on the cards, I just want to be back home. With me and Darren splitting up and the house sale going through, I feel like it's time for a fresh start.'

'I guess that means I'll have to find an actual therapist!' Hollie said, trying to disguise the lurching feeling in her stomach.

'Edinburgh's just up the road. And you can come for weekend retreats when I get settled,' said Diane as she linked arms with Hollie. 'We'll still be un-mothers united!'

'Yes, but it won't be the same,' said Hollie, aware she sounded like a sullen teenager. 'Sorry … what I should have said is I'm happy for you. And to be honest, the way Hugh is talking about Brexit I wouldn't be surprised if we end up emigrating to bonny Scotland with you!'

'How is Hugh?'

'Not good, to be honest. Stephen got married without telling him.'

'Ouch, that must have hurt.'

'Yeah. And the business isn't going well. He's convinced it will fall apart if we vote Leave. I keep saying I can't imagine that happening, but to be honest I'm starting to have my doubts. There's a funny atmosphere in the air, like things are unravelling. I'm worried about Hugh. He's becoming increasingly morose these days and the slightest thing seems to trigger him.'

'Do you think he's angry about you deciding not to have a baby?'

'I'm not sure. It feels more like he has lost hope. Like he is grieving for fatherhood but won't allow himself to actually let go.'

'Sounds like he could do with a ceremony too!'

'You're probably right, but I can't imagine him ever doing anything like that.'

'Men, eh?' said Diane.

They walked in silence for a while, listening to the seagulls and the gentle lapping of the tide.

'I keep meaning to ask, how's your dad these days, Hollie?'

'Slowly declining. I think his muscles are atrophying just lying on his bed all day. Thank God he has a good imagination. Last time I saw him he told me how he had been out walking in the woods with Lady Di. Said she was a *very nice girl*.'

'How wonderful.'

'I feel guilty as I don't see him as often as I should. Work is so all-consuming and the days and the weeks just whizz by in a blur.'

'Does he ever talk about being in the lighthouse?'

'Not since he got dementia. Come to think of it though, I never ask him. I might try next time and see if it sparks anything. I wish I'd asked him more about it when I still had the chance.'

Diane took a deep breath in. 'Ah, smell that, Hollie, the unique and pungent bouquet of seaweed. Good for the soul, eh?'

'Yeah,' said Hollie, inhaling the drain-y, mulchy smell, 'it's so easy to forget we are part of nature, with all its rhythms and squelch. It's like we preen and protect ourselves in this sterile, screened-off world … waking up in a box, driving to work in a box, eating from a box, entertaining ourselves in front of a box. Rinse and repeat. Over and over. And then we wonder why we feel like robots. That's what I mean about being on the island, it felt like coming home, back to a forgotten simplicity in harmony with nature.'

They reached the end of the beach, climbed a set of worn stone steps, and sat down on a wall to dust the sand from their feet.

'You know what, Hollie,' said Diane, 'I think maybe the world needs motherhood energy right now. To remind us that we need to nurture ourselves, and the planet, and find a better way to live in tune with nature. Maybe, instead of birthing children, this is the gift we un-mothers can bring to the world.'

'Is this the work of midlife, do you reckon?' said Hollie, standing back up.

'Yeah,' said Diane, 'maybe we need to turn up our dimmer switches and become like lighthouses, shining in the dark.'

~

A few days later Hollie was regretting that walk. Perhaps if she had just knuckled down and worked that evening, she thought, she would be feeling better prepared.

She went into the ladies' toilets en route to the meeting room. She knew these ones were usually empty. Sitting on the toilet seat in a cubicle, Hollie opened her blue leather handbag, took out her make-up case, and touched up her face in a compact mirror. Her eyes looked small and puffy.

She looked exhausted.

One final push, Hollie, she said to herself.

Forty minutes later, she felt all eyes in the room on her as she finished her presentation.

'Well, thank you for that presentation, it was most informative. It's a shame your paper didn't live up to what you've just delivered, Holl-aaay,' said Harriet Kayne in her drawling accent.

'It would be good to hear your feedback, Harriet,' Hollie said, trying to choreograph her face, but fearing her voice was a pitch too high.

'Frankly, this strategy is a bit of a camel. Doesn't know what it wants to be. Shall we go through the document?' she said with a gleeful flick of her wrist.

No one spoke.

'May I suggest,' Hollie's boss, Phil, interjected, 'rather than going through the whole document, we discuss key points at this stage, given it's just the first draft?'

'No, Phil,' Harriett Kayne said as if speaking to a naughty child who was dangerously close to getting detention. 'I think we should go through the document. Page by page.'

Silence.

The strategy was thirty pages long.

Hollie looked at her chief exec, Peter. He was sitting back in his chair, with a glazed expression of amused detachment. The three other executive directors looked blank.

'And, we have our incentive, don't we?' Harriett Kayne continued, casting her falsetto grin towards the cheap foil platter of regulation sandwiches as she shifted her long legs under the table. Hollie caught sight of black socks with pictures of Daffy Duck on them above a pair of black leather policeman-shoes. She remembered something JK Rowling had once said in an interview about her inspiration behind the character of Dolores Umbridge, about how a taste for the ineffably twee frequently went hand-in-hand with a lack of real warmth or charity.

Harriett Kayne began reading a paragraph from the first page aloud. 'No. No. No, Holl-aaay. I see what you're trying to do here, but you've got it all wrong …' she began, seeming to savour every word of her withering critique. *The bitch with the buttons*, Mike had called her, capturing her character with one deft phrase, the way a cartoonist might bring a figure to life with a single stroke of their pen.

Hollie could feel rumbling, like a fault line was cracking opening underground, so visceral it seemed like dust might come through the polystyrene ceiling tiles at any moment. She considered leaving the room for a toilet break but feared the slightest movement might release an eruption. Panicky, she shuffled in her chair and leaned to one side, trying to contort herself to make bends inside her body so it would be harder for the rising energy to come out. She glanced up at Peter, hoping he would intervene and challenge. He looked like a still, cool reservoir, just sitting there, taking it all in. He gave Hollie a small nod, as if to say, *Hang in there.*

Hollie looked back down at her paper, grabbed her pen and feigned writing notes, trying to nod sagely to indicate she was attentively taking it all on board. Harriet Kayne continued her monologue, with a tone of voice that sounded like an eternally disappointed headteacher, weary from the burden of being the only responsible adult in a room full of underachieving pupils.

Feeling lightheaded, Hollie zoned out. She looked back at the buffet platter and heard a booming voice inside her head.

I don't want to eat a fucking sandwich from another shitty fucking buffet!

She looked back down at the juddering, spidery scrawl in her notebook. It looked more like the reading from a seismograph than actual handwriting.

'Holl-aaay, are you alright?'

'Yes, Harriet,' she said, grimacing through her teeth. 'Just my stomach rumbling a bit.'

Suddenly, she remembered something Peter had told her about Harriet. *She had a son. Tragically killed in a car accident. Only thirteen years old. Marriage fell apart afterwards and don't think she ever got over it.*

Hollie looked again at Harriet.

Perhaps those buttons were a necessity? Fastened right up to her neck as a way of holding herself together. And what if the policeman shoes were the only footwear that felt sufficiently robust to keep her upright and walking, able to put one grief-stricken foot in front of the other? Maybe her son loved Daffy Duck, and kept her grounded to the memory of him?

Be compassionate, she said to herself as she imagined Ani Zopa looking at her again.

~

'How was your day?' Hugh asked that evening as they sat down to eat jacket potato and beans. 'Sorry it's a bit basic, I couldn't be bothered to cook.'

'It's okay, I'm not hungry,' said Hollie, staring vacantly at her plate.

'I've noticed you haven't been eating much recently. You're starting to look a little bit skinny.'

'Now you sound like my mother.'

'How about a drink?' said Hugh, standing up and fetching a half-empty bottle of wine from the kitchen bench.

'You been drinking?' Hollie said, immediately regretting her slightly judgemental tone.

'A couple of glasses, before you say anything,' he said, pouring a large glass to the brim. 'Sure you don't want one, might help you relax?'

'No, thanks.'

'How did the board meeting go?'

'Bitch-with-the-buttons ripped the strategy to shreds.'

'After you busted a gut to get it done! I thought it was only supposed to be a draft?'

'It was.'

Hollie leant her elbow onto the table, put her head in her hand, and pushed beans round the plate with her fork.

'What are you thinking about?' Hugh said.

'I keep having this weird rumbling feeling, like I'm splitting open. Today in the meeting, I had an outburst in my head, this loud angry swear-y voice shouting.'

'You're just stressed, babe. Why don't you speak to your boss, whatshisname? It's probably just too much stuff going on in that busy head of yours.'

'I could,' Hollie replied, already starting to regret saying anything.

'Just write down all the things on your mind, get everything out, then talk it through. Ask for help.'

'Yes,' she said, trying to sound appreciative of the advice, despite feeling pricked by the word *just*. 'But Phil already has enough on his plate, and I don't want to seem incompetent.'

'Isn't there anyone else you can speak to then?'

'Maybe Miranda, the external consultant who's helping us on the project.'

'So, you talk to this Miranda and just ask for the help you need?'

There it was again. *Just* …

'The problem is, I'm not sure what I need to ask for. Whether I actually need more resources, or the issue is just how I'm viewing things.'

Hugh looked exasperated.

'It's okay,' Hollie said. 'I'm not sure I want to talk about it.'

'You always do this,' he said. 'You make everything so complicated. Why don't you just ask for help?'

Hollie could feel her jaw tensing. She put her fork down, as if she didn't even have the energy to bear its weight.

'I feel like you're giving me solutions, but I need to work this out myself.'

'So what do you want me to do?' Hugh said, trying to contain his evident frustration.

'Ask me questions to help me understand what's going on.'

'Like what?'

'Like, what do you mean when you say you have a rumbling feeling?'

'Okay … so what *do you* mean?'

'It's like a foreboding, that something is coming.'

'An earthquake?'

'Remember years ago when there was that huge tsunami. The tide went out and there was this weird prescient atmosphere before it hit. It's like that. Like a pause point, before a gigantic wave hits.'

'So what are you going to do if a tsunami is coming?'

'I don't know.'

'Well, could you get a tractor, or a helicopter to help?'

Appease him, Hollie, he's trying to help, she said to herself, trying to counteract the annoyance of him messing with her metaphor.

'Yeah, I could do,' she said, hoping to end the conversation. She could detect a slight change in his voice now, on the verge of starting to slur his words.

'So then, what *do* you do?' Hugh asked, leaning forward.

'Run away?'

'So there is a tsunami coming towards you, and you're just going to run away? What about other people on the beach?'

She was getting really lost now. There'd been no people on her beach. She tried adding some into the picture in her mind.

'So you're comparing completing a merger to a tsunami? Do you really think it's an appropriate way to think about it?'

Hollie was clenching her fists under the table now.

'It's … just … how … I feel,' she said, carefully enunciating each word.

'Do you even want to do this job, Hollie?'

'I don't want to carry on this conversation,' she said and got up to put the kettle on. 'I know you are trying to help but you are just making things worse.'

'Great. I'm doing what you asked, but I'm making it worse. Thanks.'

Hugh walked out the room and slammed the door.

~

'Morning, everyone,' Hollie said, addressing her three colleagues in the room, and Miranda who was on the screen via video call from London.

'As you'll see from our agenda, our focus today is to decide our approach to the new terms and conditions package, so we can get key principles signed off by the Executive Team before taking a paper to Remuneration Committee next month. Before we start, let's have a quick check-in. How are you as we begin today, and is there anything you need to let us know?'

'I'll start,' said Hollie. 'I'm slightly afflicted by a silly injury. I went out for a run this morning and as I was taking my leggings off to get in the shower, my middle finger got caught and I heard a horrible crack as it bent back. Look!'

Hollie held up her right hand.

'I think that's called a hammer finger, Hollie,' said Phil, Hollie's boss. 'Probably need to get it seen to.'

'I've been calling it my ET finger,' she said, laughing as she moved it towards the screen.

'Phone home. Phone home.'

Hollie watched with detached curiosity as her finger continued to move forward as if under its own volition.

'*Phone home.*'

She hadn't intended to say this a third time, and as she heard the words come out of her mouth with more emphasis, she felt a strange sensation, as if something was beneath the guise of her joke. She withdrew her finger and looked at it in puzzlement, as if it didn't quite belong to her.

'I know this sounds odd, but I've just had a strange feeling that I need to ring my dad's care home,' she said. 'Carry on and I'll be back in two minutes.'

Hollie stood in the corridor and dialled the number. Shannon, the care home manager, answered. 'Hollie, I was literally just about to call you,' she said. 'I'm very sorry but your dad has been taken ill. He's been under the weather for a few days and had a fall. We think he might have fainted, but we don't know exactly what's wrong. The paramedics have just arrived and are going to his room to assess him now.'

'What?' said Hollie, trying to take it in.

'If he needs to go to hospital the paramedics will need to speak with you. Is this the best number to get you on?'

'Yes. I have back-to-back meetings all day, but I'll pick up if you call.'

Hollie called her mother to update her, then walked back into the meeting room.

'Are you okay?' said Phil. 'You look like you've seen a ghost.'

'Weirdly, my dad's had a fall. The paramedics just arrived.'

'Do we need to reschedule?' Phil said.

'No. Let's go ahead, otherwise we won't hit the deadline for papers. There's nothing I can do just now, but I'll have to dip out if they ring back,' Hollie said, feeling slightly dazed.

'I think you must have a very strong connection with your father,' said Miranda. 'In Hindu culture, we might call this a soul connection.'

'Yeah. My mother is always saying I'm just like Dad,' said Hollie.

'It's funny you say this, Miranda,' said Martin, one of Hollie's senior HR officers who was sitting opposite. Martin looked like an archetypal bank manager from a black-and-white Saturday matinee film – conventional and reliable, the kind of person who did the same thing, in the same meticulous order every day, a man to set your clock by, who could spot a misplaced semi-colon at ten paces. Hollie had expected him to be rolling his eyes at the mere mention of something as esoteric as a soul connection, yet he looked surprisingly engaged. 'Last year, before my mother died, I started feeling a strange pain, all down the side of my right leg. I hadn't injured myself so I couldn't understand what was happening. I was very close to my mother, and it turned out that she had also fallen and broken her right hip, at the same time as my leg began hurting.'

'Well, I must say, this Steering Group meeting is already shaping up to be infinitely more stimulating that I had imagined. Who knew that terms and conditions of employment could be so enlightening!' Phil said, chuckling. 'I'm sure good old Albert Einstein said something pertinent about this kind of phenomena … spooky action at a distance, he called it, I believe.'

Hollie felt the air tingling around her.

'I had a funny experience with our Lizzy last year,' said Margaret, an

HR manager from the other trust. 'She got pneumonia and was in intensive care for days. Her lungs had collapsed, and they had to force litres of oxygen into her every minute to inflate them. It was touch and go for a while and I remember this one night, I was lying in bed at home after a twelve-hour stint in the hospital. I had been dozing and, honestly, plain as day, as clearly as I'm hearing you speak now in this room, I heard Lizzy's voice and the sounds of her gasping for breath. Right there in my bedroom, as if she were next to me.'

'I wasn't going to say this,' said Miranda on the screen, wrapping a dazzling lime green scarf round her shoulders, 'because it sounded … well, frankly, a bit too weird, and I'm always especially hesitant when working with clients in the mental health sector, but now I feel right at home here in this conversation, so what the heck!'

Everyone, including Hollie, was now glued to the screen.

'I had a really odd dream last night. And something you just said Margaret reminded me of it. You are I were talking, Hollie, and I said to you … *It's time.*'

'Time for what?'

'No idea,' said Miranda. 'That's all I remember.'

Hollie gulped, feeling everyone's eyes resting upon her. Her mobile phone rang, breaking the silence, and she excused herself again. It was the paramedic team.

'Miss Hardwick?'

'Yes, speaking.'

'I understand you have power of attorney for health and wellbeing for your father?'

'Correct.'

'We are very concerned about him. He's fainted and is very confused and dehydrated. We also understand he's been losing weight recently.

At this stage, we aren't sure what's wrong, so he's going to need further assessments to find the cause of his illness. Given your father's age and condition, moving him is a risk, and is likely to place additional stress upon him by being in an unfamiliar environment.'

'I understand.'

'We can take him to hospital, or he can stay here and we can arrange for his GP to come and see him. Obviously leaving him here is a risk if he deteriorates, as the home are not set up to treat your father and will only be able to make him comfortable.'

'My dad hates hospitals. He would want to stay and be comfortable,' said Hollie.

'I understand, Miss Hardwick. We will make your father as comfortable as possible for now and I expect his GP will be in touch with you in due course.'

'Thank you,' said Hollie.

Later that day, as Hollie was preparing to leave the office, the doctor called.

'I have to be honest and tell you that your father is gravely ill, Miss Hardwick,' he said. 'His white blood cells are sky high, he's not taking on fluids, and his kidneys are shutting down.'

'Are you saying he's going to die?'

'I'm saying that, unless he makes a miraculous recovery, his prospects are not good. We could still take the option of moving him to hospital, but there are risks attached to this too.'

'I understand. So, unless the situation improves, my dad is going to die?'

'That is certainly a potential outcome at this juncture.'

'I know he wouldn't want to be moved. I've spoken with my mum and sister, and we are in complete agreement. He'd want to die rather than have medical intervention.'

'Okay,' the doctor said, hesitating 'And speaking off the record, in your situation I'd want the same if it were my father.'

'Thank you. That's very kind of you to say.'

'We will make him as comfortable as possible. I'll give him some morphine before I leave, help him rest.'

'How long do you think he has?'

'Unless he starts to make a recovery, I'll be surprised if he is still with us come Monday.'

That evening Hollie sat on the side of her father's bed watching him doze, propped half upright on his pillow.

He looked so pale and fragile, like a tiny bird.

She thought about the last time they had spent time together, before his dementia had really taken hold. It had been about six months before the kitchen floor moment.

It felt like a lifetime ago now.

They had visited a pretty coastal village not far from her mum's house and sat on a bench at the side of an old wooden Watch House building overlooking the mouth of the river.

'Look at this, Hollie,' he had said, removing the plastic lid from his tea. 'Even drinking tea has been beautified.'

'What do you mean, Dad?'

'Everyone walking around posing with these cups, looking pretty. Before all this marketing nonsense, we used to enjoy our hots drinks from proper mugs. Sitting down, actually talking to one another. But now it's all about being seen to be drinking tea and coffee, as people walk along looking at their mobile phones. I mean, look at this preposterous lid!' he said, holding it in front of him like an

285

anthropological specimen. 'These lids burn your lips, and they are awkward to drink out of, and when you are walking you can't actually get a good sip out of them, so you have to wait for the drink to cool down before you can actually drink the damn thing, thus defeating the purpose of enjoying a hot drink. And if you do take the lid off, you spill it as you walk. And, to add insult to injury, they have the audacity to print a pretty message on the side about how your sustainable cup is helping to save the environment. Don't make me laugh! I mean you couldn't make this up. How many landfills must be teeming with these plastic lids? But because a pretty message is printed on, and it all looks so lovely and benign, it has the image of being good, so we tell ourselves it's alright.'

'I can see what you mean,' Hollie said, marvelling once more at her father's ability to say the same thing over and over again, as if he were telling you for the first time.

'And this is happening in every walk of life, Hollie. There's no end to the ways that we enslave beauty to make money. We're not having the actual experience anymore. We're being seen to have a facsimile of the experience, packaged up to look so beautiful on the outside that we forget the substance has been hollowed out. It's a magician's trick, a collective sleight of mind.'

'Good phrase, Dad.'

'So we're left with this empty feeling that something is missing, but when we look around us we see a pretty cup, a beautiful house, a glossy car – so our brains are reassured that everything's okay because it *looks* good. Because beauty creates belief. That's why, when you walk into the head office of any large economic or religious institution, the buildings are so magnificent. This is not a coincidence, Hollie. It's the weaponization of beauty to make our brains believe that what we are seeing is truth. Beauty soothes us, it makes us feel safe. Ugly people and ugly things are not good for business. And this is the ultimate irony – we are plundering the beauty of nature to manufacture fake beauty to cover up the ugliness we are creating. And as the chasm grows ever wider, the process of beautification accelerates and extends into every aspect of our lives to reassure us that the good ship Earth is not really sinking.'

Her father had snorted with laughter and shaken his head as he sipped his tea.

'I feel as though I'm just an observer of it all now, Hollie. I am perched in the crow's nest on top of the *Titanic*, like an eagle on the rooftop of the world, just sitting watching the theatre of it all and marvelling in mankind's utter stupidity.'

Hollie had changed the subject by telling him she was writing again, a book inspired by his time as a lighthouse keeper. She had shared the first few pages, hoping he might say something encouraging.

'I think I can see where you are trying to go with it, Hollie,' he had said when she finished reading aloud, 'but the tone … it has a sentimentality to it. I mean, your writing has some nice pretty flourishes here and there, but it feels lacking in any central idea, you know, something that is going to really cut through and make an impact. I can't imagine many people would want to read it, to be honest with you.'

'I see, Dad,' Hollie had said, trying to disguise her hurt.

'You're a clever girl, but I think you are naive about the world and what's really going on.'

Hollie remembered she had taken a deep breath and looked out at the mouth of the river where a small tugboat was making its way towards the open sea, wondering whether he was right or whether it might be time to let go of seeking approval from her father.

As she replayed the scene now, Hollie reflected that perhaps her father and Ani Zopa were not as far apart as she might have first imagined. In some ways, her father had been teaching her about mind poisons all her life: warning her of the folly of becoming attached to shiny, pretty things, training her to recognise life's delusions, and urging her to go inward and cultivate her imagination.

She thought again about that time he'd come to their house to visit, commenting that it looked like 'a beautiful show home'. And this was *before* they had completed all the renovations.

Had she fallen for beautification's sleight-of-mind magic trick?

Had she built a life that looked beautiful on the outside, but was somehow hollowed out?

A life that was slowly sinking?

Hollie was brought back into the room as her father began to stir.

'I'm here, Dad,' she said, gently stroking his papery hand. 'It's Hollie.'

Her father opened his eyes and gently squeezed her hand.

'I've been waiting for you.'

She wondered whether she should pull out her notebook in case he was about to say something profound.

'Are you ready to fly off your perch now, Dad?'

He looked at her again, his head cocked to the side, just like Julian Finch had done, but his eyes were unfocused as if he were slipping in and out of realms.

Destination Joy!

Hollie was sitting in the study upstairs. She'd been awake for hours practising her father's eulogy that she would be delivering later that morning. She stared out of the window, watching the birds in the trees as the sun warmed the sky, feeling a faint stirring, as if something were out there in the ether slowly approaching from far away. She wondered whether this was her father's presence somehow communicating with her.

Suddenly, she was startled by a banging noise that came from outside.

'FUCKING BASTARDS!'

She got up from her desk and peered out of the window. The door from the lounge was open and Hugh was standing on the patio at the bottom of the garden, smashing their *Remain* sign against the wall. Hollie wrapped her velvet dressing gown more tightly around herself and went downstairs into the lounge. Hugh walked back into the room, red-faced and sweating.

'We're leaving the EU, Hollie! I told you this was going to happen! The turkeys have voted for Christmas!'

Hollie looked at the large TV screen in disbelief as she watched the ticker tape of breaking news with the sound muted.

6:00am. EU referendum result. Breaking news. Leave 52%. Remain 48%.

'Oh my God.'

'We're screwed Hollie. Can you believe they voted *leave* in fucking Sunderland, for God's sake? All these people who work for Nissan, they actually voted to come out of the EU! This country has lost its mind.'

Hollie stood like a statue, gawping at the screen, breathing heavily with her mouth wide open as tears spilled down her cheeks.

'It's game over for our business. Our main clients warned us that they'll be moving their headquarters to Holland if this happened. We won't survive without them, Hollie.'

She felt tectonic plates shifting inside her.

'I bet you what will happen next … that lunatic Donald Trump will become president of America and then the whole world will go to hell in a handcart. This is the beginning of the end.'

Hollie imagined her father standing in the crow's nest on the *Titanic*, shouting, *Icebergs ahead*! She held her hands in front of her eyes and turned them over, half expecting the edges of her outline to begin dissolving.

'Are you okay?'

'What?' Hollie said slowly, as if Hugh's voice had penetrated her mind from far away.

'You are staring at your hands like an alien who just landed inside a human body.'

'I feel death upon me,' she said, still staring in shock at the TV screen.

'What do you mean?'

'Like I'm becoming pixelated and everything is breaking open.'

'You are grieving Hollie, it's a lot to take in, today of all days.'

'It feels like it's something more.'

'More than what?'

'Bigger than Brexit and my dad dying. Like I'm being swallowed up inside a huge ending.'

'It *is* an ending. The end of our country as we know it. The end of us having influence in the world. The end of believing that people in this country actually care about the future of young people. The end of clean beaches, and open borders, and free trade. It won't be too long before we are swimming in our own sewage again, waving union jacks, and arguing over Gibraltar, just like the fucking good old days. So yes, it is an ending. It's an ending of ever feeling proud to be British.'

Hollie was still standing in front of the TV like a zombie.

'I'm going to get a drink,' said Hugh. 'Do you want one?'

'No, thanks,' said Hollie.

Hugh returned into the room a few minutes later. Hollie had still not moved.

'Is that whisky?'

'Jack Daniels,' said Hugh, swigging a big gulp from the glass. 'What time did you get up anyway? I didn't hear you leave the bed.'

She had woken up in the darkness, crying silently into her pillow. She was relieved he hadn't noticed.

'Around three o'clock, couldn't sleep again. I've been rehearsing Dad's eulogy.'

'You happy with it now?' said Hugh.

'I've managed to read it aloud about twelve times without dissolving into tears, so that's progress. I think I probably need to rehearse it in front of a live audience now. Are you up for listening?'

'Yeah. Take my mind off this shitshow,' he said pointing to the TV and searching for the remote.

~

Later that morning, Hugh and Hollie filed into the crematorium chapel and walked slowly along a cobalt blue carpet to take seats in the front row at the end. There were six other mourners. Hollie's mum and sister, two old friends of her parents, and two staff from the care home. Summer sunshine was streaming in through a large, decorative window behind the lectern where Aunty Ruby was already standing, looking glamourous as ever in a cream suit with gold accessories. Hollie gazed up at the window. It was a large rectangle about ten feet high with a rounded archway at the top, like the kind you saw in churches. It was framed by a vaulted ceiling that mirrored its shape. Her father would approve, she thought. The room had an elegant simplicity. It felt like a space where there was room to breathe and expand. A space large enough to be a container for all the love and grief that vibrated inside these walls.

The door on the right opened and the undertakers entered, carrying her father's coffin. It was plain oak with gleaming brass handles. Her father had always loved polishing brass. Hollie felt her hands trembling as the undertakers gently laid the coffin on the catafalque and Aunty Ruby stepped up to the long microphone.

'Good morning everyone …' she began as a ray of sunshine beamed through the window at the opposite end of the room, lighting her flame red hair.

'We are gathered here today to commemorate the life of my brother, Robert Hardwick. We are here to laugh together, to cry, to pause, to reflect, to wrap words around our sorrow, and to say goodbye.'

Hollie felt her heart pounding and drifted off. *It's time*, she heard inside her head. She thought back to the rehearsal she had done with Hugh earlier in the kitchen. She had been okay at first but had begun weeping uncontrollably halfway through.

'I can't do this,' she had said.

'I know it's hard, Hollie, but you can do this. You're a great presenter,' Hugh had said, standing up to give her a hug.

Hollie had put her hand up to stop him like a traffic warden.

'No, don't hug me,' she had said. 'I need to let this emotion come out and work its way through my body.'

Hugh had sat back down, shrugging his shoulders like a petulant child.

'Think of it this way,' he had said, 'it's ten minutes. You're reading what you've written down, you're a great writer, and you've rehearsed lots of times. Nobody will mind if you get emotional. And if worse comes to worst, I'll take over.'

Gazing through the arch window, Hollie took a deep breath, inhaling the stillness of the crematorium. It reminded her of Serenity Hall. The same feeling of calm and spaciousness. She imagined Ani Zopa looking at her, smiling enigmatically.

'And so,' continued Aunty Ruby, 'I will now invite Robert's daughter, Hollie, to begin our ceremony with a eulogy. The word eulogy comes from the Greek and means "to bless". Today we are blessing my brother's life. Giving thanks for it and sending him on his way with our love.'

Hollie gulped and stood up. Her legs felt drunk. *It's time ...* she heard the voice say again. She stood at the lectern. She could feel her heart pounding in her throat.

'My father ... was a remarkably unique person,' she began, looking out at the small audience.

Hugh gave her a thumbs up. Hollie's voice cracked as hot tears fell down her cheeks. She looked at her mother. She was also crying, whilst giving her an encouraging smile.

'He ...'

Hollie blew her nose and stood a little straighter, like a drunk person trying to sober up to prove they can walk in a straight line.

'He grew up in a large, drafty house on the south side of the river that looked like a worn piece of stage scenery. His mother, Lillian was a famous opera singer and his father, Frank, was vaguely self-employed, generally preferring to spend time in local bars where his gift for storytelling drew roaring crowds of admirers. His mother's steely ambition clashed with his father's genial indifference, creating an emotionally volatile environment. As he grew up, my father found solace running wild and free on the moors of his imagination. This eventually led him to become a lighthouse keeper, which seemed to fulfil a kind of prophecy uttered to my grandmother by a travelling gypsy when my father was a baby. Don't worry, she had said, *the light shines brightly upon him …*'

Hollie glanced towards her mother who now had tears streaming down her face and she began to shake.

'I'm sorry …' she said, grabbing another tissue as the flow of tears overwhelmed her ability to dab them gracefully. Hugh stood up and walked to the lectern, put his arm around her shoulder, and gently removed her speech. Hollie walked down the steps, but instead of returning to her seat she found her legs carrying her out of the chapel. Outside, she stood with her back against the wall next to the main door, breathing deeply to get fresh air in her lungs. She could hear Hugh continuing to read the eulogy.

'Sorry, Dad,' she said, looking up at the sky.

Sunshine warmed her face and a soft breeze fluttered through the leaves on the trees. She smiled, reflecting that pre-Footprint Island Hollie would have been tearing herself to shreds right now for being so flaky, willing herself to get back in there. Instead, she felt that her father would have approved of her having walked out to commune in nature, rather than following what everyone said you were supposed to do.

Hollie dug into her handbag, removed a packet of tobacco and some papers, and rolled a cigarette. She had persuaded Hugh to buy them for her earlier that morning and was comforted by the ritual as she thought about how her father would berate her for smoking. After standing for a while, her attention was caught by a small bird flying in her eyeline. It landed in a large oak tree, just across the path directly in front of her, and sat on a branch as if it was looking at her.

'Dad?' she whispered inside her head as her eyes filled with tears. 'Is that you?'

The bird stayed still.

'I love you,' she said, smiling up at the little bird.

The bird moved its head and she imagined this was her father trying to communicate.

'What is it time *for?*' she asked the bird.

It flew away across the canopy of trees and disappeared.

Hollie walked back into the chapel and sat on down as Hugh finished reading the final lines of the eulogy she had written. He stepped down from the lectern and sat back next to her, grabbing her hand. 'Thank you,' she whispered, squeezing it. Aunty Ruby stepped back to the lectern and winked at Hollie.

'Thank you, Hollie and Hugh, for that powerful eulogy. We are now going to take a few minutes for some quiet, personal reflection. As you go inwards, I invite you to call to mind your memories of my brother, and to remember your relationship and all he brought to your life. And as we do this, we will be accompanied by one of his favourite pieces of music, *Morning Mood* from *Peer Gynt Suite.*'

Hollie drifted off again and imagined that little bird flying, dipping and weaving on slipstreams of air, soaring high in the sky above a vast sea, heading towards a lighthouse.

'Now comes the time when we say our final farewell to Robert,' said Aunty Ruby when the music faded out. 'As we say our final farewell and release his body, we can think about all the ways we will remember him, and stay connected, to the energy of his unique spirit.'

Aunty Ruby turned to face the coffin.

Robert, my dear brother, we bid you farewell.
Into our memories

we let you go.
Into the cycle of living and dying
and rising again.
We let you go Robert.
May you rest in peace.

~

The following evening, Hollie walked into the utility room attached to the garage. She unhooked the rope that held the wooden pulley of clothes and lowered it, looking for her favourite little black dress. There, next to it, was a pair of her father's tartan pyjamas that she had brought from the care home and washed following her final visit. How could the body that inhabited them be gone? she thought as she stared at them. How could the normal background whirr of domestic routine continue in his absence? Why had the world not stopped, even if just for a while? She pulled the pyjamas from the wooden rail and held them up to her face, inhaling their freshly laundered scent. 'Dad ...' she whispered. Hollie slumped to the concrete floor and wept into the soft cotton folds, remembering how she sat on the edge of his bed that day.

'How long have you been here?' Hugh said, sitting down next to her and putting his arm around her shoulders. 'I heard you crying upstairs.'

'I don't know,' said Hollie. 'I found my dad's pyjamas.'

'Do you still want to go to dinner? We can cancel if you want.'

'No. It's been booked for ages, I'll be okay,' she said. 'I think it's just another wave of grief hitting me.'

Hollie wiped her eyes on the pyjama top.

'I feel hollowed out, Hugh.'

'You're feeling empty again?'

'It's different this time. Like a huge clearing is being created inside me.

As if I'm preparing for something. I keep thinking about the sound of Dad's *Titanic* bell when Aunty Ruby rang it at the end of the funeral.'

'For whom the bell tolls …' said Hugh.

'Isn't that Hemingway?' said Hollie.

'I think so.'

'I keep hearing this phrase, going round and round in my head. *It's time* …'

'Time for what?'

'No idea.'

'Maybe it's time to write your book? If your Aunty Ruby is anything to go by, there are clearly storyteller genes in your family'

'I don't know. I've tried so many times and I can never get past my inner critic voice, you know, telling me how I have nothing to say, how my writing sucks. I tried this writing practice that the woman talked about on the writing workshop, but I just don't seem able to keep up the discipline, and work is so stressful I never have the headspace. I always feel so exhausted. And I keep thinking about what the course leader said about owning and writing my story, but I don't feel like I have anything to say.'

'I know, but that won't last forever.'

'I suppose so.'

'What if …' Hugh hesitated.

'What if what?'

'What if …'

He looked as though he was about to say something but changed his mind.

'What if … we just go out and have a lovely evening? We can celebrate your dad, drink some fizz, and say *fuck it* to Brexit.'

'Okay. That sounds like a good plan.'

~

A few hours later, they were sat in the dim light of the restaurant at a table tucked into the corner, finishing off their meal.

'Would you like any liqueurs?' asked the waiter

'Yes, please,' said Hugh. 'Two double Jack Daniels, an Amaretto, two filter coffees, and the bill, please.'

Hollie stared at the tealight in the green holder on the table, trying to steady her gaze and feeling woozy from the champagne they'd consumed over the course of dinner.

'Babe …' Hugh said, reaching out to hold both her hands across the table.

'Yes?'

'There's something I've been wanting to talk to you about for a while now, but it's just never seemed like the right time.'

'Okay,' Hollie said, trying to focus.

'Might not be the right time now either, but … I don't know how to say this, so I'm just going to come out and say it.'

Hollie could feel her heart racing, adrenaline coursing through her body as if bracing herself to jump out of an airplane.

He looked at her straight in the eyes.

'I think we should move to Australia.'

Hollie blinked, feeling as though a clean, sharp incision had just been made in her stomach. As if a blade had been inserted, in and out, in a single swift move.

'What? Emigrate ... for good?'

'I know, bear with me ...'

'Are you serious?'

'One hundred percent. I've been thinking about it for a while.'

Hollie felt herself slowly pixelating again. As if invisible dust particles of energy had started to dissolve round the edges of the outline that delineated her body.

'I ...'

'I know it's a lot to take in, but just think about it for a minute. The business is not going to survive and, to be honest, I don't have the heart to reinvent it, especially given whatever the post-Brexit future is going to look like. One way or another, whatever happens next is going to be a total shit-show; either a sudden and dramatic one, or just a slow decline, and frankly I don't want to be here to see that happen. Your dad is dead now and your sister will look after your mum when the time comes. And you hate your job anyway—'

'I don't *hate* my job.'

'Okay, if you say so, but let's be honest, it's not making you happy, is it?'

'Well, no, but—'

'Just let me finish, please. I know I'm a bit drunk, but I'm serious, Hollie.'

'Okay,' she said, feeling her mind spinning its wheels.

'The business, if we sell it off, will still be worth something. Even if it isn't, we own the building, and the digital marketing company in the basement want to expand and have approached us about buying it. David and I have discussed it and we could sell to them and make a killing. I've checked it all out and, if we also sold our house, we'd easily have plenty of money to get into Australia through the points system. I reckon the house would get snapped up so I think we could be gone, within … maybe six months.'

'So, we sell our lovely house, and I leave my job, in the middle of the merger?'

'We could figure all that stuff out. Give them plenty of notice to find someone to replace you.'

'But where would we go?'

'Stephen lives in Brisbane, so I thought we could move somewhere near there. And you never know, maybe I might finally get to be in his life. And Brisbane is supposed to be a cool place. Remember my mate Dan, who I used to play tennis with a few years ago, went off travelling?'

'Vaguely.'

'I bumped into him at the gym the other day. He just got back, and we had a beer. He ended up living there for a while, and … get this …'

'What?'

'He said it was quite spiritual. Dan! Can you believe that?'

'Isn't he a mechanic or something?'

'Yeah. Fixes army vehicles. Probably the most unlikely person you'd ever expect to use the word spiritual. And I thought to myself, maybe this is a sign, you know. Time for a fresh start. A new adventure. Maybe this is what that phrase of yours means … maybe *it's time* to begin over again.'

'I don't know what to say Hugh.'

'And there's something else …'

Hugh paused as the waiter returned to the table with a tray of drinks and the bill.

'Let's raise a toast, Hollie,' he said when the waiter had gone. 'To new beginnings, whatever they may be.'

'To new beginnings,' said Hollie, clinking his glass in a daze.

'Dan also told me about this lighthouse near there, right out on the eastern peninsula. Apparently the most powerful light beam in the southern hemisphere. He told me a story about how he went there with a woman on a midnight walk, and they sat on a patch of ground and were bathed in this incredible light show.'

Hugh mimed the rotating light beam with his hand, making a noise like a lightsaber.

'He said it was like being inside a snow globe of glittering light. Can you imagine that, babe?'

Hollie felt tingles all over her body.

'And haven't you got a couple of friends in Brisbane?'

'Yes.'

'And I'm sure with your skills and qualifications you could get a job if you wanted. You wouldn't even need to work for a while, if you didn't want to. We'd have enough money to kick back and enjoy ourselves, far away from all the grey and the rain here.'

'Australia? It's not somewhere I even thought to visit, never mind live.'

'I know. But I've been thinking, maybe you were right and there was a reason we didn't have Egberta after all, because now we are free to do things like this. Maybe it's time to really take advantage of being childfree!'

It's time …

The words echoed in Hollie's mind again. Could this be it, time to leave and start a new life?

After paying the bill, they stepped out of the restaurant, and she breathed in the warm air.

It was a clear, still evening and people were coming out of the park, couples still dressed in shorts and flip flops, laughing and carrying picnic blankets.

'Just think,' said Hugh. 'In Australia, we could enjoy a more outdoor life, more picnics and sunshine.'

She wondered what her father would have thought about Australia, imagining he would lecture her on its lack of culture and sunny superficiality. 'Remember, Hollie,' he always used to say, 'the best ideas always come from the grottiest surroundings.' They walked past an imposing Catholic church on their left and Hollie felt a sudden urge to stop, as if her feet had commanded the rest of her body to cease walking before her brain had even registered the order.

'Can we go in the graveyard, Hugh?'

'A bit morbid, don't you think?'

'Maybe, but I really want to walk round … *please*.'

'Okay, but just for you.'

They entered slowly through a side entrance off the main road.

'I love graveyards, they're so peaceful,' Hollie said. 'It's like you can feel the atmosphere vibrating with love.'

'I think they're creepy,' said Hugh.

'Don't you ever wonder about all the people who have died over the centuries and wonder who they were, and how they lived, and about all the dreams and hopes they had? Whether they really lived the lives they wanted?'

'No.'

They walked down a path and Hollie stood still, looking up at the tall spire. Something rustled in the trees up to their left. 'Sssshh,' Hollie said, putting her finger to her lips as Hugh stood swaying slightly, looking as if he was about to speak. An owl hooted. 'Wow,' said Hollie, as her eyes filled with tears. 'I know it might sound a bit weird, but I feel like my dad is here.'

'Really? Not sure he would be hanging out here, babe. He was never exactly a fan of the church.'

They walked towards the sound of the owl and stopped underneath the canopy of a large oak tree. The leaves rustled, as if holy breath was blowing gently from the unseen. Hollie looked up at the imposing church, backlit by a huge ethereal moon. Light was shining from inside the building and her eyes were drawn to a round, stained glass window with a dove in the middle, carrying a branch in its beak. An image of her father flashed through her mind. She turned to face Hugh who was swaying slightly behind her about five feet away from the base of the tree, as if he might keel over at any moment. Despite the alcohol, she suddenly felt oddly clear-headed and alert.

'Hugh, I know you don't believe in God, but ...'

'What?'

'... but just imagine you died, and found yourself at the pearly gates, and came face to face with God. What would you say?'

Hollie had no idea why she said this.

'Don't believe in God ...' Hugh said, half speaking to her and half muttering to himself.

'I know, but just imagine, if this happened, what would you say?'

Hugh paused.

'God ... is just a convenient excuse for people to trash the planet. Why d'you think all these right-wingers believe in him? May as well believe in magic pixies.'

Hollie felt as though the earth had stopped turning and was momentarily holding its breath. As if an all-seeing eye was watching her.

Did *she* believe in God?

There was a time when her answer would have been no. But now …
well, she definitely believed in something. She looked at Hugh's face
clearly illuminated in the moonlight as if he was suddenly a stranger
and felt a churn of dread in her stomach. Something peculiar was
happening. Her body was standing a little taller and more erect, as if it
was making room for something unfurling inside her. She looked up at
the moon and an image of Lesley from Bensham flashed through her
mind.

Motherhood energy, it's primal Hollie.
It's howling at the fuckin' moon.

Suddenly, she heard a voice bellow out with startling clarity inside her
head.

'I don't want to be happy … I … WANT …
JOYYYYYYYYYYYYYY!!!!!!!!!!'

Hollie thought about what Billy had said on the island that day, about
hearing a voice telling him to take a flight to the UK and head north.
Was this now happening to her too? Was this a set of marching orders
… to find a destination called joy? Hollie thought about the moment
she swallowed the pill standing at the bathroom cabinet and recognised
the same feeling. A mysterious, inexplicable *knowing* in every cell in
her body.

Something, or someone, had spoken.

The Cherry Tree

Four months later, Hollie hurriedly pulled the handle of a large, heavy conference room door and opened it carefully, hoping to be as unobtrusive as possible. She was a few minutes late and could hear the speaker had already begun. There were about fifty people packed into the room. Embarrassingly, the speaker paused and turned to look at her as she closed the door.

'So, welcome to today's workshop, *How Talking About Death Can Bring Us Back to Life.*'

He seemed to pause as their eyes met and Hollie felt a flush of heat course up through her body as she stood motionless by the door.

It was him.

Just No Dave.

Hollie saw his eyes twinkle with recognition, as he broke out into a wide smile that revealed the deep dimples in his cheeks.

'Please,' he motioned to her, pointing to the only obviously available chair. 'I'm afraid you have the booby prize of a front seat.'

Hollie walked slowly to the empty seat, limping from the pain in her left leg that she had strapped up that morning. She sat down, opened her notebook, and looked up at the stage. Just No Dave was wearing a mushroom-colour suit, buttercup yellow shirt and a golden striped tie, with the collar unbuttoned at the top. He looked even more handsome than Hollie remembered.

'I have to say, I'm a little nervous, as I imagine you must all be wondering what on earth the chief executive of a veteran's charity is doing here at an HR conference, talking about Death Cafés?'

Nervous laughter fluttered round the room.

'I wondered the same thing, to be honest, the day last year when my chair told me he had invited this man to come and run one at our organisation.'

Just No Dave pointed to the next slide which featured a photograph of a tall handsome man in military uniform.

'Meet Cameron Macleod. A former royal marine who now works for the Ministry of Defence teaching mindfulness and meditation to veterans.'

Hollie shifted forward in her seat, feeling herself being magnetised towards him with the force of a gravitational pull. As she listened to his voice, she noticed an upward intonation at the end of his sentences that made him sound slightly Australian.

'What I learned changed the culture of our organisation and, I believe, has significant implications for how we lead change. I realised the reason so many change programmes fail is because we ignore endings. We are so busy trying to move quickly into the sunny uplands of new beginnings that we fail to meaningfully process our losses. And in doing so, we lose the opportunity to tap into the phenomenal store of energy that is available for our growth and transformation when we fully lean into grief …'

Later that afternoon she was standing in the exhibition hall waiting to speak to a woman on a stand about talent development when she felt a presence behind her.

'I've been looking for you,' the voice said, whispering into her right ear.

Hollie felt a rush of electricity through her body. She turned to see Just No Dave looking at her intensely.

'You smell amazing.'

Hollie thought his cheeks looked slightly flushed. Was he flirting or just being nice, she wondered?

'Oh God. I said that out loud, didn't I? Sorry, think I still have nervous energy after my presentation.'

Hollie laughed.

'It's a Clarins perfume, in case you'd like to buy some, Eau Dynamisante,' she said, wondering if he had anyone special to buy it for as she held her right wrist out toward him.

Just No Dave brushed her skin with his nose as he inhaled her scent.

Hollie felt a surge of heat.

'Mmmm,' he said, 'geranium and lemon.'

'Impressive!' she said. 'Hugh calls it Eau De Old Lady. Says it reminds him of his Nana.'

Hollie felt good for having tactfully inserted Hugh's name into the conversation, like a protective talisman against too much flirtation.

'Are you kidding me? More like Miss Dynamite! It smells ...'

Just No Dave hesitated, as if he was about to say something then stopped himself.

'... lovely.'

'Thanks,' said Hollie.

'So ... dare I ask, what did you think of my session? I appreciate the topic was probably not going to win me any prizes in a popularity contest!'

'It was great. Really. You're a good presenter, very natural. I loved your story and I agree that we don't do enough to talk about endings and messy emotion when we are managing change. Definitely made me think again on how we can help our managers move through the merger we're implementing.'

'Great. And anything you think I need to improve on if I were to do it again?'

Hollie hesitated.

'Be honest.'

'One thing I noticed. Your voice, it seemed to go up at the end of sentences. Made you sound a bit Australian.'

'I hoped no one would notice. It happens when I'm nervous, for some reason. I once had feedback about it from a woman at a job interview, and not in a good way. No idea why it happens, especially as I'm from bloody Lancashire!'

'We all have our strange tics, I guess.'

'And how did your find the actual Death Café session? I was nervous about doing it with a bunch of HR folk, but I think sometimes you just have to dive into these things and allow people to experience it for themselves.'

'I ...'

'It's okay, you can be honest.'

Hollie felt tears pooling in her eyes.

'I ...'

'What's wrong?'

'My dad died a few months ago, so it was a bit intense talking about our relationship to death.'

'Oh God, Hollie, I'm so sorry.'

He leaned towards a nearby table and pulled a tissue from a box.

'Here,' he said, handing it to her.

Hollie dabbed her eyes.

'I know it's a little early, but do you fancy grabbing a drink? Maybe somewhere quieter. I'd love to hear what's been happening since the island. And you can talk, or not talk about your father, whatever feels good for you.'

Feeling a tingle of excitement, Hollie heard herself saying yes before she had a chance to engage her brain and say no. Just No Dave began walking in the direction of the main entrance, talking about some of the places they could go nearby. Hollie walked alongside him feeling hyper present and awake, as if her body was telling her to absorb the moment and take notice of everything that was happening because it was going to be important.

What harm could it do? she thought. *Just a drink.*

It seemed that lots of other conference delegates had had the same idea, as they tried three places that were packed to the rafters, animated with noisy conversation.

'We could go to my hotel?' Just No Dave said. 'I notice you're limping, so guess you probably don't want to keep walking about?'

Hollie didn't respond. Somehow the idea of going to his hotel felt a little too intimate. He seemed to sense her hesitation.

'It's just the bar is lovely. Art deco. And it's set back a few streets, so I reckon it'll be quiet.'

'Okay,' she said, telling herself she was being silly. It was just a bar, after all. Five minutes later they turned a corner.

'This is it,' Just No Dave said, pointing straight ahead. 'The Cherry Tree Hotel.'

Hollie stopped in her tracks as she remembered the image of the two of them entwined beneath the sycamore tree.

'You just gasped. What is it?' he asked.

'Nothing. Just my leg playing up,' she lied.

You don't have to believe everything you think, Hollie, she said to herself as they walked into the hotel, past a small reception where a large flatscreen television was reporting on the latest news from the American election with the sound turned down. Just No Dave held a large, black leather-effect door open for her and she entered the cosy bar, following him down a flight of steps towards a small round table tucked in a far corner.

'Cheers, Hollie. Here's to Footprint Island,' he said, clinking his glass of red wine against hers after returning from the bar.

'Cheers,' said Hollie, holding up her gin and tonic.

'So, I'm all ears,' Just No Dave said, leaning in towards her.

'Not sure where to start. How about you tell me your story first? What has happened for you since Footprint Island?'

He looked up and to his right as if forming a picture in his mind, then back at Hollie, gazing at her intensely again with his dark brown eyes. 'I don't know about you,' he said, 'but I felt different after I came back. Like a tremor had been set off across the surface of my life, but I didn't have the language to describe it.'

'I know what you mean,' said Hollie. 'I felt something shifted for me too but couldn't quite put my finger on it.'

'Exactly. When I look back now, I see I was full of unexpressed anger, and it really started to surface during our retreat. Like the island somehow knew exactly what I needed to confront and was forcing me to open a kind of spiritual Pandora's box.'

'Good phrase,' said Hollie, feeling the hairs go up on the back of her neck.

'I think it started that day when Ani Zopa said *no* to me.'

'I remember that,' said Hollie. 'Your face was a picture!'

'Yeah. I was furious at first, but I think that was actually the start of a healing process for me. As if she saw my anger and knew it needed to be triggered.'

'Spiritual x-ray vision.'

Just No Dave laughed and removed his tie, undoing another button of his pale-yellow shirt. Hollie caught a glimpse of dark chest hair and wondered what his torso looked like underneath.

'On the island I realised I was still angry about my wife dying of cancer and saw how I'd been running away from the pain.'

Hollie nodded as she sipped her drink, inviting him to continue.

'I came back with this clear sense that I needed to process my grief, but I didn't know how to do it. I think I kept expecting this big *ta-dah* moment to happen, and a new beginning to arrive. But it didn't, and after a while I experienced a kind of comedown, like I was floating around as a spectre in my own life. So I did what any self-respecting bloke does and buried myself in work. For a while I convinced myself I was channelling my grief into something positive, when in fact I was just numbing myself to the point of being completely joyless.'

Joyless.

The word jolted Hollie.

'Then what happened?'

'Cameron Macleod showed up and got us all talking about death, and I suddenly had this lightbulb moment. He explained how repressing emotions makes our nervous system feel unsafe, and switches on our fight or flight mode. Pain is a portal he said, and death is part of life; so when we resist change, loss, or death, we are effectively saying no to life.'

'A portal,' said Hollie, tilting her head to one side and stirring her gin with a straw. 'That's a great reframe.'

'Yeah, it was a bit of a mic-drop moment for me. I suddenly recognised the truth of what he was saying – that when we resist grief, we numb the possibility for joy. And then what Ani Zopa said about suffering and impermanence really landed. I realised I was suffering because I was *resisting my grief*, running away, afraid of what Ani Zopa called *the unbearable weight of emptiness*. Trying to make a new beginning before I had really completed my ending.'

'What did that mean for you, to complete your ending?'

'When my wife died, I cried a few tears at the funeral, but that was about it. Instead of allowing myself to feel the depth of my sadness and despair, I told myself I just needed to get on with life and carry on as normal. Instead of being sad, I put on this mask of false positivity, but under the surface I was becoming more and more angry and frustrated, and it eventually started leaking out. I guess I was afraid that if I really acknowledged how I felt, I would completely unravel, lose control and fall into a deep dark pit. I convinced myself that this would lead to a total breakdown, and I'd lose my mind.'

'I get that,' said Hollie, feeling as though he could be describing her own story.

'After the Death Café session, Cameron gathered us round in a circle and got us to tell our stories – the people and events that had shaped us, life lessons, that kind of thing. He began by telling the group his story and somehow, hearing this big tough guy be so open and vulnerable about his own experiences inspired everyone else to open up. One by one, these guys started talking about some of the things they'd seen. Tough, battle-scarred men talking about friends killed, bodies blown apart, guilt they had carried for years because of a moment's hesitation. And we cried together ...'

Hollie pulled a tissue out of her handbag and handed it to him.

'Here. My turn now,' she said, feeling a thrill as she accidentally brushed the skin on his hand.

'Sorry. Don't know what came over me there,' he said, wiping his eyes.

'Must be the wine!' said Hollie.

'Yeah,' he said with a half-cocked smile that revealed his deep dimples again.

Hollie resisted the strong urge to move across the table and wrap her arms round him.

'I know it might sound strange, but it was one of the most beautiful moments of my life, sitting in this circle crying with all these men. And after we cried, Cameron offered to lead us through an exercise called *cutting the cord*. Most of the guys wanted to do it, so I thought I ought to show willing even though, frankly, it sounded completely weird.'

'What's cutting the cord?'

'It's based on the idea that our interactions with people have an energetic imprint. Ani Zopa talked about this a bit on the island, I seem to remember, when she said everything is made up of energy and space, that life is energy in motion.'

'I remember,' said Hollie.

'Turns out this applies to the people we interact with. Cameron described it as cords of connection that join us to one another. Between me and the guy behind the bar I spoke to earlier say, I imagine there is now a thread of connection between us, as fine as the threads of a spider's web. But with one of my old friends, the energy cord might be the thickness of a rope. And of course, with our nearest and dearest, the cord is even bigger and stronger.' As he said this, Just No Dave held his hands in front of his belly button, as if holding a thick pipe. 'I suppose it's a bit like acquiring cookies on your browser each time you look at a website.'

'Makes sense,' said Hollie, wondering what the energy cord between them would look like. The image of a sturdy rope came to mind, like the kind she had climbed in PE at school. Hollie wondered if she still had one connecting her to Egberta, or whether their energy cord had been cut on the island when she had done the ceremony with Krystina.

'Sometimes, we need to cut this energy cord, to allow a new, healthy relationship to re-grow.

Other times, we need to sever a cord for good.'

'So … you cut the cord with your wife?' Hollie said, leaning forward and lowering her voice to almost a whisper.

'Yes,' he said, looking straight into her eyes.

Hollie took a deep breath. She felt a holy heart tug pull at her chest as the weight of his tender yes landed on her body in the silence of their spacious, intimate moment. Just No Dave took another sip of wine and looked up at the decorative gold leaf lampshade on the ceiling, as if he were receiving permission to continue with his story.

'I finally realised I was clinging on to a version of my wife that no longer existed. I'd unwittingly mummified our marriage and was torturing myself by visiting it every day, looking at it through a pane of glass, like a tomb in a museum.'

'That's one of the saddest and most beautiful things I've ever heard anyone say,' said Hollie as two hot tears rolled down her cheeks.

'Here,' he said, smiling at her. 'Have your tissue back.'

'Thanks,' Hollie said, wiping her eyes with a corner that felt dry.

'How did you cut the cord, if you don't mind me asking?'

'We sat in a circle of chairs and Cameron Macleod walked us through a guided meditation. He got us to visualise a theatre where we were sitting in auditorium seats in front of a stage. He told us to allow our intuition to guide the process and watch as people walked onto the stage, without trying to control what was happening. Some he said, would linger on the stage, and these were the people that you needed to cut the cord with. Others would walk across it and sit in the seats, and you had to go with the idea that there was no need to alter your connection with them. It was odd, because for me, some of the people who stayed on the stage were not who I would have expected. Then I remember there was this pause before we moved to cutting the cord, and – I know it sounds a bizarre – but I heard a loud voice inside my head. Really loud. It seemed to come from nowhere. *Where is she?!* it said. And the next thing I knew, Angie walked onto the stage from the left and stood right in the centre. The cord between us was huge,' he said, making a circle with his hands like the size of a rope that would moor a massive ship to a dock, 'and made of white light.'

Just No Dave paused, took a glug of wine, and looked at her intently as if trying to gauge her reaction.

'What is it?' Hollie asked.

'I don't know,' he said. 'I haven't told anyone about this, and I'm wondering whether you think I sound, well, a bit mad?'

'Not at all,' said Hollie. 'In fact, I'm relieved to be honest, because some similarly strange things have happened to me recently.'

'So if I'm mad, then at least I'm in good company?' Just No Dave chuckled.

'Definitely,' said Hollie, relaxing a little more as she felt the gin taking woozy effect. 'So, what happened next?'

'We had to imagine wielding a sharp blade, like a samurai sword, to cleanly cut the cord with everyone on the stage. I remember looking at my wife as I swung the blade. She looked so peaceful, like she was glad it was happening. And at the moment I severed the connection between us, it felt like an umbilical cord had been cut. *Literally.* It was the strangest thing.'

'What was it like afterwards?' asked Hollie.

'I felt this immense sense of peace. And the funny thing is, in a way, I was right. I did have to lose my mind before I could heal.'

'Wow... that's an incredible story, thanks for sharing it.'

'Thanks for listening,' he said, finishing the last of his wine. 'Your turn next. Shall I get another round of drinks?'

'Why not,' said Hollie, feeling slightly lightheaded as she excused herself to go to the bathroom. Inside the ladies' toilets she took a deep breath, pulled her phone from her handbag and messaged Hugh.

Hi babe. Hope you had a good day.
Out for drinks with work colleagues.
Speak later xxx

She re-typed the message, removing with *work colleagues* but it felt uncharacteristically blunt, so she reverted back to the original, keenly aware of the small untruth of that letter 's' looking back at her like a splinter in the sentence.

Hugh messaged back instantly.

Hi babe.
Enjoy.
Watching election coverage x

Hollie was dreading the result. She had the feeling that if Trump was voted in, it would bring the subject of emigrating to Australia up again, which she had managed to avoid on account of being too busy and still grieving.

She re-applied her make up and looked at herself in the mirror.

Maybe Just No Dave is just being friendly.
Maybe he has been put in my path to help me figure something out.
That's all.

'*Yes,*' she said aloud, conflicted about whether she actually wanted this to be true. She walked back into the bar. Just No Dave watched her as she made her way slowly back to their table.

'Two for one,' he said, taking four drinks from the tray he was carrying. 'Happy hour started at five.'

'Ah, that explains why the bar just got busier,' she said, noticing it was also getting louder.

'Yeah, maybe people are bracing themselves for the election result! I have a bad feeling about the whole thing. Anyway, who wants to talk about politics, Hollie, there's nothing we can do about it. What's with this limp of yours?' he asked as she sat down, sounding genuinely concerned.

'My leg just suddenly started giving way under me a few weeks ago. Out of the blue. Not sure why. I haven't had time to go to the gym recently and can't think of anything I've done that would have triggered it.'

'I see,' said Just No Dave as he opened a packet of dry roasted peanuts for them to share. 'Have a medicinal peanut.'

'Thanks,' said Hollie, taking a few.

'So what's your story since the island?'

'Like you said, I think the island gave me what I needed too. I can't remember if I said when we met, but before Footprint Island I went through a long, soul-searching journey, to decide whether I wanted to become a mother after Hugh unexpectedly said he wanted us to start a family.'

'I remember you mentioning it, but you didn't say much at the time.'

'Up to this point, I'd always been ambivalent, so being confronted with making a decision sent me into a state of paralysis – especially when I realised writing endless pros and cons lists was a complete waste of time!'

Just No Dave giggled.

'I know. Who knew, eh?'

'So interesting, Hollie. Ignorantly, I'd assumed that for women, knowing whether or not you wanted a baby would be taken care of by maternal instinct, that you'd just inherently know you wanted to be a mother.'

'Me too. But turns out, it's not true. It was only after psychotherapy, bodywork therapy and a miscarriage that I finally experienced my truth … a clear knowing that motherhood was not my path. But then I was left with this big fat *now what?* question, tugging at me. I had this strong feeling that there had to be something more than just skimming the surface of the normal nine-to-five, climbing the ladder, going out at weekends, and a few mini breaks every year. And somehow, this question guided me to Footprint Island.'

'I'm sorry about your miscarriage, Hollie,' Just No Dave said gently.

'Thanks.'

'And did you find your answer?'

'Yes and no. I felt as though I grieved for motherhood on the island. And, as you said about grief, facing into it seemed to have a catalytic effect. I made peace with having an empty womb in the physical sense, and in doing so I began to feel filled up with a kind of motherhood energy instead.'

'What's motherhood energy?'

'It's the best way I've found to describe a primal feeling of longing I've felt since closing the door to motherhood: not for a baby, but towards nurturing and creating something from within myself. A feeling that there's this whole other life inside me that needs to be birthed. Does that sound crazy?'

'Not at all. It sounds rather beautiful.'

'The problem was, just like you, when I returned home I had no idea where to begin, and I had a disturbing feeling that life off the island was somehow less real. I thought for a while the answer might be something to do with finishing a book I tried to write years ago, so I picked this back up again. But it was like trying to catch a cloud, and I quickly ran aground like all the other times before, full of self-loathing and disappointment. Then I guess I got busy at work, my dad died and ...'

Hollie hesitated, unsure of whether she should be sharing things she had barely spoken to Hugh about.

'And?'

'And then ... well, weird things started to happen.'

'Trust me, I can do weird, Hollie. I mean, look at the things we now label as so-called "normal" – like being plugged into our phones 24/7 and advertising ourselves on a digital book called "Face". Imagine trying to explain this kind of "normal" to our grandparents! If you ask me, normal is just weird waiting to reach a tipping point.'

'That sounds like a T-shirt slogan in the making.'

'Yeah. Maybe I should copyright it!' Just No Dave chuckled.

'Absolutely.'

'So anyway, I'm not letting you off the hook, Hollie, what weird things started to happen?'

Just No Dave shuffled closer, so their legs were almost touching. 'Sorry. I am finding it a little challenging to hear and don't want to miss anything,' he said.

The lights dimmed as Hollie opened her mouth to speak.

'Lights, camera, action,' said Just No Dave. 'Looks as though the stage is set now for you to tell me whatever it is!'

Hollie took a large gulp of her gin and tonic. She felt herself swoon with the fuzzy tingle of the alcohol in her veins, the whirling chatter of the room, and the background music that was now playing.

'It's okay, Hollie. You can tell me anything.'

Surrender ... she heard inside her head.

'Okay ...' she said.

Hollie described what had happened that night in the graveyard as Just No Dave listened intently.

'You know, what you just described makes me think of something else Cameron Macleod spoke about. He said in Tibetan Buddhism they have this idea that we have demons inside us, which are just parts of ourselves that we have repressed and not yet brought to light. Maybe this was your demon speaking to you?'

'A kind of shadow self?'

'Exactly. So what does it mean, do you think ... *I want joy?*' said Just No Dave.

'I've been wondering whether it's the answer to my question ... *What does a meaningful life look like as a childfree woman*? The only problem is I don't have any co-ordinates for Destination Joy, and I definitely don't know anyone who lives in the neighbourhood to ask!'

Just No Dave smiled at her, seeming to appreciate the joke.

'Okay. So let me ask you this Hollie ... is joy actually destination, or a state of being?'

'Now you sound like Ani Zopa!' she replied.

He pretended to fold his arms into robes and pulled a face.

'Very funny. I think you need to work on your equanimity face!'

'Interesting,' said Just No Dave, resuming his normal posture. 'You have been wrestling with how to find joy, and I have been exploring how to lean into grief. Two sides of the same coin'

'Maybe that's why we bumped into each other?' Hollie said. 'To put the pieces together.'

Just No Dave looked at her. She felt sure he was looking at her lips, as if he wanted to kiss her.

'So how's it going, so far, on your quest for joy?'

'Terrible!' Hollie said.

'Oh?'

She sighed as she lowered her eyes to the floor.

'I haven't told anyone this,' she said.

'You can tell me,' he said, nudging her arm, 'by the power of Footprint Island ... scout's honour!'

'Since that moment in the graveyard, I've been feeling really strange. Like an amplified version of me. Two days ago, I was driving back from the office, late. It was dark and raining heavily, difficult to see with all the spray. And I heard another voice in my head ... *Hollie, if you just did this with the steering wheel,*' she said, making a swerving action, '*you could crash and die, and then it would all be over.* The next day I was driving to work. I came to a level crossing that I drive through almost every day, and as I approached, the red lights started flashing and I heard the same voice again ... *If you just drove onto the railway line and stopped the car now, the train would kill you, and then it would all be over.* It freaked me out.'

'I've experienced this too, Hollie.'

'What?'

'Suicidal thoughts. Cameron Macleod talked about this when he came to see our veterans. He said we often get confused by what these thoughts are telling us. He said just as a nightmare is a dream shouting at us because we're not listening, so suicidal thoughts are trying to wake us up to something important we are avoiding and *really* need to pay attention to.'

'You're saying I'm avoiding something?'

'Let me ask you this. How long ago did your leg start giving way?'

'A couple of months ago.'

'So your body has done the smartest thing it knows to do, which is to *literally* stop you in your tracks by collapsing your leg to get you to pay attention to whatever it is that needs paying attention to!'

Hollie stared at Just No Dave.

'And I would also guess, reading between the lines, that you've been too busy to do anything about it, and you have put that strap on, sucked it up and carried on, because you have too much work to do. Am I right?'

Hollie wasn't sure whether he was being caring or judgemental.

'And because you haven't been listening to your body, your psyche has upped the ante!'

'So you don't think I'm deranged?'

'I think there are many things I don't understand in this world, Hollie, and the older I get the more I've come to accept that spooky shit happens. But maybe it's only spooky because our measuring instruments haven't caught up yet.'

'Thanks for saying this.'

'I'm only saying it because I was like you, Hollie ... A-grade workaholic, burying my feelings, keeping on keeping on. And then Cameron Macleod told us that suicidal thoughts are our friend, because they are trying to point us towards something that needs to end. Not literally our lives, as most people think – but an old belief, an outdated way of living, or a redundant story. And I've come to believe that leaning into the swell of grief is the key to unblocking an unlived life.'

'An unlived life, that feels powerful,' said Hollie. 'So you think my leg and my dark thoughts have been trying to tell me that the way to joy is to find my ending, whatever that may be?'

'I can't be sure, but I can say this from my experience … there is no meaningful new beginning without a meaningful ending first.'

'And then, before you get to the new beginning, there's the messy middle to go through, as you said in your presentation.'

'Exactly. Gold star to you!'

'But I thought I had processed my ending on the island, when I let go of motherhood.'

'Maybe you did and maybe you didn't.'

'In fact, for the last two years I feel like all I've done is process endings and float about in liminal space. Going round and round and not moving forwards. It's so frustrating and exhausting. I mean, how long does it take until you can get into the new beginning part, the bit when something good actually happens?'

'If I knew the answer to that Hollie, I'd be a rich man. All I know from what I've studied and understood is that we keep getting pulled backwards on the boardgame of life, until we've completed all the necessary lessons. Only then do we get to pass go and collect our two hundred pounds!'

'My board game is more like snakes and ladders. Only without the feckin' ladders!'

'I hate to say this, Hollie, but maybe there's something else which needs still to end?'

The question hung in the air and Hollie looked down at the floor, gripping the seat with her hands. He was such a good listener, she could feel herself wanting to talk to him about Hugh's suggestion that they emigrate, but it felt risky venturing into a conversation about her marriage.

'Who knows,' she said, trying to convey a lightness she didn't feel.

'Same again?'

'Actually, I think I've had enough. I probably need to get going,' said Hollie, looking at her watch as Hugh's face popped into her mind. A wave of guilt washed over her.

'How about dinner? Get some food in your stomach. The restaurant here is very good, and I'd love to continue our conversation. You haven't even told me about your book yet and you can't leave me on a cliff-hanger!'

'I probably should give Hugh a call,' Hollie said, feeling awkward and slightly furtive.

'Of course,' Just No Dave said. Hollie was sure she detected a note of disappointment.

'Okay, tell you what. You call Hugh and I'll see if there is any space in the restaurant. If not, we can take it as a sign.'

~

Hollie struggled to open her eyes. Her head was pounding, and the room looked unfamiliar. She could hear a faint noise over to the left.

Where am I?

Hearing the question in her head, Hollie felt her stomach lurch.

Oh God, where the fuck am I?

She pulled herself upright and looked around.

She was naked and this was not her hotel room.

Shit. Shit. Shit.

She felt panic fluttering like a trapped bird in chest.

Breathe, Hollie. Breathe.

Her mind frantically scrolled backwards, as if trying to rewind a tape. She saw the doors of a lift shutting and her and Just No Dave kissing passionately as they ascended floors. Then the tape went blank. The only other image was of him putting his hand on the small of her back as she arched herself on top of him. Hollie scrabbled to find her phone which had fallen on the floor underneath the gold-rimmed glass nightstand next to her side of the bed.

No missed calls. No unanswered texts.

'Thank you,' she said under her breath, raising her eyes to the ceiling. 'Thank you'

A door to the left-hand side of the room opened and Just No Dave walked in wearing a white towel round his midriff and holding another in his hands.

She stared at him, suddenly wishing she'd had time to check her appearance.

He was breathtakingly handsome.

'You look like a rabbit in the headlights,' he said.

Hollie noticed she had balled her fists.

'I …'

'What do you remember?'

'Getting in the lift,' Hollie said sheepishly, deliberately avoiding the part about them kissing, as if not saying it aloud somehow allowed it to remain in the realm of fantasy.

'I see,' he said, putting the towel in his hands over his head and leaning backwards into it like a sling. Hollie sat frozen on the bed. Nervous to make a wrong move. Just No Dave removed the towel, put it round his shoulders and looked back at her. He seemed unsure whether to approach her or stay where he was.

'Sorry,' she said. 'I think I was very drunk. I've never done anything like this before,' she said, but instantly regretted the implication that she was trying to find an excuse for ending up in bed with him.

'Listen, Hollie, I'm going to cut to the chase here. I like you, and I enjoyed sleeping with you.'

Hollie winced. A mixture of embarrassment and shame.

'But I also know you're married. And I don't know what's going on with you and your husband, and it's really none of my business. But it sounds like, from what you said last night, you have a big decision to make.'

Hollie was about to interject but he raised his hand to stop her interrupting.

'And ... I just want you to know I don't want or expect anything from you. I feel a connection between us, that's all.'

Hollie nodded, feeling tearful and embarrassed, trapped between an impulse to run out of the room and an urge to be swept up in his arms.

'Thank you,' was all she could manage. It sounded strangely artificial and awkward.

She swung her legs out of the bed and placed her feet on the floor. Her left leg was stiff and painful. She reached for paracetamol from her handbag and took a swig from a glass of water on the side table.

'Can I ask, Hollie, who is Egberta?' he said, moving across the room to get dressed on the other side of the bed.

'Why do you ask?' she said.

'You kept repeating the name in your sleep.'

Meredith Greenway

Three months later, on a grey February afternoon, Hollie followed her satnav to a tree-lined cul-de-sac and parked outside the address Julian Finch had given her. She walked up a path at the side of the large bungalow, opened a tall gate, and entered a well-groomed garden enclosed on all sides by a neat hedge. To her the right was a wooden cabin, about six metres long, perched on top of a generous decking area lined with pots of marigolds and hydrangea. Two stone figures stood sentry-like at either side of the door, a female Buddha and an owl.

Hollie opened the unlocked glass door as instructed and stepped inside. Faded Persian rugs decorated the wooden floor, and ceiling-high shelves stuffed with books lined three of the four walls. She stepped towards them, browsing the spines in a clockwise direction: psychotherapy texts, books on social work, poetry anthologies, feminist novels, and books about sacred plant medicines. To her right was a large writing desk in front of a rectangular window, scattered with papers and books bent open, face-down. On the wall next to the desk was a well-worn cream leather massage bed.

Hollie inhaled the warm, familiar smell of pine wood and childhood memories flooded in. She saw herself in the house where she grew up: pushing up a metal latch and opening the creaky hallway door, padding down the wooden stairs salvaged from an old ship, descending into the dim light of the basement where her father's locked writing shed beckoned mysteriously. Tears pooled in her eyes as she sunk into a green leather armchair and allowed herself to be enveloped in the fuzzy nostalgia of this memory, recalling tiny forgotten details. Trailing her hand along the damp, chalky basement walls. The cold of the concrete floors. The intoxicating smell of burning paraffin mixed with the fragrance of the pine wood inside the shed ...

She was still lost in reverie when a tall woman appeared, accompanied by a shabby-looking three-legged dog. With her waist-length silver hair, Meredith Greenway looked like a Native American tribal elder.

'Hello Hollie, pleased to meet you,' she said as she stepped forward and extended her hand. 'I'm Meredith and this is Alba. She comes to all my sessions. I hope that's okay?'

'Of course,' Hollie said as she shook her hand and noticed incongruous pink diamante hair clips holding back strands of her long grey hair.

'Can I get you anything to drink? I was going to have a cup of tea myself. Just old-fashioned builder's brew.'

'Yes, please,' replied Hollie.

It began to rain as Meredith Greenway shuffled off, disappearing back into the bungalow. The rhythmic patter of raindrops and the sounds of water running into gutters was comforting.

'I love it in here. It really reminds me of my childhood,' Hollie said as they held their steaming mugs of tea ten minutes later.

'In what way?'

'My dad had a wooden shed like this, in the basement of the house I grew up in. It was his writing den and always felt like a magical place to me.'

'Sounds wonderfully romantic, like something straight out of a Lewis Carroll novel. And there's a long tradition of authors writing in sheds. Didn't Roald Dahl have one? Although admittedly usually at the bottom of gardens, not in basements. What was your father writing about?'

'He was a history professor, obsessed with maritime history. He was writing a book about the Titanic disaster and how it was a metaphor for impending ecological disaster, that mankind was speeding up the engines of the economy despite the warnings of icebergs ahead.'

'Interesting. Did he get his book published?'

'Sadly not.'

'I don't know if Julian Finch mentioned it when he referred me, but I was a peace activist living at the Greenham Common Peace Camp, protesting against nuclear weapons.'

'He didn't, but I've heard of Greenham Common.'

Meredith Greenway removed a grainy framed photograph hanging on the wall to the right-hand side of the door and handed it to her.

'That's me,' she said, pointing to a woman dressed as a witch holding a hand-drawn poster. 'It was a tough time sleeping in the mud, but so inspiring, taught me so much.'

Hollie peered at the poster Meredith Greenway was holding in the photograph. It was drawn in red pencil and depicted rows of planet Earths inside feminist symbols, encircled by spiders' webs.

'Hundreds of us women rallied together. Mothers protesting for the future of their children and the next generations. It was powerful and joyous.'

'What are the webs on the poster?'

'We used spider webs to represent networks of women coming together, fragile yet resilient. It was such a creative community. Full of witchery,' she said with a nostalgic smile. 'Anyway, enough about me. Tell me about you, Hollie, and why you are here.'

'The factual answer to that question is because Julian Finch referred me. I previously had some psychotherapy sessions with him. He told me he was retiring, but I wondered whether this was a ruse because he'd had enough of me!'

'Yes. I know Julian from way back. And I can assure you he's been intending to retire for some time … as have I, but that's another story! Anyway, back to you, Hollie.'

A torrent of words came tumbling out as Hollie downloaded her story: the kitchen-floor moment; her descent into the deadlock of ambivalence; her journey to Footprint Island and letting go of motherhood; the writing course; her father dying; the booming *I-want-joy* voice; drowning at work; her suicidal thoughts; Hugh wanting them to emigrate; and her encounter with Just No Dave.

All of it.

Meredith Greenway listened, nodding, hands cupped around her mug.

'And to answer your question, I've felt something gnawing away at me ever since I closed the door to motherhood.'

'Gnawing in what way?'

'Just this feeling that there must be something more. That this can't be it.'

'What can't be it?'

'This life. The nine-to-five. Eat, sleep, work. Rinse and repeat.'

Meredith Greenway nodded.

'And it feels as though I have arrived at another crossroads. Last time, I had to decide whether I wanted to take path A or B, to become a mother or not. Now, I need to decide whether to emigrate to Australia, and whether I tell Hugh the truth about what happened with Dave? Otherwise, I feel like our marriage will be based on a lie …. I just keep thinking, how can I not be better at making a decision this time? I feel so frustrated and ashamed!'

'And how long ago was the kitchen-floor moment, as you called it?' she asked when Hollie had finished.

'Almost three years.'

'And remind me, when was your father's funeral?'

'Six months ago.'

'Okay, I see,' she said, shifting forward in her chair, putting down her mug and looking at Hollie straight in the eyes. She had the look of a wise tribal chieftain who had just listened to the woes of her clan inside the community tipi whilst puffing on a smoking pipe.

'So you are still in the relatively early stages of grieving for a parent. A profoundly catalytic event, which invariably shines a very clear light on our lives. And, in your case, this appears to be amplified by your relationship to your father, and his very unique imprint. In the midst of this, whilst also holding down an intensely demanding job during a particularly stressful time of your career your husband has, in effect, issued you with another ultimatum, and now you feel ashamed because you slept with another man?'

Hollie simultaneously appreciated the empathy, smarted at what sounded like an accusatory tone directed towards Hugh, and flinched at hearing her betrayal spoken out loud.

'I understand he also has a lot going on, Hollie, from what you have told me and yes, in the bigger picture context, our social and political landscape is undoubtedly shifting and disrupting many people, but let's just call a spade a spade here, shall we?'

'Okay,' Hollie said, feeling that this was nonetheless uncharitable.

'And before we go any further, Hollie, I need you to know one thing. We don't do shame or judgement here. It's degenerative. It's a waste of energy. And frankly, at my age, I don't have time for it. Do you understand?'

'Yes.'

'Very good,' Meredith Greenway said. 'Also, I have been to Footprint Island too.'

'Really?'

'Yes. Like you I was guided there many years ago to a shadow integration retreat. The island has powerful healing energy. And for those of us who are open to it, fierce medicine.'

Hollie was flattered by Meredith Greenways use of us. It felt like a tacit acknowledgement of her Jedi potential by her own personal Yoda. Meredith Greenway looked at Hollie for a moment as if taking her all in, then looked up at the ceiling, tilted her head back, and gripped the arms of her chair as if she was preparing to receive a full body download. Hollie shifted in her seat, feeling the weight of the silence, and trying to breathe her way into it as she watched the rise and fall of Alba the dog's belly, snoozing on the rug between them.

After what seemed like an interminably long time, Meredith Greenway opened her eyes and lowered her gaze to meet Hollies.

'I heard the story of a woman inside the bubbling cauldron of midlife, asking herself what it is she wishes to do with this one, wild, precious childfree life,' she began. 'A courageous woman who is being guided to put her soul in charge of her life but is resisting the call. A powerful woman, grappling to implement a merger of two separate selves: a successful, controlling, corporate self, standing in the spotlight on the stage of her life; and a swelling, unbound, creative self, hidden in shadow behind the curtain. And I heard the story of a woman seeking joy, who must yet decide whether she is prepared to pay the price ...'

Hollie gulped.

'What price?'

'Death.'

Hollie felt a chill run down her spine.

'Death of what?'

'Or of whom?' Meredith Greenway said, with a penetrating stare and a fierce look on her face. She looked a thousand years old. 'Because it sounds to me like you are not fully here in your own life yet, Hollie. As though you are playing a role, rather than living into the full force of who you are.'

To her surprise, tears suddenly dripped onto Hollie's lap.

'Tell me about those tears, Hollie.'

Hollie touched her fingers to her cheek, feeling their wetness. Her tears felt oddly alien and detached, as if they had formed entirely separately from any instruction by her brain.

'I don't know what to say. I feel as though I didn't make them,' she replied looking at her fingers in bewilderment.

'Excellent,' said Meredith Greenway.

'Why?'

'Because whatever remains unwept within you is ready to be witnessed and heard.'

Hollie felt her mouth open, but no words came out. Meredith Greenway stood up slowly and walked towards the corner of the room by the massage bed and returned with what looked like a thick walking stick made of ancient, sun-bleached wood, about a metre long. Holding it horizontally at either end, she passed it to Hollie, ceremonially, without saying a word, before sitting back in her armchair. Hollie twirled it round observing its twists and knots.

'It's my talking stick, Hollie. Hundreds of people – men, women, and children – have held that stick and told their stories over the years. I like to imagine it's imbued with all the energy of their pain and triumphs, their losses and dreams; every scrap of who they are, and were in the process of becoming, is infused into that wood. It's my most treasured possession.'

Hollie stood it vertically on the floor in front of her.

'It sounds as though whatever it is that wants to come through you, it's very powerful,' Meredith Greenway continued, 'and it's okay to take yourself seriously you know, however weird or crazy you might tell yourself these experiences are. This is part of our healing, I think, especially as women in the modern world, to learn to be in communion with our intuitive, wild selves that lie beneath all our good girl conditioning. We need to reclaim our inner witches!'

'Yeah,' Hollie said, 'I definitely relate to having an inner witch!'

'Have you ever come across the work of Clarissa Pinkola Estes? She is a Jungian psychoanalyst who wrote *Women Who Run with the Wolves*,' Meredith Greenway said.

'The title vaguely rings a bell,' said Hollie.

'She talks about this idea that in midlife, we begin to feel a pull towards a process of un-becoming. That our essential, wild self begins to call out to us, like a hag in the dark woods beckoning us to meet her round a fire. I have come to believe this is a metaphor for menopause. That the heat of our night sweats and hot flushes are like a purifying fire. They purge our bodies, burning away the surface gloss of pretty appearances and all the things we believe we should be in order to be loved and accepted and belong. And from the ashes we have the chance to be re-born: to rise, phoenix-like and powerful, in the full creative force of who we are and ...'

Meredith Greenway paused and leaned forward in her chair, staring intently at Hollie.

'What just happened?'

'What do you mean?'

'You banged the stick on the floor. Just then.'

'Did I?'

'Yes. When I said, *the full creative force of who we are ...*'

Hollie felt the hairs go up on the back of her neck.

'What does this mean to you?'

'It reminds me of a phrase from my writing course. The teacher talked about creativity as *an in-dwelling force*.'

334

'And?'

'And it struck me that this was the same as *motherhood energy*. A primal, creative, life-giving force that is hard-wired into us and needs to be expressed, whether or not you do this through having a child.'

'And why is it important to be expressed?'

'Because unused creativity metastasizes.'

Unbidden tears dripped into Hollie's lap again.

'Go on, Hollie.'

Hollie looked down at her lap watching the tears fall.

Drip ... Drip ... Drip.

She could feel her grip tighten on the stick, her hands resting one on top of the other, pushing her weight onto it.

Drip. Drip. Drip.

'All of you is safe here, Hollie.'

Her chest heaved up and down as her breathing became deeper and the tears faster.

Drip-drip-drip-drip-drip ...

She closed her eyes and the tears continued to leak from her lids. It began to rain outside again. Hollie listened to the gentle patter of drops on the roof, imagining she was crying the rain as her chest continued up and down. She noticed her body began to rock gently back and forth, as if it knew something was coming up from beneath. She curled into a ball as if a flight attendant has just advised her to adopt the brace position for a crash landing. Hollie felt her face crumple and head bowed, she began to bang the stick, rhythmically up and down. She heard a strange, otherworldly sound come out. A cross between a wail and a howl. She felt the weight of her head drop closer towards her lap and hang there, as a torrent of sorrowful rain fell from her eyes and nose.

After what she imagined was about ten minutes of whole-body weeping, Hollie suddenly heard an internal dialogue.

Okay Hollie, that's enough now.
This is getting embarrassing.
You need to stop crying.
Dry your eyes.
Focus and come up with some actions you can take away.

And then she heard herself reply.

FUCK OFF!!!!!

Hollie felt her entire body heave, as her waters broke, and she abandoned herself into wanton weeping. She sank deeper into the chair, curling more tightly, rocking even harder, abandoning herself to sorrow in a way she had never done before, like leaning into a shuddering orgasm.

Crying because she was exhausted.

Crying because she felt so overwhelmed and incompetent.

Crying because everything felt too hard.

Crying because she had hoped by now she would be better than this.

Crying because she so bored of going round and round the same thought-loops, feeling seasick.

Crying because she was not enough.

Crying for sleeping with another man.

Crying because the emptiness she felt inside was like a cold stone room.

Crying because she felt so joyless.

'Bravo,' Meredith Greenway said when Hollie finally came to a juddering halt. 'You have been crying for thirty minutes. It feels as though this was, in every way, truly a watershed moment, Hollie. Well done for allowing yourself to deeply feel into your feelings. It's one thing to intellectually process something, but it's entirely another to allow our body to metabolise it. Being willing to feel inconsolable, this is courageous work.'

Meredith Greenway passed Hollie a box of man-size tissues.

She took three gratefully.

'What was that smile there, as you took the tissues?'

'I was just thinking that right now I probably look like that hag in the woods,' Hollie said as she blew her nose.

'You certainly move fast, Hollie,' said Meredith Greenway, chuckling.

'Really? I sometimes feel I'm very slow, that it takes ages for me to make things happen.'

'Not from where I am sitting.'

'Thank you,' said Hollie in a voice that sounded small and child-like, suddenly feeling exhaustion wash over her.

'Would you like another cup of tea before we wrap up for today? Give yourself a chance to come back into the room and into your body before you drive home. And if there is anything you would like to share, we can make time for this too.'

Hollie nodded.

'There is something,' Hollie said when Meredith Greenway returned with another two mugs of tea.

'I'm listening.'

'I had a visualisation. I was back in the stone egg room I told you about, the one I first saw in a session with Julian Finch.'

'This was your metaphor for fertility?'

'Yes.'

'It was empty and abandoned. A dead relic. All the dusty eggcups were lined neatly on the shelves, like empty artefacts in a museum. I sat in the middle of the floor, and it was stone cold and lifeless, as if all the motherhood energy had disappeared. And I wept for the emptiness. And I just kept thinking ... after everything I went through to make a wholehearted decision about not becoming a mother, all the soul-searching and the pain, this can't be *it* ... living a conventional life, just minus the children. Like I am *child*-free, but not *free*-free.'

Hollie could feel herself becoming upset again, but no actual tears formed, as if she did not have enough water left to make any.

'You know, Hollie, I believe that as women we need to create. That in creating we are at our most vividly alive. I don't buy this crap that the highest expression of womanhood is to have a baby; to my mind, this is just an aspect of patriarchal control. But I do believe there is an impulse within us that means we need to give birth from the womb of our self, over and over again – to projects, and poems, and paintings, and quilts, and music, and stories ... in an endless cycle of death and rebirth. And it sounds to me that this force is strong in you because you keep resisting it. This force is not something we can control. It's something wild that we need to lean into and surrender to, a force we must allow to come through us and guide us.'

'I keep getting this message, about surrendering, but I don't know how to do it,' said Hollie.

'I would suggest it's not about *doing* anything, Hollie. For now, it's about *being*. Holding yourself in a state of expectation without impatience. Listening to your intuition and grounding your energy by spending time in nature and finding small, simple ways to nourish your creativity. If you do this, the needle will jump to the magnet, and all the rest will follow. If you want to come for a couple more sessions, we can explore this some more, and I can give you some guided activities to

338

help.'

'Yes, I'd like that,' said Hollie.

'You know, when I was on Footprint Island, someone told me a story about a community of Tibetan monks who practice a very particular type of walking meditation. They get up in the dead of night and put on a pair of special sandals with a hole at the front big enough to hold the stub of a candle. In the pitch black, they go outside, light a candle, and place it in this small hole. Then, step by mindful step, they walk out into the night, carefully placing one foot in front of the other, slowly traversing the wild ground that is home to many varieties of snake. And all they have to guide their way, is a tiny circumference of light from the candle on the end of their shoes.'

'You're saying this is what I need to do, just put one foot in front of the other?'

'I'm saying that the journey of your lifetime has already begun, step by step from Footprint Island. And all you need to do for now, as you walk through the darkness, is pay attention to the tiny light on the end of your shoe.'

Part Three

Birthing a New Beginning

Departure Gates

'Going anywhere nice, folks?' asked the waiter as he arrived at their table.

'Emigrating to Australia,' Hugh said with a beaming smile. 'Flying to Sydney tomorrow.'

'The boomerang route!' said the waiter.

'I think they call it the kangaroo route,' said Hugh, correcting him, 'but who's counting, eh?'

'Sorry, yes of course,' said the waiter, rolling his eyes at himself. 'Are you going to live in Sydney?'

'No. We're heading to Brisbane. My son lives there.'

'Lucky guy. Well then, would you like to look at our champagne menu, sir?'

'We'll have your best bottle of champagne,' Hugh said, looking at Hollie. 'I know you don't normally like drinking before a flight, babe, but how about a special glass? We're never going to be emigrating again after all!'

'Yes, madam,' said the waiter. 'You can't be letting your husband drink alone tonight.'

'Go on then, just one,' said Hollie, feeling irritated at caving in so easily when she had decided not to drink.

'You know, I can still hardly believe it, that we're actually doing this,' said Hugh.

'I know,' said Hollie. 'It definitely seems a bit surreal.'

'To be honest, I never really thought you'd agree!'

'Why not?'

'You've always felt so quintessentially British. Maybe it's because of your dad. He was such a classic British eccentric, like a character from a Dicken's novel.'

'I know what you mean. But he's gone now, and I don't feel the same about living here since Brexit. I still feel heartbroken about it all.'

'Yeah. Thank God we are leaving it all behind. I bet it won't be too long before they bring back pounds, shillings and pence, the way this country is going, and probably find a reason to start a jolly good war! Anyway, let's not talk about Brexit, it's too depressing.'

'I thought about what you said as well, about making the most of being childfree. You know, taking a few risks. And the sessions I had with Meredith Greenway last year shifted something.'

'In what way?'

'I kept thinking over and over about something she said.'

'What was that?'

'She asked me, *What is it you plan to do with your one wild, precious childfree life?* … and it really made me think about how little time we have and that probably, I'm already about halfway through my life. I reflected on everything that had happened since I decided motherhood was not my path and retraced my steps back to the idea of waiting in an airport departure lounge in anticipation of a flight to my future. I started thinking that, whilst I'd found the courage to take the road less travelled by not having children, I was living – in every other way – completely conventionally. Child-*free*, but not truly free. And I started to wonder why? What would happen, I thought, if I were brave enough to be *really* wild and free?'

'You mean the departure lounge became a kind a premonition, rather than a metaphor?'

'Yeah, crazy as that sounds.'

'I don't care what has led us here to be honest, Hollie. I'm just glad you said yes.'

The waiter returned to their table.

'I brought an ice-cold bottle,' he said, pouring the champagne with a hand behind his back and leaving it to chill in a silver stand. 'I'll let you guys enjoy this and come back shortly for your food order.'

'Let's have a toast,' Hugh said, raising his glass. 'To new beginnings, and fun in the sun.'

'To new beginnings and writing our own ending,' said Hollie, sipping the sharp, icy fizz.

It tasted acrid.

'Mmm,' said Hugh. 'This is the life, eh?'

'Yeah.'

'That didn't sound too convincing. Is there something else?'

'What do you mean?'

'You just seem a little distracted. I thought you would be ... well, happier.'

'I am happy.'

'Are you still feeling guilty about work?'

'A bit,' she lied.

She had been thinking about Just No Dave.

They had swapped numbers that morning at the hotel, and he said he was leaving the ball in her court. She had clicked on his name in her phone, *Dave Juno*, hundreds of times since then, but resisted the urge to call. What would be the point anyway, especially now?

Hi Dave, just want to let you know I'm emigrating.

Have a great life.

Pop by if you are ever in Australia x

'You did everything you could, babe. Nobody could have worked harder than you, and you got the most important part of the merger over the line. Job done. Now it's time to let other people carry on and finish the rest. It's your time, for you, now. For us,' said Hugh.

'I know, you're right, it's exciting. I think I'm just tired after working so hard, packing up the house and saying goodbye to people and everything. I haven't been sleeping that well.'

Was it fair to emigrate without telling Hugh about Just No (Yes) Dave? This was the question that had really been keeping her awake at night. She had thought so many times about saying something, but she feared Hugh might throw her out in an act of karmic revenge, just like his first wife had done to him. In the context of her father dying, it had been an understandable mini midlife crisis – like trying out a Harley Davidson – and given her the jolt she needed to re-boot their marriage. Australia would be a fresh start, with a clean slate.

'Well, you can rest now. With what we've made from the house and selling the business we don't need to do a damn thing. We can leave Brexit Britain behind, lie on beaches, have barbeques and smell the roses. We can finally have some fun again, Hollie. Like we used to.'

'Can I ask you something, Hugh?'

'Yeah.'

'Do you think I've changed?'

'You're more serious than you used to be, but not surprising with all the responsibility you've carried. I'm sure a few months Down Under will help you relax, be more like your old self. And maybe you can even finally write your book?'

'Yeah,' said Hollie, taking a sip of champagne. She felt dangerously close to treading on a landmine.

'You know I was thinking the other day, remember when we first met?' Hugh asked.

'At Sally's party? Seems like such a long time ago. Like another lifetime.'

'I was thinking it's like we've come full circle.'

'In what way?'

'When we met, I remember you telling me about how your dad had been a lighthouse keeper and you were going to write a book inspired by his life, and I was so mesmerised by you. And now here we are starting a new life and you'll finally have the time to write and … you know … get it out of your system.'

'I'm not sure I want to be like my old self, Hugh.'

'What do you mean?'

'I dunno. I feel different. Like I'm not the same person I was. Ever since closing the door to motherhood and going to Footprint Island.'

'Is this the menopause?'

'What?'

'I read something the other day about how women who haven't had children can be really affected when they go through menopause, that it can trigger regret. And I wondered whether this might be affecting you, since you went to see the doctor last month?'

'I don't think so.'

'So, you don't have any regrets, about not having a baby?'

'I can honestly say, I've never regretted my decision, not for a single second. That day I swallowed my pill, I had such a strong, clear *knowing* in my mind and body, that I knew this was my truth, without question.

The more time has passed, the more deeply I've felt at peace with not being a mother. And as for the menopause, I'm trying to see it as a good thing. Meredith Greenway said it's a time when you burn away the superficial debris and clear what's no longer useful, so you can really step into your power.'

'What do you mean, then, about feeling you've changed?'

'It's hard to put into words. I don't think I want to have *fun* anymore. It feels like skimming the surface. I want something deeper and more meaningful. I want ... *joy*.'

'Joy? Isn't that just the trendy new word for happiness?'

'I ...'

'What's wrong with just being happy these days? Why is happy suddenly not enough anymore? Just enjoying the simple pleasures in life without always needing more. This is the problem these days, nobody's content with what they have,' Hugh said, shrugging his shoulders in a kind of weary resignation.

'I don't know if it's about wanting more. I think it's a state of being. Something deeper and more spiritual than being happy. I think I've learned that joy is the reward for grief, and grief is the entry fee for joy. That they are two sides of the same coin.'

'I don't understand.'

'The Buddhists have this saying, *No mud, no lotus*. It comes from the fact that the lotus flower grows in stagnant waters, which is why it's a symbol for enlightenment. I think it means we have to sink into the mud and face the abyss of our own emptiness to find joy and peace.'

'Is this what you're trying to say, that you're peering into the abyss?'

'In a way, yes.... and I think surrendering is the key ... we have to find the courage to be swallowed up, however much it hurts.'

Hugh stared at her, and for a moment Hollie thought she saw fear in his eyes.

'But no one wants to be swallowed up, Hollie. I don't understand why anyone would want to deliberately make themselves feel pain.'

'What if our path requires us to do something we know will cause us grief and pain, but we do it anyway because we trust it's necessary?'

'I'd never deliberately choose to make myself sad. But if doom and gloom works for you, that's great,' said Hugh, in a tone that suggested he'd already had enough of the conversation.

'But what if you knew,' said Hollie, continuing in spite of herself, 'that grief is the dark womb of your potential?'

'I don't know, Hollie. I think too many people these days are focused on themselves instead of other people. I understand why this is relevant, what with your dad dying last year, but all this talk about focusing on the self, it's not helping to make the world better, is it? You just have to look at Donald Trump to see that.'

'I hope I didn't interrupt there,' said the waiter hesitantly as he stood at the table. 'How's the champagne?'

'Very good,' said Hugh, sounding relieved.

The waiter took the bottle from the stand and filled Hugh's glass, then turned to Hollie with a look that suggested she really ought to have some more. She let him fill her glass. Hugh seemed pleased.

'Anyway,' he said, raising his glass again after the waiter had left with their order. 'Let's not go there, eh? This is a moment for celebration. To happiness *and* joy.'

'Happiness and joy,' said Hollie.

Maybe Hugh was right, she thought. Maybe she was becoming too hung up on semantics. What did it matter if they had different definitions and words for how they wanted to experience life? They were together, on the threshold of a new chapter, with so much to look forward to. Surely, it was perfectly possible for her to find joy in their new beginning together.

~

In the early hours of the morning, Hollie woke up breathless, her hands frantically scrabbling between her legs as if fighting off an assailant.

'What is it?' said Hugh, waking up with a jolt.

Hollie was hyperventilating.

'Breathe, Hollie,' he said, putting his arms round her and trying to calm her down.

Hollie shuddered as he held her, still feeling the presence of the figure imprinted on her body.

'There was a black figure over me. A witch.'

'It was just a bad dream.'

'It felt more like a visitation,' Hollie replied with a feeling of dread in her stomach.

'I think that imagination of yours is running wild again. Probably just adrenaline, mixed with the champagne and talking about Meredith Greenway over dinner.'

'It felt more than that, Hugh. It was *so* real. I've never had a dream so vivid and intense. I can still feel her on me. And I can see her in front of me, clear as day.'

'What does she look like?'

'Skinny with bluish skin. Pointed teeth and a large lightning tattoo across one cheek, in a kind of tribal style. But the weirdest thing … instead of fingernails, she has blades. And she was scratching me at the top of my thighs and between my legs, like she was trying to slice me, and I was screaming for her to get off …'

'No wonder you look like you've seen a ghost. What do you think it means?'

'No idea,' said Hollie.

'It's only five thirty,' Hugh said, checking his phone. 'Maybe try and get another hour of sleep? We have a long flight ahead of us.'

'Okay,' said Hollie, unconvinced.

They lay back down in the bed, which was wide enough to fit three people in comfortably. Hollie pulled up the white cotton duvet and sank into the pillow. It was like lying on a cloud. She lay for what felt like half an hour, wide awake, before deciding to put a jacket over the top of her pyjamas and creep out of bed, trying her best not to disturb Hugh. She walked along a long, deserted corridor and eventually came into the large atrium of gleaming glass and chrome which formed the central hub of the hotel. She stood on the balcony, looking down at the multiple levels of floors descending to the reception and bar area with a queer feeling of surreal normality.

Momentarily, the light seemed to change, and Hollie looked up to see an art installation hanging from a net suspended below the roof. A flock of large, white origami birds on wires of different lengths. In their midst was a piece of sky-blue cloth with a decorative quote printed on it in white writing.

When once you have tasted flight,
you will forever walk the earth with eyes turned skyward,
for there you have been,
and there you will always long to return.

~ Leonardo Da Vinci

An image of the little bird at the crematorium flashed into her mind, and she remembered a trip to the local lighthouse with her father, captured in a photograph in one of the leather-bound albums her mum kept in the sideboard. On their way home that day, they had visited the library where she'd ended up outside at the back of the building, running across concrete, chasing a sparrow. As she'd stretched out to grab the little bird that was just out of reach, she'd lost her footing and fallen on a jagged piece of glass and arrived home with rivulets of blood pouring down her leg.

Was this a metaphor for her life, she wondered, chasing something that was beyond her grasp? Searching for an abstract notion of joy she could not easily describe, even to herself? Always restless, trying to get somewhere rather than enjoying the journey, as Hugh seemed to imply. What was wrong with just being happy and having fun?

She thought of her father again, wondering what he would say.

Fun is joy, hollowed out. A pretty facsimile.

Another memory began playing in her mind. Her wedding day. She saw her father's face as he'd walked her down the aisle towards Hugh. He had looked as though he was at a funeral. She'd always assumed his expression was due to his discomfort of people looking at him, but now she began to wonder. Had he perceived something beneath the surface of that day, like Ani Zopa with her spiritual x-ray vision?

Hollie looked up at the origami birds again.

Please help me, Dad, she whispered.

She glanced back down to ground floor and noticed a few people ascending the escalator holding cups with plastic lids and smiled as she thought about that little tugboat sailing out to the open sea. Hollie hopped on the escalator and descended to the main reception and walked to the bar area where they were serving takeaway coffees. She ordered two Americanos, with extra shots.

Her phone pinged in her jacket pocket. It was a message from Diane.

Today is a new beginning my friend!
Have a good flight.
Message me when you are down under.

352

D x

Hollie paid for the drinks, returned up the escalator and stood on the balcony again, looking at the origami birds. She dialled Diane's number.

'Hollie? This is a nice surprise.'

'Yeah. I'm at the airport, just been getting some coffee and heading back to the room to get ready. Saw your message, thanks.'

'You okay?'

Hollie hesitated.

'No, I don't think so.'

'What is it?'

'I don't know if I'm making the right decision, Diane. I'm not sure emigrating to Australia is my path to joy, the thing I want to do with my one wild, childfree life.'

'What's happened?'

'I had a weird dream. A witch with blades for hands was over the top of me, scratching between my legs, as if she had something important to tell me.'

'That's definitely up there in the spooky dreams section. What else?'

'I feel so guilty for not telling Hugh about Dave. Like our new life is based on a lie.'

'For what purpose would you tell him, Hollie? What good would it do? You are human and you made a mistake. You were still grieving for your dad. And you haven't had any contact since, have you?'

'No.'

'Do you want to be in contact with him?'

'Don't know.'

'Okay, when was the last time you felt certain about a big decision?'

'When I swallowed my pill that day and closed the door to motherhood.'

'When you did your Incredible Hulk routine?'

'Yes.'

'And how does making the decision to emigrate with Hugh compare to this?'

'Swallowing that pill was like a *hell yes* in every cell of my being, I felt it in my body, whereas this decision feels like it's rattling around in my head.'

'Okay. I'm going to say something provocative now. If it's not a *hell yes*, then is it a *no*, Hollie?'

'Oh God, I don't know Diane … I really should be getting back as Hugh will be starting to wonder where I am.'

'Do you want to still be married to Hugh, Hollie? I know it's a hard question, but you get to keep on choosing, you know, and you get to change your mind.'

'Honestly, I don't know. We've really drifted apart these last few years and I guess I was hoping that Australia could be a reboot, a fresh start that would bring us back together, like we used to be.'

'But are you the person you used to be? Do you really want to go back, Hollie?'

'No … I don't know … maybe it's just an … *I don't know yet* … and I'll find out when I get there. Thanks, Diane, I'll message later.'

Hollie returned to the room carrying the two takeaway cups of coffee.

'Where've you been?' asked Hugh, sat up in bed.

'Couldn't sleep, so thought I'd stretch my legs.'

354

'Thanks,' he said as she handed him one. 'You okay?'

'Yes, I'm fine,' Hollie said.

'Great. We better get a move on then. Big day ahead. Do you want to get a shower first, babe?'

'Okay,' Hollie replied.

She walked into the bathroom, shut the door, and turned on the shower to heat up as she removed her pyjamas and stepped into the large cubicle.

She stood under the powerful jet spray, trying to gather her thoughts.

After a few moments, Hollie looked down at her body curiously, watching it like a detached observer as it began to move into a peculiar position, as if it were responding to a high frequency signal too sophisticated for her mind to process.

She felt her mind project itself out of her body as if it were filming the scene, as if she was simultaneously both the actor and director, experiencing and observing the moment in real time.

She saw a woman standing with her hands and forearms flat against the glass in a kind of brace position, as though she were preparing for a contraction.

Suddenly, another image scrolled into her mind.

She was back sitting on the toilet in their bathroom, holding that final pregnancy test, staring in disbelief at the wording in the tiny plastic window.

The image was frozen.

Why am I seeing this?

She looked again at the still image, sensing something was approaching at the periphery of her perception and felt an instruction to zoom in. She imagined taking her thumb and forefinger and expanding the image.

Is there something more to see here?

The image of the pregnancy test grew bigger and came close-up.

Pregnant.

She watched a replay of her reaction to seeing that word.

… Omigod. I'm pregnant. Me. Hollie. Pregnant. A baby. Omigod.

Hollie gasped.

She *had* missed something.

A moment that had been so infinitesimally small, she had not even registered it. A tiny bird of a moment that had flown beyond the reach of her mind in that fleeting instant, so fast she'd been unable to catch it.

There had been another word, just before her first *omigod.*

One missing word.

Shit!

And now, standing in this strange position she saw it in the full, raw light of truth. A tiny knowing that had been lying there all this time, hiding in shameful shadow.

She had not wanted a baby.

She had not wanted her baby.

Hollie slammed back into her body, shaking violently. She took a deep breath and switched the shower off with deliberate precision, then stepped slowly out of the cubicle. She pulled a white fluffy bath towel from the metal radiator on the wall and wrapped it round her body, then took another and sat on the edge of the bath holding it in her hand. She stared vacantly at the grey sparkling tiles on the floor, holding her breath.

A wave crashed upon her. A tsunami of shame and grief.

She let out a howl as she fell to the floor and wept, knocked over by a lightning strike of clarity.

'I'm so sorry, Egberta. I'm so sorry I didn't want you. Please forgive me.'

Hugh came bursting in the door.

'What the fuck? … Hollie, what's happened?'

She tried to speak, but no words would come out.

'Are you injured? Are you okay?'

Hollie waved her hands at Hugh trying to indicate she wasn't hurt.

'Hollie, what the fuck is going on? You're frightening me!'

'I … I'm o … kay,' she managed to squeak as she fought to ger her breath. 'Just hold me.'

Hugh sat on the floor, and she put her head on his lap, snot and saliva and tears soaking into his fluffy white hotel dressing gown.

'Tell me what's going on,' said Hugh, sounding panicky.

'I … I … I … I just realised …' she said.

'WHAT?'

'I … I didn't want our baby, Hugh'

'What are you talking about?'

'I'm so sorry,' she sobbed.

'I don't understand. Tell me what's happening,' said Hugh.

Hollie could hear the panic in his voice and willed herself to stop crying. She wiped her eyes on her towel and sat up.

'I … I had a vision of the moment I found out I was pregnant a few years ago. And I suddenly realised I missed my *very first* reaction. That I didn't want a baby. And I'm glad I had a miscarriage.'

She began wailing again.

'I didn't want Egberta, Hugh, and I'm so sorry. I never wanted a baby.'

'Well … Jill had a miscarriage, you know. It's really common. Happens to women all the time,' said Hugh.

Hollie could hear he was trying to be helpful, but her body absorbed his words like a cold, hard slap.

'You really shouldn't give yourself a hard time. It was just a bunch of cells at that stage, Hollie, not a baby.

Just a bunch of cells. Hollie repeated the phrase in her mind. It sounded clinical.

'What's done is done.' Hugh continued 'We're starting a new life now. It's probably best we didn't have a baby anyway.'

As Hugh spoke the last syllable of his sentence, Hollie felt the sensation of a giant umbilical cord between them being severed.

Inside her head, she heard a clear, unequivocal statement of fact, spoken calmly.

My marriage is over.

She felt the forceful, undeniable truth of these words simultaneously in every cell in her body.

She recognised this knowing.

It was the same knowing she had experienced that day when she almost tore the cabinet door from its hinges and swallowed her pill.

Her truth, revealed in the full light of day.

Shit. My marriage is over, the same calm voice said.

Hollie wiped her tears and stopped crying. She knew there was more grieving to be done, but it would have to wait.

'You are right, babe,' she said. 'I don't know what came over me. Must have just needed to get it out of my system. I'm fine now. I guess it's just a release, after the stress of the last few months, and having that nightmare before. I just got overwhelmed.'

Hugh looked at her as if not entirely convinced.

'Okay … If you're sure?'

'Yes,' said Hollie. 'Let's get ready and have some breakfast.'

She needed to buy herself some time to think.

After stopping to eat in the hotel restaurant, they walked along the glass walkway connected to the airport. Hugh jumped on the moving escalator, but Hollie continued walking slowly along the glistening, smooth floor. She could feel her heart pounding in her chest as the yellow and black signage of the airport check-in desks came into view. Hugh was standing at the end of the walkway watching her.

'You sure you're okay?' he said.

'Yeah,' she said, hoping she looked sincere.

'We need to go to terminal one. I can see the lift over there,' said Hugh, motioning forward with their tickets in his hand.

They stood side by side as the lift doors closed and Hollie began to quake inside as she remembered that night with Just No Dave. She felt her insides drop as they descended one floor and the conversation they had that evening in the bar replayed in her mind, when he had described cutting the cord with his wife. As the doors opened, Hollie felt a holy heart tug as she saw a sign.

Multi-Faith Prayer Room.

'Hugh …' she said, hearing herself sound a little shaky.

'You're not okay, are you?' he said. 'I can tell by your voice.'

'I know this sounds weird, but I need to go to the prayer room.'

'You're going to pray?'

'I just feel like I need to speak with Egberta. I don't know why, it's just a feeling.'

'Okay. Give me your suitcase and I'll get another coffee and wait for you over there,' he said pointing to a Starbucks. 'But don't be too long, Hollie.'

'I won't,' she said.

As soon as Hugh was out of sight, Hollie began breathing like a puffer fish, blowing her cheeks up like a balloon then releasing the air through a goldfish mouth. She had no idea why she was breathing like this, but it felt comforting.

She opened the door marked *prayer room* and entered a small chapel. Straight ahead was a large rectangular opaque window made of mosaic glass, bright cobalt blues and khaki greens. Tears pooled in her eyes as she felt a wave of peace wash over her, bathing in the simple beauty of the space. She walked along the aisle between rows of wooden chairs with green upholstery, facing towards a lectern in front of the beautiful window and sat on one of the chairs to the right. Hollie set down her handbag, interlocked her hands into the traditional prayer position, bowed her head and gently closed her eyes.

Hello, Egberta.

It's me.

Your mother.

I am here, to ask for your forgiveness.

Hollie felt her heart swell as she said the words and tears began to fall down her cheeks.

She sat in silence for a few moments, breathing deeply.

She smiled as she felt a sensation of being wrapped in a blanket of loving energy and given permission to ask for whatever she needed.

I am also here because I need your help.

I'm not sure if I'm supposed to go through the departures gates and I don't know what to do.

Please help.

By the power of Green Tara, give me a sign.

Hollie opened her eyes and looked up.

There was nothing but stillness.

She closed her eyes again and resumed the prayer position.

Egberta. Sorry to be annoying, but I don't have much time.

Hollie opened her eyes and laughed aloud.

'God, I'm a ridiculous woman,' she said, wondering what on earth she had expected to happen.

That moment, Hollie heard the door open behind her and then quickly shut again.

'Very funny,' she said aloud, unsure who exactly she was speaking to.

She bent down to pick up her handbag, and the door reopened.

Hollie turned round and saw a tall man walk in. He had a silver beard and appeared to be about sixty years old. Oddly, he was holding an eggbox in both hands with what seemed to be a peculiar air of reverence. He smiled as he walked towards her then stopped at the end of the aisle she was sitting on, facing towards her.

'I'm sorry,' he said. 'I nearly came in before and then lost my nerve. I hope I'm not disturbing you?'

'Not at all. I was just about to leave. I'm emigrating to Australia and my husband is waiting for me,' said Hollie, noticing her words sounded hollow.

'You are having doubts?' he said, smiling kindly.

'I ...'

'Oh excuse me, that's absolutely none of my business.'

'It's okay,' said Hollie. 'Really.'

'May I sit here?' he asked, motioning to the seats next to Hollie.

'Please do.'

The man carefully laid the eggbox down on the seat next to Hollie, removed his coat and a small rucksack, and sat down.

'Is that why you came in here? To decide if you're going to stay or go?'

Hollie nodded looking straight at him, noticing he had lovely green eyes. 'It's the first time I've ever been in one of these prayer rooms.'

'Me too. I just walked past and felt this strange pull to come in,' said the man.

'I have this powerful feeling that I'm not supposed to go through those departure gates. But how do you trust what you feel when you can't explain or understand it?'

'I don't know, but it sounds a lot like being in love to me. Sometimes we just know something even though we can't rationalise it.'

Hollie nodded.

'May I offer something?'

Hollie nodded again.

'What if the departure gates are not literal, but metaphorical?' the man continued.

'What do you mean?'

'What if the departure gates are in here,' he said, pointing towards her chest.

Hollie noticed he was wearing a copper bangle, just like one Julian Finch had worn.

'What's making you smile?'

'That bracelet,' said Hollie, 'it reminds me of someone.'

'Funny you should say that,' the man said. 'You resemble someone too. You look like the woman I'm going to visit in Paris.'

'Is she French?'

'British but lives there now. She's an artist.'

'How very seductive,' said Hollie.

The man looked up at the ceiling and laughed.

'Yes. She most definitely is,' he said, looking round conspiratorially 'Terrifyingly so!'

'May I ask, what's in the eggbox?'

The man picked it up from the seat.

'It's a gift for my love,' he said as he opened the lid with a look of bliss in his eyes. Inside, the egg tray was covered with gold tissue paper, nestling three crystal eggs and three plastic stands.

'How beautiful!' whispered Hollie.

'So this one,' said the man, taking out the green and indigo stone and gesturing for her to take it, 'is fluorite. Mainly used for absorbing negative energy and eliminating stress.'

Hollie cupped the lovely egg in her hands like a holy sacrament, feeling the smooth cool stone and its satisfying weight for a few moments, before replacing the crystal back in its golden nest.

'And this one,' he said, handing her a second iridescent black egg, 'is labradorite. If you hold it to the light, you will see lots of other colours.'

Hollie held up the egg. 'Like a peacock feather!'

'Exactly. It's a great protecting stone and increases intuition.'

'I definitely could do with some of that!' said Hollie, laughing as she replaced it.

'And this one is rose quartz,' he said, handing her a baby pink egg, 'which is recognised as the centre of universal love. It is said to open our heart, to promote love, self-love and healing.'

'What a wonderful gift!' Hollie said as she replaced the third egg. 'She's a very lucky woman.' Hollie picked up her handbag and stood up to leave. 'Anyway, I really must be going. My husband will be getting agitated.' She paused, put her hand on the man's shoulder and bent down, kissing him softly on each cheek. 'Bon voyage. And thank you for coming in here,' she said.

'You are most welcome. So, may I ask, have you made a decision?'

Hollie looked at the man. 'It's already been made,' she said.

Rising from the Ashes

The moment she felt the wooden jetty beneath her feet, Hollie felt held once again, in a familiar loving embrace. *Thank you*, she whispered under her breath as the ferry engine started up and the driver waved them goodbye. She began to pull her suitcase along behind her, feeling a deep sense of peace. She was home, returning once more to something sacred and forgotten.

At the end of the jetty, as the wheels moved from smooth wood to bumpy gravel, Hollie's suitcase flipped over. She stopped to straighten it back up, and as she resumed walking she noticed a woman running across the grass towards their group with the gleeful enthusiasm of a small child. The two volunteers who had greeted them at the ferry had stopped at the front of the party, and watched as the woman ran past, turning their heads to follow her trajectory. As the running woman drew nearer, Hollie felt her heart expand in her chest as she recognised the beaming megawatt smile.

'Krystina!'

Hollie let go of her suitcase and opened her arms out wide, bracing herself for the full force of Krystina who flung herself forwards in a move reminiscent of a scene from *Dirty Dancing* and wrapped her legs around her waist like a lover.

'Oh my God, Hollie, it's really you! I'm SO SO happy to see you, my darling! I just saw your name on the guest list.'

They held each other tightly, swaying in delightful, lingering unison.

'Let me look at you,' Krystina said as she planted herself back on the ground, extended her arms as she held Hollie's hands and looked at her. 'I can't believe you're actually here! I have so *much* to tell you!'

'Me too,' said Hollie. 'How come *you're* here?'

'I stayed on as a volunteer after you left and was about to leave yesterday but something made me stay another day. Can you believe it?'

Hollie stared at Krystina's lovely face, still trying to take her all in. She looked radiant.

'I thought I was never going to see you again.'

'I'm so sorry I haven't been in touch, I kept meaning to contact you, to say thank you and everything, but …. Omigod, I can't believe this! Here, let me take this,' said Krystina, grabbing the handle of Hollie's suitcase with one hand, and clasping Hollie's hand with the other. They began walking towards the main centre, swinging their clasped hands in a shuggy-boat motion, moving past the other passengers from the ferry who had stopped to watch.

'Petra! Joe!' Krystina shouted to the two volunteers at the front of the party who were still standing waiting for them to catch up. 'This is my Hollie!'

Hollie saw their eyes widen.

'As in … *the* Hollie?' said the man in a rolling Scottish accent.

'YES!' replied Krystina. '*The* Hollie!'

Krystina stopped and introduced her.

'I'm so glad to meet you, Hollie, the great facilitator!' he said with an earnest smile as he shook Hollie's hand.

'Me too,' said the other volunteer, shaking her hand. 'I've heard so much about you.'

'Thanks,' Hollie said, feeling her cheeks flush with a mixture of pride and embarrassment, wondering what on earth Krystina had said. Yes, she had made a small kind gesture, but the way they were looking at her, it was like she had given a kidney!

After checking in, Krystina escorted Hollie to her room. Once again, she was in Wisdom wing. They made up the single bed together with the bedding that was waiting in a neat pile and sat cross-legged facing each other in a state of excitement and anticipation.

'Look at you,' Hollie said, stroking Krystina's hair as she bathed in the light of her dazzling smile and shining blue eyes. 'You are even more beautiful than I remember. You look lit from within.'

Krystina's eyes began to well with tears.

'I am, darling,' she said, pointing to her face and laughing as tears fell down her cheeks. 'Look, happy tears! I can't begin to tell you how overjoyed I am to see you. My very own fairy godmother! I can never thank you enough for what you did. You changed my life.'

Hollie resisted the urge to shy away and say her usual, *Oh it was really nothing*, and decided instead to open herself to the grace of Krystina's heartfelt thanks. It felt beautiful to take it in. She could feel her heart swelling as she received it. Krystina leaned forward in a raised lotus pose, and hugged Hollie in a warm embrace, as if she needed to confirm that she was not a figment of her imagination.

'So, tell me everything,' Hollie said when she had sat back down.

Krystina downloaded her story at breakneck speed. It turned out that the extra week Hollie had gifted turned into two weeks on the back of another act of generosity from one of the nuns, which coincided with a very rare and auspicious visit by a group of high lamas. While they were visiting, one of them became unwell and Krystina was invited to make some herbal remedies which had such a miraculous effect that she was invited for a private interview with him.

'It was like meeting the Dalai Lama and the genie from the lamp all in one go!' said Krystina.

Paralysed by the fear of wasting her opportunity as she desperately tried to think of her magic wish, Krystina had told him the story of her life. The lama-genie had listened for a long time, asked questions, then abruptly told Krystina he had heard enough. 'Condemning yourself is a waste of time,' he had said. 'Do not try to figure out how to be better, or how to fulfil your calling. Your calling is very clear. Just allow it to be heard and seen, here on the island.'

After this, Krystina had signed up as a full-time volunteer and stayed on the island.

'It was astonishing to me,' she said. 'I ended up making all these poultices and remedies for people, and it just kept growing and growing, day by day, until eventually I had my own room with a make-shift dispensary where I conducted all these experiments with different plants and herbs picked from the gardens. It's like I became Baba Yaga, without even noticing!'

'That's amazing, Krystina. You got your wish that you made at our ceremony. Look, I have happy tears now!' said Hollie, grinning from ear to ear.

'So, tell me about what's been happening with you, since the island,' said Krystina.

Hollie downloaded her story and Krystina sat listening, enthralled.

'So basically ... the universe rushed in and cleared a huge space in your life? You became a great big eggcup, like you said at our ceremony!' said Krystina, beaming.

'I keep trying to tell myself that,' said Hollie, smiling weakly. 'But then my logic mind kicks in and says ... *What the hell have you done?* You had a well-paid secure job, a husband who loved you, a beautiful home, the chance to begin a new life adventure, and you let it all go. And for what?'

'Why did you let it all go? I mean ... *really*, really?'

'I guess I felt this *knowing* again, just like that time I almost pulled the bathroom door off the hinges. It happened at the airport hotel. I had an intensely vivid dream about a witch with scissors for hands. She was on top of me, clawing here in a frenzy,' Hollie said, pointing to between her legs.

'You know what that is?' said Krystina, her eyes growing bigger.

'My vagina?'

'This is where your root chakra is located, Hollie. The foundational energy centre in your body associated with sexuality, pleasure and creativity. When the root chakra is blocked, we feel deeply restless and fearful.'

Hollie could feel cogs inside her mind clicking into place.

'It sounds to me like your inner witch was trying to help you unblock it.'

'I think she succeeded.'

'Why?'

'Because in the shower that morning I had a flashback to the moment I found out I was pregnant, and suddenly realised I hadn't wanted my baby.'

Krystina reached out and squeezed her hand.

'I fell on the bathroom floor, howling, as I purged all this shame and grief. Hugh freaked out and tried to help, but then I had a powerful sensation of an umbilical cord of energy between us being severed with a clean cut. Then I heard this voice in my head … *my marriage is over…* and I felt the truth of it in every cell in my body. I didn't want it to be true, but I couldn't deny my own knowing.'

'It sounds like your witch unblocked you and set you free.'

Hollie's mouth fell open as the hairs stood up on the back of her neck.

'So then what happened?' Krystina prompted.

'On the way to the departure gates, I went to the prayer room and asked for guidance. And, bizarrely, a man walked in carrying an eggbox with three crystals inside, a gift for his girlfriend. A pink one, a green one, and another that looked like peacock feathers.'

'Holy shit, that's incredible. You know what I reckon that was, Hollie ... Green Tara stepped into action and brought you crystal eggs!'

'I don't understand.'

'At our ceremony, remember? We scattered those seeds ... the egg tree!'

Hollie's mouth fell open in amazement as she remembered that moment.

'You asked for a sign and Green Tara brought you eggs. Like she had been incubating those seeds waiting for just the right moment!' Krystina said, her eyes even more huge and sparkling.

'No way!' Hollie said, feeling the cogs in her brain whirring furiously. *'No fucking way!'*

'Yes, way. This is the mysterious, wild force of this island at work,' said Krystina.

'I think the last vestiges of my mind just left the building!' said Hollie, holding her hand over her mouth and staring at Krystina.

'So, tell me, what did Hugh say after you said you weren't going with him?'

'He was angry. Told me I'd lost my mind. And to be honest, in a way, I agreed. He gave me the chance to start again and create a new life and I rejected it, without even being able to give him a proper reason. I mean, I tried to explain, but it was difficult to put into words. All I knew, in every cell in my body, was that I was not meant to go through those departure gates. And Hugh still chose to leave.'

'How do you feel about it now?'

'I miss him, and I still love him. I always will. But I couldn't ignore my own knowing. It's impossible for me now, regardless of what it means I must surrender to it.'

'How are things now, with Hugh?'

'We haven't spoken much. He doesn't understand, and I think he has given up even trying to. And I can't offer any explanation that doesn't sound like spiritual woo-woo … even to myself!'

'Sounds like you had a full-on, holy-shit awakening, Hollie.'

'All I know is some days I'm not sure I can tell the difference between being completely nuts and living from my truth.'

'I'm no expert, Hollie, but for the record, you seem extremely sane to me, although granted I'm probably not the most natural go-to-choice for providing a sanity reference,' Krystina chuckled.

'Do you ever wish you could go back, Krystina?'

'Back where?'

'Normal. Pre-awakening.'

'I wasn't ever like you, Hollie. High-flying career woman and all that. My life never felt particularly well organised and together and I think I've always been prone to being a bit mystical. Although I can relate to trying to squeeze myself into being so-called "normal" … it nearly killed me! What is it they say … *If your path is clearly laid out in front of you, then it's not your path. The only way you can see your path is when you look back and see the tracks you've made.*'

'I have thought so many times about buying a plane ticket and joining Hugh, telling him I'm sorry, that I wasn't thinking straight, that I was still grieving for my father, and begging him for forgiveness, but there's nothing in my body that will allow me to do this, regardless of how much my mind might want to. In my body it feels like the journey of our marriage is completed and there's no going back. Does that sound mad?'

'It sounds profound. I'm so proud of you, darling.'

'Thanks,' said Hollie, staring out of the window for a moment. She wasn't enjoying hearing herself out loud, but at the same time felt relieved to be able to speak and be understood.

371

'What about this guy ... Just No Dave?'

'We haven't been in touch and I'm not sure what I would say. It's like, after saying no to motherhood, I know that choosing a different queue than the one marked *White Picket Fence and 2.4 Children* was the best decision I ever made. But I feel like the queue I'm standing in now doesn't have a sign, and I still don't know what I am saying yes to. I guess that's why I've come back here – to figure out what departure gates I do want to go through!'

Krystina laughed and slapped her thigh.

'Well, I'm enjoying being with you in the childfree-queue-to-fuck-knows-where! And I have come to the view that the only way we truly lose in life is when we don't honour our own experiment. When we say *yes* to things we want to say *no* to because we're afraid to disappoint people, and *no* to the things we want to say *yes* to, because we're too frightened of the unknown. I think when our truth speaks, she often whispers, or comes riding in on the crest of emotional waves. And all we can do is get still and quiet enough to hear her as she rises up and emerges through us.'

~

That evening, Meredith Greenway stood up slowly from her chair and removed a white chiffon scarf round her neck, draping it over the backrest with the reverence of a ceremonial act. She bent down and reached for a small box of matches on the floor under her chair. Then, with the precision of a tightrope walker, she put one bare foot in front of the other and walked towards a gleaming brass candlestick that stood on the floor in the middle of their circle and lit the wick of a tapered white candle.

'Welcome,' she said after returning to her chair, 'to the beginning of your rising.'

Hollie gazed at the diffuse glow around the candle, allowing her eyes to become unfocused as she leaned into the pin-drop silence of Meredith

Greenway's pause.

'I believe each of you is here because you are ready for transformation. Whether you are conscious of it or not yet, you are here because the wisest, bravest, deepest part of yourself has called you here to rise from the ashes, to claim the prize of your true self.'

Meredith Greenway looked around the circle, making eye contact with each woman, just as Ani Zopa had done. This time, the group was smaller, twelve women in total.

'I feel certain this will be powerful, sacred time and space that we will share together. Footprint Island is a special place. What would be called a power place in many ancient cultures. A numinous place that radiates a special mysterious power which has been felt by pilgrims and seekers through the centuries. The Native Americans believed Mother Earth is a living being, and that power places are like charging points where we can plug into her electromagnetic energy and heal through our reconnection to source.'

Hollie smiled as she reflected on how she had changed since that moment on the kitchen floor with Hugh, how grateful she was that this had happened and how she had been led here.

'This evening, we are gathered to set our intentions for this retreat. Intentions are like spells: they have the power to stir and conjure magic. I would like to invite you to take five minutes to introduce yourself now and I will then say a little more about the structure for our retreat and what we will be doing together over the course of the weekend. Before we begin, I'd like to ask you a question: Why are you here? And I would like you to avoid thinking of your answer too hard. Instead, simply allow the question to drop into the pool of your mind and watch the ripples that are created.'

Hollie closed her eyes and saw herself sitting at the edge of a still pool of water. She imagined a large stone plopping down into the centre, breaking the surface of the water and watched as the ripples moved outwards.

Why *am* I here?

When it came to her turn to introduce herself, she paused, pulling the sleeves of her bright yellow cashmere jumper round her wrists, feeling its comforting softness. As she opened her mouth to speak, she was not sure what was about to come out.

'My name is Hollie,' she said, looking round the circle at the other women. 'And up until recently, I would not have fully paid attention to what the rest of you were saying, because I would have been too busy pre-rehearsing my introduction in my head.'

Hollie noticed a few wry smiles on the faces of the other women.

'I've spent years expending a huge amount of effort keeping control of myself – trying to predict what is going to happen – if I say X, this person will probably react by saying Y, or if I do A the other person will probably do B – constantly editing what I'm saying, checking my appearance to make sure nothing has slipped, keeping everything planned and on track and in order. This me would've introduced myself firstly by telling you what I do for a living. I would've told you I was the people director for a large mental health trust. After that, I would've told you that I'm married and live with my husband. Now, none of these things are true.'

Hollie gripped the sides of her chair and leaned forward.

'Six months ago, my husband and I packed up our lives and were set to emigrate to Australia. But at the airport, I had a very powerful knowing that if I went through the departure gates I would be stepping into the wrong life, so I changed my mind at the last minute, and he got on the plane and left without me.'

She heard a few gasps.

'Stripped of my job title, my marriage, and my lovely home, I've been left wondering who I am, and what I *really* want to do with my one, wild precious life? I realise how attached I was to those things, how much I clung to them to define me, and how exhausting my constant

374

vigilance had become. Although I must admit, I'm still trying to get over my Italian kitchen tiles and walnut worktops!'

Several of the women laughed out loud. Meredith Greenway beamed at her like a proud mother.

'I now have this keen sense of being a divided self, that there are these two unintegrated parts of me: a controlling self and a creative self, pulling in opposite directions, and I'm sick of feeling schizophrenic. After my father died, I had a strange encounter just after the funeral in the graveyard of a local church. Something rose up inside me, a huge and powerful presence that shouted, *I WANT JOY*!!! … and I've been trying to figure out what it means ever since. After what happened at the airport, I've decided that if I am going to pass through some departure gates and take a flight to joy, controlling and creative me need to come together, as I'm not paying for two fucking tickets!'

A spontaneous round of applause broke out.

'Well, follow that eh?' said a burly woman with a Yorkshire accent, called Angie. 'With that kind of imagination, you should be a writer, Hollie!'

~

Hollie opted to sit alone on one of the silent tables at breakfast the next morning. She had decided to take up the practice of writing morning pages once again, just as Glaswegian Ronnie had encouraged her to do the last time she was here. When she finished, she climbed the steps of Serenity Hall, removed her walking boots and went inside. She was the first to arrive. She sat a chair and removed a hardback notebook from her small grey backpack. It was covered with an explosion of blue, orange and green butterflies. It had arrived through the post with a small handwritten card, just before she had set off for the island.

I saw this and thought of you. Love, Diane x

The door opened and Meredith Greenway walked in. She was wearing the same cobalt blue tunic as yesterday with a heavy purple woollen blanket wrapped around her shoulders, decorated with flowers and tiny round mirrors. Her hair was pinned up at the sides.

'Good morning, Hollie. Would you like to be our gong-ringer this morning?'

'Absolutely!' said Hollie.

She stood once more on the balcony and struck the large gong. Standing here again felt like completing a circle she thought, remembering Just No Dave teasing her that day. The scene of the lift doors closing and their lips finding each other played again on the movie screen of her mind, and she wondered what he was doing right now.

'I trust you all slept well,' Meredith Greenway began. 'Let's do a quick check-in before we start, so we can hear how you are arriving as we begin today. Who would like to start?'

Hollie raised her hand.

'I had a strange dream that I was transforming into a witch. My face was slowly becoming scaly and there was movement beneath my skin, as if something was trying to break through. And my hair was turning black and becoming matted, attaching to my scalp in a peculiar way with this strange sticky texture. I had the feeling of something important I needed to finish whilst I was still human.'

'Interesting,' said Meredith Greenway. 'It's common for people to have vivid, and sometimes prophetic dreams on the island. As if the subconscious speaks more clearly and directly here. And what did you make of this?'

'Years ago, *inner witch* was how I used to describe my vicious, internal critic voice. I tried to bury her, literally and metaphorically, when the barrage of constant criticism became too overwhelming. Then, I realised the foolishness of orphaning a part of myself and worked instead on trying to accept her. On the night before we were due to emigrate, I think I had a visitation from her through another intense dream. She appeared on top of me with scissor hands, frantically clawing at the top of my thighs and between my legs as if she was trying to cut me. If I am *becoming* her now, does this mean I'm finally integrating her?'

'You should definitely write this down, Hollie! The story of Edwina Scissorhands!' said Angie.

'Sounds like a classic metamorphosis dream, of being cocooned,' said Meredith Greenway. 'The archetypal transformation process and a wonderful metaphor for shadow work. First there is a death as the caterpillar's world ends. Then, the caterpillar goes into transition as it enters the fertile void of liminal space. At this stage it is neither caterpillar nor butterfly, simply formless goo. Eventually, when the transmutation process is complete, the chrysalis breaks open, and a beautiful butterfly emerges into a new beginning. In other words, as Carl Jung said, we have to go into the darkness if we want to become whole and re-emerge into light.'

After everyone else had spoken, Meredith Greenway repeated the candle-lighting ritual from the previous evening and invited everyone to hold hands.

'We are gathered with awareness and intention, to crystallise the lessons of the journeys that have led us here and to let go of the old stories that no longer serve us. We are here to weave a new tapestry for the future on the loom of our imaginations. We open this ceremony today by consciously calling in the energies of the four directions ...'

When she had finished the invocation, Meredith Greenway allocated the group into pairs for the first exercise. Hollie was partnered with an Irish woman called Celia.

'I enjoyed your story this morning, and your check-in yesterday,' Celia said as they closed the gate and headed in the direction of the Inner Light retreat. 'All the time I was listening to you I kept thinking, *How the fuck was this woman in the corporate world?*'

'I must admit, I've been wondering this myself recently.'

'I was enthralled by the imaginative way you described your mystical experiences. Honestly Hollie, you'd fit right in in Ireland!'

'You mean I'm a little bit leprechaun?'

'Aye, exactly,' Celia nodded smiling as she tied back her long, raven hair into a ponytail and ruffled her poker straight fringe that hung over her eyes. Hollie thought she looked a little like a pale-skinned Claudia Winkleman.

'Thank you,' said Hollie. 'Your accent is beautiful. Whereabouts in Ireland are you from?'

'The south coast, near Cork.'

'I loved listening to you yesterday evening too, describing your journey,' said Hollie.

'Thanks. I'm looking forward to going back home. Been a year since I was in Ireland and feel like my body is saying, *it's time.*'

'I know that feeling. What you going to do?'

'Going to move in with my aunt and await my next instructions. I have a little money set aside, so I don't need to do anything immediately. Just see what calls to me, you know.'

'I'm trying to do this, but I get stressed about not having a plan. I worry I'll become lazy and end up drifting. Then on other days, I find myself not wanting to do anything at all, feeling swallowed up by grief for a life I was supposed to have in Australia with Hugh.'

'Not surprising, given everything that's happened, Hollie.'

'People keep telling me I just need to sit in my patience, but it's really hard!'

'I know, don't you just hate it so when people quote Rumi at you! Bastards,' Celia said, laughing. 'You know I used to be the same until a couple of years ago. I was living in London with my girlfriend, on that corporate hamster wheel … busy, busy, busy. I was like you, so dedicated, always looking to improve myself, to be the best version of me. But I wasn't listening to my body, and I got chronic fatigue, and everything changed. Eventually, after trying everything to get better – from hardcore pharmaceuticals to crystals – I started meditating and one day I asked what my illness was here to teach me. The answer I got was … *to surrender*. So I set down that uptight, glossy, results-driven perfectionist, and I have no interest in picking her back up again.'

'That's so interesting, I hadn't pictured you being like that at all,' said Hollie.

'Thank God. The pills are working, touch wood!' Celia said, tapping the side of her head.

'So how did you get from this realization to going on a year's pilgrimage that led you to France, India, and now Scotland?'

'It was incremental. I started off getting all chanty. You know, just repeating the word in my head, over and over: *surrender … surrender … surrender*. When I was driving, as I was eating, when I put my head on the pillow at night. And after a while, I started to feel a stirring, like this word was an incantation and something was slowly being summoned. As I kept repeating it, I became more tuned in and present, really paying attention to everything that happened in my days – all the little coincidences, the peculiar things people said, and every time I stopped to look down at my feet and found something on the ground. You know, things I previously wouldn't have even noticed. And I gradually opened to the idea that they were all nudges in the right direction. After I recovered from chronic fatigue, it hit me one day in a meeting at work, the blinding obviousness of the truth: if I was to be fully alive and awakened in my own life, I needed to put my soul in charge.'

'Oooh … I just had a God-shudder!' said Hollie, feeling the hairs stand up on the back of her neck.

'A God-shudder! I've heard of a fanny flutter, but not a feckin' God

Shudder. I love that!'

'A friend of mine invented it. It's her phrase for that trippy feeling of a glitch in the matrix.'

'What was it that just resonated?'

'Putting your soul in charge of your life. I feel like that's what I'm supposed to do.'

'All I can tell you is that when you peer into the abyss for months on end, it really clarifies the mind. I did a lot of crying and purging, like a colonic irrigation of the heart, Hollie. And when I'd finished – like you – I walked away from everything. Left my job, sold our flat and my car, and left my relationship. Jo was devastated. And angry. She kept saying it was just a phase, but I knew in my marrow it wasn't. No matter what I said, she didn't understand, and I couldn't explain in a rationale way. In the end, the best I could come up with was that I'd had a kind of holy take-over!'

'As in, God bought you out?'

'Yeah,' Celia said, laughing as she grabbed Hollie's arm and lowered her voice to a conspiratorial whisper. 'Although, between me, you, and the gatepost, I still have a problem with the new branding, if you know what I mean! As a gay Irish woman, I can't say I'm exactly comfortable with the God Plc. Too much feckin' baggage and bad PR. I think of it more as a spiritual awakening, but even then, it's like … don't mention the S-word!'

'You could get that printed on a T-shirt!' said Hollie.

'Make a fortune. I tell you, Hollie, spirituality is the new feckin' coming out!'

'I'll take twelve!' said Hollie, cackling.

'Amen, sister!' said Celia, making the sign of the cross in the air with a cheeky smile.

'God, it feels so good to laugh,' said Hollie, fishing for a tissue to wipe her eyes.

'Anyway, I'm conscious we've started chin-wagging and we haven't discussed any of the exercise yet,' said Celia. 'What're we supposed to be doing again?'

'I think she said to find a place where we feel connected to the element of water and explore what might be stagnating in our life and needs flushing out so we can be more in flow.'

'Look,' said Celia, pointing to a large smooth rock with a small blue plaque attached to the stone. '*Judgement Rock* ... and right here next to it, *Healing Spring* ... I think this is our place, Hollie.'

They laid their rucksacks down on the ground.

'Stand here and put your hands on the rock, think about what is stagnating for you and see what bubbles up.'

Hollie leaned forward and placed her hands flat against the cool stone and closed her eyes.

'The first time I came here, I was searching for an answer to a question. *If motherhood is not my path, what is plan B?* The answer I got was to search for an expression of motherhood energy. I started to believe this was an invitation to connect with my creative life force by resurrecting a forgotten dream to write a book inspired by my dad's life. But every time I tried, I hit a dead end. Then, on a writing course, a teacher said to me that perhaps I needed to own *my* story first. But I didn't know how. Felt I had nothing to say. So I convinced myself this was just a cunning ruse to distract myself from reality.'

'Ah yes, reality. The province of so-called normal!' said Celia.

'I doubled down working harder and harder, and eventually felt like I'd become a kind of avatar of myself ... like I was playing a version of me – Hollie the people director, Hollie the wife. Always trying to control myself, never feeling enough. And eventually I had a dark night of the soul while driving home from work, when I heard a calm voice telling me how I could end it all. Later, I realised this was my avatar wanting to die.'

'I had something very similar, except unlike you I didn't listen and got ill!'

Hollie opened her eyes and looked at the soft grass beneath her feet.

'So, you feel your creativity is stagnating?'

'Yes,' replied Hollie. 'I think I'm afraid of being in the full force of who I am, and even this not being enough. Fuck!'

'And what would this mean? To allow yourself to be in the full force of who you are, and it still not be enough?'

'That there is nothing left in the tank. Nowhere to go.'

'Okay, Hollie … keep your hands on Stonehenge here while I get some holy water from this healing spring.'

Hollie turned her head and watched Celia cup her hand under the stream of water between the rocks. 'Here,' she said, dabbing her right hand and placing a wet forefinger on the centre of Hollie's forehead like a water-bindi. '*Anam Cara.*'

'What does it mean?'

'It's Celtic. Means "soul friend".'

'Thank you, Sister Celia,' Hollie said, smiling.

~

After lunch they sat back in the circle. In the middle was a pile of white masks and a plastic box full of pens, crayons, pencils and crafting materials.

'Welcome back. I hope you found this morning helpful and healing. As you may remember, one of our ground rules is to be lean of words, so I am going to suggest what you shared this morning remains with you for now, and you allow yourself the space to continue your journey inwards this afternoon. There will be time later for hearing and witnessing each other.'

Hollie felt relieved. She didn't feel like saying anything in front of the group before she'd had more time to process everything.

'As some of you may know, it's the autumn equinox today, a point in the year when the night and day are in perfect balance, which makes this an especially auspicious and powerful time to be doing shadow work ahead of our firepit ceremony in the Mandala Garden this evening.'

Hollie was looking forward to the fire. She was feeling ready to burn some things away.

'So … what is our shadow?' Meredith Greenway began rhetorically. 'It's a concentration of powerful energy within each of us which, contrary to what we are led to believe, is not inherently good or bad. It's simply yet to be illuminated. Our shadow is also the crucible of our creativity. As Carl Jung said, if we want to live in the full force of who we are, we have to go to the places that scare us, confront what lurks in the dark corners, and dance with the devil at some point.'

Yet to be illuminated.

Hollie opened her butterfly notebook and wrote the phrase in large, decorative letters.

Meredith Greenway continued.

'Our shadow is made up of all that we hide from others: our shame, our fears, our wounds that block the full power of our life force. The bits of ourselves we have chipped away to fit in. Aspects of ourselves we don't want other people to see. Parts of ourselves we have rejected, suppressed, denied, are unwilling to love. Everything we don't want to face.'

Yorkshire Angie put her hand up.

'Meredith, are there ever things in our shadow that we aren't aware of?'

'Absolutely. But … and here's the really interesting thing … we also have a golden shadow. This is our divine spirit, our blinding beauty and hidden talent that we also suppress for fear of appearing foolish, or too intense, or too woo-woo. Equally, unless we bring this into awareness, its power remains untapped and our full potential unexplored. So, the invitation is to liberate this unused energy, to transmute it for our highest growth.'

Hollie thought about the idea of a shining golden self inside her, waiting to be revealed. Maybe this was the Buddha-nature Ani Zopa had spoken about, the too-much creative self she was afraid to let out of captivity, like releasing a madly enthusiastic kraken. She noticed Celia glance across at her, smiling, as if she'd just had the same thought.

'So we are going to explore this idea by using masks, which are, of course, powerfully symbolic. On the outside I would like you to depict the self that you show to the world. The persona you project. On the inside, I would like you to draw, write, represent your dark and golden shadows. The shameful stuff you keep hidden, and also the shiny stuff that's too freaky to let out.'

Hollie gathered a mask and a selection of felt tips and sat cross-legged in a far corner of the room. She sat for a few moments, listening to the comforting sounds of pencils colouring-in, hands rummaging in the boxes of art supplies, and *oohs* and *ahhs* as someone held up a tube of glitter glue or a handful of pink feathers. She felt grateful to be here. Grateful to be with these willing women who wanted to mine for their hidden treasures, even if that meant wading through a lot of shit.

Around forty minutes later, Meredith called everyone's attention again. A few of the women were still picking their masks up and adding things – mostly to the insides.

'As we explored earlier, our shadow is that which is yet to be illuminated. When we accept what is in our shadow with love and compassion and bring it into the light of awareness, we begin to heal, integrate and release this stuck energy. My invitation is that you reconnect with your partner now and share with each other, to whatever extent feels good for you.'

Celia handed Hollie her mask. She received it with cupped palms, like a holy wafer. It was covered mostly with drawings and a few words. Hollie studied them and then looked up at her friend's lovely face. She was smiling beatifically, radiating a tangible ease and grace.

'I haven't known you for long, but I recognise all of this in you,' Hollie said.

Celia bowed towards her with her hands held in prayer position, nodding in a way that seemed to say, *Thank you, and bless you my child.*

'You may turn it over, if you'd like to.'

Slowly and reverently, Hollie turned the mask over and laid it in the cradle of her lap. Tears of recognition fell instantaneously as she read the inside, seeing many words that matched her own. Tears of pure connection and a profound joy for the tender intimacy of the moment. All the while, Celia calmly held her gaze.

'Thank you,' said Hollie.

Celia reached forward, hugged her, then returned to her cushion, perfectly still and at ease.

'I've done something like this before,' she said. 'At a retreat about a year ago. And I notice my mask is different from last time. Less on the inside, more on the outside now. It feels good.'

Hollie had the sense this was all she wanted to say so let her words hang in the air a moment until Celia gave a little nod that seemed to be her invitation to share.

Hollie handed over her mask, face-up. It was relatively sparse. Neat, ordered and symmetrical. She watched Celia drink it all in with shining eyes, nodding.

'May I?' she asked.

Hollie nodded and watched as Celia turned her mask over gently, like a horse whisperer trying not to scare the animals. Tears rolled down Celia's pale cheeks as she read the explosion of words inside. Words talking over each other. Words shouting in capital letters. Tiny, whispering, unspeakable words trying to take up as little space as possible. Hollie felt that she was being seen for the first time in her life. Truly, deeply seen, as her innermost self. Here, on a cushion on this magical island, alive, naked, vulnerable. This Irish Claudia Winkleman pilgrim accepting all of her. It felt chaste and erotic at the same time, like an act of tender lovemaking.

Celia returned Hollie's mask and they hugged again.

'D'ya know …' said Celia, '… there's a part of me now that wants to lie on my back and smoke a feckin' Marlborough.'

'I know what you mean,' said Hollie, laughing. 'Definitely feels a bit post-coital!'

'So then, how was it for you darling?' said Celia, laughing.

'Illuminating,' said Hollie. 'I'm struck by how much more is going on under the surface. The first word I wrote in thick green marker inside was this one … *Wild*,' she said, pointing to the large letters inside the indentation of the forehead. 'I have no idea where this came from but there was intense energy in my hands as I wrote it, as if I was watching myself write the word. I spent several minutes on it, going over and over each letter. *W… I … L … D.*'

'And what sense are you making of this?' asked Celia, clearly intrigued.

'I don't know. Wild is a word I barely use, other than to confess embarrassing anecdotes about being drunk to entertain friends.'

'I hear you!' said Celia with a twinkle in her eye.

'Yet somehow, this wasn't how the word showed up in the mask. It felt more like it was like this pulsing, thrilling energy desperate to be let out to play! As soon as I finished writing it, all the other words came tumbling out, as if *wild* was a key that had unlocked a door. And I couldn't help but notice the stark contrast between the energy of the outside and the inside, how much effort I must be using to contain what lies beneath.'

'Yeah, I thought that when I turned it over. Like, Jesus, how the hell is Hollie managing to hold all this in!'

~

That evening, under the glow of a full moon and starry sky, the group gathered in the Mandala Garden in a clearing sheltered by large trees in front of a cluster of small wooden huts where some of the long-term residents of the island lived. Meredith Greenway was sitting on a camping chair dressed in furs, in front of a rusty oil drum where a roaring fire was giving off an amber glow. She was resting a Celtic-looking ceremonial drum about the size of a car hubcap on one knee and holding a beater in the other. Hollie warmed her hands over the fire as she stood chatting to two of the women, tingling with excitement and enjoying the good-natured banter.

'It feels a bit hubble-bubble,' said Nicky, a flame-haired Glaswegian.

'It sure does,' said another woman called Anne-Marie who Hollie had chatted to over soup. She was a wellbeing coach currently training to be a grief counsellor.

'Hey, Hollie,' Angie said playfully as she rubbed her hands together in black fingerless gloves.

'Maybe this is where you *actually* turn into your witch!'

'You never know,' Hollie said.

'I dunno about that, Angie,' said Celia. 'I think she's already pretty magical meself, like.'

Hollie blew Celia a kiss.

'Or maybe this is the moment when we turn into ash and transform into a bunch of old hags,' said Angie.

'I'm not even fifty yet and I already feel like one!' said Nicky.

Hollie glanced over and saw Meredith Greenway watching them with a wry smile on her face, as if she were presiding over a graduation of a promising coven of witches. She stood up, unfurling to her full height, as the animated chatter died down.

'We all experience turning points in our lives. Like Mother Earth, we are in a constant state of flux between endings, transitions and new beginnings. We begin something new, or an important relationship, project, year, or phase draws to a close. Each threshold is an opportunity to honour what has been, to release what no longer serves us, and to write our future history.'

Hollie held hands with Celia and Anne-Marie who were standing on either side of her, and everyone else followed.

'With intention, we can use these threshold points to activate our potential, release stuck energy and accelerate healing. Tonight, on this autumn equinox, we have come together in communion to bring light to that which is yet to be illuminated. We are ready to break free from our self-imposed limits and from our stories that are holding us back. We are here to name that which we need to burn within us and to rise, phoenix-like, from the ashes. To let what needs to die fall away, so we may be re-born into the full force of who we are.'

Meredith Greenway held her the drum to the light so everyone could see the markings illuminated in the glow.

'This is a Bodhran Celtic Cross. The interlacing lines on the knot symbolise that there is no beginning and no ending; there is only the continuity of everlasting love that binds together two spirits. As you listen to the drum now, think about binding together your dark and golden shadows into one integrated whole. And, when you are ready, name that which you need to release and throw whatever you decided to bring into the fire.'

Meredith Greenway sat back down and began drumming.

Doom-doom, dum-dum. Doom-doom, dum-dum. Doom-doom, dum-dum

Nicky was the first to release her hands and break the circle. 'I'm finally letting go of trying to save my son from his heroin addiction,' she said. 'I'm throwing this feather onto the fire to remind myself that I can't ride in on my white chicken trying to rescue him. He's the only one who can save himself.'

Angie followed, trying to speak as her bottom lip began to wobble. 'I'm letting go of how angry I was at my brother for taking his life ten years ago. And my guilt for not seeing he needed help before it was too late. I love you Bobby, you fucking idiot,' she said and threw a v-shaped branch into the oil drum.

Anne-Marie went next. 'I am letting go of never feeling good enough to do this work,' she said, throwing a crumpled piece of paper into the flames.

'I am finally letting go of my old story,' said Celia, 'by throwing away this hospital appointment card I have been carrying around from when I was chronically ill.'

Hollie took a piece of paper she had torn out of her butterfly notebook.

'I am letting go of the life that I would've lived with Hugh if I had gone through those departure dates. I am letting go of the self-doubt that holds me back from trusting my inner knowing. I am putting a big full stop on the page of my life, and tomorrow I am opening a new book. Henceforth, I pledge to embrace my one, wild, childfree life … wherever the hell she decides to take me on the back of her broomstick!'

Hollie scrunched up her piece of paper and threw it into the fire.

~

After their group briefing the following morning, Hollie was the first out of Serenity Hall to begin her medicine walk. Outside, the silvery-light had an ethereal, dream-like quality to it. The sky was blue and crystal clear. It felt like a picture-postcard autumnal day.

She strode purposefully across the courtyard and turned right onto Avenue of Joy, stopping at the top of the path which was scattered with leaves. The metal gate was framed by an arch of lush foliage and from this vantage point it looked like a giant keyhole. Hollie listened to the chorus of chirping birds, the bustle and clink of the kitchen through the open window, and the faint whirr of cars moving round the neighbouring island across in the distance, trying to let everything *fall upon her eyes* as Meredith Greenway had suggested.

She inhaled deeply.

She felt potent, free, and startlingly alive.

Hollie felt herself leaning further back, her chest slowly arching as if her body was stretching her ribcage to accommodate her expanding heart, as the beauty of the moment rushed in. A wide, joyous smile spread across her face, and she raised her arms above her head as the sun shone on her face, as if receiving a rapturous kiss of light.

Thank you, Footprint Island.

She brought her arms back down by her sides and walked mindfully towards to the gate, greeting the white and yellow daisies and sprawling hydrangeas along the way like a cheering crowd. Hollie put her hand on the metal latch.

"I am ready to go through the departure gate," she whispered.

After walking a while, she stopped at the Green Tara rock painting and gave a bow of respect to the mother of all Buddhas, then laid her hands onto the soft earth at the base of the rock and gazed up at the colourful image.

It's me again, Green Tara, Hollie Hardwick.

I was here a few years ago with my friend Krystina.

Just want to say thank you for incubating those eggs seeds we planted and sending them to me in the eggbox when I really needed them.

I am hoping you might be able to work your magic again.

I think I'm finally ready for a new beginning.

Hollie stared at the blue lotus flower in Green Tara's left hand and remembered something Ani Zopa had said … *No mud, no lotus.*

Perhaps, she was going to start blossoming from all the sludge she had waded through these past few years. She opened her phone and scrolled through her notes to find the Green Tara mantra she had made a note of after her first visit.

Om tare tuttare ture soha.

Hollie repeated it three times.

She turned to leave and noticed three wild, raggedy sheep grazing in front of her. The one in the foreground raised its head and stared. Forming her hands in prayer, Hollie bowed her head again for good luck, just in case the spirit of Green Tara had momentarily apparated into this woolly brown body.

With a spring in her step, she resumed her walk towards the Inner Light retreat then followed the headland round as it ascended, enjoying the vibrant harvest-festival patchwork carpet of heathers and ferns stretching out in front of her.

As the incline became steeper, she stopped to catch her breath at a viewing point a few metres below the summit, removing a water bottle and camera from her rucksack and sitting down with her back against a large, smooth rock carved out like an ancient armchair to enjoy the view.

A tiny sailing boat was making its way slowly across the horizon and Hollie watched as it moved directly into her eyeline, positioning itself right in the centre of the sun's shimmering reflection on the water. She took a picture at the exact moment of perfect symmetry, when the boat was precisely in the centre of the shimmering corridor of light and clicked the shutter.

Hollie heard a voice in her head: *Your ship is sailing*.

She smiled as she lowered her camera and watched the tiny boat continue on its path.

As she followed its trajectory, the Outer Light lighthouse came into view, jutting out of the cliff face below, its masculine, angular shape squaring up to face the wilderness of the open sea. As she peered at the lighthouse, Hollie thought it seemed like a metaphor for her father – similarly isolated, difficult to access, imposing, and somewhat melancholic.

She turned to her right, and looked down at the small, curved Inner Light retreat surrounded by a cluster of white buildings, and well-kept allotments and gardens. Perhaps, she mused, this one was more like her – integrated into a community of women, well cared for and nurtured, and easily accessible. She began turning her head this way and that between the two lighthouses, feeling a *click-click-click* happening in her mind.

His story ... her story ...

Hollie stood up, closed her eyes, and reached her arms out horizontally, palms facing down, standing like an angel with wings spread wide.

Eyes still closed, she pushed her chest forward, reached her fingertips a millimetre further in opposite directions and tilted her head backwards, opening herself as wide as she could, in a kind of primal salutation. She felt a warm ray of sunshine beaming its blessing on her face. Hollie stood there until its warmth faded and took this as a sign that it was time to continue climbing, thanking the sun as she set off once again.

As the climb became steeper at the end of the path, she began using her hands as well as her feet to propel herself up the craggy rockface, feeling renewed strength in her body and a profound sense of wellbeing each time she found a secure foothold and pulled herself upwards.

After a while, it looked as though she had reached the top, but as she stood up and stopped to take a sip of water, she realised the actual summit was higher still. It felt like a metaphor for her journey over the last few years – no obvious path to follow, scrabbling for footholds, and thinking you had arrived somewhere only to realise there was still further to go. But, she reflected, it had all been worth it to stand right here, right now, connected to this mysterious island.

Suddenly, it didn't seem to matter what the future held. She knew she would be okay.

Replacing her water bottle in her rucksack, Hollie continued to scrabble upwards like a wild mountain goat.

She felt unstoppable.

At the end of the climb, she stood on flat ground and looked ahead at the island stretching out in a gentle undulating descent. A few metres ahead she could see a small washing line of fluttering Tibetan prayer flags and headed towards it. After a few minutes, she arrived at a stone structure, waist-high and about a metre in circumference. She didn't remember it being here last time when she had walked with Krystina. It looked as though someone had attempted to build a well using a dry-stone-wall technique, but instead of being hollow it was filled with smooth stones, with an indentation in the middle where a large round stone about the size and shape of a shotput had been placed. And there, carefully balanced on top of it, was a pure white stone. Hollie gasped as she picked it up and held it in her palm.

It was unmistakeably heart shaped.

She recalled Meredith Greenway's words from earlier.

Let your soul stone reveal itself to you. And when it does, ask it what lesson it has come to offer you.

Hollie knew instantly what it meant. It was time to open her heart.

She put the stone in the top of her rucksack and headed towards the prayer flags, taking in the beautiful scenery. If she kept going at this pace, she would make it back to the centre in time for lunch.

About ten minutes later, a sprightly older man came into view, heading straight towards her. He was the first person she had seen since leaving Serenity Hall earlier.

As he came closer, Hollie could see he was bald on top with white hair at the sides and guessed he was in his mid-sixties. He was wearing a sleeveless jacket with lots of pockets over his clothes, and was peering at the ground, pausing here and there to look at rocks, then notating into a small pocketbook.

'Hello,' he said as stopped in front of Hollie and raised his arms up to the sky. 'Beautiful day isn't it?'

'It is indeed. May I ask what you're doing, as I noticed you writing things down in your notebook?'

'Ah, yes, geocaching. A kind of outdoor treasure hunt using GPS. I'm looking for good places to hide clues.'

'Sounds brilliant!'

'All good clean fun,' he said heartily with a glint in his eye.

'I'm Hollie,' she said, extending her hand.

'Peter Bird,' he said, shaking her hand as if meeting a long-lost friend. 'Nice to meet you. It's actually my birthday today.'

'Wow. Happy birthday, Peter Bird,' she said, reflecting that today felt like a kind of birthing day for her too.

'You can call me Pete. I'm just here to do a few jobs. I'm the island lighthouse keeper, so you've just caught me on my way.'

'*What?*

394

He looked at her quizzically, which was not at all surprising given tears were pooling in her eyes and her mouth was hanging open a little.

'I know this is going to sound strange,' she said, 'but may I give you a hug please? It's just that my dad was once a lighthouse keeper, and I was just thinking about him earlier.'

'Be my guest,' he said, opening his arms with a look of delight on his face.

Hollie hugged him tightly, unable to quite believe what was happening, as if part of her was expecting to wake up.

'Well, that was an unexpected birthday bonus!' he chuckled. 'You're welcome to come with me if you like ... to the lighthouse, I mean,' he said, pointing back in the direction of the Outer Lighthouse.

'I'd love to.'

'So where was your father a lighthouse keeper?'

'On the south coast, a couple of places in Devon, before I was born. And how did you end up being a lighthouse keeper, Pete?'

Peter Bird proceeded to tell his story which lasted until they arrived at the door of the Outer Lighthouse. He had lived a colourful patchwork quilt of a life that had included being an undertaker, a fish farmer, and a carer. Hollie listened to his story with delight. There was something about him that reminded her of her beloved grandpa. He felt warm and familiar.

Peter Bird fished out a bunch of keys from his rucksack and opened a black wooden door with a large key that looked like something from *Alice in Wonderland*. It was cold and bare inside. It reminded Hollie of her stone egg room. She watched him measure a window for a frame that needed to be replaced and then followed him upstairs where they sat in the lantern room on the mesh metal floor.

'Would you like to share my packed lunch?' he said, pulling a large tupperware box and flask from his rucksack.

'Thanks!'

'So these days,' he said, continuing the conversation that had paused at the front door, 'I mostly take care of my wife and keep my brain active by writing children's stories, about a character called Stinky Pete who has lots of adventures.'

'That's amazing!' said Hollie. 'Have you had anything published?'

'No. I started writing them originally to entertain the grandkids, but I'm thinking of self-publishing my latest one. It's called *Stinky Pete and The Rat Mattress*.'

'Great title.'

'Yeah, the grandkids love it.'

'It's so funny meeting you like this, Pete. I can't help thinking it feels like divine intervention.'

'Oh?'

'I've wanted to write a book inspired by my dad's life for years now, but every time I tried, I hit a dead-end and lost my confidence. He died last year, and recently I've been thinking again about writing, but maybe trying something different this time. Oddly, this morning we did an activity on our retreat to conjure a mentor who will accompany us on our journey after we leave the island and I saw Grace Darling.'

'As in, the lighthouse keeper's daughter who famously rescued those people from the shipwreck?'

'Yes. We were sitting in a stone circle together.'

'Did she say anything to you?'

'No. She just sat there in silence, wearing a bonnet.'

'The two lighthouse keeper's daughters together, eh? It sounds to me like the island is definitely trying to tell you something, Hollie. *Really loudly*,' he said, nudging her playfully with his shoulder.

'I'm starting to think so too.'

'I reckon whatever this book is about, it's important that you write it. Footprint Island always gives people what they need. Happens here all the time.'

They finished their cheese and pickle sandwich, then shared a chocolate biscuit washed down with strong tea.

'Better get going. I've got to go to the other lighthouse before I go. Fancy coming there too?'

'The women's closed retreat? I thought nobody was allowed in?'

'They're not,' he said with a mischievous wink.

They arrived half an hour later, entered through the white metal gates and crept down past the allotments which were lined with trees and bushes. A shaven-haired woman wearing red robes was clearing leaves with a rake and waved to Pete as he bounded past but didn't seem to notice Hollie.

They rounded the corner past a beautiful temple with ornate wooden doors and walked briskly down a grassy path. Dead ahead was the diminutive lighthouse Hollie had seen from the ferry, painted white with decorative splashes of a golden butternut squash colour around the edge of the small black door and round the rim of the lantern. Peter Bird fished out his bunch of keys and inserted one in the keyhole that could easily have been the key to Rapunzel's tower. Hollie followed him inside the small round tower and stood on the opposite side of the lantern to him, looking out of the glass window reinforced with a criss-cross pattern of black metal.

It felt like a moment of holy communion.

Peter Bird rummaged in his rucksack again and pulled out a hat, like the kind a gamekeeper on safari might wear, and placed it gently over the lantern, like a tea cosy.

'What are you doing?' asked Hollie.

'Testing the light,' he said. 'You have to put it into total darkness. It's the only way you can know that the light is working properly. Or as I like to say, out of darkness cometh the light.'

Hollie felt the hairs stand up on the back of her neck.

'That's beautiful, is it from the Bible?'

'No, it's actually the motto of Wolverhampton Wanderers Football Club. Been a lifelong supporter like my dad. For my sins! I think he wanted to teach me a life lesson about heartbreak and pain,' he said, chuckling.

'And what did you learn?'

'That they are the price you pay for fleeting joy. But in the end, they're always worth it.'

Mother's Allotment

A few weeks later, Hollie lifted the latch of the wooden gate and wheeled her bicycle inside her mother's allotment. She closed it behind her and propped her bike up against the fence.

Her mother was standing on the left, bending over a patch of soil, digging with a spade.

'I can't believe I'm finally here,' Hollie said as she walked towards her, 'in the mother's sacred space!'

'I thought it was about time I put you to work!' her mother said, smiling as she handed her a pair of gardening gloves. 'Here, make yourself useful and wipe the muck off these potatoes.'

'Yes, boss!'

'So, how was Footprint Island?'

'It was … enlightening, and liberating.'

'I'm glad. And any news on Hugh?'

'We spoke briefly yesterday. He's doing well. He's been seeing quite a bit of Stephen, and he has a new girlfriend.'

'How do you feel about that?'

'I'm happy for him. Feels as though he's where he's supposed to be.'

'And what about you. Have you decided what you're going to do about work yet? I was speaking with Kristen the other day, and she says they're going to be recruiting for an HR Director soon and wondered whether you might be interested?'

'That's kind of her to say, but I don't think so, Mum. It doesn't feel like me anymore. I think I'm going to take some time off, you know, have a kind of sabbatical year.'

'What you going to do?'

'First off, I'm going to finish unpacking all my boxes and do some decorating. I want to make a lovely writing den in the room that overlooks the sea.'

'You're definitely your father's daughter. Your dad would have loved your new place.'

'Yeah, I think so too. Even he would approve.'

'So, you're working on your book about the lighthouse keeper again?'

'Actually, I'm thinking about writing my story. A kind of memoir, slash self-help book.'

'Speaking of which, I heard an interesting programme on *Woman's Hour* the other day. There was a discussion about the decision of whether or not to have children, and they were talking about a growing trend for women to be childless by the time they hit their forties. There was an interesting woman speaking who wanted to have children but couldn't and talked about her experience of living in what she called a "pronatalist culture". You should have a listen, it was really interesting.'

'Thanks, Mum, I'll check it out.'

'Something she said really got me thinking. She talked about how she had constantly experienced micro-aggressions, all these little things people did and said that made her feel she was less-than because she hadn't had children. And ...'

Her mother stopped digging and looked at her.

'I hope I didn't do this. You know, to you, Hollie, when you were agonising over your decision and everything. I tried to help ... didn't I?'

Hollie paused.

She could feel a small part of her wanting to make her mother understand how deeply hurt she had felt, but what would be the point now? She could hear the earnest tone in her voice, and the uncharacteristic chink in her self-assurance. No, she thought, her mother had done the best she could with the resources she had.

'I know you did. Although I did feel a bit judged at times.'

'Sorry. I didn't mean to make you feel judged or less-than. I just hated watching you torturing yourself.'

'I know, Mum. It's okay. I'm totally at peace with it all now. Deciding to be childfree is the best decision I ever made.'

'I was thinking as well, Hollie ... if I'd actually thought about whether or not to have children, properly, like you did ... you know, I mean *really* thought about it, I would probably never have had them either. In fact, I'm not sure anyone would because, let's face it, logically, having kids doesn't stack up.'

Hollie felt her mouth hanging open.

'I can't believe you just said that, Mum. You of all people!'

'Well, I just want you to know, I'm proud of you. You've paddled your own canoe and done what's right for you.'

'Thanks. That means a lot. Actually ...'

'What?'

'While we're on the subject, there's something I've been wondering about telling you.'

'Oh? Well, I know it can't be that you're pregnant!' she said, playfully shoving Hollie's arm as she took a plant out of its pot.

'No ... But I was.'

'What? Pregnant?'

'Yes.'

'Why didn't you tell me?'

'I don't know. It was just too much to process, and then, as time moved on and I made my peace with it, there just didn't seem to be any point … I lost her at ten weeks.'

'Her?'

'Yes. I just felt that it was a girl. I nicknamed her Egberta.'

'Come here, you,' her mother said, putting down the pot in her hand and opening her arms.

Hollie folded herself into her mother's firm embrace.

'You're just so you, in every way!' she said.

'I love you, Mum,' Hollie said as her eyes welled with gratitude. 'I'm sorry if I don't tell you enough.'

'I love you too,' she said, pulling away. 'Now come on, let's finish off these potatoes, and I can show you how to tell when your spring onions are ready to pick. Then you can come back to my house on your way home. I have something to give you.'

An hour later, Hollie followed her mother through the hall and into the kitchen at the back.

'Your garden looks beautiful, Mum,' she said, looking out of the large picture window.

'I remember when we moved into this house. You were only ten years old, and you were so excited that it backed onto a railway line. Do you remember?'

'Yeah. I thought it was magical, thinking about all the people on those trains and where they were going to.'

'I think it probably made up for us moving. I know how much you loved our old house.'

'Yeah. I often think about it, you know, and how happy my childhood was. I remember the way the afternoon sun used to bounce off the yellow walls in the kitchen. And how the whole room was filled with this soft golden light. And you would be standing at the sink, bustling away, wiping something or other, while I was sitting playing on the lino floor. It still gives me the tingles now, the feeling of being enveloped in a hazy glow of love.'

'That's very poetic, Hollie. Like your father.'

Hollie smiled.

'Do you still miss him?'

'Yeah, I think about him a lot. In a funny way, I feel closer to him now he's gone. As if he is somehow watching over me. When I was on the retreat, I had an amazing experience where I met the island lighthouse keeper, and he took me inside two of the lighthouses and showed me around. It felt like Dad was with me.'

'Funny you should say that. Wait there.' her mother said, disappearing into the hall.

Hollie sat down at the table and looked at the power cables of the railway line. Finally, she thought, I'm on the right track and the right train, just enjoying the journey.

She thought back to her dark night of the soul, driving back from work in the rain that night, when she had heard the voice inside her head wanting to end it all.

She felt so different now.

Like she had been re-born.

She replayed what her mother had said in the allotment.

If I had REALLY thought about it like you, I would probably never have had children either.

Hearing these words felt like a great circle had been completed. From that kitchen-floor moment on her mother's birthday, and all the agonising she had gone through, to sitting here ready to begin a new chapter of her life. She finally felt whole and at peace with herself, and it seemed the world around her was now mirroring this back.

Hollie smiled to herself as she thought about the man she had met at the airport and the question he had asked her in the prayer room that morning as he'd pointed to her chest.

What if the departure gates are in here?

'Here,' her mother said, returning into the kitchen as she handed her a large homemade envelope of thin brown paper. 'I found it in the loft the other day and I thought you might like it.'

Hollie opened the package and pulled out a painting, about ten inches wide and fourteen inches tall.

A lighthouse.

'You painted it at school, when you were seven years old. It says the date on the back.'

Hollie laid it gently on the kitchen table as if it were a sacred relic and stared at it.

The sky was powder blue, with Van Gogh-esque brushstrokes that seemed to imbue it with energy and movement. In the foreground was a small white brick wall with dark blue waves lapping in front. The lighthouse was white and yellow and had a weathervane on the top.

Hollie gasped.

'What is it?' her mother said.

'The lighthouse. It reminds me of the one I visited on the island with the lighthouse keeper. It's called *The Inner Light*,' she said, pointing to the painting, 'it has the same colouring here ... butternut squash yellow.'

Hollie felt as if a great set of gates was slowly opening inside her chest.

'You look like you're about to cry, Hollie, what is it?'

'On the way back from the allotment, my mind was ticking over as I pedalled my bike. I suddenly had an idea for my book. A title that appeared, like a download.'

'What was it?'

The Lighthouse Keeper's Daughter: How to Find Your Courage and Shine.

'Good title! You better write it down.'

'It's already imprinted up here,' Hollie said, pointing to her head. 'And … in here,' she said, cupping her hands over her chest, in the same spot she'd first felt the holy heart tug.

'Maybe your father has passed his torch on to you. Maybe it's time for you to be the keeper of the light.'

Hollie could feel her face crumpling.

'Soft as clarts you are, Hollie. Always were a sensitive soul. Here …' she said, passing a tissue.

'Thanks, Mum.'

'Here's an idea … maybe in your lighthouse you could have a plaque above the door made of brass, with your father's favourite saying.'

'The best ideas come from the grottiest surroundings,' said Hollie laughing.

'Yes,' said her mother.

'You know, the older I've got, the more I think he was onto something there. The Buddhists have a similar saying, *No mud, no lotus.*'

'Well that definitely sounds true to me,' said her mother, smiling. 'In my experience, you need a good stinky fertiliser for anything to really grow.'

~

That evening, Hollie walked upstairs in her new house, carrying a cardboard box with the lighthouse painting balanced on top.

She stopped on the landing, looking at the bare cream wall adjacent to a long, gold-rimmed rectangular mirror that the previous owner had left. It seemed a perfect spot to hang the painting.

She set the box down and opened the door to the room that overlooked the sea.

As she pushed the door open, a beam of light illuminated her face and swept across the room like a giant lightsaber, bouncing off the walls. It was the light from the North Pier lighthouse standing guard at the mouth of the river further up the coast, near where she and her father had watched that time as the tugboat had chugged out to sea.

She opened her arms out wide like the Angel of the North.

As the beam swept round again, she stood, bathed inside a glittering snow-globe of light.

Hollie's eyes filled with tears of gratitude for the conversation with her father that day and the kitchen-floor moment with Hugh, and all that had unfolded in their wake.

She had found her inner light and was finally ready to fly through the departure gates, to destination joy.